FINAL RECKONING

It had become appropriate to know things beyond Kutath . . . The Kel was the caste which veiled, the Face that Looked Outward. That Outward had become more than the next rising of the land; it was outsiders and ships and a manner of fighting which the ages had made only memory on Kutath. Pride and the Holy that the Kel defended forbade that he should flinch from facing it, since it came.

They had a kel'anth who had come out of that Dark. They had a she'pan young and scarred with the warrior scars on her face. Fit, he thought, that she should bear kel-marks, which testified she had attained skill with weapons. A she'pan of a colder, fiercer stamp, this Melein . . . She was a chill wind, a breath out of the Dark. And as for her kel'anth, her warrior-leader. . . .

THE FADED SUN: KUTATH

KUTATH

C. J. Cherryh

DAW BOOKS, INC.
DONALD A. WOLLHEIM, PUBLISHER
1633 Broadway
New York, N.Y.   10019

FIRST PRINTING, FEBRUARY 1980

1 2 3 4 5 6 7 8 9

 DAW TRADEMARK REGISTERED
U.S. PAT. OFF. MARCA
REGISTRADA. HECHO EN U.S.A.

PRINTED IN U.S.A.

I

There was chaos about the docking bay; Galey observed it as he was coming in, heard it, a chatter of instructions in his ear, warning him to keep his distance. He held the shuttle parked a little removed from the warship, watching kilometer-long *Saber* disgorge a trio of small craft. Blips showed on his tracking screen, an image supplied him by *Saber*-com, from *Saber's* view of things. One blip was himself; one other was blue and likewise human—that had to be *Santiago* . . . *Saber* had deployed the insystem fighter between itself and the red blip that was *Shirug*.

The outgoing blips were likewise red: regul shuttles in tight formation. Galey read the situation uneasily and kept his eye to the steady flow of information on the screen. There was one dead regul to be disposed of: that was likely what was in progress out there . . . the late bai Sharn Alagn-ni, ferried out to her own ship for whatever ceremony the regul observed with their dead. Sharn: ally, as all regul were allies according to the treaties . . . according to the agreement which had brought a human and a regul warship into orbit about this barren world, this home base of the mri. Regul made Galey's skin crawl. It was a reaction he did not speak aloud: promotions in the service were politics, and politics called regul friendlies.

Mri, now, mri were near human-looking, whatever the insides of them might be like. Galey hated them with a different dutiful hate. He was Havener, of a world lost and retaken in the mri wars. Parents, a brother, cousins—had vanished into the chaos of that war-torn world and never surfaced again. It was a remote kind of grief, rehearsed guiltily in every other scene of slaughter he had witnessed, but he could not recover the intensity of it. His kin were lost, in the sense of not found, misplaced in the war and gone: dead or alive, nor knowing for sure. He had not been home when the strike came, and in the years after, the service had become home, *Lancet, Saber, Santiago,* whatever ship received his papers, wherever his current ship took him, live or die. Mri were like that. Just soldiers behind their black robes and veils. Nothing personal. He had a friend who had gone mri . . . he had seen a different look on him after the years of absence, disdainful, remote; there was something heart-chilling in standing close to a man in that black garb, something intimidating in gazing close at hand into a face of which only the eyes were visible—amazing how much of expression depended on the rest of the face, concealed behind black cloth. But for all of that, a human could understand them.

Regul . . . regul had hired the ships, the weapons, the mri themselves, and planned, and named the strikes, and profited from them. Forty years of war, bought by regul. An investment . . . Galey sounded the words out in his mind, distastefully. Po-li-cy. Cash on the table. Big folk, the regul, who sat fat and safe, who made the decisions and put out the cash, sending their mri mercenaries out to war. Humans and mri killed each other, and the wise old regul, reckoning a forty-year war nothing against their centuries-long lifespans, and reckoning the tally of gain and loss—kept the war going just so long as it profited them.

In the same way the regul turned up on the human side during the cleanup—had turned on their own mercenaries, slaughtering them and the mri's civilian population without warning. That was the mri's final payoff for serving regul. A simple change of policy: regul knew the right moment to move. And, truth be told, everything human breathed a sigh of relief to know the mri were gone, and that someone else had pulled the trigger.

Regul came now, having tracked the last two survivors of the mri who had served them, to their homeworld, to Kutath, the far, far origin of their kind. Regul had rushed ahead to destroy a peace message from Kutath before humans could hear it, had fired on a quiet world and elicited answering fire before humans understood the situation. More mri were dead down there. The last remnants of dying cities were shot to ruin; the last of a dying species were made fugitives on their own world . . . the last place, the very last, that mri existed.

Something tight and unpleasant welled up in Galey's throat when he thought of that. Somehow it was Haven again, and civs getting killed. He had come very far to feel something finally. It was ironic that he felt it for the enemy, that deep-down sickness at the belly that came of seeing an unequal contest.

It would have been that kind of blind, helpless death for his own kin. It gave him nightmares now, after so many years. No fighting back; a city under fire from orbit; no ships; no hope: folk armed with handguns and knives against orbital strike.

Everything dead, and no way out.

There was a little drift in his position. It had been minor, but the shuttles were still in his path and he had to maintain a while longer. He corrected a fraction. Sweat was running down his sides. He tried to stop thinking, tried to concentrate on his instruments for a time. There was no reason for uneasiness. The feeling simply grew. And in time the thoughts crept back again. His eyes traveled inexorably and unwillingly toward the outward view. Kutath's dying surface was barely in his visual field. The rest was stars, fewer than he ever liked to see. He sweated. He had never been in a place where the goblins got to him so thoroughly, those ancient human ghosts that tagged after a man in the deep. They dogged him, kept, as proper ghosts should, just behind him . . . gone when he would look.

Look back, they whispered against his nape, stirring the hairs, *Look again.*

The stars hung infinite in his drifting view, as deep down as up, as far on left as on right; and a near star, Na'i'in, the mri called it, which would make even *Saber* a mote of dust beside it. All, all those little lights which were suns, and some cloudy aggregates of suns, themselves reduced to dust motes by distance which reached out from himself, who was the center of the universe, and then not—an insignificance, less than the mote of a world, far less than a sun, infinitely less than the vast galaxies, and the distance, the cold, deep distance that never stopped, forever.

Move it, he thought at the ships which held him off. He wanted in, wanted *in,* like a boy running for his front door and warmth and light, with the goblins at his back. It had never gotten to him, not like this.

The mri had a word for it: the Dark. Scientists said so. Anyone who had traveled the wild places in little ships had to have a word for it. Except maybe regul, who could not imagine, only remember.

Mri felt it. He understood beings who could feel it.

He worked his hands on the controls, heard the chatter in

his ear, the thin lifeline of a voice from *Saber,* proving constantly his species was real, however far they sat now from friendly, trafficked space.

Real. Alive. Men existed somewhere. Somewhere there were human worlds, less than dust motes in the deep, but living. And that somehow affirmed his own reality.

Was it this, he wondered, for the two mri, last of all their company . . . who had run this long, desperate course home? *Their* little mote was dying, an old world under an old sun, and what fragile life of their kind survived here, regul refused to leave alive. Was it such a feeling, that had made *home* more urgent for them than survival—to come in out of the Dark, even to die?

He began to shiver, catching a moving dot of light among all the others. *Shirug.* The regul shuttles were too far and too small to see now. It had to be regul *Shirug,* catching the sun.

"NAS-12, come on in," *Saber*-com said. "Shuttle NAS-12, come on in."

He kicked the vessel into slow life and eased onward, resisting the temptation to close the interval with a wasteful burst of power. There was time. The bay was all his.

"Priority, NAS-12."

They gave him leave to move. His heart started thudding with a heavier and heavier weight of premonition. His hands moved, throwing the little ship over into rightwise alignment and hurtling it at *Saber* with furious haste.

"Sir," the intercom announced, "Lt. Comdr. James Galey."

Adm. Koch scribbled a note on the screen, hit FILE and disposed of one piece of business, touched the intercom key in silent affirmative. A second screen showed the busy command center: Capt. Zahadi was taking care of matters there at least; and Comdr. Silverman in *Santiago* was currently linked to Zahadi, keeping a wary eye over the world's horizon. Details were all Zahadi's, until they touched policy. Policy began here, in this office.

Galey arrived, a sandy-haired, freckled man who had begun to have lines in his face. Galey looked distressed—ought to be, summoned directly to this office for debriefing. The eyes flicked to the corner, where a high-ranking regul had lately died; Koch did not miss it, returning the offered courtesies.

"Sir," Galey said.

"You set SurTac Duncan downworld in good order?"

"Yes, sir. No trouble."

"You volunteered for that flight."

Galey was masked in courtesies. The face failed to react to that probe, only the eyes, and that but slightly, betraying nothing.

"Want you to sit down," Koch said. "Relax. Do it."

The man looked about him, found the only chair available, drew it over and sat on the edge of it. Koch waited. Galey dutifully eased himself back and positioned his arms. Sweat was standing on Galey's face, which might be from change of temperature and might not. Careers rose and fell in this office.

"Why?" Koch pursued him. "The man walks into this office wearing mri robes, asks for a cease-fire, then guns down a ranking regul ally. Security says he's gone entirely mri, inside and out. Science department agrees. You imagined some long-ago acquaintance, is that it? You volunteered to ferry him back—why? To talk with him? To satisfy yourself of something? What?"

"I—worked with him once. And I'd flown guide for *Flower's* landing, sir; I happened to know the route."

"So do others."

"Yes, sir."

"You worked with him—on Kesrith."

"One mission, sir."

"Know him well?"

"No, sir. No one did. He's SurTac."

The specials, the Surface Tactical operatives, were remote from the regul military, in all ways remote: peculiar rank, peculiar authorities, the habit of independence and irreverence for protocol. Koch shook his head, frowned, wondering if that was, even years ago, sufficient explanation for Sten Duncan. Governor Stavros, back in Kesrith zones, had trusted this wildness, enough to hand Duncan two mri prisoners and their captured navigational records. It had paid the dividend Stavros had reckoned: they were here, at the mri home world; and Duncan, with the mri contacts no one had ever been able to establish, came suing for peace. . . .

Then shot a regul in the same interview, bai Sharn, commander of *Shirug*, lieutenant to humanity's highest placed ally among regul, and all plans were off.

I have done an execution, Duncan had said. *The regul know what I am. They will not be surprised. You know this. I can give you peace with Kutath now.*

Mri arrogance. Duncan had been acutely uncomfortable, asked for a moment to drop the veil with which he covered his face.

"You worked with the man," Koch said, regarding Galey steadily. "You had time to exchange a few words with him in getting him back to Kutath. Impressions? Do you know him at all now?"

"Yes," Galey said. "It's what he was, back on Kesrith. Only it wasn't—wasn't all the same. Now and again it's there, the way he was; and then . . . not. But—"

"But you think you know him. —You . . . were in the desert together back at Kesrith, recovered the records out of that shrine . . . had a little regul trouble then on the way back, all true?"

"Yes, sir."

"Hate the regul?"

"No love for them, sir."

"Hate the mri?"

"No love there either, sir."

"And SurTac Duncan?"

"Friend, sir."

Koch nodded slowly. "You know the pack he was given has a tracer."

"I don't think that will last long."

"You warned him?"

"No, sir, didn't know. But he's not anxious to have us find the mri at all; I don't think he'll let it happen."

"Maybe he won't. But then maybe his mri don't want him speaking for them. Maybe he told the truth and maybe he didn't. There are weapons on that world worth reckoning with."

"Wouldn't know, sir."

"Your first run down there, you took damage."

"Some. Shaken about. What I hear, it's old stuff. I didn't see anything to say different; no fields, no life, no ships. Nothing, either time. Only ruins. That's what I hear it was."

"Less than that down there now."

"Yes, sir."

A dying world, cities decayed and empty, machines drawing solar power to live: armaments returning fire with mechanical lack of passion; and the mri themselves. . . .

Rock and sand, Duncan had said, *dune and flats. The mri will not be easy to find.*

If it's true, Koch thought. *If—there are no ships in their control, and if all the cities are machine life only.*

"You think they pose no threat to us," Koch said.

"Wouldn't know that either, sir."

There was a feeling of cold at Koch's gut. It lived there, sometimes small, sometimes—when he thought of the voyage behind them—larger. It grew when he thought of the hundred twenty-odd worlds at their backs, a swath which marked the trail mri had followed out from Kutath to Kesrith, a trail eons old at the beginning and recent at the farther end, in human space, where the mri had been massacred. Before that, along that strip—all worlds were scoured of life . . . more than desert: dead.

Mri hired themselves for mercenaries. Presumably they had done so more than once, until the regul turned on them and ended them.

Ended a progress across the galaxy which left no life in its wake, a hundred twenty-odd systems which by all statistical process should have held life, which might have supported intelligent species.

Void, if they had ever been there . . . gone, without memory, even to know what they had been, why the mri had passed there, or what they had sought in passing.

Only Kesrith survived, trail's end.

I have done an execution, Duncan had said, black-robed, mri to the heart of him. And: *The regul know what I am.*

"Bai Sharn," Koch said, "is being transported back to her ship. There *is* no regul authority with us now; the rest are only younglings. They can probably handle *Shirug* competently enough, but nothing more, without some adult to direct them. That puts things wholly into our laps. *We* deal with the mri, if Duncan can get their holy she'pan to come in and talk peace. *We* run operations up here. And if we misread signals, we don't get any second chance. If we get ourselves ambushed, if we die here—then the next thing human space *and* regul may know is more mri arriving, to take up the track the others left at Kesrith, and this time, this time with a grudge. The thing we've seen . . . *continued.* Is that understood, out among the crew?"

"Yes, sir," Galey said hoarsely. "Don't know whether they know about the regul, but the other, yes, it's something I think everybody reckons."

"You don't want to make a mistake in judgment, do you? You don't want to make a mistake on the side of friendship and botch a report. You wouldn't hold back information you could get out of SurTac Duncan. You understand how high the stakes are . . . and what an error could do down there."

"Yes, sir."

"I'm sending *Flower* and the science staff back down. Dr. Luiz and Boaz are friends of his. He'll talk with them, trust them, as far as he likely trusts any human now. I have need of someone else, potentially. What we want is a substitute for a SurTac, someone who can operate in that kind of terrain." He watched the apprehension grow, and a twinge of pity came on him. "Our options are limited. We have pilots we could better risk. You're rated for *Santiago*, and you know your value . . . don't have to tell you that. But it's not a matter of skill in that department. It's the land, and a sense of things—you understand what I'm saying."

"Sir—"

"I want you first of all *reserved*. Just prep. We keep our options open. Maybe things will work out with mri contact. If not . . . you have a good rapport with the civs, don't you?"

"I've been in and out of the ship more than most, maybe."

"They know you."

"Yes, sir."

"In some things down there, that could be valuable; and you've been in the desert."

"Yes, sir," the answer came faintly.

"I want you available, whenever and wherever SurTac Duncan comes into contact with us; I want you available—if he doesn't. Willing?"

"Yes, sir."

"You'll have some semblance of an office, whatever scan materials we come up with, original and interpreted. Whatever you think you need." Koch delayed a moment more, pursed his lips in thought. "It took Duncan some few days to get from the mri to groundbase; allow—ten, eleven days. That's the margin. Understood?"

It was; it very much was, Koch reckoned. He had a sour taste in his mouth for the necessity.

One covered all the possibilities.

A private office: that was status. Someone had put a card on the door, the temporary sort: LT COMDR JAMES R GALEY, RECON & OPERATIONS. Galey keyed open the lock, turned on the light, finding a bare efficiency setup, barren walls, down to the rivets; and a desk and a comp terminal. He settled in behind the desk, shifted uncomfortably in the unfamiliar chair, keyed in library.

ORDERS: the machine interrupted him with its own program. He signalled acceptance. SELECT COMPATIBLE CREW OF THREE AND RESERVE CREW, GROUND OPERATIONS, REPORT CHOICE ADM SOONEST.

He leaned back, hands sweating. He little liked the prospect of taking himself down there; the matter of selecting others for a high-risk operation was even less to his taste.

He made up a demanding qualifications list and started search through personnel. Comp denied having any personnel with drylands experience. He erased that requirement and started through the others, erased yet another requirement and ran it again, with the sense of desperation he began to understand what Koch shared.

They were Haveners on this mission, and for all the several world-patches on his sleeve, won on this ship, there was nothing they had met like this save Kesrith itself; there was no time at which they had relied on themselves and not on their machines. *Saber* had not been chosen for this mission: it had gone because it was available. As for experience with mri— none of them had had that, save at long range.

Devastation from orbit: that had been their function until now. Now there was the barest hope this would not be the case. He was not given to personal enthusiasm in his assignments; but this one—a means of avoiding slaughter—that possibility occurred to him.

Or the possibility of being the one to call down holocaust: that was the other face of the matter.

He did not sleep well. He sat by day and pored over what data they could give him, the scan their orbiting eyes could gather, the monotone reports of comp that no contact had been made.

Flower descended to the surface. Data returned from that source. Day by day, there was no reply from Duncan, no sighting of mri.

He received word from the admiral's office: SELECTIONS RATIFIED. SHIBO, KADARIN, LANE: MAIN MISSION. HARRIS, NORTH, BRIGHT, MAGEE: BACKUP. PROCEED.

The days crawled past, measured in the piecing of maps and vexing lapses in ground-space communication as Na'i'in's storms crept like plague across its sickly face. He took what information Saber's mapping department would give him, prowled Supply, thinking.

The office became papered with charts, a composite of the world, overlaid in plastics, red-inked at those sites identified in scan, mri cities, potential targets.

He talked with the crew, gave them warning. There was still the chance that the whole project would be scrubbed, that by some miracle *Flower* would call up contact, declaring peace a reality, the matter solved, the mri willing to deal.

The hope ebbed, hourly.

II

Windshift had begun, that which each evening attended the cooling of the land, and Hlil tucked his black robes the more closely about him as he rested on his heels, scanning the dunes, taking breath after his long walking.

The tribe was not far now, tucked down just over the slope by the rim, where the land fell away in days' marches of terraces and cliffs, and the sea chasms gaped, empty in this last age of the world. Sen-caste said that even that void would fill, ultimately, the sands off the high flats drifting as they did in sandfalls and curtains off the windy edges, to the far, hazy depths. Somewhere out there was the bottom of the world, where all motion stopped, forever; and that null-place grew, yearly, eating away at the world. The chasms girdled the earth; but they were finite, and there were no more mountains, for they had all worn away to nubs. It was a place, this site near the rims, where one could look into time, and back from it; it quieted the soul, reminded one of eternity, in this moment that one could not look into the skies without dreading some movement, or reckoning with alien presence.

The ruins of An-ehon lay just over the horizon to the north, to remind them of that power, which had made them fugitives in their own land, robbed of tents, of belongings, of every least thing but what they had worn the morning of the calamity. There was the bitterness of looking about the camp, and missing so many, so very many, so that at every turn, one would think of one of the lost as if that one were in camp, and then realize, and shiver. He was kel'en, of the warrior caste; death was his province, and it was permitted him to grieve, but he did not. There was a dull bewilderment in that part of him which ought by rights to be touched. In recent days he felt outnumbered by the dead, as if all the countless who had gone into the Dark in the slow ages of the sea's dying ought rather to mourn the living. He did not com-

prehend the causes of things. Being kel'en, he neither read
nor wrote, held nothing of the wisdom of sen-caste, which sat
at the feet of a she'pan alien to this world and learned. He
knew only the use of his weapons, and the kel-law, those
things which were proper for a kel'en to know.

It had become appropriate to know things beyond Kutath;
he tried, at least. The Kel was the caste which veiled, the
Face that Looked Outward. That Outward had become more
than the next rising of the land; it was outsiders and ships
and a manner of fighting which the ages had made only
memory on Kutath, and pride and the Holy the Kel defended
forbade that he should flinch from facing it, since it came.

They had a kel'anth, the gods defend them! who had come
out of that Dark; they had a she'pan who had taken them
from the gentle she'pan who had Mothered the tribe before
her . . . young and scarred with the kel-scars on her face; fit,
he thought, that the she'pan of this age should bear kel-
marks, which testified she once had been of Kel-caste, had
once attained skill with weapons. A she'pan of a colder,
fiercer stamp, this Melein s'Intel; no Mother to play with the
children of the Kath as their own Sochil had done, to spend
more time with the gentle Kath than with Sen-caste, to love
rather than to be wise. Melein was a chill wind, a breath out
of the Dark; and as for her kel'anth, her warrior-leader. . . .

Him, Hlil almost hated, not for the dead in An-ehon,
which might be just; but for the kel'anth he had killed to take
the tribe. It was a selfish hate, and Hlil resisted it; such resentments demeaned Merai, who had lost challenge to this
Niun s'Intel. Merai had died, in fact, because gentle Sochil
had turned fierce when challenged: fear, perhaps; or a
mother's bewildered rage, that a stranger-she'pan demanded
her children of her, to lead them where she did not know.

So Merai was dead; and Sochil, dead. Of Merai's kinship
there was only his sister left; of his tribe there was a fugitive
remnant; and the Honors which Merai had won in this life, a
stranger possessed.

Even Hlil . . . this stranger had gained, for kel-law set the
victor in the stead of the vanquished, to the last of his kin
debts and blood debts and place debts. Hlil was second to
Niun s'Intel as he had been second to Merai. He sat by this
stranger in the Kel, tolerated proximity to the strange beast
which was Niun's shadow, bore with the grief which haunted
the kel'anth's acts . . . which could not, he was persuaded, be
distraction for the slaughter of a People the kel'anth had not

had time to know—but which more attended the disappear-
ance of the kel'anth's other alien shadow, which walked on
two feet.

That the kel'anth at least grieved . . . it was a mortality
which bridged one alienness between them, him and his new
kel'anth. They shared something, at least; if not love . . .
loss.

Hlil gathered up a sandy pebble from the crumbling ridge
on which he rested, cast it at a tiny pattern in the sands
downslope. It hit true, and a nest of spiny arms whipped up
to enfold the suspected prey. Sand-star. He had suspected so.
His hunting was not so desperate that he must bring *that* to
the women and children of Kath. It wriggled away, a disturbance through the sand, and he let it. A pair of serpents, a fat
darter, a stone's weight of game; he had no cause to be
ashamed of his day's effort, and there was a stand of pipe
growing within the camp, so that they had no desperate
need of moisture, certainly not the bitter fluid of the star. It
nestled into safety next to some rocks, spread its arms wide
again, a pattern of depressions in the sand. He did not torment it further; it was off the track so, and offered no threat.
Kel-law forbade excess.

And in time, with the sun's lowering, kel'ein came. Hlil sat
his place, sentinel to the homecoming path, and marked them
in, as he had known by the fact that this post was vacant,
that none had come in before him. They saw him as they
passed, lifted hands in salute; he knew their names and put a
knot in the cords at his belt for each—knew them veiled as
they were, by their manners and their stature and simply by
their way of walking, for they were his own from boyhood.
Had there been one of higher rank than he that one would
have come and relieved him of this post, to take up the tally;
there was none, so he stayed, as they entered the perimeter of
the secure area of the camp.

They came in groups as the sun touched the horizon, appearing like mirages out of the land, so well they judged their
time, to meet at homecoming after hunting apart all day:
black-robed, like drifting shadows, they passed in the amber
twilight, while the sun stained the rocks and touched the hazy
depths of the sea basins, going down over the far, invisible
rim as if it vanished in midair, drawing out shadows.

The knots filled one cord and another and another, until all
the tale was told but two.

Hlil looked eastward, and of certainty, at the mid of sunfall, there came Ras. He need not have worried, he told himself. Ras would not be careless, not she—kel'e'en of the Kel's second highest rank. No reasoning with her, nothing but ordering her outright, and he could not, even if it were wise.

Ras s'Sochil Kov-Nelan. Merai's truesister.

Of that too, Niun had robbed him. They had been a trio, Hlil and Merai and Ras, in happier days; and he had dreamed dreams beyond his probabilities. He was skilled: that was his claim to place; he had had Merai's friendship; and because of that—he had been always near Ras. He had taught her, being older; had gamed with her and with Merai; had watched her every day of her life . . . and watched her harden since Merai's death. Her mother, Nelan, had been one of those who failed to come out of An-ehon; of that Ras said nothing. Ras laughed and spoke and moved, took meals with the Kel and went through all the motions of life; but she was not Ras as he had known her. She followed Niun s'Intel, as once, as a kath-child, she had followed him; where Niun walked, she was shadow; where he rested, she waited. It was a kind of madness, a game lacking humor or sense; but they were all a little mad, who survived An-ehon and served the she'pan Melein.

Ras arrived, in her own time, paused on the path below the rocks—began, wearily, to climb up to him. When she had done so, she sank down on the flat stone beside him, arms dropped loosely over her knees, her body heaving with her breaths.

"Did you hunt well?" he asked, although he knew what game she hunted.

"A couple of darters." It was not, for her, good. And it was a long walk that brought Ras back out of breath.

Hlil looked out, and in the darkening east, there were two dots on the horizon. The kel'anth and the beast, strung far apart.

"East," Ras said beside him, finding breath to speak. "Always east, along the same track. He would have brought back no game at all, but the beast routs things out for him. He delays only to gather it, and he takes long steps, this kel'anth of ours."

"Ras," he objected.

"He knows I am there."

He gathered up another stone, rolled it between his fingers. Ras simply rested, catching her breath.

"Why?" he said finally. "Ras—let him be. Anger serves no purpose; it dies unless you go on nursing it."

"And you do not."

"I am the kel'anth's second."

"So you were," she said, which was a heart-shot; and a moment later she looked on him with something like her old fondness. "You can be. I envy you."

"I have no love for him."

She accepted that offering in silence. Her fingers stole, as they would, to one of the many Honors which hung from her belts. Merai's death gift, that one, from Niun's hand.

"We cannot challenge him," she said. "Law forbids, if it were revenge for Merai; but there are other causes. Just causes."

"Stop thinking of it."

"He is very good. If I challenged him, he would kill me."

"Do not," he said, his heart clenched.

"You want to live," she accused him. And when he did not deny it: "Do you know how many generations of Kel-birth lie behind me?"

"More than mine," he said bitterly, heat risen already to his face: his plain birth was a thing of which he was deeply conscious.

"Eighteen," she said. "Eighteen generations. It comes to me, Hlil, that here I sit, last of a line that produced kel'ein and she'panei. Last. They are dead, all the rest; gods, and they would never understand such times as these. I look around me; I think—maybe I do not belong here; maybe I should go too, end it. And I think of my brother. Merai saw it standing in front of him—saw just the edge of the horizon waiting for us. And I think . . . he *died*, Hlil. He was not himself against this stranger; he missed a blow he could have turned. I know he could have turned it. Why? For fear? That was not Merai. It was not. So what do I believe? That he stepped aside—that he let himself die? And why so? At one word from these strangers that they are the Promised, the Voyagers-out? Could he stand in the way of such a thing?"

Hlil swallowed heavily, "Do not ask me what he thought."

"I ask myself. He could not see ahead. And then I think: *I see*. I am here. I am my brother's eyes. Gods, gods, he died knowing it was for a thing he would never see or understand. To clear the way, because he was set where this man had to stand. And I am desperate to see— Truth, Hlil: this kel'anth of ours will live under my witness; and if he cannot bear that, if he feels guilt, it is his guilt, let him bear it; and if he turns and strikes me—you will know. And what you do about that—I leave in your lap, Hlil-my-brother."

"Ras—"

"I leave it there, I say."

They sat still, staring alike at the shadowing land.

The beast arrived far in advance, a great warm-blooded animal, down-furred, pug-nosed and massive. Its feet turned in when it walked, its head wandered from side to side close to the ground as if it had lost something and forgotten what it was. It was probably nearsighted. Ras hissed a soft sound of distaste when it came up the rise toward them. Hlil felt a crawling at his gut whenever it was by him, for the length of those claws (venomed, the kel'anth had warned them) and the power of those sloping shoulders argued its way wherever it went, and something in the creatures set nerves on edge when they were disturbed. It came now, nosed wetly at each of them. Ras cursed it and pushed it, and Hlil set his hand at the side of its head and heaved to turn it aside, for all that those great jaws could take the hand entire. It moved, rebuffed finally. It put fear into him, and no beast Kutath had bred had ever done that; it consumed, gods, it surely must: it rolled with fat and moisture. On hungrier days Hlil had looked at it resentfully . . . but the thought of eating warm-blooded flesh nauseated him, like cannibalism.

Another gift of the kel'anth, this creature.

"Go on," he said to Ras. And when she delayed still: "Go on back."

She muttered soft agreement and rose, slipped away down the rocks, vanished into the shadows.

The beast made to follow her, snorted and came back again, nosed about and found the sand-star with uncanny accuracy. The star had not a chance. The beast—dus, its name was—lay down with the tendrils wrapped about one massive paw and ate with noisy relish. The sound became a rumbling, mind-dulling, pervasive.

Contentment weighted Hlil's limbs, at odds with the distress that tugged at him from another direction. It was as if he grew two minds, one warring with the other. The dus—he connected the sensations, the slow purring, felt his senses dulled. . . .

"No!" he said.

It stopped, a silence like sudden nakedness, devoid of warmth. Small, glittering eyes lifted to him.

"Go away," he told it. It did not. He sat and watched Niun come, weary and limping more than a man should from a day's ordinary hunting. He ought to walk down to the path, signaling to the kel'anth that he might simply take the way into camp, being the last.

He did not. He sat still, let Niun walk up the stony walk to her perch among the rocks.

"Is someone still out?" Niun asked, hard-breathing and in a manner of some concern.

The accent with which he spoke was also different; they had in common only the hal'ari, the high tongue, preserved changeless in the city-machines, and the kel'anth struggled badly in what he had learned of the mu'ara, the tribe speech.

"No," Hlil said, rising, ignoring the kel'anth's vexation. "You are last; I will walk down with you."

The beast rose up, shambled out to rub against Niun as he started down; Hlil walked as close to it as he must.

"You walked far," Hlil said.

"Ai," Niun muttered as he walked, evading him.

"So did Ras."

That stopped him. Niun turned a veiled face toward him, looking up on the shadowed slope. "Your sending?"

"No."

"She wants a quarrel—does she not, kel Hlil?"

"Perhaps. Perhaps she is only curious where you go . . . daily."

"That too, it may be. I beg you—intervene."

That was not the answer he had expected to provoke. He slipped his hands into the back of his belt, far from his weapons, evidencing reluctance for quarrel. "I beg *you*, kel'anth . . . bear with her."

"I do," he said. "What more can I do?"

Hlil regarded him, the alien fineness of him, the familiar Honors which winked among his robes: easy to hate—this too-fine, too-skilled stranger. The dus laid its ears back and rumbled an ominous sound, stilled as Niun touched it.

"Ras and I," Hlil said, "have little more to say to each other. You speak to her if you like. I cannot."

The kel'anth did not answer him—turned and picked his way to the bottom, walked onto the sandy track toward camp, the great dus ambling along behind him. "Yai!" he snapped at it then, and it fell back, turned aside from the trail into camp: it rarely did come in.

Hlil followed, seething with resentment, as if the kel'anth

abandoned him equally with the beast . . . followed the
kel'anth's straight figure in among the shadows of overhang-
ing cliffs, and out into light again . . . the rim itself suddenly
on the left hand, a dizzying drop to the cut which gave them
refuge from the kel'anth's enemies aloft.

"Tell the sentry we are in," Niun turned to bid him. "Here,
I will take your pouch."

The dismissal further angered him. He shed the pouch con-
taining his day's take into the kel'anth's outstretched hand
and left the trail, going up into the high rocks.

It was a reasonable order. Had Merai ordered, he would
have felt no least resentment; he argued so with himself,
through the heat of anger. *To claim my hunting for yours?*
he wondered, a petty suspicion, when in fact the kel'anth did
him a great courtesy, to offer to bear his burden that little distance: rank forbade. It was always like that between them,
that bitterness underlay whatever dealings they had one with
the other, that they could not speak the simplest words without offense; that they could not take loyalty for granted between them, which they ought to be able to do, for the tribe's
sake.

It was Ras, who committed slow suicide . . . Ras's eyes
were on him too, surrogate for Merai.

It had been so when Merai was alive, that Merai's was the
greater soul, the higher-tempered, the quicker—a great prince
of the People, kel Merai; and he was only Hlil s'Sochil, born
of Kath-caste and no special father—no shame, but no great
distinction; no particular grace, nor handsomeness—
weapons-scars had not improved him in that; never quickness
of tongue. Only skill, and stubborn adherence to the kel-law
and what seemed right.

Those two things had never diverged, save now.

Niun hesitated at the bottom, in the shadows, staring into
the camp. Ras was not waiting for him. He had thought she
might be; she had, then, gone her way to Kel. Mad she was,
but not enough to discommode herself, sitting out in the
dark. He summoned a little of that cold-bloodedness of hers
and slung the two pouches of game over his shoulder, walked
his unhurried course in the shadow of the cliffs.

It was a place which offered at least the hope of concealment from humans, this deep maze of eroded overhangs . . .
a stream course, perhaps, while water had flowed the high
plain and seas had surged from rim to rim of the great

basins. The cut ran down and down the vast terraces, more and more steeply, to lose itself in the evening murk. Between these cliffs was a sandy floor, dangerous at the rimside, the seam of a sandslip running a good stone's throw up the center; farther along the sands were stable. Infrequent gusts carried clouds of sand down into the cut, making veils necessary even for children on windy days. It was no comfort, but it was shelter of a sort, a bad place in storm, on which account the seniors of the Kel had objected; but he had overridden them. They had experienced fire; they knew the theory of machines and strike from orbit; but they still did not realize how thorough an enemy's scan might be. There were deep places within the maze, decent separation for the castes, Sen to the north, with the she'pan; Kel to the south, nearest the entry, to protect it, if it were a question of enemies who dared face them; and farthest back, deepest, the Kath, the child-rearers and children: the strongest place of all for the children, of whom they had lost most in An-ehon, in the ruin of the city.

One strike from above, only one, and they were done. He much feared so.

He turned in at the shelter which served for kel-hall, walked deep within. The glitter of weapon hilts and Honors pierced the gloom, shadowy faces showed in the light of oil-wood flame. One came to him, a kel'en who had not yet won the kel-scars: Taz, his name was; on such as he he fell the burden of all labor in the Kel. Niun slung the game pouches into his hand. "Mine and Hlil's. Carry it to Kath."

His eyes located Ras, inevitably, among those who stood to welcome him. He slid his glance aside from her and the others, unveiled and turned to make the token respect to the empty shrine, the three stones piled in symbol of the Holy, which they had lost in their flight. The whole place smelled of oilwood, the fiber of which served for incense.

The others had settled at his dismissal; he walked among them, sank down nearest the small fire which served them. On a square of leather which served them for a common-bowl, was supper, an *ab'aak* Kath had contrived out of other days' hunting—the pulp of pipe and whatever flesh could be spared: more pipe than meat, truth be told, and done without salt or utensils or other amenities. They had fared worse, and better. He ate, in the others' silence.

Hlil returned, sat with him, took his own share. There was idle talk finally, a muttering of small matters, the sort of

things passed among folk who had spent all their lives in
each other's company, but self-consciously, in the hal'ari and
not in the more natural tribe speech. It faltered. Constantly
there was a silence ready to enfold them, as every evening.
Niun sat staring into the fire, letting the chatter flow through
him, about him, unparticipant. He scarcely knew their names,
let alone those of the dead, who figured all too often in their
rememberings; old jokes were lost on him; too much had to
be explained. In truth his mind was elsewhere, and perhaps
they knew it.

He remembered, when he let himself. Memory was where
his own Kel lived; his House; his friends and companions. He
remembered the ship: that was most vivid. Reminiscence
could become a disease with him, and he did not permit it often, for even the most unpleasant things involved the familiar, and home, and past pains were duller. Wise, he thought,
that the law of the People had commanded them to forget, in
each between-worlds voyage . . . even to cease to speak the
language or think the old thoughts. To go into the Dark was
to return to the center of things, where only the hal'ari was
spoken, where worlds were not important, where no past existed, or future.

Even on Kutath it was done, the deliberate forgetting, by
all but the scholars of Sen-caste. It was, he suspected, the
sanity of a world so very old. Sen remembered, No kel'en
might, save in the chants of legends, of which he was one.

The Ships which went out,
they sang of his kind,
With the World at their backs . . .

The noise of their voices oppressed him as silence. He
looked up, realizing his lapse, looked about him, at Hlil, and
the several survivors of the first rank of the Kel, the Husbands of the she'pan.

"We—" he said, and silence fell, flowing to the rearmost
ranks. "We should consider a matter. Our supplies . . . in
An-ehon. And what we do next."

"Send us," a young kel'en exclaimed from the middle
ranks, and voices seconded him. "Aye," another said. "Day
by day, we could bring them out, if we hunt that way."

"No," he said shortly. "It is not that simple. Listen to me.
Putting a limb of the Kel into An-ehon . . . gods know what
we could stir up. Ships may have landed there. The place

may be watched, and not alone with eyes. Rubble may have buried what is left . . . no knowing; and if we go to the open land again—chances are we will be seen. What hit An-ehon could come down on us when we have only canvas over our heads. We need the supplies; I am sick of seeing Kath struggle to make do with what little we have. And I agree with you, we are pressing luck staying here. But I prefer rock between us and them for now. I am thinking of moving up into the hills."

"Not our range," objected Seras, eldest of the Husbands.

"Then we take it," he said in a small and bitter voice.

The fusion of tribes, the merging of Holies . . . oil and water. It was trouble; he saw their faces, and it was the hardness he expected to see.

You cannot hold this tribe well, they were thinking. *What power have you to hold two at once?*

"The she'pan's word?" Seras asked.

That too was challenge.

"I have not talked with her. I am going to."

"So," said Seras.

There was silence after that, no murmur of suggestions, no expressions of opinion. Their faces, alike scarred with the kel-scars, regarded him, waited on him, set as stone. He considered asking again for their free discussion, reckoned that he would have only silence for answer. He brushed at his robes, gathered himself up and walked through their midst as they rose, perforce, a respect which might be omitted, which they never omitted, which began, to him, to have the flavor of mockery.

They would do their talking after he was gone, he reckoned. Hlil and Seras and the rest of the Husbands led them, in truth; him they only obeyed. He veiled himself, walked out along the narrow trail which followed the curving of the cliffs in the dark, back farther in the cliffs where in places not even starshine reached. A sandfall sheeted down, daily building at a large cone of sand with a constant, hissing whisper. He walked between it and the cliff, ducked his head from the windblown particles. He missed the dus, which probably hunted somewhere above, in the rocks: well that it had not come in with him, this night, with resentments smoldering in the Kel.

And on that thought he looked back, half expecting Ras to be there. She was not.

At the sharp bend of the cliff he walked across the open

center, past the stand of pipe, which rose at an assortment of angles, its greater segments thick as a man's waist. Good fortune that it grew here, making far easier their existence with its reliable moisture; it was the only good fortune they had to their account.

Faint light showed in Sen's retreat. Gold-robes who sat in contemplation at the entry looked up in mild inquiry, scrambled up in haste when they recognized him, and stood aside in respect for the kel-first. He walked farther, into the shadow and lamplight of the inner sanctuary, disturbing more of them from their evening's meditations. He unveiled out of respect to their elders, and one went ahead while he waited, to ask permission, and returned with a gesture bidding him pass.

He rounded the turning, into the last secrecy, where a few gold-robes sat about the piled stones which served Melein for her chair of office, in this little recess which served as the she'pan's hall, primitive and far from the honor she was due. Her robes were white, her face always unveiled: Mother, the tribe ought to call her, and she'pan, keeper-of-Mysteries, the Holy.

Truesister, Niun thought of her, with a longing toward that companionship they had once had. Often as he had seen her in the white robes and surrounded by sen'ein, he could not forget kinship.

She motioned dismissal of the others, summoning him; he bowed his head and waited as the sen'ein passed, murmured courtesy to the seh'anth, old Sathas—received back a grumbled acknowledgment, but that was Sathas's way with everyone.

"Come," Melein said.

He did so, took the offered place at her feet.

"You look tired," she said.

He shrugged.

"You have some trouble?"

"She'pan—Kel does not admit this is a safe place to be."

"So. Are not others worse?"

That was a drawing question; impatience. "Others require taking. But perhaps that is what we have to do."

"Kel agrees?"

"Kel offers no opinion."

"Ah."

"The Holy, the things we lost in the city. . . . I think by

now if there were ships we would have seen them. Give me leave to go in. I think we can get them out. And for the rest—maybe it is not something in which Kel should have an opinion."

"You have begun to stop waiting."

He looked up at her, made a small gesture of helplessness, disturbed more than he wanted her to see. "I know the old kel'ein say weather change is a little distance off yet . . . on the average of years. But we ought to prepare our choices. This cut will be headed for the basins when the wind starts up; I believe that. We have to do something; I have been trying to think what. Chance is lying heavier and heavier on our shoulders."

"You have talked with the Kel."

He shrugged uncomfortably. "I have told them."

"And they have no opinion."

"None they voiced."

"So." She seemed to stare past him, her eyes focused on something on the ground beyond him, her face half in shadow, gold-lit by the oilwood flames. At last her eyes flickered, the membrane passing twice before them, betraying some inner emotion.

"Which way would you go?" she asked. "Down, into the basins? They tell me tribes range there too, that the air is warmer and moisture more plentiful; we would find larger tribes, likely, or smaller ranges. You would win challenge. I have no doubt that you would. Your skill to theirs—is far more than they would want to meet: nine years with the finest masters of the Kel—I have no dread of that at all. We could, yes. Even seize upon a Holy to venerate, take their supplies, if our own are lost . . . the gods forbid. And what more?"

"I am kel'en; how should I know?"

"You were never without opinions in all your life."

"Say that I find no better hope in them."

"You are missing one of your *j'tai*."

His hand went to his chest belt before he caught her meaning, touched the vacant place among his Honors.

"It was one of your first," she pursued him. "A golden leaf, a *leaf*, on Kutath. Surely it would not have dropped away and you not notice it. I have—for many days."

"Duncan has it." It was no confession; she knew: he knew now she always had.

"We do not discuss a kel'en who left without my blessing."

"He went with mine," he said.

"Did he? Even the kel'ein of this tribe consult me; even with the example of you and Duncan before them. I have waited for you to come to me to tell me. And I have waited for you to come to speak for the Kel. And you do neither, even now. Why?"

He met her eyes, no easy matter.

"Niun," she murmured, "Niun, how have we come to such a pass, he and you and I? You taught him to be mri, and yet he could defy my orders; and now you follow after him. Is that the trouble I hear from the Kel? That they know where your heart is?"

"Perhaps it is," he said faintly. "Or that theirs is constantly with Merai."

"Because you constantly push them away."

There was a long silence after.

"I do not think so," he said.

"But that is part of it."

"Yes. Probably that is part of it."

"Duncan went back," she said, "of his own choice. Was it not so?"

"He did not go *back*. He went to the humans, yes, but he did not go back. He still serves the People."

"So you believed . . . or you would never have given him your blessing. And have you talked of this with the Kel?"

"No."

"Humans would surely not let him go again, if he even lived to reach them."

"He *has* reached them." Niun made a gesture which included An-ehon, northward, the wide sky above the rocks. "There have been no ships, no more attacks. She'pan, I know that he has reached them, and they have heard him."

"Heard him say *what*?"

That struck him dumb, for all his faith in Duncan did not bridge that gap of realities, that could span what was mri and what was human with a request to go away.

"And you talk of regaining the means to move," she said. "So I have thought in that direction too, but perhaps with different aims. You always hunt eastward. I have heard so."

He nodded, without looking at her.

"You hope to stay close hereabouts," she said. "Or to move east, perhaps. Do you hope, even after so many days—that he will find us?"

"Some such thing."

"I shall send Hlil to An-ehon," she said. "He may arrange his own particulars; he may take whatever of the Kel he needs, and a hand of sen'ein."

"Without me."

"You have other business. To find Duncan."

On two thoughts his heart leaped up and crashed down again. "Gods, go off with the Kel in one place and yourself left with no sufficient guard—"

"I have waited," Melein said, as if she had not heard him. "First, to know how long this silence in the heavens would last. We need what is in An-ehon, yes; a hand of days or more: Hlil will need a little time in the city, and more returning if they are successful, and carrying their limit. But alone, with no burden at all—I daresay you could search even to the landing site and reach us again here in that time."

"Possibly," he said. "But—"

"I have weighed things for myself. I doubt you will succeed; Duncan surely went with his dus, and if it were still with him, he could have found us by now . . . if he were coming. But I loved him too, our Duncan. Take it at that value, and find him if you can; or find that we have lost him, one or the other. And then set your mind on what you have to do for this tribe."

"You need not send me, not to satisfy *me*."

"Lose no time." She bent, took his face between her hands, kissed his brow, delayed to look at him. "It may be, if you are too late getting back—you will not find us here. There are other cities, other choices."

"Gods, and no more defense there than we had in An-ehon. You know, you know what humans can do—"

"Go. Get moving."

She let him go, and he rose up, bent to press a farewell kiss to her cheek. His hand touched hers, fingers held a moment, panic beating in him. He was skilled enough to fend challenge from her; Hlil was; she was parting with both of them.

"My blessing," she whispered at him. He went, quickly, past the wondering eyes of the sen'ein, averting his face from their stares. He was halfway back to the Kel before he recalled the veil.

And suddenly, by the sandfall, a shadow startled him, kel-black and somber. Ras. He finished tucking the veil in place, met her. "Ras?" He acknowledged her courteously, attempting comradeship.

But she said no word. She never did. She walked behind him, a coldness at his back.

Silence fell in Kel, at his coming. They waited, a ring of black, of gold-limned faces. He came among them and through their midst with Ras in his wake as far as the ring of the second rank; they stayed seated when he motioned them to do so. He dropped to his knees nearest the lights, across from Hlil; and he removed both veil and headcloth, *mez* and *zaïdhe*, in token of humility, of request.

"Kel'ein," he said in that silence. "Yes—at least to the matter of recovering our belongings from the city." He leaned his hands on his knees and drew breath, gazing at their shadowed faces, row on row, to the limits of the recess. "Hlil will be in charge of that party; Hlil, surely the she'pan will give you some advice in that matter. If not, seek it of her."

"Aye," Hlil muttered with a quizzical look on his broad face.

"I warn you this much: be wary. A kel'en should go in ahead, searching for any traces of landing. There could be machines set to sense your presence, very small. Anything that does not seem to belong there—O gods, kel Hlil, be suspicious, of every small thing. And if you should see ships aloft, do not lead them; go astray, lose them, until the wind has blotted your trail. They do not depend on eyes, but on instruments."

"You refuse leading, kel'anth?"

"I am sent elsewhere." His heart set itself to beating painfully. "Kel Seras, be in charge over the Kel that stays in camp; Hlil, I have said. Good evening to you."

They did not question him; he desperately did not invite it. He rose, gathered up an empty pouch for food, slipped on the headcloth again and veiled himself.

And turned to face kel Ras, who had risen among the others, whose cold face was veilless, eyes hard above the kel-scars. "Ras," he said in a voice he wanted to carry no farther than it had to. "Ras, in this—go with Hlil."

"If Hlil wills," she said likewise quietly; but in the silence of the Kel it surely carried. It was more reasonable in her than he had expected, which itself made him suspect some tangled motive.

"Thank you," he said, and started away, through their midst.

"Kel'anth," Hlil called out; and when he stopped and looked back: "Will you take nothing with you?"

"Kath and Sen will be short of hunters. The dus and I will manage."

"That beast—"

"—cares for me," he said, knowing their disapproval of it. "Life and honors."

Hlil omitted any wish to him in return. Only Ras came and with irony watched him out onto the path. She did not follow. He looked back to be sure, and once again; and then put her from his concerns and walked on, the long corridor outward.

He alarmed the sentry, coming out at such an hour. He gave the signal, a low whistle, and passed, hearing the kel'en high in the rocks settle back to his place.

Dus, he called when he had reached the outside, the level of the plain.

It was there. He kept walking and felt it before he heard it, a heavy shape moving among the rocks, a whuff of breath suddenly at his heels as he passed a boulder. He sensed disturbance in it, an echo of his own troubled mind, and tried to calm himself, as a man must who walked with dusei.

He took the way he had taken daily, from which he had come this same evening. He was footsore even in starting out; day after day he had pushed himself farther than he ought. Sense said he should rest now; but he could do that on the journey, when he must. Time was precious—life itself, if one ran out of it.

And anxiously as he walked he scanned all the heavens, to be sure that they were empty of watchers, gazed over all the flat horizons, the rounded hills. The night-bound desolation dismayed him, starker than it was by day. Dead stars above. And enemies.

A soft surge of strength came into him then, beast-blank: dus mind, offered to his need. It wished to comfort, brushing against him in its waddling stride.

He took the gift, bearing eastward.

The place where their own ship had landed: that was surely where Duncan had gone, to the first place humans would have come in trying to locate them. He walked steadily—did not dismiss the dus from his side to hunt, not now: he needed it by him to find a safe way, exhausted as he was, for the open sands held ugly surprises.

It made him no complaints. Dusei were night walkers by preference. It tossed its massive head and ranged either at his side or a little ahead of him, snuffing the wind, panting a little at times from the pace he set.

Duncan . . . had never been able to match his stride. Always he had had to shorten his steps when Duncan was by him; and the very air of Kutath was hostile to a human's lungs. It was madness that Duncan had ventured this desert alone.

The chance was—he admitted it to himself—that the odds had overtaken Duncan, coming back, if not going. Only one thing Duncan had had in his favor, that he might have been mri enough to handle: the company of his dus.

Find it, he willed his own, casting it the image. Dusei, it was said, had no memory for events, only for persons and places. He shaped Duncan for it; he shaped the other dus, so long its companion. *Find them; hunt.*

Whether it understood clearly or not he could not tell; on the following day it began to radiate something in answer, which prickled at the nape and tightened the skin behind his ears.

Friend, he shaped.

It tossed its head and kept casting about anxiously, making occasional puffs of breath. Its general tendency was eastward, but it had no track, no more than in all the other treks they had made, only a vague, persistent nervousness.

He slept by snatches, day or night, whenever he could go no farther, curled up against the dus's warmth until he could regain his strength. He was by now out onto the wide flat, where the land went on forever, save for the rim and the void beyond, world's edge. He drove himself, not madly, as one who did not know his limits, but as one who did, and thought he might pass them by a margin.

He caught a darter or two in his path, and for all he hated raw flesh, he ate, and shared with the dus, which persisted in its distress.

And finally he looked back, at the west, where the sun set with a shadow on it, amber and red and darker tones.

Not moisture-bearing cloud, not on Kutath.

Dust across the sun.

He stared at it, and beside him the dus flicked its ears uneasily and moaned.

III

The weather had held steady for days, out of Kutath's eternally cloudless sky, but the west bore a murkiness this dawn which boded trouble.

And the back trail . . . daylight showed nothing, no hint of movement.

Duncan kept moving, looking frequently over his shoulder; it was the land's deceptive roll, a trick of the eye—on his side for once. He made what time he could, looking to the storm with hope.

Cover, he desperately needed.

And again and again he sought the presence of his dus. The beast ranged out at times, hunting, perhaps, exercising a little fear-warding on those who followed, kel'ein, strangers. He was full of dread whenever it was parted from him, that it might try to attack his pursuers, that they might kill it.

Here, he ordered it, but it did not touch his mind, so that he went alone, blind in that sense he needed. He walked steadily . . . cut off a bit of the blue pipe which he carried among his other supplies, and slipped it into his mouth beneath the veils. Doubled, he wore them, like the robes, for although he had become acclimated, he had no business carrying the smallish pack he bore, no business doing anything that taxed his breathing. *We are not bearers of burdens,* mri were wont to say, disdaining manual labor and any who would perform it; and he had long since understood the common sense in that attitude, in which a mri kel'en walked the land with no more burden than his weapons, often taking not so much as a canteen, where no free water existed. He pushed himself too hard. He knew it, in the rawness of his throat, the headaches which half blinded him. He played just beyond the convenient reach of his mri shadows—curious, he reckoned them, keeping an eye on a stranger, and it was not to his advantage to increase the pace. He kept himself constantly alert to the horizons and the sand underfoot, stayed to sandstone shelves and domes where he could, not alone to avoid leaving tracks, but to avoid the dangers of the sand. *Mez* and *zaidhe*, veil and visored headcloth, and the several layers of the kel-robes: these he had chosen, although others had been offered; and a pistol and the ancient *yin'ein*, the weapons-of-honor . . . these he had by similar choice. He reckoned he might try a shot to dissuade his followers, but firing *at* them . . . all the kel-law abhorred such a thing; he had more than the robes to mark him mri, and he would not.

The dust began to kick up in discernible clouds, wave fronts borne on the wind. The sand ran in moving serpentines like water across the broad shelf of sandstone which he followed.

He turned his head yet again, half-blinded by the sand, lowered his visor against the dust.

And when he looked back again before him there was a black figure on the northwest horizon, nearer by far than he had expected, and in a different quarter.

Panic tugged at him, bidding him swing away south, and perhaps that was what they wanted him to do. He glanced to that horizon and saw nothing but naked land and naked, sand-fouled sky. There was an incline: his eye had learned to pick variations out of the vast samenesses, the incredible flat expanses. Ambush was possible there.

He bore west, summoning his dus with all his might, apprehensive now of every quarter of the horizon. They might cut him off to question him; and even a stone's-throw sight of him would tell them he did not belong here, that some connection might be made between ships and destroyed cities and a stranger-kel'en.

Only the dusei, if they had not killed them, his own and the wild ones which were its offspring, might set fear enough into them, sendings of nameless dread.

But time would come when that fear itself drove them to attack, for kel'ein were trained to caution, not cowardice. They would fight the fear as readily as they would an enemy.

His heartbeat hammered in his temples; there came times when he walked blind, sight blurred, numbed by want of air. He dared not, as he wanted desperately to do—abandon the pack. They would come on it, know by the alien things of it that here was a mystery they could not leave unsolved. A sand-laden gust rocked him, rattled off his lowered visor, stinging his hands, the only part of his flesh exposed. He leaned into it, hands tucked into the wide sleeves of his robes. The battering gusts made him stagger, and after a time he was less and less sure that he remained true to west. The rock underfoot was uneven, and dipped and rose, misguiding him when he needed to catch his balance.

Dus, he sent, desperate, cursing it for its tendency to be elsewhere when it was most needed. The wind blasted body heat away from him, weakened his limbs. He began to be afraid, wondering whether to take shelter for fear of the wind itself, or to keep walking, trying to lose his pursuers while the wind erased tracks and obscured vision.

He slipped suddenly, rock peeling under his feet; he hit soft sand, caught his balance, tried to retreat onto the sandstone shelf, but it had run out. He tried vision without the visor, a mistake; he lowered it again, and in that little time he stopped to clear his eyes his limbs were chilled to the bone, shaking so that it tore his joints.

He was blind and out on open sand; and of a sudden he began to be very much afraid, that he was making wrong choices, that he should have stayed on the rock surface. It was not panic fear, only deep dread; he kept moving, into the wind, the only means he had of determining west.

Fear grew. He looked behind him and the bleared eye of Na'i'in showed through the storm and the visor like the ghost of a sun, wan and sickly hued. In all the world there was neither up nor down, neither horizon nor sand underfoot, only the sun strong enough to penetrate the murk. He swung about again, sucked dusty air through the veils, weary with the battering. If he went down, he thought, he would die.

"Dus," he muttered aloud, wishing, pleading it back to him. The wind drowned all sound, the demon voice becoming an element in itself. His knees tottered under him, his joints wearied from the slipping sand and the force of the gusts, until at last he slipped to his knees and hunched away from the wind, fumbling with shaking hands after the bit of pipe he carried. His fingers were stiff; he bit the piece instead of using the knife, stuffed the rest back. His mouth was so dry it stuck, and his eyes stung with the dryness. "Dus," he murmured again, despairing.

A curious paralysis had settled on him, the cessation of pain. The wind vibrated into his very bones, masked every other sound, and became no-sound. He had no more force at his back; sand was piling up there, sheltering him, making an arc about him, drifting into his lap.

And fear—grew. Sweat prickled on his skin, sucked dry before it could run. He began to think of something creeping up on him, something better adapted than he to the wind and storm—it seeped into him, so that slowly he moved, stirred himself, thrust himself to his feet and staggered farther against the wind. Panic drove him, a dread so strong he tore his knees with his driving strides.

Dus-fear, not his own: he recognized it suddenly; not his own beast, but another, and near. It drew on the images of the rational mind, shaped itself. Ha-dus, wild one, wild-born, of the tame pair the mri had brought here . . . and dangerous without his own to fend it back.

He moved; it was all he could do.

And suddenly a shadow came at him on the other side.

He snatched at the shortsword, staggering aside—knew suddenly, recognized it.

His dus. It materialized out of the murk, pressed against him, and he sank down with its great body between him and the wind. It wove this way and that between him and the gusts; and another shape and another joined it, slope-shouldered, massive, weaving him a circle of protection. He knew his own, flung his arms about its hot, fat-rolled neck, and the beast heaved itself down beside him, five hundred kilos of velvet-furred devotion, venom-clawed, radiating a ward-impulse that meant business.

The other dusei, the wild ones, settled about him so that among the three he was warm and sheltered from the wind. Sand built up about them too, but each time they rose and shook it off, their great strength untroubled by the effort. He lay against the shoulder of his own, breathing in great gasps—found strength enough finally to shrug out of the pack, to fumble out packets of dried food. He put bits in his mouth, sipped at the canteen, holding water there to moisten them, and finally gained control enough to chew and swallow.

His dus nudged at him, begging; he offered it a piece of dried meat. The massive head pushed at his hand, flat face inclined; the prehensile upper lip picked the tidbit off so delicately he felt nothing but the hot breath on his hand. The other dusei crowded him, and for one and then the other he offered the remainder, in either hand, fingers carefully out of the way, for the jaws could crush bone. The bits vanished as daintily as the other. He tucked down again, hands within sleeves, conscious of vibration, first from his own dus and then from the others, pleasure-sound, inaudible in the shriek of the wind. Eyes shut, ears down, nostrils opening only slightly, filtering through fringed internal hairs and membranes, the dusei were not suffering in the least.

Duncan snugged down between, wiped what he reckoned was a trace of blood from his nose and bit himself off another bit of pipe, as safe as any man could be in Kutath's wild, companioned by such as these.

IV

The younglings huddled, muttered in hissing whispers. Occasionally one looked up, shifted weight uncomfortably.

Suth loathed them, once companions. They came near the bed when they must, offering food rich and elaborate. They trembled until it was accepted. They mourned one elder on the ship; another was in the making. Suth Horag-gi clenched degh's bony lips and groaned in the agony of Change.

Suth: *it*, neuter until the hormonal shifts had begun to course hot and cold through degh's body, until appetite increased and temper shortened to the verge of madness. The ship *Shirug* moved far apart from human ships orbiting Kutath, and ignored inquiries. There was the Wrapping of the departed elder; there was mourning; there was *ag-arhd*, the Consuming. These were secret things, in which Suth felt an instinctive vulnerability. Degh was not capable of full function in degh's hormone-tormented state, moving toward Change. Humans inquired, offered help, doubtless deviously motivated, hoping to learn enough to gain control . . . offered regret, soliciting information in the process. Degh commanded degh's attendants to silence.

Degh ate. Already the pallor of youngling skin was diminishing, and each move freed tissue-thin sheets of former skin, exposing elder-dark new skin beneath, a complete skin change twice since the Consuming. Suth was sore, sensitive new skin like a bleeding wound. The joints of degh's facial plates ached, aggravated by the need to eat, to drink, constantly. Degh burned with fever, heightened metabolism, and most of all those parts which had not yet determined function burned, swollen, maddening with pain.

A youngling ventured near with *mul*, water-soaked, to ease the skin. Suth suffered it, sucking on a straw from a mug of soi, occasionally reaching to a platter for a sweet.

Suddenly there was pain, and Suth screamed and flung the

platter and struck. Something cracked, and when the grayness cleared, other younglings were bearing away the dead one and cleaning up the spilled sweetmeats. Suth hissed satisfaction, annoyance departed. Another took up the washing, more carefully.

"Report," Suth breathed, clenching degh's hand about a new mug of soi. Degh sucked at it, looked at the frightened younglings. "Witless, the news: report."

"Favor, Honored, there is no report available; storm is covering the land."

"Storm."

"A vast and violent storm. Honored, 687.78 *koingh* across. We attempted to penetrate it, but at this range, and with the dust—"

Suth breathed a sigh of weary pleasure. "Perhaps the human Duncan will die."

"Perhaps, Honored."

Degh wished this earnestly. This human had killed the reverence bai Sharn, in command of *Shirug*. Human elders on *Saber* had then dismissed this Duncan as if this act were inconsiderable to them. Degh had been only youngling then, neuter, confused, horrified by the death as all the younglings had been horrified.

Now degh yearned toward the death of this human; it was anomaly, perverted; it no longer knew what it was, this Sten Duncan. It had killed younglings, it and its mri allies, and now it killed an elder. Its kind excused this . . . threatened now even to treat with mri, through this mri-imprinted youngling. The very thought set Suth's hearts to hammering and made deghn short of breath.

Forty-three years the mercenary Kel had served regul against humans, and now at war's end came a new arrangement to trouble regulkind: mri, intriguing with humans.

Adult authority was desperately needed in this crisis, a mind to make decisions on which the survival of other elders might rest, back at Kesrith, even on homeworld itself. Sharn was dead; elder Hulagh was years removed, on Kesrith. Someone had to make the decisions.

The pain. . . .

"Honored, Honored, be easy," a youngling murmured, sponging gently with the *mul*. Suth panted and strove to rise, fell back again, amazed at the feel of degh's own body, the increase in girth. The bony carapace which covered the face ached maddeningly. Degh closed degh's eyes and breathed in great gasps, aching in degh's lower belly until the pain was intolerable.

"Degh is in crisis," a youngling moaned. "Days, days of this; it must end, it must end, or degh will die."

"Silence!" degh shouted, and shouting helped; the pain ebbed somewhat. Muscles contracted. The hearts sped and the temperature rose.

It was true. Degh was in deep trouble. Degh had served bai Hulagh, male, and approached Impression; degh had looked to the time of Change, knowing degh's future gender with smug certainty, female to Hulagh's male . . . ambition, to mate the Eldest of great doch Alagn: security, and vast power.

But to Suth's lasting dismay there had been transfer; Suth, most honored of Hulagh's youngling attendants, passed as special favor to bai Sharn, who undertook a mission on which but one elder could be risked: Sharn, female, on a voyage years in length. Maleness tempted; Sharn herself was very high in doch Alagn.

Sharn, female, fourth eldest of one of the greatest of the docha, and murdered by a deranged human youngling.

Degh had been Impressed in witnessing that incomprehensible act. To replace bai Sharn . . . to *be* Sharn . . . that desire came with the Consuming.

And degh could not complete the Change, poised between, for days neither Hulagh's nor Sharn's, neither female nor male.

Degh screamed aloud and cursed the human who had done this thing, who allied with mri and tried to lure others of his species after. A hundred twenty-three stars, a hundred twenty-three . . . dead . . . lifeless . . . systems. And even after seeing the deadly track the mri had cut through the galaxy . . . humans approached these killers and spoke of peace.

Degh must live. Species demanded. *Life* demanded. More than personal ambition, more than doch, than the chance of elevating degh's little doch of Horag, allying to powerful Alagn at its highest levels: these things were motivation . . . but this touched something at depth Suth had never felt, which perhaps no regul had ever had to feel, for no regul had ever confronted such a possibility, death on such a scale. Degh must live, generate, produce lives to deal with this threat, innumerable lives.

There came another touch at degh's body, faint, tremulous.

It was Nagn, an older youngling. And it tore back with a shriek of dismay.

"Honored," it cried, "I burn!"

It had happened: next eldest had gone prematurely into Change. Suth cried out with relief and shut degh's eyes.

The pain moved lower. Muscle contractions began at last, fever increasing, skin sloughing and peeling. The younglings brought food, and bathed deghn, and applied unguents to the swollen parts.

Scarcely supported by the younglings, the Honored Nagn moved again to degh's side, touched, shuddering in degh's own pain.

The choice was Suth's. Suth's body was making it. The swelling continued as one vestigial set of organs was absorbed, and the other began, in convulsive heaves of Suth's body, to press down into the membrane covering the aperture . . . descended, evident as it would never be henceforth save in mating.

"Male!" a youngling declared.

Nature's logic. Suth smiled, a tightening of the muscles beneath his eyes, and this despite the pain. Elsewhere Nagn writhed in the throes of Change, but Nagn's choice was set, and swifter. Tiag cried out in agony, and Morkhug, the hysteria of Change settling upon all the eldest.

The pain ebbed in time. Suth moved, supported by younglings. Never again would he stand long unaided. His bulk, already increased by his appetite, would increase twice more. His legs, once strong, would atrophy until little muscle lay under the abundant fat, although his arms, constantly exercised by the operation of the prosthetic supports, would remain strong. Senses would dim hereafter, save for sight. The mind dominated. Regul memory was instant and indelible; he would live, barring accident or murder, for three hundred years more, remembering every chance moment and every minute detail to which he paid attention.

He had lived to be adult, and only thirty percent of regul did so; he was, by virtue of being the first adult on the ship, remote from others of greater age . . . an elder, in command of *Shirug* and of whatever other adults matured; only one percent of regul reached such status.

And by the Change which had come on him he could not now meet his old bai Hulagh as mate . . . but as a rival of another doch. He was senior to Nagn and Tiag and Morkhug, who were Alagn, and therefore this great Alagn ship, the pride of the doch, became Horag territory. Hulagh of Alagn had miscalculated, reckoning every eventuality but Sharn's premature death and a Horag sexing ahead of the others. Suth smiled.

Then he looked on the three who were in the throes of Change, . . . on Nagn, who was flushing with the swift completion of agonies which had held him for days.

"Out!" he shouted at the other younglings.

They fled. He struck at those who supported him, and they joined the others in flight. He could not long stand, but sank down on his weakened legs, panting.

"Honor, reverend Nagn," he said.

"Honor, bai Suth." She struggled to sit. He had deprived her of younglings to help her, but she was female and would always be more mobile than he save in the final stage of carrying.

And she had not near attained his dignity of bulk, nor suffered the several skin changes. Those were, for her, only beginning.

"Favor," said Suth, "Nagn Alagn-ni."

"Favor, Suth Horag-gi."

She came to him, the order of their age of Change, although it was established by mere moments. He mated her, with dispatch and twice, for honor to her precedence of the others. She was next eldest and would hold that rank while he held the ship. He moved then, necessity, and mated the other two, which likely would produce no young, but which would Impress them with more haste, painful as it was for them. He would mate them until all three were with as many young as they could carry. These were his officers; it was economical, his maleness. There was need of rapid reproduction of Horag young: eldest claimed all young in any mating. As other younglings aboard *Shirug* sexed, they would sex under his Impress, female.

Horag young would increase on the ship at first by the factor of the litters these three would bear; and more, with more females. Had he sexed female as he had first tended, the Alagn youngling Nagn would have sexed male in complement, and the next two would have sexed randomly, with himself bearing three to five young as female, some by Nagn, some by any other young male that might develop, and though he could claim such young as Horag, as female he could make only a small nest of Horag young on an otherwise Alagn ship.

It was indeed nature's logic—and politics—but Suth was smug in it, suffused with a feeling of power and rightness after his long suffering. There would be a new order on this ship, *his* ship. And for Horag to succeed in an operation where great Alagn had failed miserably. . . . Ambitions occurred to him, incredible in scope.

"It is not necessary," he said, "that humans know we exist."

"No," Nagn agreed, "but until they realize we have an elder on this ship, they will be continuing on their own course of action. They will do what pleases them without consulting us."

"If all witnesses die," said Suth, "—there is no event."

"Eldest?"

"We are far from human bases; we can do what pleases us."

"Strike at elders?"

"Secure ourselves."

Nagn considered this, her nostrils flaring and shutting in agitation. Finally they remained open. "With their rider ship and their probe as well, they have mobility we do not."

"Mri could even the balance."

"Even mri have some memory, eldest. They will not hire to us."

"On that world, Nagn Alagn-ni, there is power. It struck back at our ship; we experienced it and we know the sites of it. If both mri and human witnesses perish—then regul worlds are freed of an inestimable danger; and humans can ask questions—but regul need give no answers."

Nagn grinned, a slow relaxation of her jaws and a narrowing of her eyes.

V

Yet again the beasts shifted position, not to be buried, shaking the sand off with a vengeance. The gale had fallen off markedly, and Na'i'in shone brighter this morning than it had yesterday noon. Duncan stumbled to his feet, muscles aching. He had slept finally, when the dusei no longer roused so often; and he was stiff, the more so that the great beasts had pressed on him and leaned on him: instinct, he reckoned, to keep his chilling body up to their fever warmth. They milled about now, blew and sneezed wetly, clearing their noses. Duncan shivered, folding his arms about him, for the cold wind threatened to steal what warmth he had gathered.

Time to move. Anxiety settled on him as he realized he could see horizon through the curtain-like gusts; if he could see, so could others, and he had lingered too long. He should have been on his way in the night, when the sand had ceased to come so heavily; he should have realized, and instead he had settled down to sleep.

Stupidity, his mri brother had been wont to tell him on other occasions, *is not an honorable death.*

"Hai," he murmured to the dusei, gathered up his pack, shrugged into it, started off, with a protest of every muscle in his body, making what haste he could.

He took a little more of the dried food, with a last bite of the pipe, and that was breakfast, to quiet his hunger pangs. The dusei tried to cajole their share, and he gave to his own, but when he offered to the others, his began a rumbling that boded trouble.

He at once flung the handful wide, and the two stranger dusei paused, themselves rumbling threats, letting the pace separate them. After a moment they lowered their heads and took the food, and the curtaining sand began to come between. The storm-night was over, truces broken. His heart still beat rapidly from the close call, the injudiciousness of his own dus to start a quarrel while he had his hand full of something the others wanted. He glanced back; one of them stood up on its hind legs, a towering shadow, threatening their backs; but his own whuffed disgust and plodded on, having evidently dismissed the seriousness of the threat. His was tame only in the sense it wanted to stay with him, which dusei had done with the mri of Kesrith for two thousand years, coming in out of their native hills, choosing only kel-caste, bonding lifelong; and not even the mri knew why. Kath'ein had no need and sen'ein minds were too complex and cold for the dusei's taste: so the mri said. But for some mad reason, this one had chosen a human—its only existing choice, perhaps, when mri on Kesrith had perished.

He had a dread of it someday departing his side, deserting him for the species it preferred; truth be told, that parting would be painful beyond bearing, and lonely after, incredibly lonely. He needed it, he suspected, with a crippled need a kel'en of the mri might never have. And perhaps the dus knew it.

He walked, his hand on the beast's back, looked over his shoulder. The other two were only the dimmest shadows now. They would choose, perhaps, other kel'ein. . . . He hoped not the kel'ein who followed him now; that was a dread thought.

His rumbled with pleasure, blowing at the sand occasion-ally, shambling along at his pace, turning its face as much as might be from the wind.

But after a time that pleasure-sound died, and something else came into its mood, a pricklish anxiety.

The skin contracted between his shoulders. He looked back, searching for shadows in the amber haze—coughed, blind for a moment.

The dus had stopped too, began that weaving which ac-companied ward-impulse, back and forth, back and forth be-tween him and some presence not far distant.

"Hush," he bade it, dropped to his knees to fling his arms about its neck and distract it, for a determined pursuer could use that impulse to locate them.

A mri who pursued . . . could well do that.

The impulse and the weaving stopped; the beast stood still and shivered against him, and he scrambled up and started it moving again, facing the wind, blind intermittently in the gusts, and with the beast's disturbance sawing at his nerves like primal fear.

The land did not permit mistakes. He had made one, this morning, out of weakness.

Turn, he thought, and meet his pursuers, plead that he carried a message that might mean life or death for all the mri?

One look at his habit and his weapons and his human-brown eyes . . . would be enough. Mri—meant the People; outsiders and higher beasts were tsi'mri: not-People. He and the dus were equal in their eyes; it was built into the hal'ari that way, and no logic could argue without words to use.

It was a stranger behind him, no one of the tribe he knew: they would have showed themselves long since if that were the case; there was more than curiosity involved, if pursuit continued after the storm. He was sure of it now, with a gut-deep knowledge that he was in serious trouble.

Kel'ein did not walk far alone, not by choice. There was a tribe somewhere about, and a Kel which had set itself to trail an invader.

Hlil stopped with the sand-veiled shadow of the city before him, sank down on his heels on the windward side of a low dune and surveyed the altered outlines of the ruin tsi'mri had left.

An-ehon. *His* city. He had never lived in it; but it was his by heritage. He had come here in the journeyings which attended the accession of a she'pan, when he was very young; had sat within walls while the Sen closed themselves within the Holy and the Mother gained the last secrets she had to know, which were within the precious records of the city.

No more. It was over, the hundred thousand years of history of this place—ended, in his sight, in an instant. He had seen the towers falling, comrades slain on right and on left of him, and for so long as he lived he would carry that nightmare with him.

What he had to do now . . . was more than recover the tents, the Things, which concerned only life; it was to retake the Holy, and that . . . that filled him with fear. The stranger-she'pan had laid hands on him, giving him commission to handle what he must: perhaps she had the right to do so. He was not even certain of that. An-ehon was destroyed, the means of teaching she'panei gone with it, and they must trust this stranger, who claimed to hold in herself the great secrets. It was all they had, forever, save what rested here.

Merai, he had thought more than once on this journey,

with even the elements turning on them, *Merai, o gods, what should I do?*

He did so now, thinking of the city before them, of the tribe—gods, of the tribe, pent within that narrow cut and the sand moving. In his mind was a vision of them being over-whelmed in it by sandfalls, or the sandslip building all down the cut, gravity bearing them in a powdery slide into the basin, a fall which turned his stomach to contemplate.

He had sent five hands of kel'ein back when the storm be-gan, to aid if they could. That far he went against the she'pan's plans, dividing his force. Perhaps she would forgive; perhaps she would curse, damning him, cutting him off from the tribe for disobedience. That was well enough, he thought, tears welling up in his throat, if only it saved the rest of the children. There was following orders and there was sanity; and the gods witness he tried to choose aright . . . to obey and to disobey at once.

Sand slipped near him. Ras had caught up with him, came over the crest and slid down to a crouch at his side. In a mo-ment more came Desai, third-rank kel'en, blind in one eye, but the one that saw, saw keenly: a quiet man and steady, and after him came Merin, a Husband, and the boy Taz . . . an unscarred, who had begged with all his heart to come. There were others, elsewhere, lost in the rolls of the land and the gusting wind. He took to heart what the kel'anth had said of ambushes and ships, and kept his forces scattered.

He waited a moment, letting the others take their breaths, for beyond this point was little concealment. Then he rose up, started down the trough, keeping to the low places where possible, while his companions strayed along after him at their own rate, making no grouped target for the distance-weapons of tsi-mri.

But when they neared the buildings and crossed the track by which they had fled the city, and came upon the first of the dead, anger welled up in him, and he paused. Black-robe: this had been a kel'en. He gazed at the partially buried robes, the mummy made of days in the drying winds, ravaged by predators: they must have held feast in An-ehon.

The others overtook him; he walked on without looking at them. Ahead were the shells of towers, geometries obscured in sand, horizonless amber in which near buildings were dis-tinct even to the cracks in their walls and the distant ones hove up as shadows. And everywhere the dead.

"This was Ehan," Desai said of the next they came to; and

"Rias," said Merin of another, for the Honors these dead wore could still distinguish them, when wind and dryness had made them all alike.

From time to time they spoke names of those they saw among the passages between the ruined buildings; and the dead were not only kel'ein, but old sen'ein, gold-robes, scholars, whose drying skulls had held so much of the wisdom of the People; young and old, male and female, they lay in some places one upon the other, folk that they had known all their lives; among them were the bodies of kath'ein, blue-robes, the saddest and most terrible—the child-rearers and children. Walls had fallen, quick and cruel death; in other places the dead seemed without wound at all. There were the old whose bronze manes were dark and streaked with age; many, many of their number, who had not been strong enough to bear the running; and in many a place a kel'en's black-robed body lay vainly sheltering some child or old one.

Name after name, a litany of the dead: kath Edis, one of his own kath-mates, and four children, two of whom might be his own: that hit him hard; and sen'ein, wise old Rosin; and kel Dom: they had come into the Kel the same year. He did not want to look, and must, imposing horrors over brighter memories.

And the others, who had lost closer kin, Kel-born, who had kin to lose: Taz, who mourned trueparents and sister and all his uncles; and Ras—Ras passed no body but that she did not look to see.

"Haste," he said, having his fill of grieving. But Ras trailed last, disobedient, still searching, almost lost to them in the murk.

He said nothing to that: matters were thin enough between them. But he looked at no more dead; and the others grew wise, and did not, either, staying close with him. Chance was, he thought, that they could run head-on into members of their own party, if they were not careful in this murk, come up against friends primed to expect distance-weapons and primed to attack . . . an insanity: he had no liking at all for this kind of slipping about.

Suddenly the square lay before them, vast, ribboned with blowing sand which made small dunes about the bodies which lay thicker here than elsewhere in the city. At the far side hove up the great Edun, the House of the People, Edun An-ehon, sad in surrounding ruin. It was mostly intact, the four towers, slanting together, forming a truncated pyramid.

The doorway gaped darkly open upon steps which ran down into the square. The stone of the edun was pitted and scarred as the other buildings; great cracks showed in the saffron walls, but this place which had been the center of the attack had also held the strongest defense, and it had survived best of any structure in the city. Hope welled up in him, hope of success, of doing quickly what they had come to do and getting away safely.

He moved and the others followed, on a course avoiding the open square, taking their cover where they could find it among the shattered buildings and the blowing sand. Finally he broke away at a run, up the long steps, toward that ominous dark within, hard-breathing with the effort and thinking that at any moment fire might blast out at him.

It did not. He slid through the doorway and inside, against the wall, where dust slipped like oil beneath his feet, where was silence but for the wind outside and the arriving footsteps of the others. They entered and stopped, all of them listening a moment. There was no sound but the wind outside.

"Get a light going," he bade Taz. The boy fumbled in the pouch he carried and knelt, working hastily to set fire in the oilwood fiber he had brought. Ras arrived, last of them. "Stay out there," Hlil ordered her, "visible; others will be coming soon."

"Aye," she said, and slipped back out again into the cold wind, a miserable post, but no worse than the dark inside.

The flame kindled; Taz shielded it with his body and lit a knot of fiber impaled on an oilwood wand. They all, he, Merin, and Desai, kept bodies between the fire and the draft from the door. Merin lit other knots and passed them about. Outside, Ras's low voice reported no sight of the others.

Hlil took his light and walked on. The inner halls echoed to the least step. Cracks marred the walls, ran, visible once eyes had adjusted to the dim light, about the higher walls and ceilings, marring the holy writings there.

The entry of kel-tower was clear, and that of Sen, the she'pan's tower and Kath . . . affording hope of access to their belongings. But when he looked toward the shine his heart sank, for that area of the ceiling sagged, and the pillars which guarded that access were damaged. He felt of them and stone crumbled at his least touch on the cracks.

He had to know; he went farther into the shrine, thrust his light-wand into a cracked wall and passed farther still.

"Hlil," Merin protested, behind him.

He hesitated, and even as he stopped a sifting of plaster hit his shoulders and dimmed the light.

"Go back," he bade Merin and the others. "Stand clear."

The Holy was there, that which they venerated and the Holy of the Voyagers; his knees were weak with dread of the great forbidden; but in his mind was the hazard of losing them once for all, these things which were more than the city and more than all their lives combined.

He moved inward; the others disobeyed and followed: he heard them, saw the lights moving with him, casting triple shadows of himself and the pillars and the inner screen.

Beyond that—the stranger-she'pan had given him her blessing to go: *that first,* she had bidden him. He was shaking unashamedly as he put out a hand and moved the screen aside.

A tiny box of green bronze; figures of corroding metal and gold; a small carven dus and a shining oval case as large as a child: together they were the Pana, the Mysteries, on which he looked, on which no kel'en ought ever to look. He thrust out a hand almost numb, gathered up the smallest objects and thrust them, cold and comfortless, within the breast of his robes. He passed the box to Merin, whose hands did not want to receive it. Last he reached for the shining ovoid, snatched it to him in a sifting of dust and falling plaster. It was incredibly heavy for its size, staggered him, hit a support in a cascade of plaster and fragments. He stumbled back at the limit of his balance, hit the steadying hands of Desai who snatched him farther, outside, as dust rolled out at them and they sprawled, shaken by the rumble of falling masonry. It stopped.

"Sir?" Taz's voice called.

"We are well enough," Hlil answered, holding the pan'en to him, bowed over it, though the chill seemed to flow from it into his bones. Other hands helped him rise with it: the light of the door showed in a shaft of dust, and the figures of Taz and Ras within it, casting shadows. He carried his burden to the doorway, past them and out into the light and the storm, knelt down and laid the pan'en and the other objects on the top of the steps. Merin added the ancient box, stripped off his veil to shield the Holy objects . . . so did he, and Ras and Desai too. He looked up into the faces of the others, which were stark with dread for what they had in hand. He looked from one to the other, chilled with a sense of separation . . . for kel'ein died, having touched a pan'en: such was the law.

Or if they lived, then forever after they were known by it: *pan'ai-khan*, somewhere between Holy and accursed.

"I have dispensation," he said. "I give it you."

They crouched down, huddled together, he and the others, protecting the Holy as if it were something living and fragile, that wanted mortal flesh between it and the elements.

The boy Taz was not with them.

"Taz—are you well?" Hlil shouted into the dark.

"I am keeping the fire," the boy said. "Kel-second, the dust is very thick, but there is no more falling."

"The gods defend us," Hlil muttered, conscious of what he had his hand on, that burned him with its cold. "Only let it hold a little while longer."

Duncan paused, where a scoured ridge of sandstone offered a moment's shelter from the wind, flung his arms about the thick neck of the dus and lowered his head out of the force of the gusts. He coughed, rackingly; his head ached and his senses hazed. The storm seemed to suck oxygen away from him. He uncapped the canteen and washed his mouth, for the membranes were so dry they felt like paper. . . . He swallowed but a capful. He stayed a moment, until his head stopped spinning and his lungs stopped hurting, then he found the moral force to stand and move again.

There was a bright spot in the world, which was the sun; in the worst gusts it was still all that could be seen. The dus moved, guiding him in his moments of blindness.

Then something else grew into reality, tall shadows like trees, branched close to the trunk and rising straight up again, gaunt giants. Pipe. He went toward it, consumed with the desire for the sweet pulp which could relieve his pain and his thirst better than water. The dus lumbered along by him, willingly hurrying; and the shadows took on more and more of substance against amber sky and amber earth.

Dead. No living plants but pale, desiccated fiber materialized before him, strands ripped loose, blowing in the wind, a ghostly forest of dead trunks. He touched the blowing strands, drew his *av-tlen* to probe the trunk closest, to try whether there might be life and moisture at the core.

And suddenly he received something from the dus, warning-sense, which slammed panic into him.

He moved, ran, the beast loping along with him. He cursed himself for the most basic of errors: *Think with the land* the mri had tried to teach him: *Use it; flow with it; be it.* He had found a point in the blankness. He had been nowhere until he had found a point, the rocks, the stand of dead plants. He was nowhere and could not be located until he made himself somewhere.

And childlike, he had gone from point to point. The dus was no protection: it betrayed him.

Think with the land, the Niun had said. *Never challenge beyond your capacity; one does not challenge the* jo *in hiding or the burrower in waiting.*

Or a mri in his own land.

He stopped, faced about, blind in the dust, the shortsword clenched in his fist. Cowardice reminded him he was tsi'mri, counseled to take up the gun and be ready with it. He came to save mri lives; it was the worst selfishness to die, rather than to break kel-law.

Niun would.

He sucked down mouthfuls of air and scanned the area around about, with only a scatter of the great plants visible through the dust. The dus hovered close, rumbling warnings. He willed it silent, flexed his fingers on the hilt.

The dus shied off from the left; he faced that way, heart pounding as the slim shadow of a kel'en materialized out of the wind.

"What tribe?" that one shouted.

"The ja'anom," he shouted back, his voice breaking with hoarseness. He stilled the dus with a touch of his hand; and in utter hubris: "You are in the range of the ja'anom. Why?"

There was a moment's silence. The dus backed, rumbling threat.

"I am Rhian s'Tafa Mar-Eddin, kel-anth and daithon of the hao'nath. And your geography is at fault."

His own name was called for. They proceeded toward challenge by the appointed steps. It was nightmare, a game of rules and precise ritual. He took a steadying breath and returned his *av-tlen* to its sheath with his best flourish, emptying his hands. He kept them at his sides, not in his belt, as Rhian had his. He wanted no fight.

"Evidently the fault is mine," he said. "Your permission to go, kel'anth."

"You give me no name. You have no face. What is that by you?"

"Come with me," Duncan said, trying the most desperate course. "Ask of my she'pan."

"Ships have come. There was fire over the city."

"Ask of my she'pan."

"Who are you?"

The dus roared and rushed; pain hit his arm even as he saw the mri flung aside. "No!" Duncan shouted as the dus spun again to strike. The dus did not; the mri did not move; Duncan reached to the numb place on his arm and felt the hot seep of moisture.

Two heartbeats and it had happened. He trembled, blank for the instant, knowing what had hit, the palm-blades, the *as-ei,* worn in the belt. The dus's attack, the mri's reflex—both too quick to unravel: dusei read *intent.*

He shuddered, staggered to the dus and found the other blade, imbedded in the shoulder . . . fatal to a man, no serious thing to the dus's thick muscle. He was shaking all over . . . shock, he thought; he had to move. It was a kel'anth who lay there, a whole Kel hereabouts . . .

He leaned above the prostrate form, still shaking, put out a hand to probe for life, his right one tucked to him. Life—there was; but the kel'en had dus venom in him, and sand already covered the edges of his robes. Duncan gasped breath on his own, started away—cursed and shook his head and came back, seized the robes and tugged and struggled the inert form to the stand of pipe, left him sitting there.

"Dus," he called hoarsely, turned, veered off into the wind again, running, the dus moving with lumbering haste at his side.

They would follow; he believed that beyond question. Blood feud if the kel'anth died and someone to tell the tale of him if he did not. He coughed and kept running, sucked in dust with the air despite the veils, slowing when he could no longer keep from doubling with pain. Dus-sense prickled about him, either the animal's alarm or its sense of a new enemy. He held his injured arm to him, running a little, walking when he could not run, making what speed he could.

Two mistakes on his own; the dus had accounted for the third.

"Storm is diminishing," the voice from *Flower* reported. "No chance yet to assess conditions outside."

"Don't," Koch said, passed a hand reflexively over the stubble on his head. "Don't risk personnel, in any limited visibility."

"We have our own operations to pursue." *Flower's*

exec was Emil Luiz, chief surgeon, civ and doggedly so. "We know our limitations. We have measurements to take."

"We copy," Koch muttered. The civs were indeed under his command, but they were trouble and doubly so since they were the potential link to the SurTac. "We are dispatching *Santiago* to a survey pattern. We wish you to observe unusual cautions for the duration. Please do not disperse crew or scientific personnel on outside research. Keep everyone within easy jump of the ship, and no key personnel out of reach of stations. This is a serious matter, Dr. Luiz. We fully sympathize with your need to gather information, but we do not wish to have to abandon personnel onworld in case of trouble. Understood?"

"We will not disperse personnel outside during your operation. We copy very clearly."

"Your estimation of mission survival down there?"

There was long silence. "Obviously natives survive such storms."

"Unsheltered?"

"We don't know where he is, do we?"

Koch tapped his stylus nervously against the desk. "Code twelve," he cautioned the civ; they used scramble as standard procedure, but there was a nakedness, sending information back and forth after this fashion. He misliked it entirely.

"We suggest further patience," Luiz said. "Anything will have been delayed in this storm."

"We copy," Koch said.

"We request an answer," Luiz said. "*Flower* staff recommends further patience."

"Recommendation noted, sir."

"Admiral, we request you take official note of that recommendation. We ask you cease flights down there. These are clearly reconnaissance and they're provocative. Our personal safety is at stake and so are our hopes of peaceful contact. You may trigger something, and we are in the middle. Please discontinue any military operations down here. Do you copy that, sir?"

Koch's heart was speeding. He held his silence a moment, reached and coded a number onto his desk console. The answer flashed back to his screen, negative.

"We will look into the matter," Koch said. "Please code twelve that and wait shuttled reply."

Now there was silence for a few beats on the other end.

"We copy," Luiz said.

"Any other message, *Flower?* We're moving out of your range. *Santiago* should be in position soon to serve as relay and cover. Ending transmission."

"We copy. Ending transmission."

The artificial voices and crawl of transcription across the second screen ceased. Koch wiped sweat from his upper lip and punched in Silverman of *Santiago.* The insystem fighter was in link at the moment, riding attached to *Saber's* flank as she had ridden into the system. "Commander, Koch here. Report personally, soonest."

He received immediate acknowledgment. With matters as they were, key personnel kept communicators on their persons constantly.

He punched up security next, Del Degas. The man was in the next office and available, there as soon as four doors could open.

"Sir."

"Someone's overflying *Flower's* scan down there. Who?"

Degas's thin face went tauter still. "We have no missions downworld right now."

"I know that. What about our allies?"

"I'll find out what I can."

"Del—if they're regul . . . theoretically younglings can't take that kind of initiative. If someone's data is wrong on that point, if *Shirug* can function in their hands—that's a problem. Theoretically those shuttles the agreement allows them—aren't armed."

"Like ours," Degas said softly.

"Want *Santiago* out there where she has a view, Del; scan operations have to be subordinated to that for the time being. They won't let us inside; we do what we can."

Regul could not lie; that was the general belief. Their indelible memories made lying a danger to their sanity. So the scientists said.

Likewise regul were legalists. To deal with them it was necessary to consider every word of every oral agreement, and to reckon all the possible omissions and interpretations. Regul memory was adequate for that kind of labyrinthine reckoning. Human memory was not.

Degas nodded slowly. "Try again to open contact?"

"Don't. Not yet. I don't want them alarmed. *Santiago's* maneuvering is enough."

"And if they're not regul doing those overflights?"

"I consider that possibility too."

"And act on it?"

Koch frowned, Del Degas had his private anxiousness in that matter. Conviction, perhaps . . . or revenge. A man who had lost both sons and a wife to mri might harbor either.

"The SurTac," Degas pursued uninvited, "is a deserter. That may have been planned by the office that sent him; but his attitudes are not a calculation; the attitude that dumped that tracer and the transmitter into the canyons . . . was not carelessness. His behavior is clear; he's not human; he's mri; he *says* there are no mri ships. But the psychological alteration he must have undergone, years alone with them on that ship. . . . Those who think they know him may recognize a role he's playing, if he's playing at being SurTac Duncan."

Duncan had refused to debrief to security, only willing to talk to *Flower* staff, with Degas to frame the essential questions and take notes. Degas had been outraged at the order that permitted it.

"The SurTac is a fanatic," Degas said. "And like all such, he's capable of convolute reasoning in support of his cause. There's also the possibility he saw only what the mri wanted him to see. I strongly urge an attempt to get direct observation down there. Military observation. Galey's mission—"

"Will not be diverted to that purpose."

"Another, then."

"Do you want an objection to policy put on record? Is that what you're asking?"

Degas drew a deep breath, looked down at the floor and up again in silent offense. They had grown too familiar, he with Degas; neighbors, card players; a man had to develop some human associations on a voyage years in duration. They were not of the same branch of the service. He had found Degas's quick mind a stimulation to his own. Now there were entanglements.

"We don't use Galey," Koch said. He considered a moment, weighing the options. "The regul matter first; it may not be youngling shyness that keeps them over-horizon from us. If they can operate, they have powerful motivation for revenge. That's a motive you're not reckoning."

"Assuming human motives. That may be error."

"Who's our regul expert now?" It had been Aldin, Koch recalled. Aldin was dead: old age, like *Saber's* former captain, like the translations chief. Repeated jump stresses took it out of a man, put strain on old hearts. "Who's carrying that department?"

"Dr. Boaz is Xen head."

Boaz, Duncan's friend, the mri expert. Koch bit at his lip. "I'll not pull her up. She's important down there."

Degas shrugged. "Dr. Simeon Averson specialized in language under Aldin; ran the classification system for library on Kesrith. He would be the likely authority in the field after Aldin and Boaz."

The man's knowledge of the unbreachable intricacies of *Flower's* departments did not surprise him. Del Degas was a collector of details. Pent in a closed system of humanity for the years of the voyage, he doubtless had turned his talents to the cataloging of everyone aboard. Koch dimly recalled the little man in question. He tried to call on *Flower* personnel as little as possible, disliking civs operating underfoot, delving into military records and files. Kesrith's civilian governor had saddled him with *Flower*, and Mel Aldin had once been useful in the early stages of the mission, conducting crew briefings and studies, settling matters of protocol between regul elder and humans unused to regul. But the years of voyage had passed; things had found a certain routine, and Aldin had diminished in necessity and visibilty. *Flower* held its own privacies.

"You'll want him shuttled up?" Degas asked.

"Do it." Koch leaned back impatiently, rocked in his chair. "Galey moves down: Harris. Two shuttles. Every time we drop a rock into that pond we risk stirring something up. I don't like it. We don't know that machinery's dead. We'll draw ourselves a little back. I don't want us a sitting target."

"I can have armaments moduled in, and scan; a very short delay. As well have several shuttles downworld as two. While we're making one ripple in the pond, so to speak, we might as well take utmost advantage of it. Your operation with Galey might benefit by the information."

Koch expelled a slow breath. A long voyage, a mind like Degas's . . . security had gone incestuous in the long confinement. "Everything," he said, "every minute detail of those flight plans will be cleared with this office." He tapped the stylus against the desk, looked at Degas, turned and keyed an order into the console.

VI

Others came, across the square, up the steps, shadows out of the storm. Hlil gathered himself up to meet them. "It is safe," he said to kel Dias, who commanded them, and looked beyond her to the ones who followed, sen'ein. He set his face, assumed the assurance he did not feel, met the eyes of the gold-robes who were veiled against wind and dust. "I secured the Pana first; that was my instruction."

They inclined their heads, accepting this, which comforted him. They took charge of the Holy, one spreading his own robes to cover it, for the kel-veils blew and fluttered in the wind.

He left them and went inside with the others, where Taz began to share his light, where knot after knot of fiber flared into life. "Haste," he urged them, "but walk lightly; there has been one collapse in here already."

They moved, no running, but swiftly. He watched them scatter with their several leaders, one group to Kel, one to Kath, one to Sen, and another to the storerooms, and two to the she'pan's tower, so that in a brief time all the building whispered to soft, quick steps, the comings and going of those who had come to loot the House of all that was their own.

"Go," he murmured distractedly, finding Taz still by him. "If there are any proper lamps at hand, get light in that middle corridor. The rubble is unstable enough without some-one falling."

"Aye, sir," the youth exclaimed, and made haste about it.

Even now some were beginning to come down with bur-dens, stumbling in the dark, having to choose between light and two hands to steady their loads. Hlil stationed himself to guide them to the point where they could see the doorway; the flow began to be a steady to and fro. There was no science in their plundering that he could see; he forbore to complain of it. In their haste and dread of collapse they snatched what they could, as much as they could.

Taz managed lights, two proper lamps, set in the area of the fallen shrine; and to Hlil's vast relief the essential things began to appear, the heavy burden of the tents, the irreplaceable metal poles, wrapped meticulously in twisted and braided fiber; their vessels, their stores of food and oil; a sled of offworld metal; lastly hundreds of rolled mats, the personal possessions of the tribe.

And two sen'ein came inside, gathered up one of the lamps from the hall, passed out of sight into the entry of sen-hall.

He disliked that. He walked a few steps in that direction, fretting with the responsibility he bore for them, and his lack of authority where it regarded sen-matters. He stared anxiously after them, then turned for the door, where a diminishing trickle of kel'ein tended. Shouts drifted down from the heights of the edun, that they had gotten all of it, to the very last.

Hlil walked out onto the steps and into the particle-laden wind, where the two sen'ein who had remained with the Pana struggled to load the Holy onto the sled, padding it with rolled mats below and above. Merin and Dias and Ras had charge, directing the division of goods into bearable portions. They were not going to leave any portion of it if they could help.

He stood idle, fretting with the matter, prevented by rank from lending a hand to it. Perhaps, he thought, they should all have gone back to the relief of the tribe in the storm; or perhaps he should never have divided his force, and should have trusted the she'pan and kel Seras to do the necessary. The load was no easier for the driving wind; and it was a long trek back.

Yet there seemed some lessening in the storm. Excessive optimism, perhaps; the wind would diminish for a time and then return with double force. He could see the top of the ruined building nearest, of many of the buildings, which he had not been able to do when they came.

And the dead, revealed in their numbers, stretching in a line from the bottom of the steps to the far side of the square. Those he had to look on too.

"We might bury them, sir," said a young voice. He looked to his left, at Taz. The boy had lost all his kin in the rout. All.

"No. We have strength for what we do, barely that."

"Aye," Taz said . . . scarless, no one yet in the Kel; but he had great grace, and Hlil was grateful for that.

"Forgive, kel Taz."

"Sir," Taz said quietly, and turned away, for a few moments finding something essential to do with the packing.

It was that way with many of them. The Kel-born had lost most, knowing their kin in certainty. He looked on Ras, who labored with the others, and hoped, seeing that energy in her, that there might be some healing worked.

He could set his hand to none of the work; he paced back inside, restless, saw the last kel'ein returning from the storerooms. "Do not take the lamps yet," he bade them. "Ros, wait here; we have two still up in sen-tower."

"Aye," the one of them said. Hlil walked out again with the other, counting them, counting those outside, making sure he had all their whereabouts. They were all there. He reassured himself, stood in the cold with arms folded, watching while the readied bundles were carried down the steps, piled there, a little to the side of a heap of the dead.

"Ras," one of those at the bottom called up. The kel'en gazed down at that pitiful tangle of black and lifted his face upward. *"Kel Ras—"*

O gods, Hlil thought, cursing that man.

Ras left the others at the top and walked down the steps, no haste, no show of dread. Hlil watched, and after a moment followed. It was Nelan s'Elil who lay there; there was no doubting it. He stood by as Ras knelt by the body of her truemother, watched Ras take from among the dusty black robes the beautiful sword which had been that of Kov her father. The *j'tai,* Ras did not touch, the Honors which her truemother had won in her life; those passed only in defeat, and Nelan had never suffered that.

"Ras," he said. She sat still, the sword across her lap, the wind settling sand in the folds of her robes. No one moved, not she, not kel Tos'an who had summoned her. "Ras," he said again.

She straightened, rising, turned her unveiled face toward him, the sword gathered to her breast. There was no expression; to a friend even a kel'e'en might have shown something. He was consumed with the need to get her away from this place.

"Go back," he said. "We cannot attend to one lost, and not others. Duty, Ras."

She took the fastenings of the sword in hand, carefully

unhooked her own and replaced it, laid what was hers against Nelan's body.

And walked away, to stand supervising the others, having spoken no word to him.

He walked away too, up the steps, not looking back, cast a naked-faced scowl at kel'ein who had paused in their work. There was a hasty return to it. He reached the top, started to turn and look down.

And suddenly, from inside, a snap of power, a flare of lights.

Everyone stopped in that instant; and there was a heart-stopping rumble.

"Run!" he shouted; they moved, raced ahead of a cloud which billowed out from the door. But the full collapse did not follow.

The two young sen'ein outside started back up the steps running. "No!" he forbade them, and went himself, paused in the doorway, in the choking dust. "All of you," he shouted back, "stay out."

He tucked the tail of the *zaidhe* across his face for a veil, entered the white cloud which the wind whipped away as rapidly as it poured forth. Somewhere inside one cold light shone undamaged, giving no help in the swirling dust: no light of theirs, but a powered lamp.

The whole center had given way. He looked at the ceiling, waded farther through the rubble, disturbing nothing he could avoid, the membrane of his eyes flicking regularly to clear the dust and sending involuntary tears to the outer corner of his eyes.

At one such clearing he saw what he had feared to see, a white-dusted bundle of black amid the rubble.

"Ros," he called, but there was no answer, no pulse to his touch, which came away wet-fingered. He looked up, heart-sick, at the ruined ceiling where electric light cast a blinding haze, saw, to his left, sen-hall's access, likewise alight.

"Sen Kadas," he shouted, and obtained only echoes and the steady sifting of plaster.

He left the kel'en's body, entered the access, coughing in the dust. Cracks were everywhere in the spiral corridor. Bits of the wall crumbled to his touch. He trod carefully, ascended to sen-hall itself. The window there had given way, admitting daylight in a huge crack through which the wind swirled patterns of dust.

And beyond . . . lights gleamed through a farther doorway.

"Sen Kadas," he called. "Sen Otha?"

There was no response. He ventured in, within a room of row upon row of machinery . . . knew what he was seeing, which was the City itself, the mind, which had taught she'panei and sen'ein time out of mind. This too was a Holy, a Mystery not for a kel'en's sight. He walked farther, stopped as he realized the cracks which ran everywhere, the ruin which had plunged down through the very core of the tower, taking machinery and masonry, everything.

"Sen'ein," he called.

Light pulsed, a white light which glared down at him from the machine. He looked up at it, blinking in that blinding radiance.

"Who?" a voice thundered.

"Hlil s'Sochil," he answered it, trembling creeping through him.

"What is your authorization?"

"From the she'pan Melein s'Intel."

Lights flared, points of red and amber visible through the white glare, from somewhere beyond it.

"Where is the she'pan?" it asked.

He retreated from it in dread; the light died. With all his heart he would have fled this place, but two of his company were lost. He crept aside to the walls, trod the vast aisles of machinery amid the lights. More lights were being added constantly, places which had been dark coming alive, like something stirring to renewed power.

"Sen'ein," he called hoarsely.

Suddenly the floor slipped underfoot, a tiny jolt, that penetrated to his heart. He edged back.

And gazing down into the rubbled collapse at the core, he saw what ended hope of the sen'ein, gold cloth in the slide, amid blocks larger than a man. He could not reach them; there was no means—no need.

"Gods," he muttered, sick at heart, and, reckoning the disrespect of that here, shuddered and turned away.

"I am receiving," An-ehon thundered. The white eye of the machine flared. "Who?"

He fled it, walking softly, quickly as he could—gained the doorway into the sen-hall and kept going, breathless, into the spiraling passage down.

A shadow met him in the turning: one-eyed Desai, who

had not followed orders. He grasped the kel'en's arm, grateful
for that living presence.

"Haste," he said, turning Desai about; they descended together, past the ruin at the bottom, and out, out into the anxious gathering at the door. Hlil drew breath there, coughed,
wiped his face with a sleeve which was powdered white with
dust.

"Away," he ordered them. "Get these things away from the
edun. There is nothing we can do here. Lately-dead have no
more claim than the others."

They obeyed, with small murmurings of grief. He disre-
garded proprieties and took burdens himself, took up one at
the bottom of the steps, for kel Ros, while the remaining
sen'ein prepared to draw the sled holding the Pana alone.

"Move out," he ordered them, watched them all form file
and begin the journey. Ras passed him, lost in some thought
of her own, bearing a burden too heavy for her; but most
did. He gazed on her with a personal misery which dulled itself in other things, anxiety for all his charges. Nothing which
he had touched had gone right. They had lost lives, had lost
sen'ein—helpless even to bury the lost ones.

His leading.

He looked back, last of those who left the city, blinked in
the wind—turned from the ruin which was not the city he
wished to remember.

Three lives lost; and the tribe itself—it was not certain that
anyone survived there to need the things they had gathered.
It was his decision to go on, his decision now, to take all that
was theirs when they might have halved the weight and abandoned the possessions of the dead.

He understood one rule, that waste was death; that what
one gave the desert it never gave back, to world's end.

He did what he knew to do, which was to yield nothing.

The bleeding had started again. The wound sealed and
broke open again by turns, whenever the slope of the land
put him to effort. Duncan clenched the arm against his body
and tried to move it as little as possible in his walking. A
cough urged at him, and that was worse—much worse, if that
set in. He tried desperately to pace his breathing, tasting copper in his mouth, the sky occasionally acquiring dark edges in
his sight. He was followed; he knew that he was, and the
slow rolls of the eternal flat gave him and them cover. He

sought no landmarks, but the sun's last light, a spot of lurid flame in the west, tainted with the thinning dust.

The dus beside him radiated occasional surges of flight impulse and of anger, confused as he, driven. Occasionally small life rippled the sand ahead, clearing their path, a surreal illusion of animate sands.

And one did not. He stepped into yielding sand, cords whipping up his leg. He snatched out his shortsword and hacked at the strands . . . sand-star, a smallish one, else it had been up to his face: they grew that large. This one recoiled, wounded; and the dus ate it, the while he stumbled on his way, half-running a few steps in sickened panic. Whether it had gotten above the boot or not, his flesh was too numb to feel. He walked with the blade in hand after that, finding the hilt comfort in the approach of dark. He ought to take the visor up, he reckoned, before he stumbled into worse; but the sand still blew, and when he tried it for a time his eyes stung so he was as blind without as with. He lowered it again to save himself the misery, and trusted to the beast and to the sword.

The sun sank its last portion beyond the horizon and it was night indeed; whether stars shone or not, whether the dust had cleared that much he could not tell.

He rested in the beginning of the dark; he must. After the tightness had relaxed from his chest and his head pounded less severely he began with dull stubbornness to gather himself up, reckoning that if he were to go on living he had no choice about it.

And suddenly the dus sent him strong, clear warning, an apprehension like a chill wind on their backtrail. *Come,* he sent it, and started to move at all the pace he could.

Madness, to begin a race with mri. He had lost it already. Better sense by far to turn and fight: they would give him the grace of one-at-a-time.

And that was worth nothing if one lost in the first encounter. He gasped breath and tried to hit a steady pace.

Abruptly the dus deserted him, headed off at a tangent to the left. Panic breathed at his shoulders; he turned with it, staying with the beast, having lost control of it. It was taking him to the attack, into it; he felt the wildness surge into his brain—and suddenly—fragments.

It hit from all sides, dus-sense, all about him.

The others.

They had come. His skin contracted in the rage they sent;

they had made a trap, the dusei. A fierceness settled into his bones, an alien anger—danger, danger, *danger*—

A dus reared up out of the dark in front of him, higher than his head; he shied from it, spun, met a kel'en a sword's length from him.

He flung his sword up, low; steel turned the blade as the kel'en closed with him, shadow and hard muscle and a dus-carried wash of familiarity that stopped him cold. A hard hand seized his arm and hurled him back.

Niun.

He gasped breath, struggled for mental balance, spun left in the sudden awareness of others on them, dus-sense warning them.

"Who are they?" Niun asked him, shortsword likewise in his hand. "What have you stirred?"

"Another tribe." He gasped for air, shifted his grip on his hilt as he tried to make figures out of the darkness about them. Dusei were at their backs, more than their own two. He drew a shaken breath and lifted his visor, made out a dim movement in the dark before them.

"Who are you?" Niun shouted out.

"The hao'nath," the answer came back, male and hoarse. "Who are you?"

"Kel'anth of the ja'anom. Get off my trail, hao'nath! You have no rights here."

There was long silence.

And then there was nothing, neither shadow nor response. Dus-sense went out like a lamp flame, and Duncan shivered convulsively, gasped for the air that suddenly seemed more abundant.

Steel hissed into sheath. Niun tugged down his veil, giving his face to him; Duncan sheathed his sword and did the same, and Niun offered him his open hands.

Duncan embraced him awkwardly, aware of his own chill and the mri's fever-warmth, his own filthiness and the mri's fastidious cleanliness.

"Move," Niun said, taking him by the shoulder and pushing him; he did so, and about them the shadows of dusei gave way, scattered, save his own and the great dus which was Niun's. He struggled to keep Niun's pace, no arguments or breath wasted. That was trouble at their backs, only gone back to report; Niun's long strides carried them off southerly, to rougher land—broke at times into a run, which he matched for a while. It ended in his coughing, doubled up, trying only to walk.

Niun kept him moving, down a gentle roll of the land, an ill dream of pain and dus-sense, until his knees began to buckle under him in the sand and he sank down before a joint should tear and lame him.

Niun dropped to his heels beside him, a hand on his shoulder, and the dusei, his and the other, made a wall about them. "Sov-kela?" Niun asked of him: my-brother-of-the-Kel? He caught his breath somewhat and gripped Niun's arm in return.

"I reached them. Niun, I have been up there, in the ships."

Niun was silent a moment; disturbance jolted through the dus sense. "I believed," Niun said, "you had gotten through when there were no more attacks; but—not that you would have gone among them. And they let you go. They let you go again."

"Regul have come," Duncan said, and felt the shock fed back to him. The membrane flashed across Niun's eyes. A human might have cried aloud, so intense that feeling was.

"Regul and not humans?"

"Both."

"Allied," Niun said. Anger fed through. Despair.

"No more firing. Regul did the firing; humans have realized by now . . . Niun, they have listened. The she'pan— they sent a message. She can contact them. Talk with them."

Again the membrane flashed across. Duncan shivered in that feeling.

"Have you taken hire?" Niun asked. It was a reasonable question, without rancor. The Kel was mercenary.

"I take no hire."

The dusei caught that feeling too, and wove them together. Niun reached out and caught the wrong arm, let it go at his flinching . . . rubbed at the blood on his fingertips.

"I thought," Duncan said, "I could reason with someone. The hao'nath kel'anth came up on me. He knew something was wrong. Knew it; and he or the dus moved before I did."

"Dead?"

"I left him against the pipestalks; dus poison, broken bones or not—I stayed to keep him out of the sand: no more than that."

"Gods," Niun spat. He faced him away, took the pack from him, hooked a strap over his own shoulder and started them moving. Duncan blinked, blear-eyed with relief at having that weight gone, and tried to keep his pace, staggering somewhat in the loose sand. Niun delayed and flung a fever-hot arm about him, hurrying him.

"What are they likely to do?"

"I would challenge," Niun said. "But that would suit them. It is the tribe that is in danger now."

"Melein—"

"I do not know." Niun pulled at him, for all his efforts to keep stride. "Gods know who is with the she'pan at the moment. I am here; Hlil, in the city . . . The hao'nath have gone back to their own she'pan; they will not challenge the kel'anth of a tribe without her consent, not if she is available. . . . But they will not stop that long. If—" He caught his breath. "If they take us here, I can challenge, aye, but one after the other. The meeting of she'panei . . . is different. The she'pan is our protection; we are hers."

He said nothing else, hard-breathing with a human burden. Duncan took his own weight, cupped the veil to his mouth with his hand to warm the air, went blindly, by sound, by dus-sense, at last with Niun dragging at him.

They found a place to rest finally, hard ground, a ridge which stretched a stone's cast along the sands. Duncan flung himself down in an aching knot and fumbled anxiously after the canteen, trying to ease his swollen throat . . . offered to Niun, who drank and put it away. The dusei crowded as close to them as possible as if themselves seeking comfort, and for the time at least there was no intimation of pursuers. Duncan leaned against his dus, his sides heaving harder than those of the beast, wiped at his nose beneath the veils and wanted nothing more than to lie still and breathe, but Niun disturbed him to see to his wound, soaked a strip torn from his veil in the saliva of his dus and bandaged it. Duncan did not question; it felt better, at least.

"These tsi'mri in the ships," Niun said. "You know them?"

"I know them."

"You talked with them—a very long time."

"No. A day and a night."

"You walk slowly, then."

"Far out of my way. Not to be followed; and I walk slowly, yes."

"Ai." Niun sat still a moment, nudged finally at the pack he had carried. It was question.

"Food." Duncan reached for it, to show him. Niun caught his wrist, released it.

"Your word is enough."

Duncan took it all the same, opened it and pulled out an opened packet of dried meat. He put a bit in his mouth, tugging the veil aside, offered the packet to Niun. "Tsi-mri, you would say. But if they were offering—I took. Food. Water. Nothing else."

Niun accepted it, tucked a large piece into his mouth, put the packet into his own pouch; and by that small action Duncan realized what he had perceived in deeper senses, that Niun himself was almost spent, quick-tiring . . . hungry, it might be. That struck panic into him. He had thought the tribe a reachable walk away. If what they had yet to face had undone Niun, then for himself—

He chewed and forced the tough bits down a throat almost too raw to swallow. "Listen to me. I will tell you what happened. Best both of us should know. The beacons I left when we landed . . . to say that there was no reason of attack— regul came in first, took out the beacons and our ship; humans never heard the message. Regul were determined they should not."

Niun's eyes had locked on his, intent.

"Regul attacked," Duncan said, "and city defenses fired back; humans came in and were caught in it, and believed the regul; but now they know . . . that they were used by the regul, and they do not like it. The regul elder tried to silence me; I killed her. Her younglings are disorganized and humans are in command up there. They are warned how they were misled."

The membrane flashed.

"I told them, Niun, I told them plainly I no longer take their orders, that I am kel'en. They sent me with a message to the she'pan: come and talk. They want assurance there will be no striking at human worlds."

"They ask *her.*"

"Or someone who would be her voice. They are reasoning beings, Niun."

Niun considered that in silence. There was—perhaps—a desire in Niun's expression that he would never have shown a human.

"The landing site," Duncan urged at him. "They will be waiting there for an answer. An end to this, a way out."

"The hao'nath," Niun said hollowly. "Gods, the hao'nath."

"I do not think," Duncan said. "that humans will go out-side that ship. At least—not recklessly."

"Sov-kela—the comings and goings of ships, the firing over An-ehon—are the tribes deaf and blind, that they should ig-nore such things? They are gathering, that is what is happen-ing. And every tribe on the face of the world that has seen cities attacked or passings in the skies—will look to its defen-ses. An-ehon is in ruins; other cities may not be. And now the hao'nath know it centers on this plain; and that its name is ja'anom."

City armament. Duncan bit at his lip, reckoning what in his dazed flight he had never reckoned . . . that some city in the hands of a desert she'pan might strike at warships.

That through the city computers, messages could pass from zone to zone with the speed of comp transmission, not the migration of tribes.

He had rejected everything, everything security might have tampered with: cast gear into the basins, kept only food and water, only the things he could assure himself were safe and light enough to carry. He made a tent of his hands over his mouth, a habit, that warmed the air, and stared bleakly into the dark before him.

"Your thought?" Niun asked.

"Go back; get to that ship—you and I. Put machines on our own side. And I know we cannot."

"We cannot," Niun said.

Duncan considered, drew his limbs up, leaned against the dus to push himself to his feet. Niun gathered up the pack and also rose, offered a hand for support. Duncan ignored it. "I cannot walk fast," he said. "But long—I can manage. If you have to break off and leave me, do that. I have kept ahead this far."

Niun said nothing to that; it was something that might have to be done: he knew so. He doubled the veil over his lower face, left the visor up, for the wind had slacked some-what: there were stars visible, the first sky he had seen in days.

And after a time of walking: "How far?" he asked.

"Would that I knew," Niun said. A moment more passed. They were out on open sand now, an occasional burrower rippling aside from the dusei's warding. "Cast the she'pan for the dusei. The storm, sov-kela . . . I am worried. I know they will not have stayed where I left them; they cannot have done that."

"The tents—"

"They are without them."

Duncan drew in a breath, thinking of the old, the children, sick at heart. He shaped Melein for the dusei, with all his force. He received back nothing identifiable before them, only the sense of something ugly at their backs.

"I sensed you," Niun said. "And trouble. I thought to turn back in the storm; but there was no getting there in time to help anything . . . and this . . . the dus gave me no rest. Well it did not. Even the wild ones. I have never felt the like, sov-kela."

"They are out there," Duncan said. "Still. They met me on the way." An insane memory came back, an attempt to reach them, to show them *life*, and choices. Survival or desolation. He shuddered, staggered, felt something of his own dus, a fierceness that blurred the senses. Both beasts caught it. Somewhere across the flat a cry wailed down the wind, dus.

Melein, Duncan insisted.

Their own beasts kept on as they were heading; it could be answer; it could be incomprehension. They had no choice but to go with them.

VII

Luiz appeared in the doorway of *Flower's* lab offices, leaned there, his seamed face set in worry. "Shuttle's down," he said. "Two of them. They're coming in pairs."

"The dispatch is nearly ready." Boaz made a few quick notes, sorted, clipped, gathered her materials into the pouch and sealed the coded lock: Security procedures, foreign to her. She found the whole arrangement distasteful. In her fifty-odd years she had had time to learn deep resentment for the military. Most of her life had been wartime, the forty-three-year mri wars. Her researches as a scientist had been appropriated to the war in distant offices; on *Flower* they had been directly seized. She had to her credit the decipherment of mri records which had led them here, which had led to the destruction of mri cities, and the death of children; and she grieved over that. A pacifist, she had done the mri more harm with pick and brush and camera than all of *Saber's* firepower and all the ships humans had ever launched; she believed so; and she had had no choice—had none now that she was reduced to writing reports for security, reckonings of yet another species for military use.

She had had illusions once, of the importance of her freedom to investigate, the tradeoff of knowledge for knowledge, for a position in which she, having knowledge, could sway the makers of policy; there had been a time she had believed she could say no.

She put the pouch into Luiz's hands, looked beyond him to the other men who had come into the lab: Averson, Sim Averson, a balding fellow who walked as though he might break. He came, and she offered her hand to him. Three years Averson had worked aboard *Flower* before the Kesrithi mission, which made him one of the seniors of the present staff, a sour, fretsome fellow who took his work in Cultures and his library more seriously than breathing, and lived for

71

the increase of data and systems to his personal credit in libraries back home. Averson had taken naturally to specialization in regul, as slow and methodical as they, pleased with the mountains of statistics which regul tended to accumulate. He had taken over Aldin's office with a sour intimation of satisfaction, as if Aldin's death had been fate's personal favor to him . . . appropriated Aldin's notes and materials and immersed himself in more cataloging. It likely did not occur to Averson now that the military might have interests wider than specific questions, that what he did might have moral implications . . . or if it did, it did so at a distance outside Averson's more vivid concerns. He looked now only annoyed, roused out of his habits and his habitation and his work.

"Be careful," Boaz urged him. "Sim, something's wrong up there."

Dark eyes blinked up at her, somewhat distantly. Averson had grown into the habit of looking down. He shrugged his bowed shoulders. "What can we do? When they ask, we come, however inconvenient it happens to be. My tapes, my programs, everything disarranged. I told them. Of course it's wrong. I'll be a week putting things in order. Can I explain this to them? No. No. Security has no comprehension."

"Sim, I mean that there's something wrong with the regul."

Averson's brow fractured into different wrinkles, distant recognition of a fact both germane and foreign to his research: he was slow of habit, but not slow-witted.

"I queried about the overflights," Luiz said. He folded his arms and set his back more firmly against the doorframe . . . his knees troubled him; he had gotten old, had Luiz, fragile as Averson. *We have all grown old,* Boaz thought desperately. *None of us will live to reach humanity again, not with all our functions intact. I will be near sixty, Luiz seventy-five if he makes it through the jumps again: Koch seventy at least; and some of us are dead, like Aldin.* "Koch went silent on me in a hurry. Now he wants you up there. And files on the regul. Boz is right. Something's astir up there with our allies."

Averson blinked slowly. "Metamorphosis. We reckoned . . . a longer time required."

"Stress conditions," Luiz surmised.

"Possibly." Averson chewed at his fingernail and frowned, staring at nothing in particular the while he followed some train of thought.

"Sim," Boaz said, "Sim, watch out for security."

Averson blinked at her, drawn back from his musing.

"Don't trust them," Boaz said. "Don't trust what they do with what we give them. Think. *Think* before you tell them something . . . how ignorant men could interpret it, what they could do with it. They aren't objective. We daren't trust that. People want statistics to justify what they *want* to do. That's the only reason we're ever asked."

"Boz," Luiz protested, with a meaningful glance at the intercom. *Flower's* operations staff was all military.

"So what do I care? What can I lose? Promotion? Assignments in the future? None of us are going to be fit for another after this one; and it's dead certain they're limited on replacements for us."

"Influence, Boz."

"What have we been able to influence? Between *Saber* and the regul, invaluable sites have been blasted to rubble, the greatest cities of the world in ruins, an intelligent species maybe reduced beyond viability . . . and we observe, we take notes . . . and our notes provide information so that regul and mri can kill each other. And maybe we can join in. Duncan took his own way out. I look at this and suddenly I begin to understand him. He at least—"

A shadow fell in the corridor doorway. Boaz stopped. It was Galey, from *Saber*, with another man. Vague surprise struck her, that Galey should have come down: an old acquaintance, this man . . . a freckled young man when he had set out from Kesrith, full of promise; a man in his thirties now, with a perpetually worried look. Youth to man to senior by the time he could get back to human space again, Boaz thought; mortality was on them all. The thought began to obsess her.

"Dr. Averson?" Galey inquired, came with the black man into the main lab. He proffered Luiz a cassette, had it signed for, passed the tab to his dark companion. "Lt. Harris," Galey identified the other. "Running shuttle up for Dr. Averson. Orders explain matters. Myself and my crew, we're staying on down here; cassette explains that too, I think, by your leave, sir, doctor."

There was a moment's cold silence.

"What's going on up there?" Boaz asked.

"Don't know," Galey said, and avoided her eyes. "Sir?" he said to Averson. "We have a limited access here. Better move as quickly as possible."

Luiz handed over the dispatch, received a signature in turn, from Harris.

"Suppose," Boaz said, "you see him settled, Mr. Galey."

Galey gave her that perplexed stare he could use; she did not relent. "Doctor," he murmured, and took his leave with Harris, shepherding Averson along with them in some haste.

"My tapes," Averson was saying. "My records—"

The door closed.

"Blast!" Boaz spat, and sat down.

"There's no help for it," Luiz said.

"His whole life," Boaz murmured, shaking her head; and when Luiz looked puzzlement at her: "Theirs, mine, yours. Spent on this thing. More than just the years. We can go home. But to what? What's the chance Stavros is still governor on Kesrith? No, new policies, a new governor—the whole situation years without our input. And what do we bring back? What do we tell them about what we've seen out here, a track of dead worlds—saying *what?* No one's asking the right questions, Emil. Not we, not the regul . . . no one's asking the right questions."

Luiz wrapped his thin arms about him and stared at the floor. "We can't get out there to ask the questions."

"And now we've got the military."

"We're vulnerable here; *That's* what's on my mind. Boz, whatever's afoot, I'm going to request all but essential personnel shuttled up. Fifty-eight people is too many to risk down here."

"No!" She thrust herself to her feet. *Flower* has to stay here, right here; we have to make it clear to them we're staying."

"We have to wait for Duncan as long as there's hope of waiting. That's our purpose; our only purpose. The Xen department has to understand that. There's no chance of doing more than that, and there's sure none of making gestures of principle with fifty-eight lives. Forget it, Boz."

"And when that fails?" She stalked to the door, looked back at him. "We'll lose the mri, you know that. How do we win, in a waiting game with regul?"

"We apply pressure . . . quietly. It's all we can do."

"And can't they figure that out? It's their game. Our generations are a fraction of theirs. Our whole lifespans are nothing to their three centuries. If you're right, if there is an adult developing among them, they can even out-populate us in the long run. And if there isn't one now, there will be, sooner or

later, this year or the next. Sooner or later, *Saber* will give up
and pull us out. We're mortal, Emil. We think in terms of
weeks and months. The regul will get the mri in the end. Do
you see *Saber* tying itself up here for longer than a few
months? And do you think regul wouldn't wait fifty out of
their three hundred years to have their own way with the
mri? And we can't. Fifty years . . . and we're all dead."

Luiz gazed at her, his dark eyes shrouded in wrinkled lids,
his mouth pressed to a fine line. "Don't you go on me, Boz.
We've lost too many to that kind of thinking. I won't hear
you start it."

"Four suicides and six on trank? It's Galey's sort who go
that route . . . the young, who had illusions of a life after
this mission is over. You and I, we're too old for that. We at
least have a past to look back on. They don't. Only the
jumps. And more of them to face on the way home. The
drugs may not last; we were handing out doubled doses at the
end. And what after that? You tell me what that voyage will
be like *with no drugs*."

"We'll find something."

"We can *try*." She made a shrug that was half a shiver.
"This world, Emil, the age, the *age* of it—one vast tomb; the
seas dried up, the cities frozen and waiting for the sun to go
out—and all space about empty of life. Dear God, what is it
to be young among such sights as these? It's bad enough to
be old."

Luiz came and took her by the arms, gathered her to him,
and she held to him until the shivers stopped.

"Emil," she said, "promise me something. Talk to the staff.
Let me talk to them. We can hold *Flower* here, right where
we sit, with all her staff. No lessening the stakes, no making
it easier for them, regul or human."

"We can't. We can't make gestures, Boz. Can't. I don't
know what Koch has in mind up there or down here, but we
can't cripple our own side by making independent moves. We
have to protect our people and we have to be ready to lift on
the instant the orders come. We're the other star-capable ship
and we've no right to gamble with it."

"We've no right not to."

"I can't listen to you."

"Won't." Boaz turned aside, drew a long breath, glanced
back again. "And what answer does Koch have for us?"

Luiz drew the cassette from his pocket, stared at it as at

something poisonous. "I'll lay bets what answer he has; that those overflights aren't ours."

"Play it," Boaz said. She closed the door. "Let's both hear it."

He looked doubtful, frowning, but after a moment walked around her desk to push it into the player.

Gibberish filled the screens, codes, authorizations, *Saber's* emblem. Boaz came and sat on the edge of the desk near Luiz, arms folded, heart beating hard with tension.

". . . *request Xen staff cooperation with military mission,*" the tape meandered to its point, "*in on-site recon if this should prove necessary. Your base is base for this operation; request your staff conduct advance briefings prior to start of mission. Mission head is Lt. Comdr. James R. Galey. All decisions mission Code Dante to be made by Comdr. Galey, including final selection among* Flower *staff volunteers for mission slot. Suggest staff member D. Tensio. Your full cooperation in this matter urgently pleaded. Mission is recon only, stress, recon only, effort to comprehend nature of civilization and establish character of city installations. Failure of* Flower *cooperation will jeopardize search for alternative solutions.*"

She flung herself off the desk edge and started for the door.

"Boz," Luiz called after her.

She stopped. The tape had run out.

"Boz," Luiz said, his wrinkles drawn into lines of anguish. "You're fifty-two years old. There's no way you could keep up with those young men."

She looked down at herself, at a plump body that resisted diets, that ached with bad arches and wheezed when she had to carry equipment in standard gee. She had not been good to herself in her life: too much of sitting at desks, too much of reading, too much of postponing.

And the sum of her life rested in the freckled hands of a whipcord young soldier with no sense what he was about.

"I'm going," she said. "Emil, I'm going to talk to young Mr. Galey and he's going to listen."

"Jeopardize the operation for your personal satisfaction."

She turned a furious look on him, took a breath and drew herself up to her small height. "I'm going to give them the best they can get, Emil, that's what; because I know more than Damon Tensio or Sim Averson or any three of the assistants put together. Say otherwise."

He did not. Perhaps, she thought halfway down the corridor at as fast a pace as she could manage—

She glanced back, half-expecting to see him in the doorway. He was. He nodded to her slowly—too old himself, she realized; he knew her mind, knew to the bottom of his heart. He would be down the hall ahead of her if he could.

She nodded, a tautness in her throat, turned and went hunting Galey.

Harris kicked in the engines, took a cursory glance at the instruments, his mind wandering to *Saber*, to a hot cup of coffee; and to the next day off-duty, which was the reward of a downworld flight. Last of all he cast a glance to his right, at the little man who fussed nervously with the restraints.

"They're all right," Harris said. Groundling, this Dr. Averson, a dedicated goundling. He decided, humanely, to make the lift as gentle as possible; the man had some years on him. Averson blinked round-eyed at him, the sweat already broken out on his brow. Harris diverted his attention again to the instruments, advised *Flower* bridge of his status, began slow lift.

The shuttle responded with a leisurely solidity. He watched the altimeter, leveled gradually at 6,000 m and banked to come about for their run.

"We're turning," Averson said; and when he gave no answer: "We're turning." Averson raised his voice well over the noise of the engines. "We never turned. What's the matter?"

"We're coming about, sir," Harris said, adjusted the plug in his left ear to be sure he could hear warnings over Averson's clamor. He set the scan to audio alarm, wide-range. "Shuttles handle different than *Flower*. We're just heading where we should be."

They came to course. The desert slipped under them by slow degrees, with the indigo to pink shadings of the sky above and the bronze to red tones of the desert, the great chasm which might once have been a sea—passed the area of the recent storm and across the chasm. Scan clicked away the whole route, the instruments moduled into cargo. They crossed no cities this way and made no provocations. It was a tame run, toward a gentle parting with Kutath's pull. He relaxed finally as Averson settled down; the man took enough interest to lean toward the port and look down, though with a visible flinching.

Quiet. Sand and sky and quiet. Harris let go a breath, settled for the long run out.

Suddenly a tone went off in his ear and he flicked a glance

at the screen, his heart slamming in panic. He accelerated on the instant and their relation to the blips altered in a series of pulses as Averson howled outrage.

He angled for evasion and the howl became a choked gasp.

"Something's on our tail," he said. "Check your belts." The latter was something to take Averson's mind off their situation. He was calculating, glancing from screen to instruments. Two blips, coming up at his underbelly.

He veered again. The blips were in position to fire on the rise, could; might; he felt it in his gut. He increased the climb rate and the ship's boards flashed distress at him.

For the first time the bogies separated, shifting position and altitude. His heart went into his throat and he flipped the cover off the armscomp, ready. "Hang on," he yelled at Averson, and punched com, breaking his ordered silence. "Any human ship, NAS-6; we've got a sighting."

He banked violently and dropped; and Averson's scream echoed in his ear. The bogey whipped by and a screen flared; they had been fired on. He completed his roll and nosed up again as rapidly as the ship could bear.

"Get us help!" Averson cried.

"Isn't any." He punched com again, hoping for someone to relay to *Saber*. "Got two bogeys here. Does anybody read?"

The pulse in his ear increased, nearing. He whipped off at an angle that wrung a shriek from Averson, climbing for very life, trying at the same time to get an image on his screen. The sky turned pink and indigo, the pulses died, went offscreen. In a little more the indigo deepened and they were still accelerating, running for what speed and altitude they could attain: the sound of the engines changed as systems began to convert.

Averson was sick. Harris reached over and ripped a bag out of storage and gave it to him. For some little time there was the quiet sound of retching, which did no kindness to his own stomach.

"Water in the bottle there," Harris said. And fervently: "Don't spill anything. We're going null before long." He devoted his attention the while to the vacant scan, to making sure all the recorders were in order. He heard Averson scrabbling about after the water, the spasm seeming to have passed. His own stomach kept heaving in sympathy. "Disposal to your right."

Dayside was under them, and *Saber* was over the horizon. The instruments had nothing, not a flicker. Harris calculated.

Somewhere on this side of the world lay regul *Shirug*, beyond their scan; and somewhere downworld were cities with weapons which could strike at craft in orbit, if they once obtained a fix on so small a vessel as themselves.

Or if they had it already.

Averson snatched at another bag, dry-heaved for a time. They were in a queasy wallowing at the moment. Harris gave them visual stability with the world, wiped at the sweat that coursed his face, trying to reckon where *Shirug* might be. He had a dread of her coming up in forward scan, and the bogeys coming up under him again.

"Going to go back on course," he said to no one in particular. "At least that way downworld isn't so likely to have a shot at us."

Averson said nothing. Harris reoriented and Kutath's angry surface swung under their forward scan.

There was no reaction anywhere. A slow tremor came into Harris's muscles, a knee that wanted to jerk against his will. He reckoned that somewhere over the horizon *Saber* would grow concerned when they failed schedule, that somewhere near them *Santiago* must be on the prowl over dayside, regul-watching.

Then a tone sounded in his ear and a blip appeared on the edge of the screen, on and off. He kept his eye on it, his pulse pounding so that it almost obscured his audio. He did not tell Averson. It was of no use yet. He considered another dive into atmosphere. Maybe, he thought, that was what he was being encouraged to do. There had been two of them.

The sweat ran, the single blip grew no closer, and he wiped at his lip and tried to reckon his chances of being allowed to go his way. He could find himself up against some outrunner for *Shirug*, against which he was a gnat-sized irritant.

"How much longer?" Averson asked him.

"Don't know, sir. Just stay quiet. Got a problem here to re-calculate."

There was no way it avoided having him in scan, traveling so neatly at the edge of his own.

Suddenly it disappeared out of range.

That gave him no feeling of safety. It was back there; there could be any number back there.

The ruddy surface of the world slipped under their bow and whitened to polar frost. Ahead was the terminator.

Be there, he entreated. *Saber, Saber, for the love of God, be there.*

Averson fumbled after something in his pocket, a bottle of pills. He shook one out and put it into his mouth. He was looking gray.

"Things are going all right," Harris lied. "Relax, sir."

"We're alive," Averson muttered.

"Yes, sir, we are."

And a blip appeared at three o'clock of the scope, coming up fast. The pulse erupted in his ear, faster and faster, deepening as the instruments gauged size: it was big.

A screen flared, a computer flashing demands to his comp. Hasty pulses flurried across, coded; he punched in, braced for recognition or for fire.

"Shuttle NAS-6," a human voice said, "this is *Santiago*."

He punched com, weak with relief. "This is NAS-6. Two bogeys downworld, fire on their side, coming in with a bogey on my tail."

"Affirmative, NAS-6, we copy. Correct course our heading. Proceed to *Saber*."

He made the adjustments, recalled Averson, looked into the round-eyed face and nodded confirmation of the hope he saw there.

They crept farther into night, within the protective cloak of *Santiago's* scan. He had *Santiago's* scope on-screen now; it showed reassuringly clear, all but human shuttles and a friendly blip that was *Saber*.

Harris shifted footing uncomfortably, received the nod that sent him into the admiral's office . . . stood there, staring down at the hero of Elag/Haven and of Adavan, at the balding visage which up till now he had never had to face alone.

The formalities were short and on his own part unsteady. "Averson?" the admiral asked him, and his voice was grim.

"Meds have him, sir. A little shaken up."

"Close?"

"Close, sir."

"Security will have your tapes running now. Sit *down*, lieutenant. Did you get a clear image on your attackers?"

Harris sank into the offered chair, looked up again into that lean, ruddy face. "No, sir. I never managed it. Tried, sir. Not big, not quick on high gee maneuvers; had me, if they could or wanted, . . . harassment or just too slow, maybe."

"You're suggesting by that remark that they could have been regul?"

Harris said nothing for the moment. A mistake, a mistake

in that opinion: he reckoned where that led; and swallowed
bile. "I couldn't be a hundred percent sure of anything. They
were about that size; they shied off from high gee turns and
climbs. I've flown against mri. Mri feel different. Fast. Apt to
outguess you and crosscut your moves." He silenced himself,
embarrassed before a man who had been in it before he was
born, who sat regarding him with cold calculation. Koch
would know, all the same. The impression would make sense
to a man who had flown against both.

"I'll view the tapes," Koch said. Harris reassured himself
with that, desperately relieved to believe someone else would
be counter-checking his observations. "Did you," Koch
asked, "have your armscomp engaged?"

"Yes, sir."

"Maneuver to fire?"

"No, sir; they came up at my belly and I zigged and got
out without firing."

Koch nodded. It might be approval of his actions or simply
introspection. Koch leaned aside to key something into the
desk console. There was delay; finally a response lit the
screen, but Harris could not read it at his angle.

"Dr. Averson's under process in sick bay," Koch said; and
Harris reckoned that hereafter would be complaints. He was
caught in the vise, civ and military. Someone gave the orders
and the complaints ended up on his record. "Meds indicate
he came through in good shape, Koch said, "but they're going to keep him a little while. We'll be talking with him. Did
he have any comment on the scanning pass?"

"Said nothing, sir. Wasn't much to see."

"And the ships?"

"Don't think he observed much, sir."

"Point of origin?"

"From my view, east and low, veered to my heading and
tailed."

Koch nodded slowly, leaned back. "I appreciate the job,
lieutenant. That will be all. Dismissed."

"Sir." He rose, saluted, left, his knees still wobbling in carrying him past the secretary in the front office and down the
corridor outside. There would be other flights, he suspected
so; backup or not, there would be use found for him. He had
beaten the odds in the war, and the war was supposed to be
over. He had believed so. Every human alive had believed so.

He took the turn down to the prep room, half seeing the
scatter of men and woman who were ordinary about the

place, preferring this company until he had his nerves steady again. It was the unofficial center for preflight meetings and for beating the goblins after; it had hot coffee around the clock, an automat, and human company that made no demands—a clutter of zone charts on the walls, unofficially scrawled with notes—*home*, one wit had scrawled on a system chart, with an arrow spiraling forlornly off the board—a screen linked to scanning; tables and hard chairs, lockers for personal gear.

He wandered over to the coffee dispenser and filled a cup, stirred ersatz cream into it, suddenly aware of silence in the room. A group of men and women was clustered about the center table, some standing, some seated. . . . He looked that way, found no one looking at him directly, and wondered if he was the subject of the rumor. James, Montoya, Hale, Suonava—he knew them . . . too well for such silence.

He ventured among them, stubborn and uncomfortable, and Suonava moved a foot out of a seat for him: his rumpled blues and their crisp ones marked which had priorities at table in this room without rank. He sank into the chair and took a sip of his coffee.

The silence persisted. No one moved, some seated, some standing. He set the cup down, looked about him.

"Something wrong?"

"NAS-10's failed rendezvous," one said. "Van is missing down there."

His heart began that slip toward panic, the same as it had when the ships turned up in scan. He took a drink of coffee, hands shaking, set it down, his fingers still curled around the warmth. He knew Van. Experienced at Haven. One of the best. He looked for others who had flown out with him, on his tail and Galey's. There was no one else; likely they were still tied up in security's triplicate-copy debriefing . . . if they had returned.

"Any details?" he asked them.

"Never showed, that's all," Montoya said. "Everyone else is in; should have come in ahead of you that went to *Flower*. But Van didn't show."

"There's bogeys out there," Harris muttered, guilty at contributing to the rumor mill that operated out of this room; it would be traced; there would be a reprimand for it. But these people were flying out into that range next. Lives rode on such rumors; apprehension made reflex quicker.

"Mri," Suonava spat. "Mri!"

Harris brought his head up. "Didn't say that," he insisted, forcing the words. And because he was already committed: "And I don't think so. The feel was wrong. I don't think so."

There was silence after, sober-faced men and women settling about the table. No one spoke. It would be all over the ship by the next watch, on *Santiago* by the next. Harris did not plead for discretion. Suddenly advancements and careers shifted into small perspective.

"That doesn't leave us in a good spot," Montoya said, "does it?"

"Quiet," Hayes muttered.

Cups were refilled, one after the other retreating to the dispenser and returning. Pilots settled back at the table and drank their coffee, grim-faced. No one said much. Harris stared into the lights reflecting off the coffee, thinking and re-thinking.

It was a joyous sight, the appearance of a kel'en standing high among the rocks near the camp. Hlil flung up an arm and waved, and the sentry gave out a cry taken up by others. The very rocks seemed to come alive, first with black figures, and then with gold and blue. The weary column hastened, finding new strength in galled limbs and aching backs, as brothers and sisters of the Kel hurried out to their aid, as even blue-clad children came running to lend their hands, shouting for delight.

Only the sen'ein who drew the Pana accepted no help until others of the Sen could reach them to take the labor from them. And Hlil, freed of his burden by another kel'en, walked beside them up into the camp. Where the Pana went there went a silence in respect, a pause, a gesture of reverence, before celebration broke out again.

But all was quiet when they drew near the center of the open-air camp, where the she'pan waited, conspicuous in her white robes, seated on a flat stone. The sen'ein who drew the sled on which the Pana rested stopped it before her, and Hlil watchd with a tautness in his throat as she lifted her eyes from that to him.

"Kel-second," she said. He came, half-veiled as he was, dropped to his knees in the sand before her and sat back.

"There are three dead," he said in a calm, clear voice that carried in the silence about them. "Sen Otha, sen Kadas, kel Ros. At An-ehon . . . a collapse killed them. The edun is in ruin."

Her eyes lowered to the Pana, lifted yet again. "Who recovered it?"

"I," he said, "for any harm that attaches." He removed the headcloth, for all that there were children present. "Merin and Desai and Ras—by my asking."

"And the power in the city . . . live or dead, after the collapse?"

"Live," he said. "I saw: forgive."

"How far alive?"

For all the dignity kel-law taught him, his gesture was uncertain, a helpless attempt to recall what he had tried to wipe from his mind. He built back what he had seen, shut his eyes an instant, recalled with the meticulous care with which he had been trained to retain images. "Each row . . . some lights, mostly red, some gold; generally two hands of lights; more, the third row of machines. It spoke; I gave it my name and yours; it called for you."

She said nothing for the moment. He stared into her face . . . young and cold and scarred with kel-scars. A curse, he thought, that would be her gift to him. A chance for her to be rid of him, who was of the old order.

"Was the Pana damaged, kel Hlil?"

"No."

"You sent back half the force you took. We here thank you for that. We are without deaths in this camp because you sent us strength enough to shelter us. We could hardly have kept the sand clear without that help."

He blinked at her confused, realizing dimly that this was honest, that this cold young she'pan offered him praise.

"*J'tai* are owed you," she said. "Every one." She bent forward, kissed his brow, took his hands and rose, making him rise.

"She'pan," he murmured, and stepped back to let others through. One by one, to the very last and least, she took hands and kissed them, and there were bewildered looks on the faces of more than one of the Kel, for she had no reputation for such gestures.

Only Ras hung back, and when she was too obviously the last: "The kel'anth is not back," Ras said to his hearing and that of too many others. "Where is he, she'pan? I ask permission to ask."

"Not back yet," said Melein.

And Ras simply turned her back and walked away.

"Ras," Hlil hissed after her, his heart sinking; he hesitated

between going after her and staying to plead with the
she'pan, who must reprimand the rudeness; someone must. It
could not be ignored. It was on him, kel-second, and he stood
helpless.

But Melein turned her face away as if not to notice Ras's
leaving. "Make camp," she said into that deathly silence . . .
clapped her hands with a sharp and commanding energy.
"Hai! Do it!"

"Move!" kel Seras called out, and clapped his hands, an
echo of hers. Kath'ein called to children and sen'ein joined
kel'ein in helping Kath divide the loads they had brought.

Hlil stood still, caught the she'pan's eyes as she glanced
back across an intervening distance. Her calm face considered him for a moment, face-naked as he was, and turned
from him.

There was canvas overhead this night, the brightness of
lamps, the comfort of mats spread on the ground, in the
place of the cold sand and rocks which had been their bed;
enough to eat, and warmth besides closeness of bodies. But
most of all . . . the Pana. Melein kept it by her—once
opened, to be sure that the precious leaves within were intact.
She had her chair, robes for her lap, and outside, evident in
laughter—happiness in the camp, after all past sorrows.

Concerning Niun, she refused to give way to fear; there
had been the storm, and the desert and Niun's mission kept
no schedules. He could fend for himself no less than those
born to this land; she convinced herself so.

She sat, throned in her chair, the pan'en beside her, veiled
again. She reached out her hand and touched it from moment
to moment, this object which had come with her all her long
journey and which contained all the voyage of those before.
She feared . . . not personally, unless it was a fear rooted in
her pride, an unwillingness to fail when millennia of lives
rested on her shoulders. It was a burden which might drive
her mad if she allowed herself to dwell on that. Kel-training
had given her the gift of thinking of the day as well as of the
ages, as Sen thought. It was said that she'panei—the great
and true ones—acted in subconscious foreknowledge, that the
power of the Mystery flowed through their fingers and the
shapings that they shaped were irresistible—that they sat at
the hinge-point of space and time. From such a point—events
flowed about one, and all who stood nearest. Time was not,
as Kel and Kath perceived, like beads on a string, event and

event and event, from which Darks could sever them, breaking the string. There was only the Now, which extended and
embraced all the Past which she contained and the pan'en
contained, and all the past which had brought Kutath to this
moment; and all the future toward which she led.

She was not single, but universal; she inhaled the all and
breathed it through her pores. She Saw, and directed, and it
was therefore necessary to do very little, for from the Center,
threads ran far. It was that, to believe in one's own Sight.
There was no anger, for nothing could cross her. There was
no true pride, for she was all-containing.

And at other moments she left that vision, suspecting her
own sanity. She was kath Melein, kel Melein, sen Melein,
who desired most of all to shed the burden and take only the
black robes of Kel . . . to have freedom, to take up arms, to
strike at what should offend her honor and to walk the land
empty of past and future.

Years in voyaging, and, but for an occasional hour . . .
quite, quite alone, to study and meditate on the pan'en. One's
meditations could become convolute and bordering madness.

Did she'panei truly believe the Sight? Or was it pretense?
She did not know; she had become she'pan in the People's
dying . . . last, quite lost; and her own she'pan had not
prepared her . . . had herself been on the edge of madness.

If she entertained one keen fear, it was that: that she was
similarly flawed, that she was heir to madness, that the ancestors who had gone out had spent themselves and the World's
life to no sane purpose—or that the Sight had perverted itself, and had brought her home as the logical end of things,
the mad she'pan of a mad species, to destroy.

"She'pan."

A shadow moved, gold-robed as it entered the light. Sathas,
sen'anth. She blinked and lifted her hand, permission; and
the aged sen'en came and sat at her feet. She had called the
anth'ein, the seniors-of-caste; she drew a deep breath, regarded Sathas with quiet speculation.

New to his post: none of the original anth'ein had survived
the march out of An-ehon, save if one counted Niun; the
tribe was crippled by that loss of experience. But of all castes,
Sen was the rock on which she stood.

"Sathas," she said softly, "how goes it?"

"Surely you mean to ask us that."

"I ask of the tribe, Sathas."

He frowned . . . kel-scarred like herself, one of very few

of this Sen who had come up through that caste as she had;
and she treasured him for that, that core of common sense
that came of kel-training. Wind and sun and years had made
of his face a mask in which the eyes alone were quick and
alive, the planes of his countenance creased with a thousand
lines.

"As she'pan . . . or as Mother?"

It was well-cast. She lowered her eyes and declined answer,
looked up and saw the kath'anth and Hlil in the parting of
the curtains. "Come," she bade them.

The kath'anth seated herself, inclined her head in respect:
Anthil, a fiftyish kath'en, and never, perhaps, beautiful; but
the weathering of years had given her the placidity that
kath'ein attained. Young Hlil s'Sochil—quite otherwise, she
thought; he would have a face like Sathas's some day, all
grimness.

That it was Hlil, and not Niun . . . she tried not to think
on that.

"She'pan," they murmured greeting.

"Anth'ein," she responded, folding her hands in her lap.
"Can we move camp tomorrow?"

Heads inclined at once, although there was no happiness in
the face of the kath'anth, and that of kel Hlil was as impassive as one could look for in a kel'en.

"Understand," she said, "not . . . back to your own range;
but to a place I choose. We have come home; there are old
debts; a service to discharge."

Membranes flickered in the eyes of the kath'anth and of
Hlil, disturbance. "The Kel," Hlil said hoarsely, "asks permission to ask."

"We have lost An-ehon, kel-second; but what you saw
there confirms what I hope, that we are not without resources. There is a city beyond the hills, youngest of cities, one
never linked to us in the attack . . . nor ever one of our
own."

"Elee," Hlil murmured, shock plain in his unveiled face.

"The city Ele'et," said sen Sathas. "Sen agrees with the
she'pan in this undertaking. We may perish. We do as we
must."

"She'pan," Hlil murmured faintly.

"Elee were our first service," Melein pursued him. "Is not
the return . . . appropriate? Of the races which came of this
world, are we two not the last? And in the trouble that at-
tends us—I think it an appropriate direction. I have consulted

Sen, yes. Long since." She flicked a glance at Anthil. "I have
seen Kath withered in the House of my birth, kath'ein and
children lost by my own she'pan, who killed them in the forg-
ing that shaped my generation, on a world too harsh for them
. . . but not so harsh as Kutath itself. You are stronger,
Kath. But ask, and I will part you from the tribe, give you
into some shelter and set kel'ein to guard you."

"No," the kath'anth exclaimed at once.

"Think on it before answering," Melein said.

"We go," the kath'anth said, a voice gentle as befitted her;
and unyielding. "I shall ask; but I know Kath's answer."

That pleased her. She inclined her head, accepting—
glanced at Hlil. Not unthought, that she appealed to Kath before Kel: the others were true anth'ein, no surrogates; and
the others knew their authority. "Kel-second," she said, "do
you undrstand now . . . what the matter is before you? My
own kel'anth—we came of such a struggle, he and I: of
tsi'mri, and ships, and the serving of a service. It has been a
long time, has it not, for this Kel? Nigh a hundred thousand
years you have served to the service of living, of surviving
the winds, of providing for Kath and Sen . . . and perhaps
. . . of waiting. Do you hear me, kel Hlil? The world has
tsi'mri over its head . . . and you, for the moment, wield the
Kel; you are my Hand . . . and the People have need. I
may be the last age, kel-second. Can you lead if you must
. . . even into the Dark?"

The membrane flicked rapidly across his eyes; the kel-
marks stood stark upon his face. Such distress was for her to
see; he did not give her the blankness that was for strangers.

"I beg the she'pan put kel Seras in my place."

"He is experienced," she agreed, and felt pain for this man,
that he should make such a retreat . . . fear, perhaps, She
met his eyes and a curious sense came on her that something
very tough rested at the core of this kel'en. "No," she said. "I
ask you: why did kel'anth Merai s'Elil set you to be kel-second?"

Hlil looked down at his hands, which were like himself,
unlovely. "I was his friend, she'pan, that is all."

"*Why?*" she returned him; and when he looked up, plainly
confounded: "Do you not think, kel-second, that it had something to do with yourself?"

That was a heart-shot; she saw it. After a moment he
bowed his head and lifted it again. "Then I have to report,"
he said in a still voice, "that we are missing one of the Kel.

That kel Ras—is not in camp. Should we do something in that matter, she'pan?"

She let go a slow breath, looked on the man and read pain. The eyes met hers, quite steady and miserable.

"I shall not ask what the Kel would do," she said. "You would judge harshly because you want not to. I am afflicted with an unruly Kel; can I heal it with impatience? Perhaps I should be concerned; but I am more concerned for those who remain. Let her go if she will; or return. I do not forbid. And as for the matter at hand," she said, going placidly about the matter of orders and looking instead at Anthil, "we abandon nothing, except by Kath's discretion, I do not urge it. Some of the least kel'ein can walk burdened, and some of the lesser sen'ein too. Settle that within your own caste. Divide the property of the dead according to kinship and need. I trust the Kel can bear another trek?"

"Aye," Hlil said quietly, earnestly. Sathas and Anthil added soft assent.

"Then at dawn," she said, dismissing them with a gesture. They rose, pressed her hands in courtesy. Only Hlil held a moment more, looked at her as if he would speak . . . and did not.

They withdrew. She leaned back in her chair, touched at the pan'en, stared before her with an unfocused gaze on the lamps.

To manage others . . . had a bitter taste in the mouth, a taint of Intel, her own she'pan, who had known how to seize her children and wring the hearts out of them, who could choose one to live and one to die, who could use, and move, and wield lives like an edged blade.

So she had sent Niun; and in cold realization of necessity, selected another weapon, for its hour.

Only Ras. . . . She attempted, consciously, to use Sight, to know whether she was a danger or no: and Sight failed her, a vast blankness all about the name of Ras s'Sochil.

The vision was at times not comfort enough; when she doubted it altogether, it was far less.

VIII

They were still there. Duncan rolled aside on the dune face and turned his head to regard Niun, who still rested on his belly and his forearms, though he too had slid down somewhat. The beasts rested down in the trough, needing nothing of vision to tell them where their enemies were, spread wide about the horizon of dunes under a morning sun.

"Yai!" Duncan said hoarsely, stopping that impulse, lest their followers use it to track to them.

"We need to keep moving," Niun said. "When you can."

Duncan considered it, lay there, content to breathe. Food nauseated him; but he accepted the dried strip of meat Niun offered him while they waited. He thrust it into his mouth and finally chewed it and choked it down his raw throat. Things tasted of blood and copper, even the air he breathed. There were frequent moments when he lost vision, or when his knees threatened to bend the wrong way in walking the uneven ground. His head pounded. Alone, he would have burrowed into the first stony cover he could find and prepared to fight if hiding failed; Niun would make other choices, that would get him killed.

"Much farther?" he asked.

"Some," Niun said. "Tonight, maybe."

Duncan lay still and considered that, which was better than he had thought. "And then what? You fight duel? You have walked twice their distance."

"So," Niun said. "But it remains what I said: that between she'panei . . . the challenge is single; must be. If we started the matter here, we would have bloodfeud, and no end of challenges." He drew a short breath, himself near panting. "Hai, and their kel'anth may not be with them; in that case challenge falls to their kel-second. That can only be in our favor."

90

Niun was very good. So, Duncan reckoned, might others be.

"Do you want to go on from here?" Duncan said. "They do not have us always in sight; if I walk over your tracks you might be a good way back to—"

Dusei stirred below, uncomfortable. "No," Niun said. He touched his own face, where the veil crossed his cheeks and the blue edge of the kel-scars was visible. "You are unscarred; no kel'en should challenge you; but alone—gods know what they would do."

"That is my difficulty, is it not?"

By the look in Niun's eyes it was not.

"Aye," Duncan said. Much, Niun had taught him aboard the ship, much is mind; what one will, one can. He had survived jump without drugs, as mri did, and that was called a physical difference. He sucked air slowly, measuring his breaths, warming the air through his hands, finally gathered himself up off the face of the dune and started moving. Niun swiftly overtook him, and the dusei, shambling along at a better pace than they had been making.

"Do not overdo it," Niun said.

He slacked a little, went blind to his surroundings and concentrated on breathing and pace and the little bit of sand about them. Until night. He reckoned he might last that long.

It was back, the human ship *Santiago*, despite all maneuvers to shake it. Bai Suth glared at the image of it, which was, even against *Shirug's* vast teardrop shape, a threat. An elder human commanded *Santiago*, bai Silverman. Were there only human younglings in question, *Shirug* might dispose of that nuisance and argue the point with bai Koch later, in confidence that human anger would not ascend to a hostile move against *Shirug* itself: humans had three ships; regul, one. It was a clear question of proportional damage.

The fighter simply maintained orbit, observing. The shuttles sown into atmosphere during the evasive maneuver could not return without another such. They performed maneuvers frequently, whether or not shuttles were going; and each brought *Shirug* closer than Suth liked to come to the planet. There was no means to lose the human craft: a hard run and a threat toward jump might keep *Santiago* from their vicinity for days, but in fact all the fighter needed do was to sit at the objective, orbiting Kutath close-in, and all elusive maneuvers came to naught. The fighter was far more maneuverable in close planetary orbit than was *Shirug,* being able to cut lower and get out again, as *Shirug* possessed similar advantage over giant *Saber,* and therefore *Saber* had the ultimate advantage while it had *Santiago,* a two-point flexibility which made eluding them nigh impossible.

To remove that ship—permanently—might well be worth the hazards of human reaction, if that reaction could be understood in advance.

No doubt remained at least that humans had decided an adult existed among regul. Suth fretted with disappointment that this realization had come sooner that he would have wished, but it did give them added safety—assuming elder status meant what it should to human minds.

But elder status had not at all protected bai Sharn from death. It might be argued that the youngling Duncan was thoroughly mri, and that what Duncan did, did not speak for humans; it might even be argued that Duncan was mad, and therefore apt to any act. But the fact remained that humans had not shown sufficient disturbance at Duncan's act of elder-murder. Distress . . . of course that was not to be anticipated; Sharn's death was a political convenience to humans, and they could only be pleased at the opportunity which fell into their hands . . . but the lack of emotional disturbance in the presence of a dead elder, the cold haste in which they had been ejected from the ship and sent back to *Shirug,* in which they must wait a day on the release of their elder's body—that was a reaction without sane emotion, a void where some emotion ought to exist and failed. Suth turned this circumstance over and over in his mind, day by day, smothering his own anger in an increasing preoccupation with this illogic. A reaction existed in regul which—perhaps —humans did not feel at all. This insensitivity had vast implications, and Suth felt keenly the lack of experience which was his. What he had once heard, what he had once seen, what things had impinged on his life or what he had studied, every minute detail, he recalled unshakably.

Humans, he had observed, recalled things in time-ahead. *Imagination,* they called this trait; and since they committed the insanity of remembering the future—Suth had been tempted to laughter when he first comprehended this insanity—the whole species was apt to irrational actions. The future, not existing, was remembered by each individual differently, and therefore they were apt to do individually irrational things. It was terrifying to know this tendency in one's allies—and worse yet not to know it, and not to know how it operated.

They might do anything. The mri suffered from similar future-memory. Presumably two such species even thought they comprehended one another . . . if two species' future-memories could possibly coincide in any points; and *that* possibility threatened to unbalance a sane mind.

This was one most profound difference between regul and human, that regul remembered only the past, which was observable and accurate as those who remembered it. Humans accustomed to the factual instabilities of their perceptions, even *lied*, which was to give deliberate inaccuracy to memory, past or future. They existed in complete flux; their memories periodically purged themselves of facts: this was perhaps a necessary reflex in a species which remembered things that had not yet happened and which falsified what had occurred or might occur.

Disrespect of temporal order; this was the sum of it. Anything might alter in them, past, present, future. They *forgot*, and wrote things on paper to remember them; but they might not always write the truth; and the possibility that they might accurately *imagine* the truth . . . Suth backed his mind from that precipice, refusing the leap.

Humans had not experienced disorientation in the killing of a regul reverend with the accumulated experience of nearly three hundred years. It was as if they could *forget* all this information, not valuing it—perhaps because they could change whatever they pleased, or *imagine* backward as well as forward.

And it evidently did not matter to them whether they remembered accurately; it did not disorganize the species, who were accustomed to divergency in future-memory, and therefore—perhaps—cared nothing for divergence in past-memory.

How did they view the present? Did it likewise shift about?

Could they likewise *forget* the killing of a human elder, if it was not useful to remember it?

If he could reach a correct conclusion, it would be of great value in determining policy.

He sat now, in his sled, which supported his increasing bulk and provided him on rails and wheels, swift transport about the spiraling corridors of *Shirug*, if he needed it. In fact there was little need for him to stir from his office, and he did so seldom. Every control on the ship was accessible directly or indirectly from his sled console. Only actual flight operations demanded more meticulous attention to incoming data than he could conveniently handle, and a nervous clutch of Alagn younglings attended the controls constantly. He had killed several for inattention . . . and also because they were older Alagn younglings, and there was the remote chance of one of them sexing male, once the immediate hysteria of Change had eased on the ship, and while the fact of his command was still new to the crew.

The younglings who survived his tempers had improved markedly in efficiency, working feverishly whether or not his eye was immediately on them; this was to the good of the ship. They learned; he would Impress them, so that even years hence he would have no rivals.

Therefore he was prepared to deal with humans. He had absolute power on his own ship, and he was calmer about entering the maze of regul-human relations that he might have been.

Therefore he allowed himself to contemplate confrontation.

He keyed the position of *Santiago* to the screen on the panel of his sled, and widened the schematic to include the latest plotting of the position of *Saber*, over the horizon. *Flower* was a third dot, below, on Kutath's surface. There were four other points, two human shuttles aloft, two regul shuttles left on Kutath: younglings, expendables.

He stared in prolonged speculation at the screen, his nostrils flaring and shutting in dislike as he sorted all past action to determine present ones, combining and recombining pieces like a stoneworker, seeking those which made coherent structure.

A light flashed on his board, signaling someone wishing his personal attention. He cleared the screen and received a notation from Nagn: *Urgent. Direct-contact, favor.*

He flashed back his permission. "Door," he shouted at the youngling who kept the anteroom, and it stirred out in haste: Ragh, its name was, clever and zealous and mightily fearful.

The other doorway opened. Not one but three sleds arrived, Nagn and Tiag and Morkhug, with attendants and commotion. Ragh showed them through, directed the other attendants, stumped this way and that offering drink, murmuring anxious courtesies.

"Out!" Suth snapped; Ragh daringly slipped a cup into his hand and fled with all possible speed, herding the other

younglings into the anteroom. "Report," Suth asked of his mates. "What is the urgency?"

"Important news," Nagn said. "Favor, reverence bai: analysis of the new tapes indicates a resurgence of power in the sites."

Suth hissed softly, delayed for a drink to stabilize the out-of-phase beating of his hearts. "Details."

"Scant, reverence. The readings are faint. More might be done . . . but the likelihood of triggering fire with *Shirug* in range. . . ."

The hearts tended apart, and then toward unity. "Mri with weapons. This can be domonstrated in plain data. Mri with weapons."

"Every site," Nagn said in a low voice. She keyed a graphic to their screens, the world rotating, sites lighting, all edging on the great chasms. "Concentrated life signs indicate moisture in the depths of the basins; what is there, is patently available for use at such sites. Life requirements are available to a technology advanced sufficiently to draw the water up. The area out of which the youngling Duncan appeared . . ." The graphic reversed its revolution and narrowed in field. ". . . possesses more than one such site."

"Old," Suth murmured, staring at the distance between the diminished water sources and the city sites. It was shattering constantly to realize how old. Data available in home space had indicated the mri to be a young species, and regul oldest of all—regul, who had risen on the cycles of famines and the dread of famines, to seek resources outward, warless, with errorless passing of knowledge from one generation to the next. But not the oldest. Far from oldest. Millions of years lay even in the decay of Kutath.

Of mri who, like humans . . . *forgot*.

Data existed in such cities, recorded as *forgetting* species must record such things: a treasury of eons, knowledge of all these regions of space, records of the dead worlds which the mri had killed, of all this aged, alien species had done and known and been. To destroy this knowledge. . . .

The very thought sent a wave of revulsion through him, almost unbearable in intensity. It was the death of elders. It was murder. He sucked air, his hearts paining him. Sharn had committed such destruction, without understanding what she did. He was cursed to know. But what was down there was knowledge inaccessible to regul, in language mri had never given regul to learn, of experiences which had to make sense only to mri—or to those who could speak the language, who could become mri.

A human could. Duncan spoke the mri tongue, and assumed the robes and the manners and the thoughts of mri. A human *forgot* his own way, and crossed that boundary which regul in two thousand years had not crossed nor wished to.

Humans would gain access to such knowledge with the fall of the mri world, or with the peaceful accommodation they sought with it. They would possess the experience of millions of years which would be recorded down there. Would become . . .

. . . mri. Imitating, as Duncan so facilely imitated. The model was before them, in the youngling Duncan.

To let this happen . . . to allow to exist information which regul could not use, and allow it into the hands of a species which could *forget* its own nature and assume that of another . . . or which already shared tendencies which mri had—

"Eldest?" Nagn murmured. "Eldest?"

"We have a difficulty, bai Nagn. One which affects policy. Heed: I shall tell you a thing. Once . . . in the memory of doch Horag, a dispute of Horag elders was to be resolved by the combat of mri kel'ein. And one kel'en said that he sought this particular combat gladly, because he understood that the other Horag elder had abused her mri mercenary. Yet the first mri killed the second."

"That is mad," said Tiag.

"Not so. The regul who lost the challenge, lost territory and younglings and influence. Thus the dead mri was avenged powerfully, and his killer was indeed his avenger as he had purposed to be. Mri are fully capable of understanding revenge. And they do not value survival above status as humans do."

"Their lives are short by nature," Morkhug said with contempt. "And they *forget* what they are told."

"Do not reckon that they lack wit, mate-of-mine. Errors have been made on this account, serious errors."

"There is a human with them, reverence. He is the dangerous one. He has made them dangerous, as they were not before his coming among them. Humans are capable of some memory functions, if only on paper and tape. Remove this one human and the mri are disorganized."

"No," Suth said flatly. "No. Sharn and doch Alagn erred, because Alagn never employed mri directly and did not understand them. Alagn came from homespace . . . as you do.

But Horag doch has employed mri in the colonies, for two thousand years. *I remember.*"

This silenced them all, Alagn-born that they were; they were tied now to Horag, and lifted their faces to him, respectfully expecting enlightenment.

"I shall share my knowledge," he promised them, "as it becomes needful. Alagn erred. Bai Hulagh Alagn-ni of Kesrith failed to ask into the experience of his predecessors. Therefore Alagn does not remember. I do not make that error of omission. If any of you has pertinent information or acquires it, I order you to give it to me at once."

One after the other they solemnly confessed ignorance of mri.

"Attend," said Suth with a pleased hiss. "It is necessary to touch that mri characteristic I named."

"This is not Kesrith," Nagn said. "Bai—"

"Does a question occur to you?"

"There are cities. Machines. Do mri construct such things? Have mri ever constructed such elaborate things themselves? This is not consonant with observation."

"Mri have always worked . . . among themselves, or for their own benefit. They would not lift a pebble at our bidding; but to house themselves, yes, they have built their own edunei, and they handle complex machinery—expertly. Does Alagn estimate the mri edun on Kesrith was built by regul? Does Alagn not know that kel'ein have handled regul ships—with controls designed for regul minds and memory, which humans have greatest difficulty grasping? Alagn has failed to observe, until now. I congratulate you, bai Nagn, at least on an appropriate question."

The three Alagn-ni fretted in visible discomfiture.

"Further question," Suth pursued. "As this is the mri homeworld—we accept human reckoning this is so—do associational structures here operate as they did in mri for hire far from the authorities of this world? It will not be wise to make simplistic conclusions based on data from Kesrith. Facts too soon recorded are sometimes imperfect."

"But," Tiag said, her nostrils fluttering still under the sting of sarcasm, "this is an armed world, reverence. Facts not swiftly enough recorded are not available for our defense, reverence bai."

Suth swelled in pique, not overmuch. Logical that Tiag had sexed as she had; she had always had a brusqueness that disturbed. "Physically, bai Tiag, we could launch further fire into those sites. But humans are onworld; humans must perceive the origin of the threat clearly as mri. We are within range of human ships as well as mri cities." In exaggerated lack of haste he reached for the sled-console, sipped at his cooling cup from one hand while he keyed in library functions with the other. He obtained memory-films, meant to chronicle the mri wars for any youngling which might be born on board; and he smiled, having obtained what he sought. Editing them on the spot was a simple matter, ordering the machine to duplicate, beginning and ending at certain points, and to arrange scenes into desirable sequence.

Human faces showed on the screen: Duncan's face. The mri slaughter at Elag lay tangled in smoking ruin; the towers of Nisren's edun fell in fire and human troops rushed across a field strewn with mri dead; human warships hovered above mri ruins.

He composed, sent the result to the others, watched their faces conceive excitement.

"We do not speak the mri tongue," he said, "but these powered sites surely have the facilities to receive simple transmissions. And demonstration speaks all tongues."

"Bai," Nagn murmured.

"We have ten shuttles. Several can be dropped; we reserve four for maneuverings where humans can keep them in sight. The ones sent down are at very high risk. But I tell you this for your information, honored mates: these mri . . . all the laughter regul have indulged in over species whose memory is lost without their paper . . . and these humans too. . . . Does it occur to you that in the Alagn debacle at Kesrith, these aforesaid humans gathered up a great deal of regul paper and tapes? The library was lost. Your great Alagn bai Hulagh salvaged machines and ships and lives of younglings and let the library fall into human hands; a minor loss, so long as the minds which contained that—doubtless trivial—information were packed onto ships and sent back to home space and safety, true? Or perhaps Hulagh would have fired the library before leaving . . . if he had had time. Observe this youngling Duncan, observe how exactly he imitates mri. A minor loss, a poor colonial library on a mining colony? Regul lost nothing; but humans gained. Did humans much fret for the loss of the machines Hulagh lifted off? No. But humans swarmed over that library in the first days of Kesrith's occupation like insects over corruption. Does no conclusion yet occur to you?"

"We erred," Nagn said after a moment, her nostril edges showing pallor. "Reverence, why have we failed to note such things?"

"Because, Nagn Alagn-ni, the bai of your doch lacked experience, for all his years; so did Sharn. I have realized it. This question has occurred to me; but even as a youngling I possessed something great Alagn did not have—experience of non-regul. You were insulated, safe, in home space. Horag is colonial. We dealt with mri, with humans, with mri beasts. We gained models against which to compare actions. You have lacked such models. Your comprehensions are wise within your limitations, but there are other species in the universe . . . and Horag has been dealing with them for two thousand years."

"Mri and dusei and humans," Tiag exclaimed in disgust. "What can they discover that some regul has not already discovered and remembered the first time?"

"Lackwit, observe what Nagn has correctly observed and think! What would humans do with the records of our own homeworld? And what world is this before us?"

"The mri homeworld," Morkhug said. "Cities, storehouses of data—"

"To which this Duncan has already gained access," said Suth. "Mri . . . value revenge. The revenge they owe Alagn is considerable, and I do not want that inheritance. But that is not the only cause for which we should fear. Of how many years might be the experience logged in cities which were built to surround seas which are no longer there?"

"Mri," said Tiag, attempting scorn, but her nostrils kept dilating.

"Mri with ships," said Nagn, "who made the desert of stars as far as our own space, and turned back only when they ran out of lives. And humans, who keep their memories only on paper, gather the memories of this place. Millions of years, Tiag."

"But we cannot destroy it," Tiag moaned.

"Mri," Suth said, "and incomprehensible to us. Valueless to us, in a language we cannot read. But do you observe, mates-of-mine, that the mri mind and the human . . . are compatible?"

"What shall we do, then, bai?"

"What do we do with irrationalities? We remove them from the present. Alien minds are able to bridge these irrationalities. The reflexes of *forgetting* are not all detriment, to my observation. We cannot operate by such absorptions. Already we are troubled by impossible combinations of concepts. We talk in paradoxes when we carry on any lengthy discourse with humans. We have walked into a morass. We do not extricate ourselves by swallowing mud. Remove it: that is what has to be done. It is not the weapons which are the danger; it is not the feud with mri, it is the combination, mates-of-mine, the *combination*, this absorptive tendency in our allies . . . with what we have seen in coming here. How did we first involve ourselves with humans at first hand? A human named Stavros imitated our ways. How did mri involve themselves with humans? A human named Duncan imitated theirs so successfully he has been transformed. This is beyond courtesy. This is a mechanism. This is a biological mechanism by which this species survives. There is one human, in each instance, there is one human who walks from among them, who allows himself to become Impressed, who *becomes* the enemy . . . who then bridges the gap, and gains knowledge. One sacrifice. One transformation. Who of us, who of the mri, is able to become human? Can you, Tiag? Can you define, having observed Stavros and Duncan and Koch, even what *is* human?"

Tiag shuddered visibly, eyes rolling aside.

"We shall never be quit of humans," Suth said bitterly. "By Alagn's grievous error, we let them inside. But we can see to it that what belongs to this world . . . stays here. Ends here. And we can go back to home space and give our information and observations to regulkind, without mri in the equation. We can cut off this branch, so that there is no hazard at least from this source: we can focus human attention here, where it can no longer profit them, and buy us time."

"We have one ship," Morkhug protested. "One of their three. How can we deal with them?"

"More of Alagn's negotiation. We should initiate a new negotiation. My presence gives us that option, being of different doch. We should see to the arrangement of advantages, maneuver as best we can." He set his cup aside, empty, stared grimly at the three of them. Carrying, all three; the young could not come to term in any reasonable time to be of assistance: they had not the time of years, but time as humans reckoned it, and actions had to be undertaken . . . quickly.

The tribe was not there. Niun felt it from the time that they passed the great rounded rock which had been his landmark returning from many a hunt . . . and where once he had felt a sense of occupancy—there was nothing from the dusei, only that feeling which nagged at their shoulders, warning that their pursuers were, if anything, nearer.

They had made good time, the best that Duncan could do, from nooning till now, that the sun began its midair vanishing out over the basins, and shadows were beginning to fade. Duncan kept the pace still, his breathing loud and raw. At times Niun caught him walking with eyes shut: he was doing so now, and Niun took his arm and guided him, breaking rapport with the dus, wishing to shed none of his despair on Duncan. He tried it again in the shadows' deepening . . . shaped again what he sought of the dusei, received back nothing comforting, no sense of friendly presence. There was a prickling of something else as they neared the rocks, a sense which might come of one of the ha-dusei, remote, disturbed.

Melein had warned him: other cities, she had said. Other choices. Hlil had gotten back; must have.

And somewhere they must find a place to rest, a place for Duncan. They had entered into a trap, a triangle of land with the rim on one side, the chasm of the cut on the other, and the enemy behind them, on the third. The dusei had led them here; they had followed, hoping and blind, reliant on them.

Still that blankness: dusine obsession, perhaps, with what followed . . . they were notoriously single-minded. But the dread grew in him, that that emptiness might be death, might be that Hlil had failed, that the storm had been too much for them. Dusei could not comprehend death, minds that would not respond; a bewildered persistence even without answer.

"Sov-kela," he said finally, himself hoarse with exertion. "They have moved on."

Duncan did not falter, did not answer. Some emotion came back through the dusei, a kind of panic, quickly smothered.

"We . . . go across the cut," Niun said. "We know where they are not; and the dusei probably mean . . . we should keep going south. The cut goes half a day's march around its farther end; a long diversion for our followers . . . a cautious approach this way, to go down . . . where they could meet trouble. Where I know the ground and they do not. Stay with me. Stay with me."

"Aye," Duncan said, a sound hardly recognizable.

Colors began to fade from the land. In the treacherous last light they entered the trail itself, passed under the place where a sentry should have challenged them. Sand had filled here, unreadable in the constant gentle wind, a thick blanket which lay knee-deep over the old trail, half burying rocks which had once stood clear. The dusei gave neither alarm nor sense of contact, shambling along before them.

Suddenly the way opened to the terrible vista of the sand-slip, which admitted the last amber light upon a sand-surface widened and seamed much farther than it once had been. "Yai!" Niun exlaimed, willing the dusei to stay close to them, giddy even to contemplate that fall and tormented with an abiding fear, that the dusei had brought them here because they had no other track, because there was nothing farther, and the others were lost, down that, down *there*.

Duncan breathed an exclamation beside him, a choked sound; Niun reached back, flung an arm about him, guided his unsteady steps as they came down along the edge of the cliffs. The least breath might set it into motion again, might rip loose not only that unstable surface but reach far back into the canyon.

He and Duncan walked the edge of the cliffs, the dusei throwing their heads in mistrust of this place . . . by instinct or some knowledge gleaned of his mind, they hugged the cliffs as well, shouldering against the rock, rolling nervous eyes on that outer surface.

They reached the place which had belonged to Kel, and within was nothing but shadow, sand filled halfway up to the roof of the recess. Beyond that the sandfall continued, pouring down onto what was now the face of the slip, having lost much of the cone which it had built up before. They crossed under the whispering fall and back and back in the canyon, where it had begun to be night, where the seam of the slip did not reach.

"Now," Niun said. "We cross here. No delicacy and no delay: it goes or it does not."

He sent stern command to the dusei and seized Duncan by the arm, and such as they could, they ran, crossing the stone's-throw of sand. There was a natural slipping underfoot, no more than that; and the rocks loomed before them, received them into safety. Duncan stumbled and caught himself against the rocks, moved when Niun seized him and pulled him on, up, into the tangle of rocks and wind-carved stone.

The dusei climbed, no natural activity for them, with a clatter of stone and scratching of claws, and Niun clambered after, up and up where there had been an ascent from the far side.

And halfway up, a shelf, a tilting slab, hardly more than a dus's width. The beasts went on climbing, sending down small rocks; Niun stopped there, tucked up in a cramped position, dragged Duncan as much onto the ledge as he could. Duncan coughed, a racking, heaving cough, lay face down and curled somewhat; and Niun crouched there listening, his hand on Duncan's heaving shoulder.

The dusei reached the top, perhaps to move on, perhaps to wait; Niun willed them to wait, felt Duncan's breathing ease at last to deep gasps and finally to a quick, shallow pace. There was no bed but the cold stone, no place but this to rest. In his mind Niun hoped their pursuers would try the cut in the dark—one grand slide to oblivion for that carelessness, going into that place not knowing it was there. Or if they came around it, they would go some distance out of their way, some far distance. There was time to rest, enough, at least, to give Duncan a little ease.

Melein, he cast out toward his dus, hoping, desperately hoping. There was nothing, but only that remote unease that had begun this day and continued. He dared not yield to sleep; tired as he was, he might go on sleeping, until the moment he found himself surrounded by hao'nath.

He did sleep, came awake with a guilty jerk, an attempt to focus his eyes on the stars, to know how long. The moon was up. For a moment it seemed a star moved, and his strained eyes blinked and lost it: illusion, he persuaded himself. There was still a star there, stable and twinkling with dust. He watched that patch of visible heavens until he found his eyes closing again, despite numbed limbs and the misery of a point of rock in his back; Duncan's back moved evenly under his hand. He stayed still a long time, finally moved his hand and shook at Duncan, as reluctantly as he would have struck him.

"Move," he said. "We have to move."

Duncan tried, almost slipped off the ledge in trying to push himself up to his knees; Niun seized him by his Honors-belt and steadied him, moved his own stiffened limbs and pulled, secured a better grip on him. Somewhere above them the dusei stirred out of a sleep, and vague alarm prickled through the air, a re-reckoning of positions. The enemy had a new direction . . . going around the cut, Niun reckoned.

Where Melein might have gone, to be set in their path before he might.

He climbed, hauling Duncan's faltering steps higher with him, bracing himself and struggling by turns. At last the upper rocks were about them, and a sandy ridge, a last hard climb. Duncan hung on him and made it, carried his own weight then, though bent and stumbling. The dusei met them there, comfort in the dark and the moonlight; and before them stretched another flat, and the low southern hills.

A land with no more limits than the one they had just passed from; and no sight of a camp, nothing.

"Come," he urged Duncan, against complaints Duncan had not voiced. He caught Duncan's sleeve, gentle guidance, started walking, a slower pace than before. It was almost the worse for rest; aches settled into bones, rawness into his throat: Duncan's hoarse breathing and occasional coughs caught at his own nerves, and at times he hesitated in a step as if his joints yielded, minute pauses, one upon the next.

And suddenly there was sense of presence, familiar presence, home, home, home.

"They are out there," Niun exclaimed. "Sov-kela, do you feel it?"

"Yes." The voice was nothing like Duncan's. It managed joy. "I do."

And out of some reserve of strength he widened his steps, struggled the harder, a hand cupped to his mouth, attempt to warm the air.

Rounded domes of rock existed here and there, knobs of sandstone wind-smoothed, sometimes hollowed into bowls or flattened into tear shapes. A skirl of sand ran along the ground, a wind for once at their backs, helping and not tormenting, for all that it was cold; and a lightening began in the east, the first apricot seam of dawn.

Dus-sense persisted, a muddle of confusions, urging them south, unease in one quarter and another, as if the evil had fragmented and scattered; there was hope amid it; and a darkness that was nearest of all, a void, a shielded spot in the network.

It acquired substance.

There was a stone, a roughness in the land: dus, perhaps . . . a ha-dus might have such a feel, nonparticipant; might look so, a lump of shadow in the dawn.

The shape straightened, black-robed, weapons and Honors aglitter in the uncertain light. Niun stopped; Duncan did. And suddenly dus-sense took hold of that other mind, a muddle of distress before it closed itself off again.

"Ras," Niun murmured. He started walking again, Duncan beside him. The dusei reached the kel'e'en and edged back, growling.

"Ja'anom," Duncan breathed.

"Aye," Niun said. He walked closer than stranger's-distance to her; it was no place for raising voices.

"You found him," Ras said.

"Where is the rest of the tribe?"

She lifted a robed arm south-southeast, as they were bearing.

"Are they well?" Niun asked, bitter at having to ask.

"When I left."

Duncan made a faltering move and sat down, bowed over. Ras spared him a cold glance. Niun swallowed pride and knelt down by him, fended off the dus that wanted close to him, then let it, for the warmth was comfort to Duncan. Niun leaned his hands against his own knees, to rest, the reassurance of Ras's message coiling uncertainly in his belly. He put aside the rest of his reserve and looked up at Ras. "All safe?"

"Kel Ros, sen Otha, sen Kadas . . . dead."

He let it go, bowed his head, too weary to go into prolonged questioning with Ras. He had not known the sen'ein; Ros had been a quiet man, even for a kel'en; he had never known him either.

Ras settled with a rustling of cloth, kel-sword across her knees to lean on.

"There are others out there," Niun said at last. "Hao'nath. They have been following some few days."

If that perturbed Ras she did not show it.

"Did Hlil send you?" he asked.

"No."

The old feeling returned, that tautness at the gut that assailed him whenever Ras turned up in his path, or behind him. Brother and sister was the obligation between them; it was mockery. For a moment the hao'nath themselves seemed warmer.

"Come," he said. "Duncan, can you?"

Duncan moved and tried. Niun rose and took his arm, lifting him up, and at the unsteadiness he felt, slipped an arm about him, started in the direction the dus-sense indicated.

Ras walked beside him this time, a shielded blankness in the dus-sense. Mri of Kesrith had learned that inner veil, living among dusei; Ras had, of loathing or of necessity, ignoring even a warding-impulse to stay with him.

The light brought detail to the land, the rounded hills, the limitless flat, the shadowy gape of the cut they had passed.

There was nothing in all of it that indicated a camp.

The preparations had that cold and lonely feeling which always came of dawn hours and broken routines. Galey meddled with his personal gear while the three regs with him did the same, and all of them waited on Boaz.

Ben Shibo, Moshe Kadarin, Ed Lane, two legitimate regs and Lane, who was more tech than not, in armscomp. Shibo was backup pilot; Kadarin he had picked for a combination of reasons the others shared, the several world-patches on his sleeve, a personnel file that indicated an absence of hatreds, a phlegmatic acceptance of close contact with regul.

They took to Boaz's presence the same way: quietly, keeping misgivings to themselves.

At present the misgivings were his own, a fretting at the delay, wondering if at the last moment Luiz might not confound them all by interposing his own orders.

But at length she came, Luiz trailing anxiously in her wake. She had a clutter of gear with her, photographic and otherwise; and Galey objected to nothing—it was civ business and none of his. She paused to press a kiss on the old surgeon's cheek, and Galey turned his head, feeling oddly intrusive between these two. "Load aboard," he told the others; Kadarin and Lane gathered up the gear and went out. Shibo delayed to offer a hand for Boaz's gear.

"No," she said, adjusting the straps. Fiftyish, stout to the extent she could not fit into one of their flight suits, she wore an insulated jacket and breeches that in no wise made her slighter. Her crown of gray-blonde braids lent her a curious dignity. She looked at him, questioning. "Out," he said. She paused for another look at Luiz and went.

The question had occurred to him more than once, how much *Saber* knew, whether Luiz had communicated to Koch precisely which civ had been included. There was at the back of his mind a doubt on that point, the suspicion that he was ultimately responsible, and that Koch would lay matters to his account. Boaz was not expendable.

So what good, she had cornered him, *what good is some assistant of mine with good legs and no comprehension of what he's seeing? What's known of mri customs is my work; what's known of the mri writings I broke in the first place. You need me to get the answers you're going for. I'm your safety out there.*

He wanted her, trusted her attitudes that did not want holocaust. He offered his own hand to Luiz, forbore the question and walked out, after the others.

Cold, thin air. Without the breathers for the short trip between hatch and shuttle, they were all panting by the time they had the shuttle hatch closed, and settled into the cheerless, cramped interior. Galey took his place at controls, gave them light other than what came in from outside, started up the engines.

He cast a look back and to the side of him, found nothing but calm faces in the greenish glow . . . wondered if Boaz was afraid: no less than the rest of them, he reckoned.

He cleared with *Flower* and started lift, disturbing the sand. He did not seek any great altitude; the ground ripped past in the dawning, a blur of infrequent irregularities in the sands. Eventually the chasm gaped beneath them and he banked and dropped. He passed no orders, kept scan audio in his ear, and Shibo, beside him, watched as intently.

They went for the nearest of the sites; and it was the safest approach in his calculation, the best approach to that site potentially ready and hostile . . . to fly below rim level. Dizzying perspective opened before them in the dawn, rocks blurring past on the left. Air currents jerked at them. In places sand torrented off the heights before them, cables and ribbons of sand which fell kilometers down to the bottom of the sea chasm . . . stained with sun colors. Rounded peaks rose disembodied out of the chasm haze.

And nearer and nearer they came to the city, to that point at which he had designated on their charts a limit to air approach.

His hands sweated; no one had spoken a word for the duration of the flight. He gathered a little altitude, peering over the rim and hoping to live through the probe.

"No fire," Lane breathed at his shoulder . . . for confirmation, perhaps, that they were still alive.

The ruins were in sight now; he slipped over the plateau, settled down, shut down the engines.

No one seemed to breathe for the moment.

"Out," Galey said, freeing himself of the restraints. There was no question, no hesitation, no sorting of gear: all of that on their part was already done. They went for the exit and scrambled down, himself last, to secure the ship. After that there was the ping of metal cooling, the whisper of the sand and the wind, nothing more. They shouldered the burden of breather-tanks, pulled up the masks which rasped with their breaths, adjusted equipment.

And walked, an easy pace, heavily booted against the denizens of the sands. Breathing seemed easier out of the vulnerable vicinity of the ship.

Boaz meddled with a pocket, fished out black and gold cloth which fluttered lightly in the breeze. "Suggest you adopt the black," she said. Galey took one, and the other three did, while Boaz tied the conspicuous gold to her arm.

"Black is Kel," he said, "and gold is scholars."

"Noncombatant. If they respect that, you've a chance in an encounter."

"Because of you."

"It's something they might at least question."

It was something, at least. There was the city before them, a far, far walk, and a lonely one. They were smaller targets apart from the ship, less deserving of the great weapons of the city.

Most of all was the cold, the knife-sharp air, and an abiding consciousness that they had no help but themselves.

Mri did not take prisoners. Humanity had learned that long ago.

IX

The tents were in sight, appearing out of the evening and a roll of the land, and there was still no forcing. Duncan tried, and had soon to sink down and rest all the same, senses completely grayed for the moment, so that all he felt was his dus and the touch of its hot velvet body.

More came, then: dus-carried . . . Niun's presence, the cold blankness that was Ras Kov-Nelan. It was one with the sickness that throbbed in his temples, that muddle of anxiousness and cold.

"Go on," Duncan said after a moment. "Am I a child, that I cannot walk to what I can see? You go on. Send someone out for me if you must."

Niun paid no heed to him. He moved his numb hands over the shoulder of the dus, his vision clearing finally. Niun was kneeling near him, Ras standing. Somewhere was consciousness of what they sought; somewhere was the sense of their pursuers, anger and desire, an element in which he had moved for uncounted time, that gnawed persistently at them, far, far east and north, dus-carried.

"Duncan," Niun urged at him.

Unjust, that they would not let him walk his own way, in his own time; he began to reason like a child, and knew it, at some remote distance from his own intelligence. Niun seized his arm and pulled him up, and he stayed on his feet, moved when they did, reckoning to make it this time. He shut his eyes and simply followed dus-impulse, lost to it for a time, feeling occasionally Niun's touch when he would falter. The coppery taste of blood grew more pronounced. He coughed, and the moisture began to trickle inward, so that he wove in his steps and began to shake in his joints . . . frightened, mortally frightened. A knee gave, and Niun had him before he fell, keeping him on his feet. There was a touch at his other side, likewise holding him. He bent and coughed and

109

cleared his senses, dully aware of both of them, aware of dus-sense, that was roused and angry.

Kel'ein. Ahead of them, between them and the camp in the dusk, appeared a shadow like fluid rolling across the land. It moved out toward them. Dus-feelings moiled in the air like the scent of storm. *"Yai!"* Niun rebuked them both, and stilled it. "Send them away, Duncan. Send them off."

It was hard. It was like yielding up a part of him. He dismissed the dus, felt suddenly cold, and clearer minded. The beasts strayed off a distance. He took more of his own weight, looking at that line of kel'ein who stopped before them, recognized the one who walked forward, saw sudden yielding in the line which flowed about them and included them. Hlil. He remembered the name as the kel'en tugged the veil down.

"She is well?" Niun asked.

"Well," Hlil answered, and it dimly occurred to Duncan that *she* was Melein. "Ras," Hlil said then, acknowledging her presence with a curious prickle of coldness in that tone. And for only a moment the kel'en stared directly at him, no more warmly.

"Hlil," Niun said, "there are hao'nath—" He pointed northerly. "Within this range, and with blood between us, it may be. Let the Kel keep an eye to that direction."

"Aye," Hlil said in that same still tone.

Niun shed the pack he had borne so far into the hands of a young kel'en, reached and took Duncan again by the sleeve, urging him to walk. Duncan did so. His vision blurred, cleared again. There was silence about them, not so much as a whisper from the Kel as they walked back toward the tents that now shone light-through-black in the gathering dark.

There was a stir as they reached the tents, other castes venturing out to see, kath'ein veilless and solemn, gathering children to them as they saw what had returned to them . . . sen'ein too, who whispered together.

They went to the greatest of the tents . . . realization struck him: the she'pan; he had that before him, need of wit and sense and whatever eloquence he could summon.

Warmth hit their faces like a wall as they swept within: warmth and gold light of lamps lit the antechamber of the tent, and the smell of incense choked him. They paused there, and beyond the veil which shrouded the center light gleamed on ovoid metal, a shimmer through gauze.

The pan'en. They had gotten it back. He was numbly relieved that among their other possessions they had gained this
again, this most precious thing to them. Niun paid it respect;
and respect to the Mystery he reverenced. He thought that he
ought, but it was not something Niun had shown him fully,
this last and most secret aspect of the People. He stood back
instead, intimidated by the fervor of the others, made a token
gesture toward removing his veil as they had unveiled before
the Holy, but he kept his head down and his alien face incon-
spicuous.

Then Niun came and took his arm, drawing him through
the curtain at their right, into the huge area of assembly,
among the others.

Gold sen-cloth was the drapery; and golden the lamplight;
gold-robed sen'ein made a bow about the single white figure
which was Melein. She took her chair as the shadow of the
Kel flowed about the walls to left and right; and a few older
kath'ein insinuated themselves next Sen like a touch of bright
sky. Duncan tried to walk steadily through the parting ranks
without Niun's hand, which hovered at his elbow. Manners
came back to him, recollection of courtesies which had to be
paid, things told him by kel-law, though he had never been so
much the center of matters.

Niun went beyond the place he should, took Melein's
hands, kissed her brow and was kissed in return, whispered
low words which had to do with hao'nath and strangers. Her
amber eyes flicked once with distress, and she inclined her
head.

"So," she said in a low voice, "that will come as it will."
Very slightly her hands moved, beckoning.

Duncan came the few steps forward, settled to his knees as
Niun did, head bowed; and because he did not come with favor, he reached and swept off the *zaidhe* in humility, baring
his shoulder-length hair, so unlike a mri's bronze mane. Un-
shaven, bloody about the nose . . . he even stank, and knew
it. Humans smelled differently; he had always been careful of
cleanliness and of shaving. He felt a nakedness in this ex-
posure he had never felt in his life.

"Kel Duncan," Melein said softly.

"She'pan," he breathed, head down, hands clenched upon
the veil and headcloth in his lap. The calm control of her
voice made silence in which there was scarcely even the
rustle of cloth in the assembly. His temples pounded, and his
throat was tight.

"Where was your permission to leave us, kel'en?"

"No permission." His voice broke. A cough prickled at his throat and he tried to swallow it, succeeded with difficulty, his eyes watering.

"And you have been—"

"To the ships, she'pan. Into them."

For the first time there was a breath of protest from the gathering. Melein lifted her hand and it died at once.

"Kel'en?" she prompted him.

"Three ships," Duncan pursued past the obstruction in his throat. "Regul have come with the humans; regul did the firing on you and on the city. I killed their elder. No more . . . no more regul."

The membrane betrayed disturbance. Melein understood him if no others could. "How was this done, kel Duncan?"

"The regul was aboard one of the human ships . . . attacked when I had finished speaking to the human kel'anth. I killed her. Regul have no leader now. Humans . . . never received my message; now, now they have listened. They are offended by the regul; they asked me to bear word to you—" The name of what he was to say slipped him, untranslatable in the hal'ari. He had composed it . . . lifted a shaking hand to his brow, tried in humiliation and panic to organize what he had prepared to say. Niun moved; he brushed off the hand and stared up at Melein. "No attack; no . . . wish for attack, if the People assure humans likewise."

There was no sound but anger gathered on naked faces about the she'pan, and on Melein's cold face a frown appeared.

"What have mri to say to tsi'mri?"

It was inevitably the attitude. Millennia of contempt for outsiders, for other species. The hal'ari had four words for peace, and none of them meant or imagined what humans hoped for; one of them was sinister: the obliteration of potential threat. He found both hands shaking visibly, the bitter taste of defeat in his mouth, and the tang of blood.

"Kel Duncan—the Sen will consider the matter you have brought to council. Your effort has great value. The People thank you."

He did not hear it clearly. Perhaps others in the gathering did not; there was no stir, no move. Then it dawned on him that she had not outright rejected the offer of conference . . . more, that she leaned forward, took his filthy, rough face between her hands, and kissed him on the brow as one of her

own. Her fingers pressed something into his hand, a little me-
dallion of gold, a *j'tal* of service.

There was a muttering in the assembly at that. And then
he shamed himself thoroughly, for when she drew back from
him and he sat staring at what he held in his hand, the tears
slipped his control, and he had no veil to hide them. He put
the Honor within the breast of his robe, trying not to show
his face, trying to swallow the pain in his throat.

And coughed; blood stained the hand he put to his mouth
and nose. There was a great deal of it. He began shaking
again, and heard a murmur of distress as he lost control of
his limbs. Niun seized him, held him hard against his trembling.

He was able, after a moment, to be helped to his feet—to
walk, at least to the outside of the tent, into the cold night
air. Niun held him. So did another. He heard his dus nearby
in the dark, moaning with distress, wanting him. He shook
free and tried a few steps, not knowing where he was going,
save to the dus, and then he had to reach for support. Someone caught him.

"Help me," he heard Niun say in anger. *"Help me!"*

Eventually he felt another touch. He struggled to bear his
own weight, and then coughing came on him again and he
forgot everything else.

Niun ate, only a token amount, from the common dish. He
had no hunger, and allowed others his share. He sat now, unveiled, his hands in his lap, and stared across the tent to the
Kel to the corner where Duncan lay with his dus, propped
sitting against the beast, unconscious as he was, for he bled
inside, and might strangle. He was no lovely sight, was
Duncan, and there were many in the Kel who cast furtive
looks at him, hoping, likely, for his death.

For the end of both of them, it might be, if their enemies
called them out in the morning. It was a dire thing, the merging of two tribes; they had not wanted it . . . but perhaps
many existed in this tribe who would count it better to accept
that, and gain another kel'anth, another she'pan. He ought to
clear his mind, to take food, to sleep, against such an event;
he knew these things clearly.

He made attempt, and the food stuck in his throat; he
swallowed that, and no more, sitting still again.

There came a slow silence in the Kel. Movements grew
quieter and less. Voices hushed. No hand now reached for

the bowls; no one spoke. He knew that they were staring at him, and eventually he grew as quiet within as without, remote from his pain.

Challenge me, he wished certain of them, not excluding Ras. *I will kill, and enjoy the killing.*

"Kel'anth," Hlil said.

Niun paid no attention to him.

Hlil sat silent a moment, offended, doubtless; and finally Hlil leaned closer to the fen'anth Seras, who sat next him; and then to Desai. There was some muttering together, and Niun removed his mind from all of it, letting them do what they would, reckoning that it would come to him when it was ready.

He rose instead, and withdrew to Duncan's side, sat down there, against the dus. The beast rumbled its sorrow and nosed at him, as if begging solace or help. Duncan breathed with a slow bubbling sound, and his eyes were open a slit, but they were glazed, dimly reflecting the lamplight.

The others resumed their meal, but for a small cluster about Hlil who withdrew together to talk in the opposite corner of Kel-tent, and for Ras, who came and sat down against one of the great poles, her face no more angry, only very weary, eyes shadowed.

She had, at the last, helped; he was mortally surprised for that . . . practicality, perhaps, that Duncan slowed them too much. He had long since ceased to try to account for what Ras did. He watched the others in their group, and anger moiled in him for that; he remembered the dus and stilled it . . . put a hand on Duncan's shoulder and pressed slightly, obtained a blink of the eyes.

"I know you are there," Duncan said, a faint, congested voice. "Stop worrying. Is there word yet—about the hao'nath?"

"No sign of them. Do not worry for it."

"Dus thinks they are still out there."

"Doubtless they are. But they have to think about it now."

"More . . . more than one. Back . . . side . . . front. . . ." Coughing threatened again. Niun tightened his hand.

"Save this for later."

Duncan's strange eyes blinked, and tears fell from inner corners, mixed with the dirt and the blood, trailing slowly into the hair of his face. "Ai, you are worried, are you? So am I. There are many . . . Dusei, maybe."

"You are not making sense, sov-kela."

"Life. I tried to show them life. I think they understood."

"Dusei?"

There was movement; a sudden apprehension came into Duncan's eyes, focused beyond him. Niun turned on one knee as a shadow fell on them, a wall of black robes about them. The dus stirred; but those foremost moved to kneel, restoring a little of the lamplight, and Niun moved his hand ashamedly from his weapons. Hlil—Desai, Seras, and young Taz. Niun frowned, thrust out his hand in confusion when Taz set a smoldering bowl near Duncan.

"The smoke will help," Seras said.

It was some portion of the oil-wood, which they used for lamp fuel, a greasy smoke with the cloying sweetness of some other herb added. Niun held his hand from striking it away at once, distracted between the harm it might do and his failure to have comprehended their honest intent. He settled his hand on Duncan's shoulder instead, with the other hand poised to refuse their further intervention.

"Kel'anth," said Hlil coldly, "we know some things you do not. We were born on this world."

Duncan feebly reached for the smoldering bowl. Taz edged it closer and Duncan inhaled the smoke fully. It was true. Niun felt his own raw throat eased by the oily warmth. The smoke offended the dus, which turned its great head the other way with a deep whuff of displeasure, but of a sudden the beast caught up feelings utterly naked and wove them all together uninvited, Kutathi mri and Kesrithi.

"Yai!" Niun rebuked it, and faces averted slightly one from the other in embarrassment. He looked on Duncan, who breathed deeply of the fumes, and then gazed at Hlil until Hlil looked up at him.

"S'sochil," Niun said very quietly, "I thank you; I should have said that; forgive."

"Ai," Hlil muttered, and soured the moment with a scowl and a gesture of contempt toward Duncan.

There was an explosive breath at the door. Niun looked about, saw his own dus, which had decided at last to come in out of the dark, drawn by some inner impulse. Kel'ein moved out of its path in haste as it came across the mats, head down and seemingly preoccupied; and when it had come to him, it nosed at him and sank down against Duncan's breast.

Niun rested an arm on its shoulder, tugged at its ear to distract it, lest it reach his mind and Hlil's together. For a long moment he stared at Hlil's scarred, unlovely face, fearing that the dus did indeed broadcast what moved in him. Or perhaps it came from both sides, that longing: even one who knew dusei could not always tell. Beside him Duncan rested, breathing in larger breaths, as if the smoke had taken the pain away.

Niun loosed one of his own Honors, offered it, his hand nigh trembling. He thought surely that Hlil would reject it, offending and offended; but he was obliged to the offering.

"For what service?" Hlil asked.

"That I find the tribe . . . well in your keeping. You and Seras . . . if you would."

Hlil did take; and Seras too . . . of the Honors which had been Merai's, which were his to give away; of the friend for whom, Niun thought with a sudden pang, Hlil would always grieve. It surged through the dusei unasked, the desolation and the loneliness.

"We have watchers out," Hlil said. "You did not seek this, with the hao'nath. This was not your purpose."

"No," Niun said, dismayed to realize how things had fit such a thought. "You do not know me, kel Hlil, to have wondered that."

Hlil's eyes wandered briefly to Duncan, up again.

"They tracked him," Niun said.

"They have come to the cities," Hlil said. "So should we . . . if we had not already. Kel'anth—it will not stop with the hao'nath. You understand that. Word will spread . . . of this . . . stranger with us"

"I know," he said

Hlil nodded, glanced down, rose, excusing himself as if there were nothing more he could say; so, one by one, did the others. Taz lingered last, silently produced a small handful of dried roots and pale fiber from the breast of his robe, along with a small leather sack.

"Sir," Taz said, laying it beside the pot. "I can find more, if need be: Kath surely has to spare."

The boy went away. Niun started to speak to Duncan, to ask if he was comfortable; and looked, and saw Duncan's eyes shut and his breathing eased.

He leaned against the dus, with the knot that had been so long at his belly somewhat less taut, watching all the Kel settle for the night, each to their mats that composed the flooring of the tent. The lamps were put out, all but the one that hung nearest them, and the little bowl of smoldering fibers curled up smoke about them.

Only Ras remained, sitting; she stirred finally, and he reckoned that she too would seek her mat and sleep; but she returned after a moment, a shadow in the haze of smoke and the lamps, came close and knelt down by them with something in her arms, a roll of matting, which she set down by him.

"What is it?" he asked of her. "Kel Ras?"

She said nothing . . . withdrew to the shadows, lay down finally and seemed to sleep.

He drew the matting into his lap, unrolled it, uncovering the *cho*-silk bindings of his longsword, the coarser work of Duncan's, left behind in An-ehon. He bit his lip, fingered the ancient work of the hilt, drew the fine steel a little distance from the leather sheath, eased it back again. It was precious to him, the solitary vanity of his possessions: he had counted it lost.

Challenge, he thought, to hold what he had taken. *It will not stop,* Hlil had said, *with the hao'nath.*

Time after time, while Kutath bled its strength out, and tsi'mri waited for answers.

He laid the swords beside him, settled back again. In the quiet which had settled, Duncan's breath still bubbled, and now and again he stirred and coughed and blotted at his mouth with the soiled veil. But much of the time he did sleep, and at last the bubbling ceased.

At that sudden silence Niun roused anxiously—but Duncan's chest rose and fell with peaceful regularity, and the blood which stained his lip was dried.

He rested his eyes a time then—jerked awake at a whisper of cloth by him, saw the boy Taz kneeling and feeding more of the fiber into the bowl.

"I shall wake, sir," Taz said.

He was dazed somewhat, and ungracious—simply looked at Duncan, whose breathing remained eased and regular, and let his head down again against the shoulder of the dus, moved his slitted eyes over all the Kel, that made huddled heaps in the darkness—shut them again.

The lamp gave feeble light for study; Melein turned in her hands the golden and fragile leaf from the casing of the pen'en, laid it on her knee and drew another forth, replacing the first in sequence. She canted it to the light and the lamp picked out the graven letters like hairline fire. She read, as for years and years before this she had read, the record of the People's travels. They were incomplete. Nigh on a hundred thousand years the record stretched; in so blindingly swift a few years they had come back, she and Niun and Duncan. There would come a time when she would write her own entry into the leaves of gold, the last of the People of the Voyage, the last statement, the seal.

And she shivered sometimes, thinking of that.

The hand which held the tablet lowered to her lap. She gazed at the flickering lamp, thinking, centered in the Now.

Where do I go? That was determined.

What do I do? That too, she knew.

But other questions she did not. Some of them extended to human space and regul, and dead worlds; some of them centered on Kutath itself, on the past in which mri had known another service. And they were one question.

A touch descended on her shoulder. She drew herself back, and shivered, looking into the gentle face of Kilis, the young sen'e'en who attended her, whose hands robed and disrobed her, and whose young eyes witnessed all her life.

"She'pan—the Council of the Sen is waiting. You sent for them, she'pan."

She smiled at that, for at times the dreaming was too strong; it was not so for her, at least—not often. "I will see them," she said, and carefully gathered the leaf of gold from her lap, slipped it into the casing with the others.

The curtains stirred and the Council entered, the first and second ranks of the Sen, to settle on the mats before her. Most were very old, older than kel'ein tended to live, hollow-cheeked and wrinkled; but there was among them Tinas, who had a kel'e'en's robustness about her, and kel-scars slanting across her cheeks. Foremost among them, Sathas also bore the scars, sen'anth; grimness on him was a habit, but more than one face was frowning this night.

"Has the Sen questions?"

"You appreciate our present danger," Sathas said. "It is what we warned you, she'pan."

"Indeed."

"It does not disturb you."

"It disturbs me. I would wish otherwise. But that is not ours to choose. Is that your question?"

"The she'pan knows our questions. And they are all tsi'mri."

"We have choices, sen'anth, and kel Duncan has given them to us."

"Did you send him out?"

She looked into the guarded offense of Sathas's eyes and tautly smiled, opened her hand palm up. "He is self-guiding. I let him go."

Eyes flashed, nictitating with inner passion.

"You seriously consider this offer they have made?" asked Sathas.

"It is a matter we will consider . . . for the worth in it. You do not care for his presence, doubtless. But he has brought us choices; and knowledge of what hangs above our heads; he comprehends them . . . and serves the People. His life has value. You understand me."

"We understand."

"And dislike it."

"We are your only weapon, she'pan, and you are ours. Do you turn aside?"

"From our course? No. No, trust me in this, sen'ein. *I am not yet done.*"

No one spoke. For a moment eyes glittered hard with speculations. *Believe me:* it was Intel who spoke, her old she'pan . . . who could persuade when reason counseled otherwise, with a voice which had wrapped silken cords about herself when she was younger; she had learned it, wielded it . . . consciously.

Perhaps all she'panei had had such arts; she did not know. It was the nature of she'panei that they never met, save the one by whose death one rose.

It was true that Intel had controlled her children when they would have rebelled, and persuaded elders who had power in their own selves: that half-mad force of her that chilled the spine and held the eye when the eye would gladly turn away . . . that followed after, so that even out of her presence the most cynical reason had no power to utterly shatter that argument.

Intel still held her; and she . . . held them.

X

The chief of security was back again, to trouble the labs. Averson blinked and focused on him, this dark man so persistent in his patrols. He glanced likewise at the collection of papers beside him on the desk, made a nervous snatch toward them as Degas gathered one up and looked at it.

"You've made progress with the regul transmissions?" Degas asked. "There's some urgency about it."

"It's—" Averson held out his hand for the paper and received it back. Degas favored him with a sardonic smile as he shuffled it back into order. "It's couched in idiom, not code. It might be clear if we understood Nurag."

"Nurag."

"Homeworld has bearing on language," Averson answered shortly, and experienced a little uneasiness as Degas sat down on the edge of the desk facing him. Degas put down cassettes, click, click, click, on the desk top before him.

"There's a great deal going on, Dr. Averson. Our time is escaping us. The onworld mission has decided to go . . . prudently or not rests elsewhere; they've moved out, to whatever they may find. And they may stir something up. There's always that chance. Now we have a request for permission for a regul shuttle to go down and sit with *Flower*."

Averson gnawed at his lips.

"The admiral is stalling," Degas said.

Perhaps he was supposed to make some observation on this. He did not like the thought of regul in *Flower's* neighborhood; he did not reckon what to do about it.

"The admiral," said Degas, "understands from your reports and your advisements, that the regul may move in with or without our permission."

"They may," Averson allowed. "They would reckon we would not move to stop them."

"This:" Degas reached across the desk to the spot directly

in front of his hands, tapped it with his forefinger. The man was dark in manner, dark in dress, but for the weapons and the badges; he glittered with them, like kel'ein, Averson thought, much like them. "This, Dr. Averson: you've paralyzed us with your yes and no. You've said nothing, except that there's no action to be taken. Wait, you say; and what is your general feeling on the regul? Where are your opinions?"

"I can't, I've told you. I can't pronounce with any surety—"

"Your *guess*, doctor."

"But without supporting data—"

"Your guess, doctor. It's more valuable than most men's studied opinion."

"No," Averson said. "It's more dangerous."

"Give it."

"I—find it possible . . . that there is more than one adult. One to remain here, one . . . on that ship they want to send down. Logically, you see—they don't function without elder direction. You think there are regul ships down there now; I agree. But no elder. I think they would like to get one down there if they could."

Degas's breath hissed softly between his teeth.

"The hydra's head," Averson said. Degas looked at him with no evidence of comprehension. "An old story," Averson said. "Not the star-snake . . . the old one. Cut off the head and two more take its place. Kill a regul elder and more than one metamorphoses to take its place. Shock . . . some biological trigger . . . ."

Degas frowned the more deeply.

"One thing that bothers me," Averson said. "How do they learn?"

"A question for the science department," Degas said, rising. "Solve that one on your off time. What about the rest of the data I gave you? What about the transmissions?"

"No," Averson said. "Listen to me. It's an important question. They don't write everything down."

Degas shrugged in impatience. "I'm sure that's solved somehow."

"No. *No!* Listen to me. They *remember* . . . they remember. Eidetic memory. What died with bai Sharn . . . is forever lost to them. They have to lose something in the transitions. Young regul metamorphosing and taking over adult function by themselves and without outside influence, without the supporting information of their docha-structures and adults—"

"The easier to deal with them. There's no reason for panic."

Averson shook his head, despairing. "Not necessarily easier. You want guesses, good colonel Degas. I shall give you guesses. That we have here regul without home ties, regul without past, regul who can't imagine what they're missing, regul more likely than any others to act as regul don't act; and that is dangerous, sir. A spur, a splinter of Nurag maybe; maybe of Kesrith, maybe that. On Kesrith, regul *attacked*, and these young regul *learned* that. They overcame mri. It became reality. The psychology of the eidetic mind . . . is different. That's why you asked me up here, is it not, to tell you these things? Those ships that attacked us on the way up here weren't mri; they were regul."

"Prove it."

Averson made a helpless gesture. He was confused in the motivations of this man, so supremely stubborn. He understood regul, and failed with this member of his own species, and suddenly he doubted everything, even what he knew he understood.

Degas leaned again toward him, laid his hand on all the papers in the stack. "Prove it, when none of our analyses could. By *what* do you know? Point it out to me."

"The action is consistent with the pattern. It makes a larger pattern."

"Show me."

Averson shook his head helplessly.

"I have a tight schedule, doctor. Explain it to one of my aides when you think of it. But in the meantime, I have to work on *all* the possibilities. The cassettes, doctor, come from a downed ship and the one that recovered the recorder. A man died down there. How does that fit your patterns?"

"I've told you, if you would listen."

"I'll listen when there's consistency in your advice." Degas gathered up one of the cassettes. "Landscan. Can you handle this or do we shuttle it down to *Flower*?"

"I'm not qualified. Wait. Wait, I—would like to look at it before you send it on."

"Inconvenient, to have the science staff split here and there. You say that you can't handle it expertly; someone downworld can. I'll have your affidavit on that. You'll record it."

"If you wish."

"Now." Degas ripped paper off a pad, shoved it across the desk at him, put a stylus down by it. "Write that."

"Now?" Averson took a deep breath, mustered his anger. "I am also a busy man, colonel. You could wait."

"Write it."

He did not like Degas. The man was forceful and unpleasant. Capitulation would get him out of the lab. Averson picked up the stylus. *Suggest transfer of landscan tape to more affected department,* he wrote, and looked up. "I have some notes of my own I'll want to send down when this goes."

"If they make the shuttle, fine." Degas tapped the paper. "Sign it. Write 'Urgent.' "

"I will not be bullied."

"Sign it."

Averson blinked and looked up in shock, blinked again, thinking of things going on outside his comprehension, of motives in this man which intended things outside his own interests.

"I should consult with the admiral," Averson protested.

"Do your job. If you can't do it, pass it to those who can. Sign the paper. Note it as I told you. The shuttle will have it down within the hour."

"Excuses for more flights."

"Sign it."

"I'm right, aren't I?"

Degas put his hands framing his and leaned on them, gazing into his face at short range. "Do you know what happens if security is hamstrung, Dr. Averson? Do you comprehend your personal hazard? We have a shuttle down there poking about old sites and weapons, and ships loose we *don't* have identified; science department is giving us cautions we already understand. We want information. We're in orbit in range of ground-based weapons. Do you comprehend that? Sign it. And put 'Urgent' on it.'

Averson did so, his hand shaking. He did not understand security's function in this. He understood personal threat. Degas collected the note and the cassette.

"Thank you," Degas said with great nicity.

And walked out.

Averson clenched his hands together, finding them sweating. Such men had had great power in the days of the mri wars. Some evidently thought that they still did.

This one did, where they sat, with the mri below and the regul above, and themselves neatly in the middle.

He reached for the pad and dashed off another note:

> Emil: Boaz was right. Security is involved in this, something maybe personal or political. I don't figure it out. Watch out for the regul. Don't let them into the ship. Please, be careful. All of you be careful. And send Danny up here if you can spare him.
>
> I begin to understand things. I can't make these soldiers comprehend simple logic.
>
> Sim.

He folded the paper in all directions, put it into an envelope, and sealed it. *Luiz,* he wrote on it, *Personal Mail.*

And then he sat holding it on his lap and doubting where it would finally go.

The cassettes. He suddenly regretted the loss of the landscan tape, the tiny morsel of information now denied him. He manipulated the new data into the player on the desk, rapid-scanned it.

It told partial tales. All the mosaic was not there. Bioscan. He read it with an amateur's eye, split screens, readouts, instruments he did not know. What he did told him only of an intermittent vegetation, more than they had yet seen.

With fevered haste he rejected that tape and pushed in the second. It made even less sense to him, ship's instruments or some such, data with symbols of fields outside his specialization: physics, numbers that made no sense at all except that they might be electrical or some such power symbols.

A man dead, Degas had said. There was a pilot lost; he had heard that, a man named Van. The flow of data rippled past, with a man's death in it, and told him nothing. They took landscan, of which he could have made at least a modicum of sensible interpretation, and left him this jargon . . . in payment for his signature. It was the signature security had wanted, to get another shuttle launched, a ship down there, nothing more than that. They had made games of him and he had let them. Perhaps what motivated them really was locked in these incomprehensible records . . . and Degas placed them in his hands for mockery.

They must not even need interpretation of the data . . . or they would have taken it all.

Harris: he thought of the pilot Harris, one man he knew on the ship who had some expertise in shuttles and the kind of scan they were carrying, who at least might know what field these strange notations came of. He cut off the tape with a jab of his finger, punched in ship's communications.

Com answered, a young voice.

"This is Dr. Simeon Averson down in lab. Request you locate one Lt. Harris, pilot, and ask him to come to my lab as soon as possible."

"Yes, sir."

He thanked com, broke connection and leaned back, gnawing at his knuckle.

And in a moment the screen activated again. "Dr. Averson," said a different and female voice.

"Yes."

"Dr. Averson, this is Lt. McCray, security. Col. Degas's regards, sir, but your last request violates lines of operations."

"What request?"

"For communication with the military arm, sir. Regulations make it necessary to deny that interview. Lt. Harris is on other assignment."

"You mean he's not on the ship?"

"He's on other assignment, sir."

"Thank you." He broke connection, clenched his hands a second time.

And after a moment he snatched up a pertinent handful of his notes, his notebook, and the tapes, stalked across to the door and opened it.

There was a young man in AlSec uniform just outside, not precisely watching—or moving, or with reasonable business in the otherwise deserted corridor.

Averson retreated inside and closed the door between them, feeling a prickling of sweat, a pounding of his heart which was not good for him. He walked back to the desk and sat down, slammed his notebook at the cassettes and the papers down, fumbled in his breast pocket for the bottle of pills. He took one and slowly the pounding subsided.

Then he stabbed at the console and obtained com again. "This is Averson. Get me the admiral."

"That has to go through channels, sir."

"*Put* it through channels."

There was prolonged silence, without image.

"Dr. Averson," Degas's voice came suddenly over the unit. "Do I detect dissatisfaction with something?"

Averson sucked in his breath, let it out again. "Put me through to the admiral, sir. Now."

The silence again. His heart beat harder and harder. He was Havener. In the war, such men had had power there. Absolute power. He had learned so.

"Now," Averson repeated.

More silence.

"That comes by appointment," Degas said. "I will make that appointment for you."

"This moment."

"I will meet you at the admiral's office. If there is some question regarding security operations, it will be necessary."

The heartbeat became painful again, even more than in the terror of the flight up.

"I trust you won't be needing transfer back downworld," Degas said blandly. "Flights are very much more hazardous than they were when you came up. I would not risk it."

"No," Averson said, short of breath.

"Perhaps you have come up with some new advice. I would like to hear it."

"A complaint. A complaint about security's bullying tactics. I want that man taken off my door. I want access to anyone I choose. I want contact with the admiral."

"In short, the whole ship should arrange itself and its operations to accommodate you. Dr. Averson, I have tried to be helpful."

"You have taken away data I could use."

"A copy will be sent you. But I have your statement that you aren't qualified in that area. Precisely what direction are your researches taking now, Dr. Averson? The admiral will want to know."

"I object to this intimidation and harassment."

"Stay there, Dr. Averson."

Panic set in. He sat still, hearing the connection broken, sat still with the realization that there was no contact he could make past this man; nowhere he might go without encountering the man in the corridor. Sensibly he suspected that no violence would be done him if he tried to leave, but he was not a physical man; he flinched from the possibility of unpleasantness and confrontations, which touched on his medical condition. He dared not, could not, would not.

He had to sit and wait.

And eventually the man arrived, closed the door and crossed the room to him, quiet and looking ever so much more conciliatory than needed be.

"We have a misunderstanding," Degas said. "We should clear that up."

"You should get that man off my door."

"There is no man out there."

Averson drew in his breath. "I object," he said, "to being intimidated."

"You are free to object—as I am free to state otherwise."

"What is the matter with you?" Averson cried. "Are we on opposite sides?"

"Opposite sides of opinion, perhaps." Degas settled again on the edge of the desk, towering over him. "We are both men of conscience, doctor. You have an opinion colored by panic. Mine rests on convictions of practicality. A pattern, you say. Have you *met* mri, doctor? Have you dealt with the agent who became mri?"

"We are all Haveners. All of us—remember . . . but—"

"Some interests here want to throw over alliance with the regul for protection of the mri. Do you understand that?"

He blinked, realized his mouth was open and closed it. The matter of politics began to come clear to him. "I—don't see where it is . . . No. Breaking up the regul alliance is insanity."

"And unnecessary."

"Unnecessary, yes." He lifted a hand and wiped perspiration from his upper lip, gazed up at Degas, who backed off from him a few paces.

"You do not counsel this," Degas said.

"No. It's possible to deal with the regul. I know this; I would never say otherwise. It is possible to deal with them. But dangerous . . . dangerous under present conditions."

"Do you really understand the situation, doctor? Certain interests are pro-mri. Why they have taken this position . . . leave that to them to answer. It is a very dangerous position. The mission onworld, the personnel on that mission—the mission leader, your own Dr. Boaz, if you will forgive me, who is with them . . . are predisposed to find the mri nonaggressive, to counsel us into an approach to them. Regul do not threaten us; *regul* are not an aggressive species. Regul don't pose the primary threat. Do you agree: they don't pose the primary threat?"

"We're in a dangerous position here. You yourself said—"

"But the mass of mankind, back home . . . a threat to them?"

"No. No danger from regul. No possible danger."

"Do you see what these well-meaning influences would have you do? And what the result will be? From which species is the real threat of conflict, doctor?"

"I—see what you're saying. But—"

"Application of humanitarian principles. But Cultures above all ought to see through our moralistic impulses. We're talking about a species of killers, Dr. Averson, a species that lives by killing, parasites on the wars of any available power, who cultivate wars as regul cultivate trade. We may lose the regul here. And save what we'll regret. You understand me?"

"I—"

"I suggest, Dr. Averson, that these are points worth considering. Those reports you make should be carefully considered for effect on policy at high levels. We have new data from the surface, a disturbing resurgence in the destroyed sites. The mri do not offer to contact us. So we send a peace mission stirring into the ruins. We have allies taking on independent operations thanks to these changes in our policy and the killing of their leader by a mri agent. . . . You can't interpret their intention . . . or won't. How do we proceed? Do you have answers? Or do we let the situation go others' way?"

Averson sat and sweated and slowly, after considering, wadded up the envelope in his hand, put it into his pocket under Degas's stare. "You found life in the old sites and the mission went anyway."

"We learned it this morning. We don't have direct contact with the mission . . . can't reach them without endangering everything."

"Can't call them back?"

"Officially," Degas said in a low voice, leaning close to touch a finger before him, "not without blowing what we're doing wide open to the regul, among other things. And how do regul take that? What reaction could we anticipate? You should appreciate the significance of your own reports, doctor. They set directions. You should understand that."

"I do not intend to set directions."

"You're in that position. What do you say about the regul? I should have hoped your peculiar insights into their culture would have balanced . . . other interests in Cultures. What do you say?"

"We should not lose them, no. We should not let that happen."

"Make it clear, then." Degas leaned there with both hands. "We have dissenting views. We need this in writing, in recommendations with practical application, or we slip toward another line of policy. We're sitting up here blind, over active weapons. We're protecting mri at the expense of all we've gained by the treaties. We're alienating a species from whom the gains could be enormous. I suggest, Dr. Averson, that you and I have a long conference on these matters."

"I will—talk about it."

"Now," Degas said.

XI

Someone stirred close by; Niun drew a sudden breath, lifted his head, remembering Duncan with slight panic. . . . He looked toward him and found him sleeping.

Kel Ras was sitting on her heels just the other side of him, veiled, staring at him in the shadow, leaning on the sword which rested across her knees. "They are out there," she said. "Kel'anth, I really think you should come and see."

The Kel had begun to rouse at the whispering. Hlil was there, and Seras and Desai and Merin, the youth Taz, Dias, others. A chill came over him, a profound sense of loneliness. He gazed down at Duncan, who remained oblivious to what passed, quietly disengaged himself from the dusei, a separation which had its own feeling of chill, physical and mental.

Whatever befell, they might leave Duncan in peace, at least until he was stronger; he was kel'en and some ja'anom might take that as a matter of honor. For himself and Melein. . . .

He gathered himself to his feet, shook off the concern that urged at him, bent again to gather up his sword and slung it to his shoulder. He walked outside into the beginnings of dawn, with Ras and Hlil and Desai close to him.

"Has anyone advised the she'pan?" he asked, and when no one answered he sent Desai with a gesture in that direction. It was necessary to think of no more concerns, to settle his mind for what had to be met and what had to be done. He had no feeling of comrades at his side, rather that of witnesses at his back, and the loneliness persisted.

There was no possibility yet of seeing clearly what had come. Halflight tricked the eye, made the land out to be flat when it was not. A thousand enemies could be hidden in that gentle rolling of the sands. They walked out to the rear of Kel, and Ras lifted her arm silently toward the northeast,

130

where a faint hint of rocks marred the smoothness of the land.

No one was in sight now, and that was perhaps another of the land's illusions.

Kel'ein joined them out of Kath, rousing out in some haste; and kath'ein came in haste with bowls of offering to the Kel. The word had spread through all the camp by now; sein'ein came, but the children were held in Kath, concealed.

A kath'en he knew brought a bowl to him, offered; he recalled another morning, when there had been the illusion of safety, and love with this gentle, plain-faced kath'en. "Anaras," he murmured her name, and took the bowl from her hands, ate a very little, gave it back, lonelier than before. He was afraid; it was not an accustomed sensation.

The kath'en withdrew; all that caste did, having no place in what might come. Sen remained, and turning, he saw Melein's pale figure among them, caught her eye. She had no word for him, only a nod of affirmation, a beckoned permission. He went to her and she touched lips to his brow, received his kiss in return; and from that dismissal he went out, past the tents, with all the Kel at his back.

They stopped after a space; and he walked as far again alone, stopped on the verge of a long slope, facing the open and seemingly empty land. It was cold in the wind, which swept unhindered across the land.

He had not been wise, after running so long, not to have spent all the night before in the indulgence of his own needs, forgetting Duncan; but he could not have done so, could not have rested—went at least with clear conscience for the things that he had done. He veiled himself, as one must facing strangers, as all the Kel was veiled. He put aside Niun s'Intel, slipped from himself into the Law, into the she'pan's hands, and the tribe's, and the gods'.

He waited.

The city depressed, the crumbling aisles of stone, the sad corpses, the alleys resounding to their footsteps and the rasp of the breathers, the whisper of the wind. Galey kept an eye to the buildings, the hollow shells which seemed long untouched by any living. It was such a place and such an hour as made him glad of the weapon under his hand and several armed companions about him, Boaz the only one of them who carried no weapons.

It was at once relief and discouragement, that there was no

stir from the place, neither the attack they had dreaded nor
the approach they had hoped. Nothing. Wind and sand and
shells of ruins.

And the dead.

There were only kel'ein corpses at the first, black-robed;
then others, gold-robes and blue, and children. The blues
were without exception women and children, and babes in
arms. Boaz stood over a cluster of sad husks and shook her
head and swore. Shibo touched at a kel'en's body with his
foot, not roughly, but in distaste.

"There's nothing alive here," Boaz said. She was hard-
breathing despite the mask, overburdened with the equipment
and her own weight; she hitched the breather tank to another
place on her shoulder and drew a gasping breath. "I think
they'd have buried them if they could have."

"But it was inhabited," Galey said. "Duncan maintained
the cities were empty." The suspicion that in other particulars
Duncan's data might have inaccuracies in it . . . filled him
with a whole array of apprehensions, a cowardice that
wanted to go running back to the ship, pull offworld and de-
clare failure, so that guns could blast at each other at a distance where humans had advantage. Another part of him said
no . . . looked at dead civs and children and turned sick inside. Kadarin, Lane, Shibo . . . what they felt he had no idea
but he suspected it was something the same.

"Isn't saying," Boaz said, walking farther among the dead,
"that the city was inhabited. Just that people were killed here.
Children were killed here. Duncan's mri. I think we've found
them . . . just the way he said. He talked about dead cities;
he'd seen one, been there . . . with the mri. He talked about
a woman who died; and the children . . . he'd seen that too."

"He talked about machines," said the tech Lane, a young
man, and worried-looking. "Live ones."

"I don't doubt," said Boaz, "We'll find that here too." She
paused again in the crossing of two alleys, with the sand skirl-
ing about her feet, looked about her, looked back, made a
gesture indicating the way she wanted them to go.

"Come on," Galey said to the others, who from time to
time laid nervous hands on their weapons as they passed the
darkened entries, the alien geometries of arches which led
into ruin, or nowhere. *Walk like mri*, Boaz had advised them.
Keep your hands away from guns. It was not easy, to trust to
that in such a place.

A black line materialized out of the slow swell of the land opposite their own, grew distinct, stopped. Niun stood still, his legs numb with fatigue, waiting, silent declaration of the resolution of the ja'anom. The enemy had come, waited now for bright day. Sun-born, legend said of the People; the hao'nath had not chosen to move upon them by night. Neither would he, given choice. To face an enemy of one's own inclinations . . . had an eerie, homely feeling about it.

Dus-sense played at the back of his mind. The beast was quiet, far from him . . . would stay there. It had an instinct that would not intrude on a fight on equal terms, like mri, who would not attack in masses. It knew. It drank in the whole essence of the camp and gave it to him, drank in the presence of the enemy and fed him that too, threads complex and indefinable, a second dimension of their reality, so that the world seemed the same when it stopped, only faded somewhat, less intense, less bright.

He banished it, wishing his mind to himself.

The light grew, colors became fully distinct. In the east the sun blazed full.

And with it other shapes took form, a new line of kel'ein, separate from the others, and apart from them. Niun's heart skipped a beat in alarm. Had it been his native Kel at his back he might have turned, might have betrayed some emotion; they were not, and he did not. He moved his eyes slowly, and saw with a slight turning of his head that there were yet others, a third Kel ranged to the south.

They had been herded. Runners must have gone, signals passed, messages exchanged among she'panei. Three tribes were set against them. Three kel'anthein . . . to challenge.

One by one or all at once; he had his option. He saw the trap, and the warmth drained from his limbs as he thought on Melein, who would die when he fell . . . flooded back again with anger when he thought of all that had been sacrificed to bring them this far, and to lose . . . to lose now—

A figure separated from the others before him; he knew the beginning of it then: the hao'nath came first. Another began to come out from among the tribe to the east; and another separated himself in the south. He detached his mind, drew quiet breaths, began to prepare himself.

Suddenly a line appeared at the extreme south; and another figure moved forward . . . a fourth tribe; and another at north northeast, a fifth.

They knew . . . all knew . . . that strangers had come

among them, and where those strangers might be found. Niun felt again the prickling touch of his dus, the beast growing alarmed, full of blood-feelings.

No, he sent it furiously. He detached his sword, the *av-kel,* and held it in his hands crosswise, plain warning to those who came toward him from five directions . . . perhaps more still; he did not turn his head and utterly abandon his dignity. If they came also at his back, they must at least do him the grace of moving around to face him. Heat suffused his face, that he had let this happen and not known it; that he had run so blindly with dusei warning him persistently of outlying presence, that Duncan in his ravings had felt it, and he had not conceived the truth.

That his own kind did this to him, repudiating all that he was, all that they had come to offer, blind to all but difference. . . . There was no talking with them under these circumstances: they could read well enough that the kel'anth of this Kel stood by himself, that not a person at his back would move to assist him.

He could see all the five at once now: tribal names, he thought, that he should have known, were he mri of this world. . . . Black-veiled, glittering with Honors which meant lives and challenges . . . they preserved decent interval from each other, separate in tribe, neither crossing the other's space. Perhaps they bore instructions from their she'panei already, as he did from Melein: that would shorten matters. They risked much, all of them: absorption . . . for what tribes he took before dying himself, the kel'anth who killed him would possess, and those she'panei die . . . a measure of their desperation and their outrage, that they combined to take such risk.

Near enough now for hailing. He did not, nor go out to them; it was his option to stand still, and he had had enough of walking these last days. His back felt naked enough without separating himself so far from his own tents.

There was movement behind him. It startled him . . . one shameful instant he tensed, thinking of ultimate treachery, tsi'mri, un-mri; steps approached him, solitary. *Duncan,* he thought, his heart pounding with despair . . . he turned his head slightly as a kel'en came to stand by him on his left.

Hlil. The shock of it destroyed his self-possession; the membrane flicked when Hlil looked at him straightly; and beyond Hlil, Seras came . . . too old, Niun thought anxiously: a Master of weapons, but too old for this. It was an act of courage more than to help to him. Steps stirred the sand on his right, and he looked that way . . . saw to his shock that it was Ras, her eyes cold as ever; suicidal, he reckoned. They were four now. Suddenly there was another, their fifth: kel Merin of the Husbands, whom he hardly knew.

That changed the complexion of the matter. He turned again toward the five who came to challenge, his heart beating faster and faster, from wild surmises that this was somehow a trap, arranged, between his own and them; to surmises that for some mad reason these kel'ein came to defend his hold on the ja'anom. He could challenge all at once, take the strongest himself, use these four at least as a delay until he could turn his hand to the next.

They would die doing that; there was no sane reason for them to preserve the ja'anom for his possession.

The five halted before them, individually.

"Kel'anth of the ja'anom!" the central one shouted. "We are the ja'ari, the ka'anomin, the patha, the mari, the hao'nath! I am kel'anth Tian s'Edri Des-Paran, daithenon, of she'pan Edri of the ja'ari. We hear reports of landings; and I ask: does the kel'anth of the ja'anom have an answer?"

"Kel'anth of the ja'anom!" shouted the one farthest right. "I am kel'anth Rhian s'Tafa Mar-Eddin, daithenon, of the she'pan Tafa of the hao'nath. And my question you well know."

There was silence after. They had spoken in the hal'ari, not the mu'ara of tribes: and that the kel'anth of the hao'nath was alive to protest in person . . . here was a stubborn man.

"Kel'anthein! I am kel'anth Niun s'Intel Zain-Abrin, daithenon, of she'pan Melein of the ja'anom and of all the People." He drew in a second great breath, clenched the sword tightly in his fists. "I am kel'anth of the Voyagers, of those who went out from the world; heir of An-ehon and Le'a'haen, of Zohain and Tho'e'i-shai; kel'anth of the Kel of the People, Hand of the she'pan of the Mysteries; for she'pan Melein I took the ja'anom, and in her name I defend it if challenged, or challenge if she so decides. The path we take is our path, and I defend her right to walk it. Be warned!"

They stood still a moment. Somewhere the dus stirred, troubling, and he willed it silent.

A rustling of cloth and steps approached behind him, a breath of holy incense, a wisp of white robes in the corner of his eye that he dared not turn from his enemies.

Melein.

"Kel'anth of the ja'anom!" shouted Rhian of the hao'nath. "Ask your she'pan for a message and we will bear it."

Any word of enemies must, by custom, pass through him. "Tell them," Melein shouted back in her own voice. "Call your she'panei here. Call them *here*."

More dead lay in the great square, corpses becoming barriers to sand which drifted in waves across the pavings, the scale of everything reduced by the great edun which towered even in ruin. "Straight through the center," Galey said in a low voice, and led the way for them. Boaz insisted it was the sane thing, that mri would not attack from ambush if the approach were direct: she had that information from Duncan.

Forty years humans had been fighting mri, and all experience denied that theory: mri had fired from ambush; had done precisely—the realization hit him with sudden irony—what humans had done. No human had ever walked plainly up to mri. He recalled stories of mri who had advanced alone against humans, berserkers, shot to rags. Of a sudden things fit, and sickened him.

And the dead . . . everywhere—alien; but dead infants were tragedy in any reckoning. Here a woman had fallen, her arms spread wide to shield a trio of children, covering them with her robes as if that could save them; here one of the warriors had died, bearing a blue-clad infant in his arms; or a pair of the gold-robes, embraced and tucked up still sitting, as if the flight had become too much for them and they had resigned themselves to die; an older child, whose mummified body preserved the gesture of an outstretched hand across the sandy stones, reaching toward what might have been its mother.

Alien and not. Regul had killed them; or perhaps he had. It was Haven, and Kiluwa, and Asgard, and Talos, and all the evils they had done to each other. It was world's end, and earnestly he wished for some stir of life within these ruins, some relief from such things.

The steps hove up before them; he kept walking, hands at his side, toward the dark inside. He knew of edunei, these places that served mri for fortresses and what else no one knew. Shrines. Holy places. Homes. No one understood. Forty years and no one understood. Forty years and no one had understood that the warrior Kel was not the whole of the mri culture; no one had known that there was Kath or Sen, that two-thirds of the mri population were strictly noncombatant.

The place afflicted all of them. From time to time the regs had stared at some sight worse than the others, stared longer than they might from curiosity, shook their heads. They were born to the war; anyone under forty could say that, but this was not a thing they had had to see first hand.

No one spoke. Boaz paused at the top of the steps to take a picture of the way they had come, of the square with its dead. Then the dark of the interior took them in, and their footsteps and the suck and hiss of the breathers echoed in great depth.

Galey took his torch in hand and switched it on, played it over the rubbble which blocked most of the accesses to the towers. "Hey!" he shouted, trying the direct approach to the uttermost; and winced at the echoes.

"Left tower," Boaz said.

"Place is like to fall in on us," Galey objected, but he went, the others with them, into the left-hand access, up a spiraling passage dark before their light and dark after, a place for ambushes if any existed anywhere in the city.

Light shone at the top; the great room there had a split wall; and beyond, through another doorway—he walked in that direction, to anticipate Boaz, who was sure to go without their protection. His heart beat fearfully as he saw the rows of machines. He had seen the like before, on Kesrith.

"Shrine," he said aloud.

Boaz paused in the doorway and looked back at him, advanced again carefully. The whole center of the floor was gone, a pile of rubble and twisted steel.

And lights burned on the panels, far into the dark.

"Don't touch anything," Lane said. The tech pushed himself to the fore, looked about him, pulled Shibo and Kadarin aside from a circle marked on the flooring. Galey's own foot had crossed that line. He took it back.

"Weapons," Lane said, "very likely controlled from here."

And the last word was choked into hush, for there was a gleam of light from above, the circle suddenly drowned in glare.

"*An-hi?*" a mechanical voice thundered. Boaz shook her head in panic, denying understanding; it asked again, more complexly, and again and again and again.

Weapons, Galey thought in sick terror. *O God, the ships up there . . . We've triggered it.*

Lane moved, thrust himself into the circle, into the light that bathed him in white unreality. He looked up at the source of it, at screens that flared with mri writings.

"*Hne'mi!*" he cried at it: *Friend!* It was one of the only words they knew.

It hurled words back, complex and then simple, repeating, repeating, repeating.

And struck. Lane sprawled, still, glaze-eyed from the instant he hit the floor. "No fire!" Galey cried, seeing a gun in Shibo's hand. Every board was alight, the screens alive, and the light flaring blue. Boaz reached for Lane's outflung hand . . . changed her mind and drew back; all of them froze. Galey shifted a glance toward the door, to Shibo and Kadarin, whose faces were stark with fright, to Boaz, whose face was fixed toward the machine, the white light turning her to shadow and silver—to Lane, who was quite, quite dead.

Eventually there was silence again. The light faded. Galey chanced a quick move, herding the two men, dragging at Boaz. They all ran, into the sunlight of the room outside, with the machine flaring to life again, thundering its questions.

"Go," he urged them. "Get out of here." He hastened them to the access, down, into the lower hall. They pelted across it, a flight close to panic; he seized at Kadarin and stopped when they reached the open air, listening.

There was only the sunlight and the square, unchanged. They stood there, their breaths hissing into the breathers, their eyes mutually distraught.

"We couldn't help him," Galey said. "There's nothing to be done for him. We get out of this—we come back for him."

They accepted that . . . seemed to.

"It was what Duncan said," Boaz broke the silence after a moment. "Machines. What he described."

There had been no firing aloft, no hostile act from the city. The holocaust had come close to them, but it had not happened. It waited, perhaps, on orders. Mri orders. Perhaps that was what it had asked of them.

Who are you?

What am I to do?

An idiot power seeking instruction.

"If there's a link between the cities," Galey said, "we may just have sent a message."

Shibo and Kadarin said nothing, only looked at Boaz, at

plump, fragile Boaz, who had become their source of sanity:
a mri world, and they needed mri answers.

"I'd say that's likely," she agreed. "Maybe it has; but they
haven't fired yet."

"And we get out of here," Galey said. "Now."

He strode down the steps, the others behind him, past a
knot of kel'ein corpses, out across the open square. His mistake, his responsibility. It had been a brave act on Lane's
part, to try to deal with the machine. He could have done
something; he was not sure what . . . pulled Lane out, it
might have been.

"Mr. Galey," Boaz said, her breath wheezing in her mask;
she pulled it down a moment, gasped as they walked. "We
have *nothing* to report. We can't go back with this."

He said nothing for a long space of walking, trying to
think in the interval, to draw his mind back from Lane and
onto next matters. He stopped when they had cleared the
square, among the ruined buildings, looked at the faces of
Shibo and Kadarin. "We get back to the shuttle," he said.
"We try another site."

"Sir," said Kadarin, "no argument, but what could we have
done that we didn't? What can we do with a thing like that?
Mri maybe, but that thing—"

"I got another worry," said Shibo, "what happens when we
try to move that shuttle with that thing stirred up."

"Mri," Boaz said, "are in open country; Duncan gave us
truth in what he told us. We should take the rest of it—look
for mri, not the machines."

"We're near enough the rim," Galey said, "I'll slide for it
and stay low, and that's the best we can do. We've got no
help but that. But we can't go off cross-country. We've got
our corridors set up, Boz, to get us from one point to the
other without crossing what we figure for defense zones, and
that doesn't give us much space in this region for any search.
But I figure we keep this mission going; another site,
maybe—in better condition." He looked at the ground, hands
in pockets, a cold knot in his belly, looked up at them after a
moment. "I reckon not to include Lane in the report; it goes
quick, no space for explaining; they have enough excuse for
canceling us off this business and going some other route. If I
were Lane I wouldn't want that. That's my feeling on it; that
we keep trying."

"While we do," Boaz said, looking straight at the others,
"we hold out hope of another solution. Of stopping what

we've seen here. We go back . . . and what else are they going to do? We stay out here; just by that we prove there's
hope in an approach to these people. We remove *fear* . . .
and we bring sanity to this situation."

The two regs nodded. Galey did, reckoning plainly it was
court martial. "Come on," he said. "It's a long walk."

It took time, that the she'panei should come from their
tribes to that sandy slope; some were very old, and all reluc-
tant. Niun stood still, aching from the long strain of standing,
watching with a sense of unreality five white-robed figures ad-
vancing from separate points of the horizon, each accompa-
nied by her kel'anth and several sen'ein.

Melein started forward eventually, to meet them on equal
ground at the bottom of the slope. He walked with her,
slowly, with sen'anth Sathas joining them. He offered no
words; if she wanted to speak, she would. Doubtless her mind
was as full as his; doubtless she had some clear intention in
this madness. He hoped that this was the case.

To challenge them all, perhaps, after giving them her ulti-
matum. So she had done with the she'pan of the ja'anom.

They stopped; the others came to them, as close as warriors might come to one another, a stone's easy toss: such
also was the distance for she'panei in the rare instance that
they must meet. Kel'ein remained veiled; she'panei and
sen'ein met without, elder faces, masked in years. One by one
they named themselves, Tafa of the hao'nath; Edri of the
ja'ari; Hetha'in of the patha; Nef of the mari; Uthan of the
ka'anomin. Tafa and Hetha'in bore the kel-scars, and only
Nef was as young as middle years.

"Your kel'anth has used powerful names," said Tafa, when
the naming came to Melein herself. "What do you use?"

"I am Melein s'Intel, Melein not-of-the-ja'anom, out of
Edun Kesrithun of the last standing-place of the Voyagers,
heir of the cities of Kutath and of the edunei of Nisren, of
Elag called Haven, and of Kesrith. For names I begin with
Parvet'a, who led us out, and who began the line of which we
two are born; and I say that we are home, she'panei. Ja'anom
met us and would not acknowledge my claim. I took the
ja'anom."

Eyes nictitated. There was not a glance or a word among
them.

"Will you challenge?" Melein asked. "Or will you hear?"

There was the sound of the wind whipping at their robes, the whisper of sand moving. Nothing more.

"I need kel'ein," Melein said, "the service of forty hands of kel'ein from each Kel; lend them. Such as survive I shall send back again with Honors which those who did not go will envy."

"*Where* will you take them?" asked Hetha'in. "To what manner of conflict, and for what purpose? You have brought us attack, and tsi'mri, and the wasting of our cities. Where will you take them?"

"I am the foretold," Melein said. "And I call on you for your children and their strength, for the purpose for which we went out in the beginning, and I shall build you a House, she'panei."

There were small movements, a glancing from one to the other, who ought never to look on one another, who were never united.

"We have trailed a tsi'mri among you," Tafa said.

"That you have," Melein answered her. "See, and trust your Sight, she'panei; by the Mystery of the Mysteries, by the Seeing . . . give me kel'ein who have the courage to fight this fight and sen'ein to witness and record it in your shrines."

"With tsi'mri?" cried Tafa. "With walking-beasts?"

"By them you know that I am not Kutathi; and by that you know what I am, Tafa of the hao'nath. See! We are at a point, she'panei, of deciding. Our ship is gone; our enemies are many; of the millions who went out, my kel'anth and I are the last alive. We two—made it home, and do you by your suspicion destroy us, who have survived all that tsi'mri have done? Sit down and die, she'panei; or give me the forces I need."

Tafa of the hao'nath turned her back, walked away and stopped by her kel'anth. A coldness settled at Niun's belly. For a moment he had hoped . . . that five she'panei who could unite against an intruder could see farther than most.

The kel'anth of the hao'nath walked forward: Rhian s'Tafa; Niun moved out to meet him, met the eyes above the veil, of an older man than he, and worn with hurt and dus-poison and the march that had worn them both. There was nothing of hate there now, only of regret. There had been such in Merai's eyes when they had met, that sorrow. He wished to protest; it was double suicide, Tafa's madness . . . but in challenge they were held even from speaking.

The kel'ein of two tribes should ring them about, shield the other castes from such a sight; here kel'anthein did that office, too few to do more than make the token of a ring.

They drew, together, a long hiss of steel; Rhian's blade lifted to guard; he lifted his own, waited, slipped his mind into hand and blade, nothingness and now.

A pass; he turned it and returned, cautiously; countered and returned. He was not touched; Rhian was not. The blades had breathed upon each other, no more. This was a Master, this Rhian. Another pass and turn, a flutter of black cloth, cut loose; his eyes and mind were for the blade alone; a fourth pass: he saw a chance and a trap, evaded it.

"Stop!"

Tafa's sharp command; they paused, alike poised on guard. He thought of treachery, of the insanity of trusting strangers. But not tsi'mri: mri. Eyes amber as his own regarded him steadily beyond the two blades.

"Kel'anth of the hao'nath," Tafa cried. "Disengage!"

Niun stayed still as the kel'anth retreated the one pace which took them out of sword's-distance. "Disengage," Melein bade him. "The hao'nath have asked."

He stepped his pace back, stood until the hao'nath kel'anth had sheathed his sword; then he ran his own into sheath, steadily enough for all the tautness of his nerves. It was challenger's prerogative, to stop the contest without a death; challenge then might be returned from the other side, without mercy.

It dawned on him slowly that he had won, that this man had gotten out alive, and he was glad of that, for his bravery. He did not relax. They might all try his measure, one after the other. He tried to subdue the pulse which hammered in his veins; one thing to fight well; the greater matter was discipline, not to be shaken by any tactic, fair or foul.

"We lend you your two hundred," Tafa said, "and our kel'anth with them. You might demand more; but this we offer."

There was a moment's silence. "Acceptable," Melein said. The breath left Niun's lungs no more swiftly, but the pounding of his heart filled his ears.

"And we lend," said the she'pan of the patha, "our kel'anth and two hundred to stay if they bring fair report of you. We cannot sit under one tent, she'pan; but let our kel'anthein do so, and bring us word again what they have seen, whether to do what you ask or to challenge. This is fair, in our thinking."

"So," said mari and ja'ari almost at one breath.

"We ka'anomin are out of Edun Zohain, far out of our range. Our allegiance is to the ma'an mri, but we agree unless the ma'an send to recall us. For a hand of days let them observe; and that long we will wait for answer."

"Agreeable," said Melein, and other heads bowed. "A hand of days or less. Life and Honors."

She turned away; the other she'panei did so, with their sen'ein. Kel'anthein remained a moment, covering the retreat.

Niun cast a glance at Rhian. A bit of cloth lay on the sand; his, Rhian's, he was not sure. He took down his veil and gave his face to the kel'anthein lately strangers, feeling naked and strange in doing so . . . glanced from face to face as they did the same, memorizing them, the fierce handsomeness of Rhian of the hao'nath; the plainness of Tian of the ja'ari; Kedras of the patha was one of the youngest, his mouth marked with a scar from edge to chin; mari's Elan was broad-faced and elder; but oldest of the lot was Kalis of the ka'anomin, her eyes shadowed by sun-frown and the kel-scars much faded with years.

He turned to follow after Melein, and they went their separate ways for the time. He looked up at the slight rise on which his own Kel waited, before the tents, where the four who had come to his support still stood . . . for the tribe's sake, he persuaded himself in clearer reason: for pride of the ja'anom and its Holy, that they would not have merged with another tribe in defeat, though much the same distress would attach to merging as the consequence of winning. It was pride. Ras's line in particular . . . had long defended the ja'anom. It was duty to her dead brother. He understood that. And Hlil was kel-second and Seras fen'anth, and Merin a friend of Hlil's. They had their reasons; and their reasons had been fortunate for him and for Melein; he took even that with gratitude.

He walked among them, spared a nod of thanks to either side as they closed behind him and the black ranks of the Kel flowed back into the camp, where anxious kath'ein and sen'ein waited to know the fate of the tribe, clustering about Melein.

"There is agreement," Melein said aloud, so that all might hear. "They will send kel'anthein into our Council; and they may lend us help. Challenge was declined."

It was as if the whole camp together drew breath and let it go again . . . no vast relief, perhaps; they still sat in the possession of a stranger, led to strange purposes. But the ja'anom still existed as a tribe, and would go on existing.

His dus ventured out of kel-tent, radiating disturbance. Niun met it and touched it, tolerating its interference as he stood for a moment staring after the figure of Melein, who retreated among the Sen.

Reaction settled on him like a breath of cold wind. He turned away, the dus trailing him, went into the tent of the Kel, dull to the looks which surrounded him . . . missed the four to whom he owed some expression of spoken gratitude; perhaps, they thought, they turned away from it. He did not seek them out, to force it on them. He went instead to Duncan's side, settled there, concerned that Duncan slept still, unmoved from the shoulder of his dus, his face peaceful as death in the faint light which reached them from the wind vents.

Niun touched the beast, recoiled from the numbing blankness the dus contained, nothingness, void that drank in sense. His own settled down, apart from that touch, and he leaned against it, unwilling to invade that quiet the dus had made for Duncan. He rested cross-legged, hands in his lap, bowed his head and tried to rest a little.

Footsteps disturbed the matting near him. He looked up as Hlil crouched down by him and tugged his veil down.

"You took no wound."

"No," he said. "I thank you, kel Hlil."

"Kel-second belonged there. For the tribe."

"Aye," he agreed, It was clearly so. "Where is Ras?"

"Wherever she wills to be. I am not consulted in her wanderings." Hlil looked down at Duncan, frowning. Niun looked and found Duncan's eyes open a slit, regarding them both; he watched Hlil reach and touch his sleeve as if touching him at all were no easy thing. "The sight of him will be trouble," Hlil said, "with the other kel'anthein."

Niun moved his own hand to Duncan's shoulder, lest Hlil's cold touch should disturb him; he felt contact with the dus, which had the same leadenness as before, mind-dulling if he permitted. Duncan was conscious, but only partially aware.

"They are coming now," Hlil said to him. "Watch has them in view. I do not think since the parting . . . such a thing has ever happened in the world." His eyes strayed back to Duncan, glanced to him again. "He is yours; no stranger will touch him. But best surely if he is not the first thing they see."

Duncan blinked; perhaps he had heard.

"No," Niun said. "Bring them here when they reach camp."

Hlil frowned.

"Let them see me as I am," Niun said. "I make no pretenses otherwise."

"This is not yourself," Hlil exclaimed. "You are not—not what the eye of strangers will see here. You are not this."

The outcry both angered and touched his heart. "Then you do not know me. Look again, Hlil, and do not make me what I am not. This is my brother; and the beast is a part of my mind. I am not Kutathi, and I am not Merai. Bring them here, I say."

"Aye," Hlil said, and rose up and walked away in evident distress.

They came, eventually, a soft stirring outside, a whisper of robes . . . kel'anthein of the five tribes with each several companions, sixteen in all, a blackness in Hlil's wake; and Hlil returned to sit by him and by Duncan.

Niun moved his upturned hand, offering them place on the mats. They sat down and unveiled; the tent stirred behind them with the arrival of ja'anom kel'ein, for it was the business of all of them, this opening of the tent to strangers.

Niun put out a hand to the dusei, one and the other, soothed them, deliberate demonstration . . . let them all look on him and them as long as they would, Rhian most of all, whose face betrayed nothing. After a moment Niun reached to his brow and swept off the headcloth in a gesture of humility, equaling their disadvantage on strange ground.

"I welcome you," he said. "I warn you against strong passions; the beasts sense them and spread them if you are not wary of what they do; bid them stop and they will do so. Sometimes one can be deceived by them into feeling their anger; or strangers share what strangers would rather not. The Kel from which I came knew such things, valued them, learned to veil the heart from them; and what hurt they have done, lay to my account: I brought them. They are as devoted companions as they are enemies: Rhian s'Tafa, it was a moment's misfortune and confusion: I beg your pardon for it."

The others, perhaps, did not understand. The hao'nath's eyes met his with direct force, slid deliberately to Duncan's sleeping form.

"He is ja'anom," Niun answered that look.

There was long and heavy silence. The dusei stirred, and Niun quieted them with a touch, his heart pounding with dread, for they could lose it all upon this man's pride.

"This came from the alien ships," Rhian said. "We tracked it. And you met with it. And that is a question I ask, kel'anth of the ja'anom."

"I am Duncan-without-a-Mother." The hoarse voice startled them all, and Niun looked, found Duncan's eyes slitted open. "I came on a *mri* ship; but I had gone to speak with the tsi'mri, to ask them what they wanted here."

"Sov-kela." Niun silenced him with a touch, glanced up at Rhian. "But it is truth, all the same. He does not lie."

"What is he?" asked Kalis.

"Mri," Niun said. "But once he was human."

What the dusei picked up disturbed, brought a shifting of bodies in instinctive discomfort all about the tent.

"It is a matter among us," Hlil said, "with respect, kel'anth of the ka'anomin of Zohain."

There was long silence.

"He is sickly," said Rhian with a wave of his hand.

"I shall mend," Duncan said, which he had the right to say, passed off in so contemptuous a manner; but it was desperately rash. Niun put out his hand, silencing further indiscretions; all the same he felt a touch of satisfaction for that answer.

And Rhian's haggard face showed just the slightest flicker of expression: not outright rage, then, or he would have been as blank as newlaid sand. "So be it," Rhian said. "We discuss that matter later."

"Doubtless," said Kalis of the ka'anomin, "we are different; gods, how not? Some we accept, at least while we observe. But what have you brought us? We have seen the coming and going of ships. The hao'nath say that An-ehon is totally ruins. We do not know the fate of Zohain. This is not the first coming of tsi'mri to this world, but, gods! never did mri bring them."

"Of the People who went out," Niun said, "we are the last; we were murdered by tsi'mri who bought our service, not by Duncan's kind. And they come to finish us here. Bring them, no. But that is the she'pan's matter, not mine. Share food and fire with us; share Kath if it pleases you; they will take honor of you. For the rest, suspend judgment."

"When will the she'pan speak to us?" asked Elan of the mari.

"I do not know. I truly do not know. She will send. We will lodge you until then."

"Your tent cannot hold us," said Kedras of the patha.

"We will do it somehow. If each caste yields a little canvas we can run cord between our poles and Sen."

"Possible," Kedras said, resting hands on knees. There was a small silence, and Kedras hissed a short breath. "Gods, all under one canvas."

"In the Kel of my birth," Niun said slowly, "we fought at the hire of tsi'mri; and went from world to world on tsi'mri ships; and it was done, that kel'ein onworld were sheltered by strange she'panei and edunei not of their birth, until their hire took them away again. Perhaps it was so on Kutath once, in the days of the great cities."

"This Kel does not remember," Kedras confessed, and others moved their heads—no.

"We will bring our kel'ein," said Tian of the ja'ari. "Perhaps each of us can spare a little of canvas."

Others assented.

"Kel'anthein," Niun gave them murmured courtesy, watched as they rose and departed, filing out of the tent, as all about them, ja'anom rose in courtesy, settled again. Hlil followed them out, gathering a band of kel'ein to serve what needed be done.

Niun sat still a moment, replaced the headcloth, sat staring at the empty doorway.

"Strangers," Duncan said beside him, and he realized that of all that had changed, Duncan knew none of it. "More than hao'nath."

"I will tell you later. Rest, be still. All is better than it was."

He rubbed at the dus's shoulder to soothe it, looked out over the faces of his kel, at eyes which were fixed on him in strange concentration . . . with distress, it might be; or simple bewilderment. Ras was there; she had come in, and Seras, and Merin. There was a curious thing in the air, a sense of madness that quivered through the dus-sense; so a man might feel with his feet on the rimsands.

"Deal with them as with our own," he said to them. He put off the kel-sword, laid it again on the matting, looked up as Taz appeared with a bowl which he offered, a small portion of liquid, a delicacy reserved for honor, and for those in need. "Kath sends," Taz told him; and he drank, though he would rather have yielded it to Duncan, who needed it more.

He gave the bowl back, thought on kath Anaras, thought that this evening would be well spent in Kath, where he might take pleasure, and ease. Rhian's skill had made him think on dying, and Kath was a place to forget such thoughts. He had much neglected them, owed Anaras courtesy which he had never paid. She was fortunate, her child had survived the flight, but the kel'anth had never come a second time to her.

Tonight there were strangers in camp, and duty, and he could not. He shut his eyes, exhaled, opened them again. "I will return it," he said.

"Sir," Taz objected; it was not custom.

He rose up, taking the small bowl with him, and walked out.

XII

Luiz stared at the screen, the message tape looping over and over again.

DUNCAN INFO CONFIRMED ON SITE ONE, the message ran tersely. DANTE PROCEEDING NEW SITE HOPING FURTHER DATA.

No way to contact them; mission Dante went its own way. That any message had come meant they had gone aloft again, messaged from one of the so-reckoned safe corridors, and flitted gnatlike to the next choice of sites.

Boz, he thought with a shake of his head; the muscles of his mouth attempted a smile as he reckoned her happiness . . . let loose in such treasuries with camera and notebook and recorder; she would be in agony if the soldiers hastened her on too soon.

Salve to the soul, for all she had given up in leaving Kesrith.

Reparations. To save something. The smile faded into heart-sickness. Guilt drove her. Would kill her. The young men would keep going—had to—she would break her heart out there in the dunes, climbing where young men went.

But she had won something. INFO CONFIRMED, the message ran.

He reached for a pad and stylus. *Tight transmission Saber,* he wrote for the ComTech, and transcribed the message in full, with transmission time.

There was another thing on his desk, which had not given him such relief. CAUTION: READINGS INDICATE LIFE RESURGENCE IN THE CITIES. POWER THERE RESTORED. MAINTAIN SHIP FLIGHT STANDBY.

And with it another shuttled dispatch: ADVISE YOU ALLIED MISSION DEMANDING LANDING: SITUATION DELICATE.

He turned from his desk and handed the slip to Brown, who was *Flower's* pilot. "Transmit," he said.

"Sir," Brown said, as if he would object.

"Do it."

Brown left to do so. It would go quickly. *Santiago* hovered over them in this crisis like a bird over eggs.

He stared at the repeating message, scowling. He would gladly get the two current messages to Boaz if it were possible. It was not. They were on their own. Presumably they knew about the power in the sites . . . and if so they neglected to mention it; neglected to warn them of potential hazard.

He bit his lip, reckoning Boaz's persuasive powers, wondered with a small and uneasy suspicion—how much else Galey's mission neglected. A deliberately optimistic message; a biased message. He sent no comment with it, guilty by silence.

Saber, he reasoned, could draw its own conclusions.

The prep room remained a haven of sanity. *Saber's* pulse went through it, this place where all had casual access, where a sharp eye might pick up what was developing, what missions went, what missions came in; and a sharp ear hear any rumor that was drifting about. Harris came by routine, in the unease that went with no missions and the lack of contact with Galey. He sat in the rhythm of the room, a frantic pace of outgoing and incoming flights, shuttles which kept their senses extended over the world's horizons . . . gamed sometimes among friends, among the others who were bound to this assignment, who came, as he did, to sit and drink and watch the scan and the boards and say to themselves, *not now, not this watch, not yet.*

Harris filled his cup from the dispenser, used his rations card to get a cellopack of dried rfuit, pocketed it while he made his usual nervous pass by the flight boards.

Regul, someone had *scrawled on the margin of the clear* plastic which overlay the system chart; and with it an eye.

Home, it had said once; but some zealot officer had erased that.

There were two ships out besides *Santiago;* that was normal. Four names on the present flight list; four more going up next. Good enough; it was all routine.

He walked next to the status board, found the point that was *Flower,* isolate as it ought to. be. He sipped at the coffee and strayed back to the table, to sit and wait as he spent his days waiting. He activated the library function, propped his feet up, drank his coffee and found himself four pages into the book he was reading, with no comprehension of it. He stared at it, heard others coming in, looked. It was the next group out, come in for prep.

"How'd it go last night?" one gibed at him; he gave a placid shrug, smug with a memory he was not going to have public, watched as they collected their flight gear from the lockers. The outward blips had made their slow way back on the scan; the outgoing team had it timed to a nicety.

Two men entered the room: North and Magee, two of his own. He moved his feet and offered them the place, while the other team walked out and on their way to the hangar deck. North went to make his own pass by the boards and charts.

And of a sudden all status on scan was arrested; the ships stayed where they were. Harris rose to his feet; so did Magee. The ships began to turn, four neat and simultaneous changes of position, oriented to different quarters, two proceeding back the way they had come, two moving wide.

The screen adjusted to wider field. Red blips were proceeding out from the larger red ship.

"Here it comes," Magee muttered. There was a cold in the air. Harris swallowed and watched. The red blips tracked not toward the world, but headed toward themselves.

The screen flashed letters: CODE GREEN.

"Going to board," North said. They knew the routine. An aisle was established from the bay to the quarantine areas near command. Regul quarters were there for use when they must be. Areas not meant for regul were put under security yellow, which meant cardlock for everyone needing passage into and out of sections.

Bile rose into Harris's throat. He swore softly.

"Guess we got our allies back," North said.

"That regul expert," Magee said. "That's what he brought us. That Averson got us *regul.*"

Koch sipped at the obligatory cup of soi, stared levelly at the regul delegation and his own staff, who sat disposed about the room, the regul adult in his sled and the inevitable younglings squatting on the carpet beside . . . not much difference between standing and sitting for their short legs. Degas, Averson, and two aides: two opinions he truly wanted at hand and two live bodies more to balance the odds in the room; protocol: there had to be youngling figures so that regul knew by contrast whom to respect.

"Reverence," said the newly adult Suth, gape-mouthed and

grinning affably. "A pleasure that we are able to deal sensibly after crisis."

"Bai Suth." Koch stared at the regul sidelong, finding difficulty to believe that he had known this individual regul before, that what bulked so large in the sled had been one of the relatively slim servitors. There was not even facial similarity. Plates had broadened and ridged; skin had thickened and coarsened into sagging folds. The metamorphosis had been radical considering the elapsed time; and yet this one had not attained the late Sharn's bulk and roughness. "We are pleased," Koch pursued, "if this meeting can prove productive; our good wishes to you in your new office."

Nostrils flared; the smile became a hiss. Experts called that laughter. "There have been misunderstandings, reverence bai Koch. One, for instance, between subordinates. . . ."

"You refer, perhaps, to my missing ship."

Eyes flickered; no, that was not what the bai had meant, but he covered with a widening of the grin. "I refer to matters between ourselves and your ship *Flower*, to which we have asked access. I seriously urge that we arrange closer cooperation . . . for mutual safety."

"You have not answered my question, bai."

The nostrils shut. That was anger. "Youngling matters and not at all productive. Are we responsible for ships which come and go without our knowledge or the courtesy of consulting us? I would prefer to continue this meeting; but if we persist in raising extraneous matters—"

"You persist, bai, in ignoring data which has been given you repeatedly: that our species is adult at a considerably earlier age than regul. We do not slaughter our younglings; we do not consider hazard to ships flown by *young adults of our species* . . . to be a minor matter."

"I repeat: I would prefer to continue this meeting."

It was there, on the table, toss them out or abandon the issue. Koch considered, scowled. "Then I think that you have answered my question all the same, bai Suth."

"No. I have ignored it, reverence bai. Assumptions between species are hazardous. I return to the previous matter under objection. You have interfered with our operations and seem offended that we want to enter yours."

"Your own bid likely to interfere with ours; you will not have our leave to approach *Flower*, take our strongest warning of that. Any ship that approaches will not be safe."

"Impasse."

"Impasse, bai Suth."

The regul shifted his weight in his sled, slowly finished off his soi, wished more of it of a youngling servitor which panted about immediately to satisfy him. "Bai Koch," Suth said when he had received the cup, "it is a matter of concern to us, this widening gap in our cooperation. We find difficulty reasoning in the unfortunate absence of the bai Sharn and the bai doctor Aldin, who had established useful rapport—" He rolled his eyes toward Averson, gaped a smile. "But we rejoice in the new elevation of this person to your councils, reverend bai doctor Averson." The eyes took in Degas, lingered there, rolled back again, the whites vanishing. "We are appreciative of any move toward understandings. We are allies. You agree. We cannot pursue differences and remain allies; I suggest we pursue cooperation. I have not mentioned the murder of an elder. I have not mentioned the discourtesy in treatment of bai Sharn's body. I have not mentioned the collapse of firm contracts between us. And I do not think it productive to mention these things. But if certain things are raised between us, rest assured that these other things can be objected . . . justly objected, now and in the future of our two species. We have, you are aware, long memory. But let us pass over these matters. Indeed, let us pass over them. Give me the benefit of your imagination, reverence bai. How will the mri respond to the situation you have posed?"

Koch did not let his face react. *What situation?* he wondered, not sure how much was known to them. "We hope for peaceful settlement with them, bai Suth."

"Indeed. Regul experience counsels that this is a vain expectation."

"Our experience counsels otherwise."

"Ah, then you are relying on records. Records from mri?"

"Of many situations, bai. Human records."

"Our experience of mri is two thousand years long; and it argues against yours, of recent duration. Mri are intractable and inflexible. Certain words are beyond their understanding. *Negotiation* is one such. The concept does not exist with them. Observed fact, bai. Where concept does not exist . . . how does action?"

Koch considered this, not alone of mri . . . glanced at Averson and back at Suth. "A question you have evaded, reverence: do you have a mri expert among you?"

The mouth gaped at once into a hiss, amusement. "He sits among you, bai Koch. I am that expert. I am, you may mark

for your memory, a colonial of doch Horag. Horag has employed mri as guards for most of the two thousand years in
question. Doch Alagn misled you; they were amateurs and
newcomers, and your believed them expert. My adulthood
has put into authority . . . a true expert in these matters.
And a new doch. You are very prudent to inquire."

"Are you fluent in their language too?"

"There are two languages. I sorrow, bai, but the languages
of mri were always a point of stubbornness with them. They
persisted in coercing the regul language into their sluggish
memories and speaking it badly."

"Meaning that they would not permit outsiders to become
fluent."

"Meaning whatever that means within their mental process,
reverence. These leaps of analysis are perhaps a natural human process, or you are withholding data. It means what the
mri wish it to mean; we are patently not mri, neither you nor
I. Are you withholding data?"

"No. No, bai Suth." Koch reflected on that matter, staring
at the bai, nodded finally. "You are an authority on mri.
Without access to their thought processes."

Nostrils shut and flared in rapid succession. "I contain information, bai, and without it you may deal in errors and ex-
perimentations at hazard of life. I tell you that we have never
been able to translate the concept of negotiation into the mri
understanding; and that should be marked for memory. I tell
you that at any time a mri was hired to fight, there was no
deviation from that path; he would kill or be killed and no offer would sway him. Trade concepts are not in their minds,
reverence bai. They hired out their mercenaries, but *hired* is
our word for the process and *mercenary* is your word. We
deal in regul and human words; what do *they* think?"

"The bai is right," Averson interjected. "There is no exacti-
tude between species. Regul *hocht* and our *mercenary* aren't
the same either."

Nostrils expanded. Koch watched and wondered how much
of his own expression the bai had learned to read. "You've
come here for some specific purpose, bai. Perhaps we could
have some definition of that."

"Understanding. Mutual protection."

"We do not desert our allies, if you are concerned."

That hit the intended mark; the flutter was clearly visible.
"Bai, we are delighted to know that. There is of course reason that the mri should bear a grudge against us. And how

will you deal with that matter in this peaceful solution you seek?"

"We will not desert our allies."

"Mri do not back up, as regul do not forget."

"Mri forget; perhaps regul can back up."

Again the flutter of emotion. "Meaning, bai Koch?"

"That mri may be persuaded to forget this act of yours at Kesrith if they have assurance that regul will not act against them here."

"Your leaps of process bewilder me, bai Koch. I have been led to understand that forgetting is not a precise act."

"We use it with many meanings, bai Suth."

Suth's nostrils heaved and flared. Suth's great fist banged the re-emptied cup against the sled and the youngling nearest raced in stumbling steps to fill and return it. Suth drank in great gulps, seeming in physical difficulty.

"Forgive us," Koch said. "Have we disturbed you?"

"I am disturbed, indeed I am disturbed." Suth drank heavily, set the cup down on his sled's rim. "I perceive great threat based on real experience and my allies leap like insects from one precarious point to the next."

"We are constantly monitoring the situation. We do not believe the threat is immediate. Information indicates we are dealing with a declined and nomadic group."

"Nomads: unstable persons."

"A stable but mobile community." He reflected on the difficulty of translating *that* to a species which regarded the least walking as agony. "They have no arms or transport sufficient to damage us. The cities are purely automated fire."

Suth's nostrils flared and shut, flared again. "Do not be angry, human bai. But can mri lie? This is a human possibility. Is it also mri? Does your experience or your imagination . . . judge?"

"We don't know."

"Ah. Do you imagine?"

"We don't have sufficient data."

"Data for imagining."

"It does take some, bai Suth. We operate at present on the premise that they can." He considered a moment, made the thrust. "In our experience, bai Suth . . . even regul can be dishonest."

"Dishonest, not honest, not . . . truthful."

"What is truth, bai Suth?"

Nostrils closed. "According to fact."

Koch nodded slowly. "I perceive something of your thinking, then. —Is there, Dr. Averson, a regul word for *honest?*"

"In business, the word *alch* . . . meaning evenly balanced advantage or observation, or something like. Value for value, we say."

"Mutual profit," Suth said. "We can spend much time at these comparative exercises, reverence. Favor, consider our position in orbit about this world. We are in range of these cities, which you imagine to be safe. I strongly urge a reconsideration."

"What would the regul wish?"

"Negation of the hazard here."

"Ethical considerations forbid. Or is that another word that doesn't translate?"

There was a silence from the other side. Koch looked at Averson. Averson muttered a regul word.

"We understand," said Suth. "We also respond to instincts."

"Sir," said Degas, "I think abstracts are in the way."

"Yes," said Suth, and grinned broadly.

Koch frowned at Degas, nodded slowly. "So the bai is concerned for our safety and that of home space. So are we."

"How much time, bai Koch, how much time? This youngling Duncan . . . how much have you given him?"

"A human matter, bai."

"We are allies."

"We are waiting."

"Humans walk very quickly. This youngling has taken far more days than needed to reach *Flower* after the attack. This evidences misfortune . . . or lack of cooperation on the part of this youngling. True?"

"Do you have information on him, bai?"

"No. Nor do you. Fact?"

"We simply wait."

"How long do you wait?"

"Does it matter?"

"Mri have had time to prepare response, bai Koch. Does this seem wise, to afford them this? They have weapons."

"Perhaps. Perhaps not."

"You balance all home space on this *perhaps,* bai."

"We are aware of the hazard."

"If they fire—"

"We adjust policy."

Suth clamped his bony lips shut, exhaled long and softly.

"We are your allies. We, we are not a fighting people. We are your very safe neighbors, rich in trade, in mutual profit. And will you trade us for mri? Go home, bai. Leave this matter to us if your instincts forbid you to settle it. You know that we do not lie. We have no interest in hiring mri."

"It isn't likely that you could, is it, reverence?"

"The situation does not make agreement likely."

"Doubtless not. Nor was the fact that bai Sharn destroyed peace messages from them and deliberately deceived us."

"The messages themselves were deceptive."

"I thought regul did not hypothesize."

"We do not leap across dataless voids. The intent of the messages was to delay your response and encourage your near approach to the world without firing. You are alive; you might now be dead. Consider this hypothesis, bai."

"We do, in all aspects."

"How long will you wait on this youngling?"

"Our patience is not yet exhausted."

"We remain, then, in danger. The dead worlds: think on them; and what if there is a mri fleet loose; and what if it comes on us here?"

"Regul imagination?"

"We make hypotheses based on data and experience. Both indicate mri are apt to wild actions which do not take into account their personal survival. We suggest you set *Saber* a little farther out in the system; one of our two ships can hover over *Flower* for its safety since you insist on its remaining on the surface; one of us can scan the other side of the world. We have not been sharing data. I suggest we do so, to our mutual benefit."

"We at least have a basis for discussion."

Suth let go a great breath. "So, indeed, I invite the human bai to my ship."

"No."

"Basis?"

"Nature of human patterns of command, bai; I have to stay near my own machines. We're not as highly automated."

Suth's nostrils puffed. Whether he believed this or whether a regul could doubt a plain declaration . . . remained uncertain.

"Compromise," Suth said. "We discuss through channels, We may also consider opening channels between *Flower* and our own onworld mission."

"You do have an onworld mission."

"Why not, reverend ally? Why should we not? A closer co-operation, I say."

Koch frowned. "I shall take it under advisement, bai Suth. I think we are at that point. —*What* regul activity onworld?"

"When we have *Flower* data, we shall give you ours."

"When we have yours we will consider the matter."

"Simultaneous exchange?"

That put it untidily fair. Koch felt the burden on himself, denied it with a hissed breath the regul might understand. "What might you have? Scan data? Our own is highly efficient."

"You have more?"

"Might." Regul feared not knowing, Averson had advised him; it seemed valid, for Suth showed discomfiture at that suggestion.

"Neither of us knows what the other has," Suth said.

"I will consult with my own staff, bai Suth. Doubtless you will want to consult with yours."

Suth's nostrils puffed back and forth, back and forth. Suddenly the grin reappeared. "Excellent, reverence bai. Soon, another conference, in which we hope specific proposals. —Younglings, move. Your favor, bai."

"Favor, reverence." Koch leaned elbows on his desk, stared at the flurry of motion as the massive sled trundled toward the door and the waiting escort, and the younglings hastened after. Koch shifted a glance toward their own two superfluous aides, dismissing them to join the group outside. They understood and went without oral command.

The regul left a musty scent behind them. They had gotten it cleared out of the ship and it was back again. Koch had not begun by hating it, but it produced now a tautness in his gut, memories of tense encounters and regul smiles.

He slid a glance to Degas as the door closed, pushed away the cooling cup of soi, the taste of which he associated with the smell. Degas offered nothing, discreetly blank. He looked at Averson.

"Advice," he said.

"My advice." Averson wiped at his mouth and felt after some object in his pocket, patted it as if to be sure it was there. "I have given it, sir."

"Your opinion on what you just heard."

Averson moistened his lips. "The maneuverings of their ship . . . this forward and back, forward and back, the eluding of watch: this is what I said . . . bluff. They have a word

for it, somewhere between status and assertion. They are here
to assert themselves after their crisis."

"Or they're screening some operation. They're very anxious
to have us move."

"Assertion. Ask more than you can get; provoke and study
the reaction."

"That can get men killed down there, doctor. Or worse."

"This is a new doch, this Horag. A new power. A totally
new entity in control. They're distressed by this silence on
our part; they lost an elder here, and that confounded all bar-
gains, because that elder was replaced by a different doch entirely. They deal only in memory; and the murder of an elder
. . . they remember vividly. They need some current reaction
from us, some approach, some substance against which they
can plan policy. Remember that they can't imagine, sir. And
we don't know what Horag remembers."

"What difference?" Koch asked impatiently. "They were all
on one ship."

"A lot of difference, sir. A great deal of knowledge was
lost with Sharn. This youngling comes out of a different pool
of knowledge. His entire reality is different."

"I leave that to the psych lads. My question is what specifi-
cally will he do? What is he likely to do in the matter with
Flower?"

Averson's hands were visibly trembling. He extracted a
bottle of pills from his pocket. . . . Koch stared at the per-
formance critically; jump-stress, maybe. There were younger
men in that condition among them.

"You have to give them data to convince them of cooperation," Averson said. "But no, sir, they haven't gone down
there because your threat is believed. They believe the line
you've drawn." Averson tucked the pill into his mouth, put
the bottle away, an annoyingly meticulous process with shaking hands. "If they fear too much they could also leave this
star. Break down the whole treaty arrangement by going back
to home space and reporting a human-mri alliance. Fact is,
we don't know that mri and humans are the only sapient life
regul are in contact with. We don't know that any exist. We
don't know anything about what lies inside or the other side
of regul space. And we know this one direction, where all the
worlds but this one are dead; and we need to get back, sir. If
no one gets back—who'll tell it?"

Koch leaned chin on his locked hands and frowned. There
were things not spread to Averson's level . . . that *Saber*

might not be the sole mission; that Kesrith would send out another, and another . . . desperate to have an answer. The way to the mri homeworld was the mri's secret, and humanity's, and regul . . . when *Shirug* reached home . . . their secret too. And if a human marker were not in place broadcasting peace to ships which came . . . human ships would move in with force. It might take time; second missions might go world by world, years upon years in searching dead worlds: they had followed mri, quick and desperate. But come they would, if humans feared enough, if men and equipment sufficed to hurl out here.

"Dr. Averson, . . . I appreciate your effort. I'd appreciate a written analysis of the transcript for our files. Things have a way of coming clear when they're written. If you would do that."

"Yes, sir," Averson replied. He looked much calmer, looked left at Degas as if to learn whether this was dismissal.

"Good day, doctor," Koch said, waited patiently as Averson made his awkward and slow retreat, with backward glances as though he would gladly have stayed.

"Opinion," Koch said to Degas.

Degas locked his hands across his belly, relaxed in his chair. "Cautious credence. I share your apprehensions about the bai; but there is merit in their position and in their offers."

"I reckon they've read the scan also. They know those cities are live again; that's what's brought them running. The question is whether they know about Galey."

"Possibly. Possibly not," Degas said. "Our strong warning has had some effect, I believe."

"On *Flower's* safety, yes. We still haven't accounted for their own operation, and the only possible motive their mission can have is provocation."

"Observation."

"Possibly."

"They aren't physically capable of getting into the sites. Chances are they suspect some operation like Galey's. We might calm them by feeding them Galey's reports openly; but I doubt they would put much weight on them."

"Because their decision is already firm."

Degas frowned; by his face he wanted to say something, finally gestured and did so. "Sir, I would suggest that we're also operating under subconscious bias."

"Meaning?"

"The regul are repulsive, aren't they? No one likes them; the crew shies from them. It's an emotional reaction, I'm afraid. There's nothing lovely about them. But the fact is, the regul are nonviolent. They are safe neighbors. Of course the mri are appealing; humans find their absolutisms attractive. They have instincts that almost overlap our own . . . or seem to; they're handsome to human eyes. But they're dangerous, sir; the most cold-blooded killers ever let loose. Incompatible with all other life. We learned that over forty bloody years. Regul don't look noble; they aren't, by our rules; they'll cheat, given the chance . . . but in terms of property, not weapons. They would be good neighbors. We *can* understand them. Their instincts overlap ours too; and we don't like to look at that. Not nearly so attractive as the mri. But the end result of regul civilization is trade and commerce spread over all their territories. And we've had a first-hand look at the result of mri civilization too . . . the dead worlds."

Koch made a face. It was truth, though something in it was sour in his belly. "But it's rather like what Duncan said, isn't it, Del—that we shape ourselves by what we do here. We become . . . what we do here."

Degas's face went flat and cold. He shook his head. "If we kill here, . . . we stop them. We stop them flat. It's our doing; it doesn't go any farther than that. We have to take the responsibility."

"And *we* become the killers we kill to stop, eh? Paradox, isn't it? We can sneak out of here regul-fashion and let the regul become the killers; or do our own killing, and how will regul look on us then, a species that looks like the mri, that could do what the mri did? Another paradox. What's the human answer to this situation?"

"Side with the peaceful side," Degas said too quickly, like a man with his mind long made up. "Blow this place."

Koch sat and stared at him, thinking that the connection of those two ideas was not half so mad as might be. Not here. Not with mri.

"Pull up Galey's mission," Degas urged him. "And *Flower* too. You can't entirely stop the regul from prodding about down there. Regul do that, keep pushing a situation. Humans can deal with that. Mri . . ."

"You're still taking for granted mri control those weapons."

"I don't believe the possibility ought to be excluded on the basis of Galey's report. There's still only one answer when it

comes down to who we want for neighbors. And preserving
the mri is—"

Degas did not finish that. Koch sat back. "I propose you
this, Del: regul are good traders. If we do what they don't
like, they'll still come back and bargain again. We can do
what we want here . . . and they'll have to negotiate from
that point, not a point of their choosing."

Degas seemed to consider, slowly and at length. "Possibly.
If there are no alternatives for them. Or if they don't reach
some instinctual limit as a result of something we do . . .
like a mri alliance."

"They're likely to hire more mercenaries. Humans, maybe;
a lot of our people are trained for war, Del; a lot are root-
less, and some are hungry. Does that make regul such safe
neighbors?"

A second and deeper frown from Degas. "I figure that's
more trouble for the regul than they want; they don't take to
human ways easily, not at depth. The mri never let the regul
know them; and maybe that's how they tolerated each other
so long. We may be more open than the regul like. But that
doesn't change my advice. We can't stay here forever. Can't.
I recommend we take the responsibility and get the ugly
business over with."

"No."

"Then land a force if those cities are dead and you trust
this report. Go in on foot and wipe out these deserted cities,
destroy their automations and their power sources. Propose
that to the regul for a compromise."

"Reckoning—"

"That if the regul are right, the mri will resist with everything they have; we'll throw it back at them doubled, and be
done with this. And if they're wrong and those sites aren't
used, then what harm would the destruction of power sources
do . . . to declined and nomadic people? Let the mri exist.
That's the humane solution you asked. One the regul could
accept; it's reasonable; one we could accept; it's moral. Give
the mri what they need to live; let them live out their natural
decline. Charity is well enough at that point."

Koch considered it, rocked back and forth, weighed the
possibilities. It began to make sense. It was, by all they knew,
something that the regul could accept. He considered it further, staring at Degas's tense and earnest face. "You wouldn't
have discussed that with Averson?"

"No. But I'm sure he could give you some sort of analysis of regul reaction, before putting it to them."

"*Flower* might accept it. Might."

"Possibly," Degas said, his eyes glittering.

"I want Averson's opinion on it. Put it to him, as from yourself. Have it written up and on my desk as soon as possible."

"Sir," Degas said with uncharacteristic zeal.

To be back in the safety of *Shirug* . . . Suth breathed a sigh of profound relief as he eased his sled free of the shuttle's confines, entered the landing bay. His youngling attendants puffed about in their own concerns, the securing of the ship. Suth locked into the nearest rail connection and punched the code of his own office.

Automation locked in, high priority. The sled shot into motion, whisking round the turns and through dark interstices of sled-passages, out into brief bright glimpses of foot corridors. Freight sleds went by with a shock air, dead-stopped at intersections as, in his case, even other adult-sleds must stop. Sunk in his cushions he accepted the accelerations, his two hearts compensating for the shifting stresses. His blunt fingers punched in a summons, and he received acknowledgment that his staff was on its way.

They were already in his offices when he braked at the door, disengaged, and trundled through the anteroom and into his own territory. Morkhug's youngling proffered him soi. He drank gratefully, having suffered depletion of his strength in this shifting about.

"Report," he asked of his three mates, who waited on him.

"The two shuttles have dropped," Nagn announced with evident satisfaction.

"Observed by any?"

"Questionable, reverence; they are at least down intact."

Suth settled back, cup in hand, vastly relieved. "Flexibility," he pronounced with a hiss. "My own operations were not without success. They are stalling, these humans. They have been set off balance by our demands, and they are talking."

"The supplies with the shuttles," said Morkhug, "will extend the life of the younglings onworld by ten days. We are considering the feasibility of recovery. We cannot afford to lose the machinery if we remain here and protract this situation."

Suth drank and reflected on the matter. In eight days, panic would begin to set in among the younglings onworld, water for the humidifiers running short; and food . . . in increasing anxiety they would eat. They had oversupplied food in relation to water: better shortage of anything but food; the presence of it would satisfy them toward the terminal stages if no provision could be made to rescue them. Fear of hunger brought madness, irrational action. It was necessary that that reaction be staved off as long as possible.

Expendables: the younglings downworld knew it as these present here did. It was the eternal hope of younglings that efficiency would win favor and spare one from dying . . . the deep-rooted desire to feed and placate the governing elders, to be constantly reassured about one's status. Recipient of such attentions and no longer bound by them, Suth settled into remote consideration of alternatives.

Deal with humans and thereby win access to supply food to the mission?

Koch's reasoning nagged at him, blind, humanish obstinacy.

Regarding forgetting . . . *We use it with many meanings, bai Suth.*

Precise forgetting?

The deliberate expunging of data?

One could alter one's reality and all time to come. Was this linked to future-memory and imagination?

Suth shuddered.

"Food," Melek breathed anxiously, tearing at the wrappings of the supply packets; its fingers were all but numb: the cold crept in everywhere, despite the wrappings with which they swathed themselves, and the biodome which, with its flooring and translucent walls, attempted to provide them some measure of moving space in their base. Four shuttles clustered about the dome, dimly visible in the dawning, where basin haze made the daybreak the hue of milk, where the shadow of a seamount drifted disembodied and lavender above the haze. All of them avoided that exterior view whenever possible; the flatnesses, they were not so bad; but the barren sand, the eternal emptiness, the color of the earth, the alienness of it . . . these were terrible. The regular thudding of the compressor measured their existence within the air-supported dome. The air was supposed to be heated, but the nights, the dreadful nights, when the sun sank and vanished in mid-sky . . . brought chill; and fearsome writhings disturbed the floor of the biodome, the life of Kutath, seeking moisture, seeking warmth; they wore footgear when they must go out to the ships, hastened, shuddering at the slithering whips and cables which attempted to impede them and to invade their suits and their doorways.

Now two more lostlings were sent among them. Melek chewed at the concentrates, its trembling somewhat abated; its comrade Pegagh sat munching on soi nuts, the while the newcomers settled in among them. Magd and Hab their names were, Alagn like Pegagh. Melek, of Geleg doch, regarded them all with suspicion, its double hearts laboring in the dull dread that they were to be held here too long, that the calculations it had made were inaccurate, and it was not valued and honored for being of another doch than Alagn . . . quite the contrary. Melek did not speak such things, certainly not to them; and made no complaints, as Pegagh did not: one never knew in what ear such complaints would be dropped should they survive. There was a swelling in Melek's throat that made swallowing difficult in such contemplations. They flew their missions precisely as told; they beamed Eldest's tape over the wide flat nothingness.

They hoped, forlornly, to be taken home and fed and comforted.

Now they were four.

There were ten shuttles in all; and four of them sat here. Two more coming down could not carry supplies sufficient to make the trip worthwhile: they would then be six marooned down here . . . a matter of diminishing returns. There would be no more supplies. Melek made the calculations with interior panic.

Perform.

Obey orders precisely.

Hope for favor and life.

It was all they had.

XIII

Duncan looked a sorry sight under any circumstances. Stripped naked and in daylight he was sadder still, scrubbing away at himself with handfuls of sand to take the blood and grime away. Niun worked at his own person, the two of them alone on the edge of camp where the slight rolling of the land gave them a measure of privacy and the wind blew clear. He rubbed dust into his mane and shook it until the dust was gone, scrubbed his skin until it stung and then quickly sought the warmth of clean robes, shivering in the wind.

Duncan managed the same for himself, although his hair-coated skin would not shed the sand so easily and the hair of his head was prone to retain the dust. Still he labored fastidiously at it, sitting somewhat sheltered from the wind, and his stress-thinned limbs shivered so that Niun took concern for him and held his robes between him and the treacheries of the breeze.

"Come, you are clean enough. Will you not make haste about it? My arms tire."

Duncan stood and shrugged into the robes, shivered convulsively, and fastened the inner robe with its cloth belt, the while Niun sat down again on the side of the slope to work his boots on.

Duncan coughed a little, smothered it. Niun looked up anxiously. Duncan ignored the matter and sat down again, began with a little oil and the blade of one *as-en*, to scrape away at the hair on his face. Niun regarded the process with furtive glances. It was a matter of meticulous care with Duncan, and a difference between them which Duncan sought assiduously to hide, which humans in general did, for Niun supposed that all had this tendency, and that all cared for it as Duncan did, not the hair of the body, but that of the face: a tsi'mri observance he continued as compatible with mri,

166

perhaps, or simply that the veil was the one portion of cloth-ing a kel'en could not maintain in the camp.

And Niun deliberately sought privacy for Duncan to at-tend to his person, so that the newcomers should not see the differences of his body. He was vaguely ashamed at this de-ception, although Duncan freely consented in it. He remained uncertain whether Duncan did so out of shame of his own structure, or out of some consideration for him, not to em-barrass him. Niun greatly suspected the latter . . . but asking Duncan why—that required delving into tsi'mri thoughts. It had been more comfortable to ignore the matter, and to provide Duncan that measure of privacy, the two of them.

Duncan lived, and that was enough at the moment. He was wan and thin and slow in his movements as an old man, but alive, and without the bleeding this bright morning. It was a good thing in a man, that he wake with a sudden concern for his appearance and his cleanliness, and an evidence of impa-tience with his own condition. It was a good thing.

This morning there seemed much of good in the world.

The dusei were out and away, lost somewhere in the haze of the amber morning . . . presumably hunting as they should be, and not out troubling the camps which lay over the horizons on all sides of them. The stranger-kel'ein had settled into camp, in a makeshift patchwork of three shades of canvas on ropes between sen-tent and Kel. There was a quiet there, sensible mri folk who were not going to provoke quarrels in stupidity, as sensibly silent and observing as folk were who knew they might be set to kill, and who could profit from understanding as much as possible and seeing clearly and without passion. Their own she'panei directed them to take orders within the camp; they did so, adapting to strangeness with the confidence that came of knowing their own tribes relied on them for eyes and ears . . . the Face-Turned-Outward of their she'panei. Even the ja'anom were unwontedly reasonable, for all Duncan's presence among them. It would not last; but it was for the moment, good.

In the camp children of the Kath played, laughing aloud and having the energy at last to skip and run. They had caught a snake this dawn, unfortunate creature which had strayed in seeking the camp's moisture. Nothing ventured into camp wily enough to escape the sharp-eyed children, who added it triumphantly to the common pot. They teased and played at pranks, amusing even the sober strangers.

And that laughter, reaching them, was a comfort to the heart more than all others.

"Why the face?" Niun asked in sudden recklessness.

Duncan looked up, wet a finger in his mouth, touched a bleeding spot on his chin. He seemed perplexed by the question, but quite unoffended.

"Why the face and not—" Niun made a gesture vaguely including his own body.

Duncan grinned, a shocking expression in his gaunt, half-tanned face, which was brown about the eyes and not elsewhere. More, he laughed silently. "It would take a long time. Should I?"

That was not the sober reaction Niun had expected. He found himself embarrassed, frowned and touched his brow. "Here is mri, sov-kela. The outside is a veil, like the other veil. You and I are alike enough."

Duncan went sober indeed, and seemed to understand him.

"My brother," Niun said, "pleases *himself* by this. For them—" He gestured widely toward the mingled camp and all the camps about.

Duncan shrugged. *"Should* I remove it all?"

"Gods," Niun muttered, "no."

And Duncan confounded him by an inward smile, a nod. "I hear you."

"My brother is perverse as a dus."

"And similarly coated."

Niun hissed, high exasperation, and found himself compelled to laugh because Duncan could so deftly lead him.

Human laughter; it was at time irreverent of most serious things; but that Duncan retained his sense of balance, that was a knowledge cheansing as a draft of wind.

"Gods, gods, I have missed you."

And that for some reason brought a touch of pain to Duncan's face, a shadow of a sorrow.

That question too he would have liked to ask, and for his peace and Duncan's . . . declined.

Duncan sat down and pulled on his boots, gave a deep breath when he had done and rose shakily, belted on his weapons and his Honors. Niun stood and resumed the visored headcloth and Duncan did likewise, until there was only the difference of the face and Duncan's lesser stature between them.

"You think—" Duncan said then, as if it were something

which had been biding speaking a long time. "You think these stranger-kel'ein would go back with us to the ship?"

"That is not for Kel to say."

"The she'pan said that she would consider. What is she considering?"

"The Sen deliberates." Niun felt exposed in the hedging, ashamed; there were times that Duncan could meet a stare with the look of a kath'en and the steadiness of a kel-Master. "Did I not teach you patience, without questions?"

"They have been deliberating the second day now."

"Sov-kela."

"Aye," Duncan answered him, glancing away. Niun made a bundle of the clothing they had shed, knotted it and rose again; he set his other hand on Duncan's shoulder, turning him back toward the main aisle of the camp, and Duncan for all his disquiet reached and took the cord of the bundle, carrying the burden with a courtesy automatic as one born to it. Niun regarded that, and felt the more uncomfortable himself.

"Do you doubt the she'pan?" Niun asked. "Do you think she would not do the best thing?"

"There are thoughts I cannot say in the hal'ari, that I am not good enough to say." They walked slowly, boots crunching on the wind-scoured sand beside their outward footprints, already wind-dimmed. "If you would hear—if you would remember human language for a small moment, and let me say in human terms—"

"Veil," Niun cut him off. "Do not breathe the wind. Manners do not apply to the sick."

Duncan did so, and was silent.

"You had years on the ship to talk to us," Niun said. "*You* are the speech you would make, and it is already well-made." He took a pass of the veil across his own mouth, for courtesy between them, not to make Duncan conspicuous, and mindfully shortened his long strides. "It is all said, Duncan."

The morning haze fell kindly about the tents, touching them all with the tranquility of the hour. Even the black fabric of kel-tent and the patchwork tent adjoining had a little of gold on their coarse surface; and gold stained the paler hue of that of the she'pan and of the others. The trampled center of the camp was alive with blue-robes, goings and comings of the children, women working by Kath in the morning light, cookfires burning. But of gold there was none; and of black-robed figures but one, and that one vanished into the main kel-tent as they approached; others came out then, jamming the doorway, and sudden apprehension gathered at Niun's belly, the morning dimmed . . . he opened his mouth to warn Duncan and did not. Duncan was wise on his own, and some things were to evil to suspect aloud.

They walked as close to the doorway as they might with the Kel blocking their way. Hlil was there in the center of matters, unveiled; some were and others were not.

"The she'pan has called half-council," Hlil said. "Ours and theirs together."

It had come, then. Niun dismissed his worse suspicions with a profound shame. "Aye," he told Hlil and started away with him at once. But a few steps away he delayed, still with that vile feeling crawling at his belly. He looked back and caught Duncan's eye, who stared after him.

"The dusei," he said to Duncan. "It concerns me . . . where they are. You might call them."

If you need them, he meant. He thought that Duncan took his meaning; that sort of glance went between them, and there was a touch of apprehension in Duncan's eyes, but no panic.

He turned then and went with Hlil.

Kel'ein settled about the doorway, showing no disposition to enter the tent . . . ja'anom, but not all ja'anom: kel'ein of the other Kels hovered about the edges, and more and more arrived, strolling up casually. The door was blocked, inconvenient to reach, and it was dark inside, lacking witnesses. Duncan settled on the sand in their midst, his back to the tent, the black bulk of which served to shelter him and them from the slight wind. He kept his head bowed, doing as Niun had suggested, thinking on the dusei, but when time passed in the quiet and extraneous conversation of those near him, he dismissed his more vivid fears and glanced furtively at the ja'anom, wondering if he understood anything at all of what game they were playing. One was old Peras, a quiet one and civil to him; he could not think evil of him. There was Taz . . . Taz's unwontedly expressionless face gave him no comfort; he had never seen the boy but that he was alive and alight to every need about him, and he was withdrawn now, watching. And Ras . . . Ras and Niun did not agree: he had sensed this thoroughly, even without the dusei. She came now and settled slightly behind him, so that she could see him and not otherwise.

Silence fell in the group. Most withdrew inside, strangers

as well as ja'anom, not into their proper tent; and that was
unwonted. Others stayed sitting. Duncan glanced down rather
than appear to question this movement, reckoning silence the
best course. Niun needed no trouble of his making; trouble
there was already, and he reckoned that a portion of it had
maneuvered to take him in. He knew names more than Peras
and Taz and Ras, but few more; there were ja'anom whose
names and reasons he ought to know, and did not, so short a
time he had been among them before. If they had helped him
live now, it was out of some sense of honor, or something
that Niun had the power to make them do; not for love: he
had no illusions of that.

The kel'en on his right touched his sleeve.

"Tsi'mri," that one said, but as if it were fact, not a calculated insult, "you say nothing."

He looked up perforce, met the unveiled face of that man
and of others, young and old, male and female. None of
them showed expression. All those left had the kel-scars, the
seta'al, time-faded on the faces of some, new and bright on
others. "Perhaps there are some who do not wish me well.
What do you wish, kel'ein?"

Silent glances went from one to the other, and Duncan followed these exchanges with anxiety he did not allow to his
face.

"You are wise," said a kel'e'en, "always to keep to someone's shadow."

Duncan felt the wind, felt his back naked without Niun,
and bowed his head to them, which was all his recourse.

"We see what is toward," another said. "Best you sit here."

He cast a look toward the aisle, toward the she'pan's tent,
into which Niun had vanished, and all that he could see was
a wall of stranger-kel'ein, listening silently on the fringes. Almost he rose to walk away from them all, to go settle at the
she'pan's door in safety, but a grip on his sleeve advised him
otherwise before he could make the move. He looked back at
them. An old kel'e'en touched the scars on her face, mark of
a skill he lacked. "You are tsi'seta. Who would challenge you
but another unscarred? And there are none such here."

"What is happening?" Duncan demanded of them, knowing that they meant something by this, and not knowing even
who ranked highest in this complex of skill and birth and seniority of mingled tribes. He scanned from face to face, lost
and betraying it . . . settled last on old Peras, whose lean,
seamed face indicated at least reverence owed, and whose

eyes perhaps showed something of sympathy. "What is hap-
pning? The Council . . . is that it?"

"Tsi'mri kel'en, there is division in the camp. Yonder stand
other tribes; ours and others come and go. They ask us questions. And while you sit here with us in this circle—there is
no one free to make a mistake."

That disparaged him; it was also the kind of insult any
without rank in the Kel had to accept as a matter of course.

"Sir," he murmured humbly, which was always the right
answer to a warrior who had won the *seta'al,* from one who
had not.

"Kel'en," Peras responded, which was more courtesy than
an elder needed use.

"He speaks well," said one of the out-tribesmen, settling
near. "It is remarkable."

Others behind him nodded, and one laughed a breath.
"This is a wonder," that one said, "to sit and talk with a
tsi'mri."

The word, Duncan reflected placidly, studying his hands in
his lap, also applied to the dusei.

"He is mannered," another said.

The old kel'e'en reached and touched at his sleeve. "Veil,
kel'en. The air does you harm; there is courtesy and there is
stupidity."

He inclined his head in thanks and did so, headcloth and
twice-lapped veil.

And now and again in the silence which followed, he
glanced in the direction of the she'pan's tent, for one by one
the standing kel'eun settled; he was anxious, for himself and
for what manner of maneuvering might have encompassed
Niun as well and for what passed in Council among those
who had power . . . all that he had tried to do, all that he
had paid his life for, and now he could not even merit to sit
at the door to hear judgment passed on his offering to them.
He sat, in their long silence, and fretted, aware finally of another presence responding to his distress.

It came padding across the sand toward them, his dus, anxious and hasty. He felt it; and it sensed hostility, and its
presence loomed dark and ominous.

He glanced about him with a gesture of appeal, to ja'anom
and to the others. "Do not hate," he wished them.

That was like asking the wind to stop; but heads nodded
after a moment. The dus came, worked quietly among them,
wended its stubborn way to his back, dislodging Ras a little

space. He cherished that warmth against him where Ras had been. And in the long silence that followed that shifting about, he drew from his belt the weighted cords, the *ka'islai*, and began to knot them in the star-mandala.

It was the *islan* of Pattern, which imposed order on confusion. It was the most complex he knew, which in his learning fingers would take long to complete.

He was, after a dogged fashion, committing an insolence. He was better in the *islai* than some who had the kel-scars; he had had long practice, on the ship, in idleness. He meant to defy them, for all it was unwise. He did not even look up . . . feeling their eyes on him, who aped their ways; felt a grating at his nerves, the shifting of his dus. Ras had her hand on it, which few dared.

He kept his mind to his pattern, refusing to be distracted even by that.

"Kel'en," said Peras.

"Ai?"

"Council deliberations can be quite tedious. Do you play *shon'ai?*"

His heart began to beat rapidly. The Game of the People was one thing played among friends; he thought were Niun at hand to hear that he would be on his feet in outrage. He carefully stripped out the complex knots and looped the *ka'islai* again to his belt. "I am mri," he said softly, "for all you protest it. Yes, I play the Game."

There were soft hisses, reaction to his almost-insolence. Old Peras took from his belt the *as-ei*, the palm-blades.

"I will play partner to kel Duncan," Peras said.

In the Game, Niun had taught him, one's life relied on seating. When strong player sat opposite weak or when grudges and alliances seated themselves out of balance in the circle, someone could die. There was only the partnering of the players at one's elbows to counsel an enemy across the circle not to throw foul. Strong beside weak was a protection, if weak were wise where he sent his own casts.

He had learned paired, only the Game of Two, patternless save for the pattern of the throws themselves, high and low.

They began to form a circle of six, with the others to witness. Duncan took comfort, for it was gentle Dias, Peras's truemate, who took the place opposing him in the circle, and those who flanked her were young, lesser in skill than some. But then kel Ras bent down and touched the sleeve of Dias. Some words passed in low voices and short dispute, and Ras, of the second rank of the Kel, replaced kel Dias of the fourth, facing him and Peras.

And suddenly Duncan minded himself what Niun had always told him of death by stupidity.

They would kill him if they wished. He suddenly realized that he did not know the limits of his skill. He had played only Niun, and Niun was his friend.

Ras . . . was no one's. At Duncan's left there was another substitution, an old kel'en, on whom the scars were well-weathered.

The dus drew back a little, rested head on paws, puffed slightly and followed all this insanity with darting moves of its eyes.

The Game; it was a means of passing time, as Peras had said. An amusement.

But the Kel amused themselves with blades, and amusements were sometimes—even unintended—to the death.

They gave their names, those Duncan did not know well; one did not play with strangers save in challenge. Duncan dropped his veil, for it was no friendly act to play veiled. There was hazard enough without that.

Kel Peras began, being eldest . . . threw to Ras. Hands struck thighs, the rhythm of the Game; and on the name-beat of the unspoken rhyme, the blades spun across the circle again.

They played about him, from man to man and woman to man and youth to youth, back and forth, weaving patterns which became established, excluding him, a Game of Five, oddly seated. Mri fingers, slim and golden and marginally quicker than human, snatched spinning steel from the air and hurled it on at the next name-beat.

At no time did he relax, knowing that the rhythm could increase in tempo and that some impulse might send the blades spinning his way, from the youths, from Ras, any of those three.

Suddenly he had warning, a flicker of the membrane as Ras stared at him. Next time: he nodded, almost unnerved by her warning, whether courtesy or reflex.

The blades spun to her, shining in the sun, and she snatched them, waited the beat and hurled them at the steady time of the Game, no deception or change of pace.

He made the catch, hurled them left of her in his time, to a young kel'en. Now a new lacery began, which wove itself star-patterned like the *islan,* the mandala of the Game, the

Game of Six, as each Game was different by every factor in it.

The pattern varied, and beside him kel Peras laughed, catching the treachery of Ras: the blades, missed, might have killed; Ras' eyes danced with amber merriment, and the blades came back to her, cunningly thrown, low-and-high. She cast them again to Peras, left-slant; he threw to her, again left; back to elder Da'on, right; and he threw to young Eran and he to young Sethan.

Tempo altered, making again a safer rhythm, the moment's sport among Masters tamed again, beating slower for lesser players.

It came back, from Ras to himself; he caught, and threw to the youngest, Sethan, tacit recognition of his status.

It returned, evenly paced; he cast back; it went to Da'on on his left, to Ras, to Peras—

And stopped, Peras signaling halt. The rhythm of the hands ceased. Duncan drew a great breath, suddenly coughed from the chill air and realized that that reflex a moment ago might have killed him.

"Veil," Da'on advised him. He did so, holding the cloth to his mouth and nose until the chill left his lungs. The dus edged up to him, settled against his back, offering him its warmth.

"An unscarred," said Da'on, "should never play the Six."

"No, kel'en," he agreed. "But when a scarred asks, an unscarred obeys."

Breaths hissed softly between teeth. Heads nodded.

"You play the Game," Peras said, "in all senses. That is well, human kel'en."

He leaned against the dus, caressed its neck, for his heart was still pounding and the dus shivered in reaction.

The tent flap stirred. Another kel'en came out and sat down on the sand, out of the wind. He looked up and two more followed, and four and three, not all of their own Kel. The black assembly widened, veils dropped, so that he felt he should take his own down, and did so, trying to breathe carefully.

He must not be afraid. The dus would catch it up and cast it to them. He must not be angry. The dus would rouse and they would sense that too. The mri of Kutath could not veil their emotions, not generally. He received a touch of resentment, and some rare things warmer, pure curiosity. It was not attack, not yet. He soothed the dus with his touch, himself master of it and not the other way about, making it feel what he wished it to feel, quiet, quiet.

Shon'ai, the mri of Kesrith said: the Game-throw is made.

No calling it back, no mending it now.

Shon'ai: it is cast!

Throw your life, kel'en; and deserve to live, for joy of the Game.

They had been there all along, and more came now, until all in the kel-tents must be there, and he was the center of it.

"Tell us," said Peras, "kel'en-who-has-shared-in-Kath, make us all to understand this thing of ships and enemies."

He cast an anguished glance toward the she'pan's tent, hoping against hope to see Nium and the others, some indication even that the Council might be near an end, that he might delay. It was a vain hope.

"Shall an unscarred of this Kel know more," asked Peras, "than the seniors of it, who sit in Council? Things are out of balance here, young kel'en of the ja'anom. That is one disease here. Remedy it."

"I am from the other side of a Dark," he protested, "and I am forbidden to remember."

"So is this brother I have gained for my brother," said Ras in a harsh voice, "who calls you brother to him. We are by that . . . *kin*, are we not? Answer. We kel'ein, are we not the Face that Looks Outward? Our eyes are used to the Dark. And the trouble has come here, to us, has it not, tsi'mri brother? Has the she'pan silenced you on that matter—or is it for your own sake you keep your secrets, ai? What arrangement did you and my brother-by-death have, that he knew where to find you?"

A muscle jerked in his face. He fought for control. "Hlil arranged this."

"Hlil would not," she said. "I. My kindred. *I* ask."

He gazed at her, kel'e'en of the second rank; daithe, kin of the last kel'anth and blood-tied to no knowing how many kindreds. A chill settled into him.

"I hear you," he said, understanding. He bowed his head then, soothing the restive dus with the touch of his fingers . . . felt her touch against the other side of it, so that the animal shivered.

It was a mutual trap, that contact. There were no lies possible, no half-truths. He laid his hand firmly against the beast.

And yielded, point by point.

XIV

"There have been arguments," the she'pan conceded, facing the Council. Niun sat nearest her, cross-legged on the mats, no Husband, but the she'pan's own kel'en, and kel'anth at once, doubly owning that place of honor. The Husbands of the ja'anom sat ranged nearest, and the several highest of the five tribes settled by them, a black mass. The ja'anom kath'anth was there, Anthil; and the whole ja'anom Sen, in a golden mass, beneath the lamps which they used in Council even in daytime. Sen'anth Sathas was foremost of them, but there were sen'ein of the five stranger-tribes there too, who had come in yestereve with the kel'ein.

"There have been strong dissensions," Melein continued, "within the ja'anom . . . for the losses we have suffered, for the choices we face. But Sen has agreed in my choices. Is it not so, sen'anth?"

"So," Sathas echoed, "Sen has consented."

"Not easy, to come home. The pan'en which is holy to us . . . what can it mean to you? A curiosity, full of strange names and things which never happened to you? And the holy relics of your wanderings on Kutath . . . how shall my kel'anth and I understand them? We struggle to do so, you with us and we with you. We of the Voyagers, we who went out . . . we want a place to stand; and you who stayed to guard Kutath so many millennia ago—perhaps you look about you and hate us, that we were voyaged out at all. Is that not part of it? Is that not a little part, that you blame us two, that of all Kutath sacrificed . . . we are all that has come home, all who will ever come home?" Her eyes moved to the Kel, traveled down to Niun. "Or is it perhaps for what we brought home with us, for what we call one of us?"

Niun glanced down. "Perhaps. It is many things, she'pan, but both may be so."

"And the ja'anom Kath?"

177

"Kath," said Anthil's soft voice, "blames no one. We only mourn the children, she'pan; those lost and those to come."

"And the songs you have taught those children over the ages . . . look for what, kath'anth? For the returning of those who went out when the world was younger and water flowed?"

"Some songs—hoped for that."

"When our ancestors were one," Melein said, "not alone the tribes, but yourselves and my ancestors . . . that was a great age of the world; and there had been many before. The cities were standing, already old, built on the ruins of others, and our ancestors walked on the dust of a thousand thousand civilizations and forgotten races. The four races who walked the world at the beginning of that age dwindled to two, and them you know. After so long there was building again: elee cities were standing, already old, built on the ruins of others, green of an old, old plant that the sands had long buried . . . but its roots were deep and it stood in the winds again. It was the last of everything that nourished it; it took from all else, so that it was the last greening . . . mri saw this: and we who had loved the land . . . knew. We built . . . the great edunei; and the great machines of the elee we appropriated to our own purposes.

"We and the elee," Melein's voice continued, low and vibrant. "We knew, and they wanted only what had always been. *Shon'ai!* we cast ourselves—to chance and the great Dark. *'Go out,'* we advised the elee, in the world's bright hour. *'We have risen on all the world's strength; now we go out, shon'ai! now . . . for the world's wind is at our backs, and we feel it.'*

"*'Go then,'* said the elee, for all they hated such an idea and pleased themselves to turn their faces away. We went and we brought greater and greater things, bringing them comfort, so that for an age the elee were very content, seeing the chance of more and more comfort and long life. We went further: we took stars for the elee, in slow years of voyaging, and brought knowledge.

"But the elee began to be afraid. They feared the Dark and hated anything strange. They wanted only Kutath, and to live with their comforts and their cities and to use up the wealth we could bring. They cared only for that. They let the stars go.

"And they let us go. They put us increasingly out of their

thoughts. Had they been able, they would have sealed us up on this world.

"Some of us . . . stayed; you held this world for mri; you entered on a holy trust, to save the standing-place from which we launched, to save the precious things and to honor the service that we served.

"Hard for us . . . to keep our ways, in our slow voyaging, always out of touch with the visible, the physical Kutath. We had to keep it in our hearts, and yet to protect the knowledge of it: only she'panei and Sen of the voyagers were permitted to remember; Kath and Kel knew only the ships . . . or between the Darks . . . the hundred twenty-five homeworlds-of-convenience. Aye," she said when Niun looked up at her in stark bewilderment. "They were *ours. Ours,* our homes, Niun.

"And hard for you who stayed behind," she said, "—to live with the visible, among the monuments, with Kutath a reality about you—and to keep contact with the invisible, with the dream.

"When we must, we moved on, shedding each world's taint, renewing ourselves like something born always new, young again and strong: we kept nothing of the Betweens. We boarded our ships and Kutath was born anew aboard them, the old language, the ways, the ancient knowledge during generations of voyage.

"When calamity fell here, you had no means to veil what resulted: the sights—were before you. You lived in the visible and looked to the promise . . . so long, so very long.

"To go on believing . . . and clinging to old ways . . . when elee mocked them; to teach the young the promise . . . which they might never see, while the seas sank further, and the world had no more strength for a new beginning, and the elee interest only in the moment. To remember skills which had passed beyond use; to sing the old chants; to look for hope, when all the sights about you counseled that the world was ending, and that there was no sane hope that this year or the next thousand years would bring what millennia before did not.

"Hardest, surely, when ships did come . . . when after centuries of waiting . . . ships came down on you—not ours—and then the elee wanted protection; then they surely wanted what they had cast from them. The world was laid waste and mri and elee were slaughtered, the land ruined so that even the enemy fled it. Enemy . . . it was the collapse of the empire which we had made; it was the last tremor of a dying power, in which the elee had refused to involve themselves, which had gone its own way; and that power died and their worlds with them perhaps. At least they did not come again.

"After that, what was there left, but to live narrowly, to find elee fighting among themselves for water and for less substantial things? Some mri took hire in these wars; some left the promise and involved themselves in the immediate and the visible. But the she'pan Gar'ai s'Hana, may her name live to all castes so long as there are mri to sing it—led a retreat from the cities and the wars, into the open land. I know her," Melein added, and there seemed not a breath in Council, the while tears flowed openly down her face, across the kel-scars. "I know such a she'pan, to do the unreasonable, and to lead others where she would fear to send even one. She foresaw, perhaps, the death of the children and the elders, of all the vulnerable ones; and for what? For what hope? To exist, and wait, singing the old songs, while the mountains wore away.

"And we Voyagers . . .

"We served—other services. Darks intervened. To my sorrow, the passing of the she'panate of the Voyagers to me was in calamity, the massacre of us all on a world named Kesrith. Some things my she'pan had no time to teach me. Most of all—the reason *why,* the reason why we went out at all, and why after so many, many ages . . . we never returned. The reason why at least . . . the she'pan who prepared me for the she'panate . . . had decided it was time to turn the People homeward."

There was disturbance in the Kel. Niun glanced that way with a forbidding frown and unfocused his eyes and stared through them, his heart leaden within him, the comfirmation of doubts he had held from the beginning.

"Is it this," Melein pursued, "for which we were met with doubt? That dreams are better than what we can touch? That Niun and I are the too-mortal flesh of a great hope? That the dream brought you destruction, and the death of friends and children, and tsi'mri, as it was in the world's worst hour?

"Why did mv she'pan refuse the offer the tsi'mri of our last service made, of a green and living world, and choose instead Kesrith, which was desolation? The Forge of the People, she named it, and gave the Sen no other answer. Why did she speak even before the danger came on us . . . of leaving the service that we served, which was to regul and against humans; and why was her mind set toward this homecoming?

"It might have been the diminishing of our numbers: we were very few when the regul decided to betray us and kill us, in the knowledge that they could no longer control us.

"It might have been that my she'pan was mad; there were some who believed so, even among her children.

"And do you think that I was not afraid, when I took up the robes, when I knew that I was charged to come home, and that I had not been told the last secret, the great *why* of all the she'panei before me. I tell you that I was greatly afraid.

"I gained the pan'en for my guide; and in the beginning I believed blindly, reading the record it holds, that guided our ship . . . the way that the People had passed, viewing world after world which our ancestors had known, and thinking them beautiful."

"She'pan," Niun objected, a breath, a pain which wrung at him.

"But they were all dead." Her voice faltered and steadied. "Dead worlds, every one. And do you think then that I was not afraid?

"I walked this world. I found the place, the very city from which most of my ancestors came . . . for we kept our chants and our lineages. And after all that time, I have found my own: the ja'anom are my far, far kindred, An-ehon's children; as are you all, even ka'anomin of Zohain . . . blood-kin to me. I spoke with the city; and with the Sen of the ja'anom, and with the sen'ein who have come from other tribes . . . and I know; I know the nature of the promise, and most of all what turned us homeward . . . in *ships, in ships*, my distant children, which cross the great Darks in an eye's blinking.

"Enemies have followed us. They have destroyed our ship and our city, but to destroy us, no, the gods forbid and the Mystery forbids. Tsi'mri do as they will. We—Niun and I— we have *done* what we set out to do. The dream is true. We have it in our hands. Tsi'mri are here, within reach of our hands, and nothing in a hundred thousand years . . . has promised such as we bring you."

It was back, that fierceness of her first night among the ja'anom; it glittered in the eyes of the Kel, ja'anom and stranger alike; even in the eyes of the Sen, and shone in the mild face of the kath'anth. Of this the shameful flight had cheated them, driving them hunted across their own land; of this they had been frustrated, hiding and cowering from tsi'mri weapons, not alone in these days but in earlier days and on other worlds, dying helpless and uncomprehending of purpose. They were suddenly Melein's, hers, clenched in her fist.

This hope . . . *within reach,* Melein had said.

Duncan.

A great cold washed over Niun, realization why Melein had been willing to cast even himself from her hand in the chance of finding Duncan, why she had remained silent while the tribe fell apart in quarrel, and had no answer—until she could find Duncan again, knowing full well where he had gone, as she had known about the messages to humans which Duncan had tried to send, which the regul had destroyed.

O my brother, he mourned, but grief stayed from his face, the habit of the Kel, that there was no link between heart and countenance, not before the adversary.

"Kel'anth," said kel Seras of the Husbands, "say to the she'pan that she isour Mother and that the ja'anom Kel is with her, heart and hand."

"And that we hear," said the kel'anth Rhian, "a message we are anxious to bear to our she'panei."

"Aye," muttered other kel'anthein.

This should have given him the most profound, the uttermost joy. It did not. He looked up into Melein's eyes, glad that there was no dus by them, to catch up the she'pan's inexorable and calculating coldness and hurl it into him, keener than any blade. "You hear," he echoed hoarsely. "And in all matters . . . I am the she'pan's Hand."

"Kel'anth," she said, "the message which came to us from tsi'mri, that we should come and speak with them . . . tell me, kel'anth of the ja'anom, what will tsi'mri do if we should fail that rendezvous they ask? Will they attack?"

"Am I tsi'mri, to answer what they will do?"

"Your knowledge of them is best of all but Duncan's. What will they do if their expectations are thwarted? What would kel Duncan have done, when he was human?"

He glanced down, lest the membrane betray his disturbance. "I would expect of a human . . . first, distress; puzzlement that things did not agree with his hopes; then anger. But—humans are more likely to come probing at us than to launch devastating attack, unless cornered. Regul . . . regul are another species; and they are up there too; and that is different. Duncan believes humans are restraining them—but humans reckon patience from moment to moment, and a day is soon to them. That is what I dread, that their patience is too short even to comprehend how slowly a man must walk in this land. They live with machines, and expect everything to come quickly."

"And once challenge has been made?"

Niun sat still, eyes unfocused, seeing a place he was forbidden to recall, fire and night, ships lacing back and forth above ruin. "Humans fight in masses; so do regul, no single combat. The People lost thousands before we learned this fact and the thinking behind it. *But*—" He struck his palm upon the floor, looked suddenly at Kel and Sen. "But they make other replies. Duncan is one. When it was all over, when regul had effectively finished us and humans had fought us to our ruin . . . Duncan came alone, as none of them had ever come alone to our challenges; and handed us himself, and struggled for us, gave us the ship in which we came here. Ask him why. He has no idea that he can express. Instinct? A response of his kind? He did not know the answer when he was human. Now he is mri. Perhaps he remembers enough that Council might call him, ask him why, or how humans think. Ask *him*."

"No," Melein said softly. "No. Can mri give a tsi'mri kind of answer? We are ourselves, kel'anth. Do not look so deeply into the Dark that you lose your balance."

He caught his breath, looked up at her, his heart beating against his ribs.

The dus stirred. Duncan caught up something, vast sorrow, and stopped in mid-word, looked about at the Kel and shivered in a sudden breeze.

Others gathered it up without understanding it. Duncan looked toward the door of the she'pan's tent, knowing direction, and a great fear bore down upon him.

"Kel'en," said Peras, and Peras in leaning forward touched the dus. The spilling of emotions touched him too, and the veteran's eyes nictitated, amazed and chagrinned.

"What is wrong?" asked old Da'on. "Peras?"

The feeling faded, like something passing out of focus. It was hard to imagine that it had been there. Duncan stroked the velvet fur with both his hands, bowed against it, lifted his face again.

"The tsi'mri called *regul*," kel Ras prompted him.

"Dead," Duncan said hoarsely. "I killed her. She stirred her younglings to attack, and I killed her and gave the matter over to humans. Only—" He found himself saying more than he wanted to and ceased, but the dus betrayed him, gathering up feelings and weaving them together, himself and his hearers, himself and Ras who sat against the beast. A dread was on him and they shared it, perhaps without knowing why.

"O my brothers." It was the idiom of the hal'ari, and he meant it in that moment. "The Dark is very wide out there, and all about this world, there is no life, none at all. They have seen it. And they are afraid."

"We move on," said Melein, "as we have been moving. I will say no more of it; I do not bind myself with words; I do as the Now asks. Tell your she'panei we move with the dawn. A double hand of Kel'ein will hunt outward from our column to feed us. If any she'pan will draw back and not lend to me, I do not permit: I challenge. If any will challenge me, well, there is honor in that, and if she will take up my robes and stand where I stand, that is well. But I do not believe the gods will permit me to fall; I shall absorb that tribe and take them for my children. The gods have not preserved me through so much to fall in tribal rivalry. If any she'pan will lend me her children in my need, I shall write her in the Holy's last table, and in the beginning of the new; and the mri who stood with me, living and dead, will mark a new beginning in the songs of their line. All things begin and end from this coming day. When I have done what I will, I shall give their children back to them with gratitude and Honors: the law prevents us of the White from standing face to face . . . but apart, we are each a point strength on Kutath's wide face. I am she'pan'anth, she'pan-senior of the Voyagers . . . she'pan'anth of all mri; and I have need. Say that to them. Is there question?"

Silence hung in the air, trembling with force.

"Go," she said, a whisper like a sword's slash. "And come back to me."

It was a moment before bodies stirred, before any had the temerity to move . . . and in a thick silence the Kel stood, the kath'anth withdrawing first in the precedence of leaving. Kel'ein waited. Niun moved, realizing it was on him, and walked out into the forechamber of the tent where the Shrine was, paid shaken homage to the Holy, wishing to gather up the threads of all that had been cast him, that drank up reason and made madmen of them all.

But others swarmed about him, a dark and fearsome presence, the blackness of Kel, his own and others', crowding the Shrine and the door out of which Sen must come. It was chaos, and he stifled in it, moved for the door and daylight, to disperse them by his leaving, but a hand caught his arm, familiarity none of them ventured with him.

"Kel'anth," said Hlil.

He resisted, but Hlil was determined. "Kel'ein?" he asked, without moving or looking particularly at any of them. "Kel'anthein?"

The hand tightened with force. "Aye," Hlil said. "You never give us your face, even when the veil is down. You have your secrets. But what the she'pan has finally said, kel'anth, we have waited to hear, and others have. She has the Seeing, is it not so?"

"That may be so," Niun said hoarsely. "I have sometimes thought so."

"You are kin to her."

"Was."

"*They* are here, other kel'anthein, other tribes; you are kel'anth to us, and we know your manner. You go out of the fingers like sand, Niun: s'Intel; you have no face, even to us, as the wind has none. We have watched you, silent with the strangers when you ought to speak, brooding over that tsi'mri, apart. We understand the she'pan. Perhaps we even understand you . . . but how can they? You are her Hand. And what she gains, you bid fair to cast away."

"That may be," he said, finding breath difficult. He no more looked at them than before. "If that is so, then I deserve blame for it."

"What *is* in you, kel'anth?"

"Let go of me, Hlil."

"Once, reach out your hand and take up this Kel. Or what will they go back and say? That the kel'anth preferred other company?"

He understood the gist of it then, set his face and glared at Hlil. "Ah. My orthodoxy. That I defended kel Duncan. That is at issue."

"Answer."

"I was taught kel-law; we kept it strictly in my House. I cannot read or write and I never knew the Mysteries. Two thousand years bounded all I knew. But my House fell. My

Kel died. I have carried the pan'en of the Voyagers in my own hands and crossed in my life all the Darks that ever were. Shall I shed this on you all? One kel'en was with me throughout; one kel'en knows the law that I knew and the songs as my Kel sang them, and saw what I have seen. I am arrogant, yes. I have all the faults you think I have. And you pick a poor time to quarrel with me, Hlil, kel-second."

He would have torn away; Hlil's hand clenched tighter still. "I hear you," Hlil said. "Long since, I have heard you. Now someone else does."

Heat crept to his face, resentment toward Hlil, toward witnesses of this humiliation. Then he thought: *before my own Kel it would not shame me to say.* And secondly: *my own Kel.* This was.

They were.

"Forgive me," he said. He let the restraint from his face, even to Rhian of the hao'nath, and the others, and it was worse to him than stripping naked. "Forgive me for offense." He recited apology docilely, like a child . . . knew that there would be murmuring when they were out of hearing. That too was just. He pressed Hlil's shoulder, felt the hand drop from his arm, turned from that quieted company to the outside, his eyes nictitating from the sudden sunlight. They cleared, and he saw the gathering by the tent of the Kel, the whole mass of them there, shoulder to shoulder.

His heart constricted.

"Duncan," he breathed aloud, and hastened, strode across the sand with strides which left the others who had followed him, met the mass of kel'ein about the tent and parted them, his and theirs, thrust his way ungently through their midst, foreseeing everything in shambles, bloodfeud, all ties unraveled.

And stopped, seeing most seated about the center, the whole mingled Kel, and Duncan in the midst of all, sitting with Ras against his dus's broad shoulder and talking peaceably to all of them.

He shut his eyes an instant and caught what the beast held, that was the essence of Duncan, a quiet thing, and strong, with the stubbornness of the dusei themselves.

And love, and profound desire for those about him.

Duncan felt his presence and looked up, rose anxiously and stood there staring at him, casting question, question, question like the beating of a panicked heart.

Niun came to him, kel'ein moving aside to give place to him and the kel'ein who came after him.

"Sov-kela," Niun said, catching him by the arm and drawing him aside from those centermost. "I was worried for you and I find you entertaining the whole Kel."

"Is it all right?" Duncan asked him. "Did it go all right?"

The question stopped him cold. What Duncan asked and what they had arrived at in Council were two different matters. The dus came between, forcing its way. Niun recoiled in his thoughts, blank to it, quickly enough, he hoped. Then the second dus made its appearance, unfelt until it came within sight around the tent corner. And all about them were listening. He set his hand on Duncan's shoulder. "Get in out of the wind, sov-kela."

Duncan went, unquestioning. Niun looked about at the others, the faces that expected answer of him, wondering the same things. "Ask of your own," he said. "We move in the morning. It would be presumption of me to wish that you will all be with us. But I do. And for my own Kel . . . give me a very little time—I ask this."

There was a murmuring. He walked through them, and into the tent, and no one followed, only the dusei. There was no one inside, but only Duncan, in the dim light of the wind vents overhead.

"I should not have asked you in public," Duncan said.

"Do not fret for it. It was all right."

"I know," said Duncan in that same faint voice, "that something is wrong. Something went wrong. But not with them and you. Am I mistaken?"

O gods, Niun thought *how much did you feel?* The dusei were there; Duncan had a talent with them . . . let them have too much, received back more than mri had ever gotten. *His nature,* he thought, *that he reserves nothing.*

"Where is your service?" he asked of Duncan.

"With the she'pan."

"And if we fight?"

"*You cannot fight!*" Duncan lowered his voice in midbreath at Niun's warning, made a gesture of helpless appeal. "You know the odds; you know, if they do not. You have no hope at all. Do you want another Kesrith?"

"If we fight—are you mri?"

"Yes," Duncan said after a moment.

"You could not be mistaken."

"No."

Niun opened his arms, embraced him, set him back at arm's-length, staring into his anguished eyes. "Sov-kela—if you are wrong, we will break your heart."

"What did they decide?"

"It was always decided. A mri way. Do you hear me? The she'pan has already determined what way she will lead; and perhaps she will use what you have given her . . . but not— not as you gave it."

"I hear you." The dusei crowded near, moaning, shied off again. Duncan caught a breath and made a gesture as he would when he was without a word, let the breath go and the gesture fall, helpless. His dus came to him and he caressed its thick neck as if that were the most absorbing task in the world. "You choose your own way," he said finally. "If I have interfered, it was because I hoped there was a way the mri could survive and keep their own way. If I was wrong, it was tsi'mri taint, perhaps, a fondness for survival."

"No. You do not understand. I am not asking whether you can *die* with us. I am talking about the she'pan's order. Your honor . . . is it mri?"

Duncan stared at him, his face stark in the dim light, and for a moment frightened. The fear passed. "I warned them. I told them."

"If they are as you once were . . . can they have believed a plain warning?"

"Some likely not. But I gave it, all the same."

There was a stirring next the walls, the soft murmur of voices, diminishing; the stranger-kel'ein were departing the patchwork tent. Niun walked to the outside doorway, looked on the ja'anom who waited, solemn and quiet, Hlil foremost among them. He beckoned, and they came, settling into council in absolute quiet. Duncan would have sought last rank, but Niun signed to him and cleared a place near him, not by rank, but in a place where those concerned in council business might be set out of their order.

"Is there any matter," he asked, "that passed out there . . . that was not resolved?"

No one spoke. But after a moment there was a stir from the second rank, and heads turned as Ras stood up. She excused herself through first rank and came to center, and in disquiet Niun stood up, and Duncan. Ras came to Duncan and embraced him, and after that to Niun, as one would with and unscarred on his first day in Kel. "I swore to be first," she said.

Others came, Peras and Desai and Hlil and Merin; Dias and Seras and all of them from first rank to last, first Duncan and then himself, in strange and quiet courtesy; to the first he was numb, and toward the last, beginning to comprehend it not as irony, but as something given from the heart. They all settled in their places, even Duncan, and the dusei by him; and he was left staring at them with heat risen to his face and a dazed lack of grace.

After a moment he sat down, hands in lap, stared at them for some moments more before he could recover his wits or reason the tautness from his throat.

"The matter before council," he managed finally in a voice which sounded distant in his own ears. "You asked to know it."

XV

No life existed here either. Boaz stared at the city from wind-sore eyes—the damaged streets, the sand-choked alleys, and hope began to ebb. Her heart pounded in her ears with the steady strain; joints ached as from long fever, and popped with sharp little pains when the sand made the going hard. The boys wanted to carry the necessary pack; she refused that stubbornly, for they had their own. Her breath rasped in her throat and came too short through the hissing mask: if she could have shed anything, irrationally, it would be that rattling tank at her shoulder, and the mask that seemed more restraint on breathing than aid, but it was life. She turned the valve from time to time, shot a little oxygen in; it made her light-headed and her throat hurt. She blamed that and not the air and the cold.

There were at least no dead; they were spared that, at least. There was no sign that mri had visited her since the seas fled. But there had been fire from this place: regul and human fire had pinpointed to areas which had fired, finding their targets by that means. Something was alive here, but not—she began to be sure—not flesh and blood. Not the mri they had needed to find.

Galey stopped ahead of her, slung his pack off and sat down on a fallen stone, arms slack between his knees; rest stop: Boaz was glad of it, and sat down, Kadarin next to her. They were three; by Galey's decision, since Lane's death—they sat themselves on strict schedule, and left Shibo with the ship, to monitor com . . . and, Boaz suspected, to get word back if they met trouble. They were out of room for recklessness. Shibo was the other pilot . . . capable of leaving them. Had those orders in certain contingencies, she suspected. Galey had not said. It was, perhaps, salve for a soldier's conscience—that truth might get back if they did not.

"Got to be close to the central square," Galey said. "Or my direction's off."

She nodded. Galey and Kadarin looked terrible, faces lined with Kutath's cruel dryness, red-marked with the masks . . . cracked lips, eyes red like sick animals'. Nails broke to the quick and skin at joints galled and cracked and crusted. Mri robes made sense, she reckoned: no way she could have persuaded the military, but mri who wore loose robes and exposed scarcely their eyes to this torment . . . had more sense than they. She would have given much for the thickness of those coarse robes between her and the wind, which buried their feet in sand even while they sat. She thought of Duncan, who had walked this land on mri terms . . . and come in strangely more whole than they: recalled the face, gaunt and changed, and narrow-eyed, smooth, as if humankind were burned out of it, and wrung out with the moisture; and placid, as if expressions were waste.

There had been a touch of the mri. Here—save for the edunei—things did not agree together. She looked about her, at stones, which had a touch of lavenders amid the apricot dust of afternoon . . . at streets and buildings. What it might have been in its prime, this great city . . . her expert eye filled in, missing angles, shaping with the remembered fragments of the saffron-hued city of so many dead: alien arches, bizarre geometries, delicate symmetry of threes.

Threes, she thought, a preponderance of triangles. Three castes. The silhouette of the edunei. The three-way intersection of streets. Buildings of slanting walls and ground-plans which made sensible geometry if the wings were divided triangularly. She shivered, recognizing an underlying geometry of alien perceptions, another thing than underlay the dualities that underlay human architecture, human relationships, human sex, either-or, up and down, black and white, duality of alternatives. The minds which built this had thought otherwise, had seen differently.

Never the right questions, she thought with a tightness at her stomach.

In any situation . . . were there *three* alternatives?

And the great edunei: always the edunei, where mri had lived in human/regul space . . . never such streets, such buildings, asprawl in triangular multiplications. Mri had used the edunei: huge ones, by report, far greater than Kesrith . . . and those were dimmest echoes of the edun of the saffron city: mud-walled echoes. Residences, presumably here as there.

And what were these outer buildings, this disorderly sprawl centering about the edun?

The triangularity was the same. The flavor was not. The logic was not. The life within the self-contained edunei . . . and in this sprawl . . . could not be the same.

"Not mri," she said aloud. "The makers of this . . . were not mri." And when Galey and Kadarin gazed at her as if she had lost her reason: "It's not the ruins we need. Duncan was right all the way in the other city; and in this one . . . no dead. Deserted, as he said. I advise we get back to that shuttle. Out in the land. There are the ship's lights . . . by night they'd be quite visible."

"Boz," Galey said, "what are you talking about, not mri?"

"Didn't Duncan tell us the truth once? And again . . . here: these cities are not where we find the mri. What *is* mri is in those machines, and we can't get at it; and what's out here in these streets is of no use to us. These buildings—are no use. We're already taking one chance, staying out here. Take a further. Go all the way. Find the mri; there may be something here we can't afford to find, whoever made the outer city. A logic we can't deal with. A language we know nothing of."

Galey stared at her, and cast a glance about the buildings, his masked face contracting in a grimace of distress. Perhaps even to his eyes things fell into new order; he had that kind of look, that of a man seeing something he had not.

"What are we into?" he asked. "Boz, are you sure?"

"I'm sure of nothing. But I suggest we take our chances on the known quantity. That if we go looking long enough . . . we might turn up something that doesn't follow the rules we know, even what little we know. And what do we do then?"

"What do we do with the mri?"

"We get a contact. We try the names we know. We get back into the range of Duncan's mri and we turn on the lights."

Galey's eyes slid aside to Kadarin, back again. "That totally breaks with the orders I have."

"I know that."

"We rest here the night; we'll go back tomorrow morning, if that's what we're going to do."

"Now." She shivered with the thought. "My old bones don't like the thought of a night walk; but how much time can we have? If we delay here, then we're giving up time; and if it comes to waiting—on the mri . . . then time is the only thing we have to use, isn't it?"

Galey sat still a long moment, staring at nothing in particular. Finally he looked at Kadarin. "You have a word in this."

"What works," Kadarin said. "What works and gets us home with it done."

"It's on my head," Galey said. "Say that I ordered you, all the way."

"Kel'anth," Dias whispered. "Watch says they are coming."

Niun sprang up from morning meal and excused himself through the Kel which scattered for their weapons. He walked along beside kel Dias, out into the dark before dawn and a stiff wind out of the south; his kel-sword he had with him, and his dus determined to follow, inanimate and living accouterments. He tucked his veil into place and felt somewhere not far from him the other dus, and Duncan, heard running steps this way and that through the camp, messengers dispatched to the other tents, to advise them of outsider approach. Hlil came up beside him, matched his pace. Ahead of him the watch stirred out, from the seeming of a rock on the crest of the eastward dune, a robed kel'en unfolding to stand and point mutely toward the east, to the dim showing of dunes in the starlight.

The Kel spread out along the crest facing that darkness, where the hint of shadow moved far, far off. Niun found himself, as he ought to be, the center of the line, with Hlil at his right hand and the dus at his left. Duncan was not far from him . . . he and his dus had no right to stand so near center; he turned his head to see, and found him by Ras, in second-rank, orderly and with second-rank distributed evenly as they ought, accepting of that presence . . . second-rank's business, he reckoned, disturbed—turned his face again to the dark and waited, the dus which touched him beginning a vibrating song, incongruous here, this over confidence. It sang against him, such that only those nearest might hear at all, so deeply that it shuddered into bone and flesh, numbing, soothing. For a moment there was awareness of the mate a few paces behind; of Duncan, anxious; and Ras, a bleeding shadow; of Melein awake in another tent and an exultation so fierce it pulsed in the ears; of sen'ein calm, kath'ein love, the sleeping peace of children . . . camps and kel'ein scat-

tered around about them, far across the dunes. Farther still,
dus-sense, contact with others . . .

He shuddered suddenly, disrupted the gnosis, pulled out of
it from deeper than he had ever fallen within it. Duncan's
manner with them . . . no restraint. No barriers. The song
reached to others, to sweep them in also. "Yai!" he said. It
stopped, and the dus threw its head, brushing against him.
There *were* others out there, beyond the dark and the shadow
which had taken on distinction on the opposing crest, that
flowed down it, weapons and Honors aglitter in the starlight.

Hao'nath: that was apparent by the direction of them; and
by the way they came, their intent was plain, for warriors
walked long-striding, with hands loose, at random intervals
and not by order.

"Ai," someone murmured nearby, the whole Kel relaxing;
a current of joy ran through the dusei like a strong wind.

Other masses appeared on the horizon, signaled by the first
breaking of daylight, the appointed time. One in the east, one
southeast, and north . . . perhaps.

The hao'nath were coming upslope now, hasting somewhat
in the nearness of the camp. Rhian s'Tafa led them, center to
center, and Niun came out to meet him, unveiled as Rhian
unveiled, embraced the older kel'anth gladly. The Kels
mingled, kel'ein who had come to know each others' faces,
finding each other again with a relief strangely like a homecoming, for veils were down and hands outstretched.

There was for the moment lack of order; and in such
chaos Niun turned, looked for Duncan, who had likewise unveiled, conspicuous among the others as the dus by him. He
turned and looked back down the slope, and saw others coming as the hao'nath had come, easily and without hostility, the
second and the third tribes, with the fourth now a shadow
against the coming dawn.

"They are coming too," he said to Hlil, overjoyed, and at a
sudden and cold impulse from the dus by him he turned
again, toward Duncan, abruptly as if a hand had caught his
shoulder.

Rhian had paused there, only looking at Duncan and
Duncan at him, and Niun cuffed at the dus to stop that
unease from building . . . but Rhian turned his back to walk
away.

"I am not sick," Duncan said, audible to all about them.
"Sir."

Rhian turned again, and Niun's heart lurched, for all he

approved that answer, for all he had some faith in the hao'nath himself. Rhian tilted his head, looked Duncan up and down, and the beast by him as well.

"You are unscarred," Rhian said, which settled any matter of challenge between them, but not of right and wrong.

"My inexperience loosed my fear; and fear loosed the beast," Duncan said. "My profound apology, sir."

Again there was long silence, for a kel'anth's pride was at stake. "You ran well," Rhian said, "kel'en." And he turned his back again, the while a murmur came about him . . . *ai-ai-ai*, that was relief and deprecation at once, Kutathi applause, as for a good joke in kel-tent, as to say it had not been so serious. Rhian shrugged and smiled grimly, touched one of his own folk and touched the hand of a kel'e'en—truemate, she might be.

Duncan stared after him soberly, as if he well knew what a chill wind had brushed him.

And suddenly the ja'ari were among them, with Tian s'Edri at their head; they had met with Kalis of the ka'anomin of Zohain and her band and theirs had joined in the madness of companionship on the way, poured among them like a black wind out of the dawn, glad to find the hao'nath ahead of them. Niun and Hlil and Rhian met the two kel'anthein, and stood atop the crest to watch the arrival of yet another group who came as the others, in haste and gladly.

"Mari," said kel Tian, who had come in nearest them. And soon another black mass had joined them, and Elan of the mari was among them, to embrace and be embraced.

"Last but the patha," Tian said, but the excitement now quickly faded, and Niun gazed out toward the lightening horizon with increasing unease. There was no sign of the fifth tribe. Quiet began to settle over the mingled Kel, until all eyes were on that vacant expanse of sand and sky.

Eventually there was total quiet, and where had been confusion, the line began to expand itself along the crest, the mood gone grim.

Light came full enough for colors, an amber and apricot dawn which flung hills into relief. "Perhaps," said Elan, "they hope for us to walk to them." And there was a murmuring at that from Tian and Rhian.

Then there was something, a darkness moving, a shadow. A few pointed, but no one spoke after that, not the long while it took for folk to walk so far, not during the intervals in which the comers were out of sight in the rolls of the land.

They vanished a last time, and reappeared on the crest facing, a huge number, nigh five hundred kel'ein, and hastening down the slope in friendly disorder.

Breaths and laughter burst from the Kel at once. "Ai, the patha cannot tell the hour," a ja'ari exclaimed, and a current of soft laughter ran the line, so that Niun himself laughed for relief and others did. It was the sort of tag that might live in a Kel for decades, the kind of gibe that a man might spend effort living down. The patha came up the slope out of breath, and met that tag to their faces, but it was not only Kedras of the patha but a second kel'anth, a young kel'en and few in Honors.

"I am Mada s'Kafai Sek-Mada," the kel'anth proclaimed himself. "Of the path'andim eastward, second sept of the patha, and here by the summons of the patha to the summoning of the she'pan'anth. Where is the kel'anth Niun s'Intel?"

"They are late," Niun said to the others, "but they multiply." Laughter broke out, in which the patha themselves could join, and Niun embraced Mada after Kedras, looked about him in the dawning at the sight of more than fifteen hundred kel'ein, a number more than he had ever seen of his own kind in all his life, more than most kel'anthein he had heard of had ever had about them, save the very greatest and most desperate struggles. The weight of it settled on him like a weight of years.

"Come," he bade them all, "into camp."

He walked through the line, which folded itself inward and spilled after him among the tents, where the kel'ein left in camp joined them, where kath'ein and children came out to stare wide-eyed at such a sight, and sen'ein bowed greeting.

Melein waited in the dawning, veilless and with her eyes shining. "My ja'anom," she hailed them, "and my borrowed children." She held out hands, and Niun came and kissed her, received her kiss in turn; and after him the other kel'anthein, the six, each a kiss; and then all, all the others for at least a touch upon the hand, a brushing contact. "She is so young," murmured a path'andim, in Niun's hearing, and then realized who heard and bowed his head and made quick withdrawal.

"Strike camp!" Melein called aloud, and kath'ein, both women and children moved to obey. "Lend hand to them!" Niun bade the ja'anom Kel, and other kel'anthein called out the same, to the confounding of the Kath and the order of things. Baggage was hastened out, tents billowed down to be sectioned and the poles laid separate. The Holy was carried out among the sen'ein, shrouded in veils; and silence went where it passed, to that place which should be Sen's on the march. Children ran this way and that, awed by strangers, darting nervously among them on their errands for Kath.

And Duncan labored with them, beside Taz and other unscarred, until Niun passed by them and quietly took Duncan by the sleeve.

Duncan came aside with him, the dusei plodding shadowwise at their heels. "Carry yourself today," Niun bade him. "That is all."

"I cannot walk empty-handed," Duncan said.

"Did you play the Six?"

"Aye," Duncan admitted, with a guilty look.

"So. You are not last-rank. And you walk empty."

The line was forming. They could not, now, walk together; rank separated them; she'pan'anth, Melein named herself, she'pan of she'panei, and he had kel'anthein for companions, on the march and in whatever came.

"What am I?" Duncan asked him.

"Walk with last for now; the pace is easier. Do not press yourself, sov-kela." He touched his shoulder, walked away toward the place he should hold. Duncan did not follow.

"Two of them," Kadarin breathed, and confirmed what Galey feared he saw: two ships, not one, a double gleaming in the haze and the sun and the desolation.

They were due a rest, overdue it. "Come on," Galey said, slipping an arm about Boaz's stout waist. She was limping, staggering, breathing heavier than was good for anyone. He expected her to object and curse him off, but this time she did not, for whatever help he was, with his height. Kadarin locked an arm about her from the other side and from that moment they made better time, nigh carrying Boaz between, until they were panting as hard as she.

Regul, he kept thinking, recalling another nightmare in the Kesrithi highlands, a ship unguarded, regul swarming about it.

Shibo. Alone there. Alone with whatever had landed next him. They were all vulnerable . . . no retreat but the desert, no help but the sidearms he and Kadarin had, against an armed shuttlecraft.

He grimaced and strained his eyes to resolve the outlines, hoped, by what he saw, and kept quiet.

"Think that's one of ours," Kadarin gasped after a moment.

He kept moving, with Boaz struggling between them, breaths rasping in sometime unison, hers and theirs. His eyes began to confirm it, the other ship a copy of their own. He had a cold knot at his gut all the same. It was trouble; it could not be otherwise.

Recall: that was likeliest, a decision to pull the mission out. Or disaster elsewhere. . . .

The possibilities sorted and re-sorted themselves in agonizing lack of variety. He had a man dead, neglected in his report; he had lost credibility by that. He had no success to claim, nothing, save Boaz's eloquence: and against distant orders . . . there was no appeal.

He tightened his arm about her, trying whether she needed to stop, whether they were hurting her. "Stop?" he asked her.

She shook her head and kept walking.

No hatch opened in advance of their coming . . . ought not: they wasted no comfort to the winds. They limped up to a blind and closed wall. No need at the last to hail them— machinary engaged, and the ramp and lock welcomed them, too small to afford them access all at once. Kadarin climbed up, Boaz next, himself last.

Two men were waiting for them. Shibo. Another, black against the light from the port. Galey pulled the breather-mask down, sought to guide Boaz to a cushion, but she was not willing to sit. She stood, braced against a cushion in the dark, seat-jammed space.

"Harris, sir," the other said. "Orders from upstairs."

Gene Harris. Galey gathered himself a breath and sank down into the co-pilot's cushion, tried to adjust his eyes to the daylight as Harris slipped a paper into his hand. Kadarin leaned past, switched on an overhead light. He rubbed his eyes and tried to focus on it, past a throbbing head and hands that wanted to shake, blurring the letters.

Mission codes and authorizations. Koch's office.

Cooperative rapprochments with allies are underway at highest levels. Agreements have been reached regarding a mutually acceptable solution to the future threat of mri retaliations . . . There was more.

"What are they wanting?" Boaz interrupted his reading.

"We're ordered to destroy the machines."

"The computers?"

He spread the paper on his knee, read aloud. " '. . . ordered to use successful techniques of access to effect demolition of high tech installations and power sources, beyond any remote possibility of repair. Allies have—applauded—this operation and will make on-site inspections at the termination of your phase of operations. Request utmost dispatch in execution of this order. Probe *Flower* will remain onworld outside estimated limit of fire of city sites. Orbiting craft will not be in position to receive or relay messages. Exercise extreme caution in this operation regarding safety of crew and equipment. Your knowledge is unique and valuable. Luiz will be your contact during this operation should mission-abort prove necessary. Re-stress extreme priority this mission, crucial to entire operation. Urge extreme caution regarding—possible allied operations onworld out of contact with allid high command. Do not provoke allied observers. Use personal discretion regarding sequence of operations and necessary evasions in event weapons are triggered. Shuttle two and crew under your command. Transport civilian aide to ground command if feasible, your discretion.' "

There was a harsh oath from Boaz.

Galey folded the paper, slid it into the clip by the seat, sat still a moment. "How many with you?" he asked Harris.

"Magee and North; we opted Bright out to get cargo in."

"Demolitions?"

Harris nodded. "Enough, at least to start."

Galey ventured a look toward Boaz, toward a face gone old, red-marked with the breather-mask, her gray-blonde braids wind-shredded. Agony was in her eyes. Kadarin rested a hand on her shoulder, his own face saying nothing.

"We lost Mike Lane," Galey said. "A mistake with those machines. They have defenses."

There was silence. He ran a hand through his knotted hair, haunted still by Boaz's eyes. His heart labored like something trapped.

"They're going to take everything we've done," she said, "and use that to destroy the sites. To wipe out their past and their power sources. They take *that* on themselves."

No one spoke. A muscle in Boaz's cheek jerked convulsively.

"And mri aren't the only ones involved. You don't know. You don't know what you've got your hand to."

He shook his head.

"Refuse the order."

He considered it . . . actually considered it. It was

madness. Harris's presence—brought sense back. "Can't," he said. "They've got us, you understand. They can blow the world under us if we don't do this. You, all of us, we're expendable in a going operation, in a policy they've got set. It's better than losing them, isn't it? It's better than killing kids."

"To kill their past? Isn't that the other face of it?"

There was an oppression in the narrow cabin, a difficulty in breathing. Boaz's anger filled it, stifled, strangled.

"No choice." He reached out toward Harris, made a weary gesture toward a cushion; his neck ached too much looking up. "Sit down."

Harris did. "We run the doctor back to base?"

Galey lifted a hand before Boaz could spit out the next word. "She's ours," he said. "She goes back only if she wants."

"She doesn't," Boaz said.

"She doesn't." Galey drew a deep breath, wiped at his blurred eyes, looked from one to the other of them. "We penetrate the sites; that's easy; we carry the stuff in on our backs, set it, the margin we know, walk out, get the ship clear . . . nothing easier. Chances are we'll trigger something that will blow us all. I figure if *Saber* says there's no one in position for relays, that means they and the regul are backing off for fear of a holocaust down here. We're in the furnace. *Flower's* safe, maybe; you understand that, Boz: you'd have a better chance on the ship; and maybe there's nothing more you can do out here."

She shook her head.

"Got a message for you," Harris told her, fished it from his pocket, a crumpled envelope.

"Luiz," Boaz said without having to read the name. She opened it, read it, lips taut. " 'My blessing,' " she said in a small voice. "That's all it says." She rubbed at her cheek, wadded the paper and pocketed it. "Who does this profit? Answer me that, Mr. Galey?"

"The mri themselves. They live."

"Excluding that doubtful premise."

"I'm not sure I follow."

"Our command ship is backing off. We've got a regul operation onworld. Whose benefit?"

He sat there with an increasing pulse, adding that up. "I'm sure that's been calculated at higher levels than this one."

"Don't give me 'calculated.' The admiral's been taking advice from Sim Averson and he can't see past his papers."

"Boz—"

She said nothing more. He gnawed at his lip and looked at Harris. "You stay on standby, here. If we go out there afoot, I want to be sure we don't have any regul prying about here."

"How do we stop them?" Harris asked.

"Shoot," he said, reckoning on protest from Boaz; he knew her principles. She said nothing. "You and Boaz stay here; if we get any regul contact, I want her by a com set in a hurry. And you listen to her, Gene. She doesn't carry guns. Doesn't approve. She knows regul. If she calls strike, she'll have reason. You monitor everything that moves; make sure Boz understands the limits of our scan and how long it takes to react. And if she says go, go to kill. Agreed?"

Harris nodded without a qualm evident. "You're going back?"

"Better," he said. He rose up in the narrow confines, rubbed his beard-rough face, wishing at least for the luxury of washing; could not. He took a drink from the dispenser and started gathering supplies from the locker, replenishing what they had used out of the kits. Kadarin did the same, and Harris went with Shibo to gather up the demolitions supplies.

He let them; that gave a little time for rest. When it was all ready he gave Boaz a squeeze of the hand and walked out down the ramp, with Kadarin, and Shibo, and Harris's man Magee. He pulled the breathing mask up and started them moving. He was cold already; his feet were numb, beyond hurting. He could have sent Harris.

Could have.

Duncan was lost. He admitted that now. Lost: dead, or lost: with the mri. There was no hope, no miracle, only this ugly act that was better than other choices.

Their past, Boaz had called it, killing the past. He looked about him; reckoned there was for this barren, dying world . . . little else left.

He shook his head, set his eyes on the city whose name he did not even know, and walked.

Pillars rose, spires of the same hue as the hills against which they stood, such that they might have been made by nature . . . but they were baroque and identical, and there were others round about them in the distance, marching off toward the south; there was beyond that a jewel-gleam, a shining the eyes could not resolve.

Ele'et.

Duncan gazed on it in sometime view beyond the shoulders of kel'ein before him . . . he was lost among them, a head shorter than most, when all his life among humans he had been tall; as for all his thinness now, he was still wider-boned than they, broader of hand, of foot, of shoulder: different, anomaly among them. And mingled with other thoughts was unease, the thought that they faced something more difficult still.

"The People served the elee," he said to Taz, who walked hard by him, with a burden slung to his shoulder. "Do you know what they look like?"

"I have not seen one," Taz said. And after a space more: "They are tsi'mri," which dismissed interest in them.

He said no more then, having enough to do only to walk, with the veils wrapped thickly about nose and mouth, and his joints remembering the pain of the long trek before. He had the dus by him, and through it, sometime sense of Niun, which comforted him.

He was afraid; it came down to that.

Why they were going to this place, what they hoped to have of the race which lived there, which—perhaps had resources uninvolved in the catastrophe, weapons. . . . he had no clear imagination. To fight, Niun had said. He had given them the breath of a chance to do so, that much; had killed the regul: that much.

They rested—had done so several times during the day, for it was Kath's pace which dictated their progress; and this time a ripple of orders went down the line: *make camp.*

Kel'ein muttered surprise, gathered themselves up from the places where they had settled, to aid Kath. Duncan began to, and remembered orders, and sat still, by the dus, his arm across it. Unease would not leave him. Dus-sense, the realization came on him; the beast itself was stirred. They were making camp as if all were well, and the dus-sense had the discomfort of a cliff's edge, a dizziness, a profound sense of strangeness.

Niun would know; would be aware of it. He rose up, ignored in the confusion of assembling canvas and the assembling of the tall poles, wended his way among them, his way blocked by a little child who looked up at him and blinked in shock, scrambled aside from him and the beast at once.

He stared that way, distracted, disturbed, walked past this kel'en and the other in search of Niun, following dus-sense.

There were others out there, shadows, following them, following them and him since the ship, all these days of walking, the young of his dus and Niun's, ha-dusei, wild. They sought. They were scattered, the senses on which their own dusei drew, eyes and ears ranging wide of their own.

His.

And they were coming in.

Niun was there, near the site of sen-tent, which was billowing in the pull of the ropes; kel'anthein were about him, and it was not a time for an unscarred to speak to him. *Niun,* he cast through the dus-sense, turned at the dark impulse of another mind.

Ras. He reached out, touched her sleeve, met her veiled face and distracted stare, began to ask her to go to Niun.

Ras. It was Ras. The dus-sense leaped through the touch. He stopped speaking and Ras looked away, following the direction that he himself sensed. "They are coming in," he said. "Kel Ras—they are coming in."

"For days—" she answered hoarsely, "for days it has been there. It will not let be. Since the time I went back from the tribe—it has been there."

The storm feeling grew, acquired other direction, another essence, male. And another.

Another still. Duncan looked, saw dusei on the sandy ridge nearest, coming down toward the camp.

"Gods!" Ras muttered. Her voice trembled; she would have backed away; he felt the tremor in his own muscles.

"It wants," he said. "There is no stopping it."

"I will kill it!"

"It has two brains, two hearts and there is a madness comes on them when they are rebuffed. Believe me, sometimes it touches the kel'en too. *Shon'ai* . . . let go. Let go, Ras. You are in its mind already. You have been."

"Drive it back."

He felt his heart laboring as it would with his own in distress, human pulse and mri and dus dragged into synch. His and Ras's and Niun's; whose else there was no knowing.

"Are you afraid?" he asked of Ras. There was nothing that might sting more.

She walked from him, through anxious, silent kel'ein, for the whole company had gone still and turned eyes toward the beasts. He walked after, heart still pounding, watched from the edge of camp as Ras went out among them, as one of the four made for her, personal nightmare: kill it she could not; it would be a knife against her own flesh.

Not hate: he understood that, which he had sensed already . . . that the signature of Ras was something else again, a stone-steadiness, a stubbornness—devotion. The stranger-dus reared up, towering above her, came down with a puff of dust and a warding-impulse which shivered through his own beast.

Then another thing, that sent dizziness through him, as dus and kel'e'en touched, as she knelt down and put her arms about the dus's neck. Power, dus-mind and mri, a thing dangerous and disciplined. Mri scattered as other dusei came in; children fled for Kath. Other bonds were forged, and he knew as his own dus had touched these minds before. . . . Hlil; the boy Taz, who was a desire so deep it shuddered through the camp; and Rhian, who feared, and stopped fearing.

"Yai!" Duncan exclaimed, dropped to his knees and hugged the beast by him, trying to shut it off, mri minds, and dusei. It would not go, not for long, slow moments. He hung still against the beast, aware finally of it nosing at him, gentle pushes that were not, to a man, gentle. He choked down nausea, free finally, of what still lodged in memory, of knowing too much, and too well, and all the veils being down.

Niun was there, as dazed as he—mri, and stable. Duncan rose to his feet, walked, aching from the convulsion of his muscles, and the dus went beside him. There was a silence everywhere, kel'ein and all the others staring at him, at them, who were also there, who assembled with Niun at center. Rhian was there, a mind he had felt all too long as hunter; Hlil, Ras; and unscarred Taz, dazed and frightened to be dragged into commonality with kel'anthein.

They met, met eyes. Duncan felt his heartbeat even yet tending from his own normal pace, struck at his dus and stopped it. Heat rose to his face, consciousness that he knew strangers as he knew Niun, was known by them.

"I am sorry," Taz murmured, as if it were his fault a dus had chosen him.

"No one answers where dusei are concerned," Niun said. "They choose. They find something alike in us—gods know what."

"They sense the strangers," Duncan said thickly. "They are here—to protect. There is another one still wild, still out here. Why . . . I do not sense. Their own business, it may be."

"We are going into the city," Niun said. "Kath and all but a few hands of sen'ein stay in camp, with a guard. They have taken service."

Duncan looked from him, to the white figure of Melein among the Sen, and beyond, to the pillar-sentinels of the elee.

Attack. He realized that of a sudden.

Alignments made sense suddenly, mri and tsi'mri, to draw the line and set all enemies across it. Mri had no allies.

"Did you not understand?" Niun asked. "We take this place."

The dusei had realized it . . . had come to take sides, as they had chosen on Kesrith.

With mri. With several in particular, who had something in common.

Madness, perhaps; Duncan reckoned so.

XVI

The ships were indeed retreating. Suth studied the screens, smiled, keyed a signal to his own crew.

Shirug began to move, a slow withdrawal from the world, keeping *Santiago* and *Saber* constantly in scan.

And on screen, bai Degas waited. "We have begun," Suth advised the human bai. "As agreed, we will keep to pattern with each other. And our communications will remain linked to yours, reverend bai Degas."

"I am instantly available in any emergency."

"Favor, bai." Suth gaped a grin; he liked this human, after a fashion. There was a pleasantness about him in sharp contrast to the others, a sense of solidity in his reactions.

And for that reason he was to be feared: not dull, this bai Del Degas-si, not at all dull-witted. He retained things very well for a human.

"I shall turn contact over to a youngling now," Suth said. "Our profound gratitude for this cooperation."

"Favor reverence," the human replied in lisping approximation of that courtesy. Suth grinned dutifully, shut off the contact for his own screen and leaned back in his sled.

Behind him the other sleds moved, entering his field of vision.

Nagn, Tiag, Morkhug.

There was no elation, no exultation. It was not a time for such.

"Keep in close contact with this office," Suth said. "When you sleep, do so in the presence of one of us four being awake. All channels are to be strictly monitored by some one of us."

"This dismantling of mri sites," said Nagn, "is *said* to be progressing. Human information is not always accurate."

"*Lie*, Nagn. The word is *lie*. Humans deceive in false statements as well as actions; but we work with this particular action . . . indeed, we work with it."

Morkhug puffed her nostrils uneasily. "I still dislike it. One threat gone: the mri sites; and I do not see the human advantage in this."

"Unless they lie," Nagn said.

"Impoverished mri," said Tiag, "must take service with someone. Or die, of starvation."

"Question," said Nagn. "Do humans assume they will take service with them?"

Suth hissed. It was insanity, that regul adults sat here contemplating trues and maybe-trues regarding human minds. They learned. They all began to think in mad terms of shifting realities. He gathered a stylus from the board before him, held it between his palms and rolled it. "Observe, mates-of-mine, the flat face of the stylus. Where does it exist? Has it a place as it spins?"

"In fractional instants," Nagn said.

"Analogy," said Suth. "A model for imagination. I have found one. The place faces all directions for an instant, a blur of motion. Human minds are and are not so many faces that they seem ready to move in any direction. They are composite realities. They apparently face all directions simultaneously. This is human motive." He laid the stylus down. "They are facing us and the mri simultaneously."

"But action," said Tiag. "They cannot act in all directions forever."

"They act for themselves. What is of value to them?"

"Survival," said Nagn.

"Knowledge," Suth said. "They *state* that they are destroying the sites."

Nostrils flared and shut in rapid alternation.

"I accept no data from humans," Suth continued, feeling the palpitation of his hearts. "Mates-of-mine, among *forgetful* species, this is the only sanity. Among species which *imagine*, this is the only alternative. I have set a sane course. I made appropriate motions by human request, to avoid unprofitable developments. Humans state that they are destroying the sites: potentially true. They omit to state that they are gathering knowledge. We know that they are using the elders of *Flower* as additional personnel. They have stated so, and if this is a lie, I do not find motive in it."

"We are letting them destroy armaments we had counted useful to us," Morkhug objected.

"No," said Suth. "We do not do that. Our base . . . will not do that."

"Nothing, sir."

Luiz leaned against the side of the cushion to the right of Brown and shook his head sorrowfully. Brown's eyes stared back at him with a bruised look . . . the man had not left this bridge, not he nor any of the rest of the military crew—had rather bedded down here near controls; the night shift was sleeping on pallets over against the storage lockers, and everyone kept movements quiet for their sakes. They had a full crew, with everyone awake; half on turn and turn about; and the men had given more than duty, monitoring scan, helping science staff with the rapid filing of data, the breakdown of delicate instruments and equipment, frantic storing of whatever might be damaged in a violent lift. There was no panic aboard; fear . . . that was an abiding guest.

They were alone, for the first time truly alone, save for—intermittently, a shuttle closer to Kutath than the big warships dared be; and Galey's mission, down with them.

They hoped, at least. There was no contact with Galey. Harris's mission could find them—if they were following the agreed sequence of sites; and the next thing they could look for was either holocaust or a progress report.

That they would delay to bring Boaz back . . . that, if it rested with her, they would not. Luiz scanned the master chart which plastered the pinup board . . . lingered on second site, where at best reckoning, she was. Eleven major targets. Even the young men had to come in for relief, somewhere in that world-spanning chain of targets; and then she would. He hoped so.

If nothing went wrong before then.

"I don't expect word," Brown murmured, evidently reckoning he was obliged to say something. "Takes a while, to get there, to lay plans, a lot of things, sir. Could be quite a while."

It was, he reckoned, a kindly attempt at comfort; he felt none.

Beyond the pillars of carved stone, the city Ele'et sat, a fantastical combination of glass and stone, aglow in the fading light. Kel'ein murmured with wonder; and Niun gazed on it thinking on his youth, on evenings spent in the hills above a regul city, looking on lights in the twilight, and dreaming dreams of ships and voyages and war, and Honors to win.

He looked on Melein, who walked among the Sen who had come with them, for all his wishing otherwise. She had no words, none, but she had simply set out with them, and what *she* would, she did. The Holy reposed in safety; she and her sen'ein, fifteen including Sathas himself, walked in the blackness of more than a thousand kel'ein, and said nothing of how they should take this place.

He had not far to reach for companions: they were near as the dusei, moving here and there throughout the column; he summoned, and they came, those not by him already, even to Taz, who was devastated by his fortunes. "Stay close," he bade them all, and at Duncan especially he looked. "You have the other gun, sov-kela; and I would you stay nearer the she'pan. These are tsi'mri."

"Aye," Duncan murmured. The incongruity did not draw a flicker from him. They were two, Niun thought, who had known the old war, on different sides as they were; who knew the Kesrithi law—distance-weapons for those who would use them: the mercenary Kel had lost its compunction in such matters.

"They must know we are here," said Hlil.

"Doubtless," Niun said.

Nearness made the rocks of the hills take on strange form in the sunset, twisted shapes, joined by aisles of stone and glass; shapes shaped by hands, he realized of a sudden, the whole face of the hills hewn into abstract geometries, as the pillars had been hewn, with glass facing the intervals: hills, whole domes of rock the size of edunei . . . carved in elaborations the north side of which the sand-laden winds had eroded, and the size—the size of it . . . only a tenth part was alight.

"Gods," he murmured, for suddenly their number seemed very small, and the sky leaden and full of enemies.

Ward-impulse prickled in the air; something started in the sand before them, and another. Soon a whole cloud of burrowers fled in distress, and the sands rippled beyond that. It was as if the very sands hereabouts lived, writhing like the mutilated stones.

Water. Outspill from the city.

And dus-sense grew more and more disturbed. "Do not loose it," he bade those about him. "You understand me. The beasts are not to be loosed."

There was murmured agreement.

"Nor the Kel," said Melein, startling them. "Take me this city. Do not destroy it. Do not kill until you must."

"Go to the center," he wished Melein. "You must have care."

To his amazement she did so, without demur. He drew breath, surveyed the place before them, which balked them with a maze of walls and no streets, nothing of accesses, nothing of pattern.

He led them straight on as the wind would blow, with contempt for their barriers and their building and the logic of their structures. He led them to a great face of glass, which showed within a hallway, and carven stones, and great carven boulders rising out of the very floor, prisoned and changed in this tsi'mri place.

He drew his gun, unfired in years, and with wide contempt, burned an access. That fell ponderously, that shattered with a crash that woke the echoes and scattered glass among the carven stones. Warmth came out at them, and moisture-bearing air.

They walked within, glass ground under their boots, the dusei snorting at the prick of slivers which let blood. His own let out a hunting moan that echoed eerily through the vast halls, and found direction, guiding them all. He kept his gun in hand, and with a wave of his arm sent a flood of kel'ein the width of the hall, to find out all sides, all recesses of the carved monuments. They were beyond the glass now, and the floor echoed to their tread, itself patterned in mad designs.

And figures stood at the end of the hall, glittering with color, gods, the colors! As one they stopped, staring at hues of green and deep blue and bright colors which had no name, none that he knew—the robes of mri-like folk who had no color, paler even than Duncan's pallor, whose manes were white and long and shamelessly naked, the whole of their whiteness bejeweled and patterned.

He had walked alone into a regul city, which shared nothing at all with mri. He had the face for this, and walked ahead, with the dus beside him and comrades about him, wondering what they would do, whether challenge, whether panic and bring forth weapons.

They ran.

Weapons ripped from sheaths with one thousand-voiced rasp of steel. "No!" he said. "But keep your weapons in hand."

He kept walking, calmly enough. They passed one archway and entered another, and into a tangle of carved stone that mimicked pipe roots, or some mad dream. Screaming began, wails, the fall of a city which had not yet struck a blow.

The steps of the great edun lay ahead, brown-hued in a lavender city, simplicity amid the maze. Galey drew in an insufficient breath through the trickle-flow of the breather, made the climb ahead of the others . . . staggering from weariness, but made it, into this sanctuary from the winds.

They brought their own lights and used them, not touching any that the place itself might have, for fear of alerting the guard systems, such as there might be. Galey looked about him at writing on the walls, at the wholeness of what the other edun had been, at a place untouched in the disaster.

"Appreciate what you're seeing," he said hoarsely, distorted in the mask. "This is a holy place to them; it's their history and their home; it's their Earth and these are its shrines. And we kill them. Remember that."

The faces of Harris's two men stared back at him, masked and demonic in the lamps' glow, eyes betraying shock. Only Kadarin . . . Kadarin, who had been with Boaz . . . he understood.

"No one ought to kill something," he said, "and not know it." He pressed the mask tighter against his face, sucked air and turned away toward the access of the machine hall . . . what must be so if the edunei were as identical as Boaz said, leading toward the tower.

And in the core of that tower must be the power accesses; structurally, it was the only place to expect them. A slender stem, which might be severed; but well-sheathed. Such a tower had stood in the other edun though all else had suffered severe damage.

"Got to get at the core in there," he said, laying a hand on the wall. "Simple job, I figure. We have a power source to worry about, maybe a lot of them. But the brain's up there, and this is the spinal cord. Isn't any coordination available without that. We blow these, and we can send cleanup teams out later, to do the job on anything left; without these, there's no danger to orbiting ships, so we reckon. You hunt those other towers. I don't think you'll find much; but we make—"

Something scuttled across the floor, a dart of silver; North ripped out a gun and Galey seized his arm, his eyes making the object clear in the next instant as mechanical, a silver dome. It wandered aimlessly, came toward them, passed blind-ly as they stepped aside, sucking up dust.

"Maintenance," Kadarin said in a shaken voice.

"Move out," Galey said. "Don't touch any switches and don't fire at anything. Alert this thing and we'll all be sorry."

They parted in the directions he indicated to them, moving quickly, a rippling of lights and shadows. Dark then, as they probed the towers one by one, steps echoing high up in the building, descending again, all but the machine tower, where they assembled finally.

"Nothing," Kadarin said. "Just service machinery." The others agreed.

"Then set the charges at the stem of the second tower, at every level, and assume it's shielded. —Kadarin. Come with me."

Kadarin hastened after him, quietly, up into the spiral of the machine tower. They moved with caution, the light cast-ing into reality only a portion of the spiral at a time and darkness following as swiftly after.

It opened upon a room eerily like the other place, the same grill-worked window, identical as if one mind, one architect had conceived it. But this one was whole, lacking the crack, as if some all powerful hand had healed it.

They walked with soft steps to the room beyond, found what had been in the other place. Galey cut off his light and motioned Kadarin to do the same, not wishing to provide any photosensitive alarm among the banks of machinery with a fatal stimulus.

"Could be a high-threshold audio alarm," he whispered. "Lane set it off when he crossed that circle there on the floor. Avoid it, We set charges on every bank and make the least sound possible. Then we get out of here. A quarter-hour trig-ger. Right?"

"Sits right over the core," said Kadarin. "Core's right un-der this first unit here."

"Likely."

Galey moved in, set that charge himself, trod carefully down the aisles, Kadarin a gliding shadow as fast-moving as he.

They tripped a maintenance robot. It shot out of an aisle, a red telltale glowing on its side, jerked about, stopped, moved off on its own business.

And in feverish haste Galey fixed the last charge, walked back to the door, met Kadarin there. "Go!" he hissed.

They still walked, quietly, across the hall outside, entered the spiral descent, and ran it, met the others below.

"Done, sir," he heard. He motioned them to move, and they crossed the foyer at a dead run, ran down the steps outside, were still running as they crossed the courtyard and took shelter in an alley among the lavender buildings, leaning there, their breathing harsh and hollow in the breathers, interspersed with hissing jets of oxygen.

It should not blow with great violence. The mind should go, the automations fail, whatever regulation the power sources needed likewise go. Quiet oblivion, likely noncontaminating power which would simply stop.

Suddenly it happened; the building disjointed itself on the left side, a dissolution with fire in the joints; a collapse, a sound which started with a dull clap and became a vibration in the bones. Galey flinched without willing it, every muscle taut, a sickness clutching at his belly as the collapse became an upwelling of dust, and the dust began to swell outward, carried away from them by the wind.

It comes, he thought, expecting at any moment the flare of weaponry to protect the city, that might annihilate the shuttles, annihilate them, wake the world to war.

It did not.

The dust settled, some of it drifting aloft. There was silence. Behind him North swore softly.

"We're alive," Galey muttered, finding that remarkable. They still could not see the place clearly where the edun had stood, only that there was a great deal of dust, and that the tower was completely down.

"No way those machines do anything again," said Kadarin. "We got it, sir, and no one's dead."

His muscles wanted to shake. He gathered himself up, shot a considerable jolt of oxygen into his breather and fought light-headedness. Another thing dawned on him, as it had during the walk to the site: that they were not alone in this land.

"We just sent up a considerable signal," he said. "We'd better set better time getting back to the shuttles than we set getting here."

There was no argument at that. They had fought mri in the wars; and the tendency of mri to ignore their own casualties was legend. Four men with handguns was no deterrent; they had not Boaz's yellow scarf with them, not on this walk.

And he reckoned that with that thought at his heels he might last to the ships.

Elee clustered among their monuments. Chattering in tremulous voices, tall, pale bodies over-weighted in robes crusted with jewels and embroideries, manes . . . incredible manes, like white silk . . . flowing before the shoulders and halfway down the back, trimmed square or braided, on some making the ears naked, immodesty that sent a rush of heat to a mri face. Niun held up his hand, with more vast corridors before them and more elee scattered here and there about them and beyond; the Kel halted, and the elee nearest clung together in dread.

"You," Niun said, pointing at one tall enough to be male, and at least not Kath: the robes masked bodies and faces were alike, delicate. "You, come and speak."

The white face showed its terror, and hands clung to companions. The elee hesitated, and came with small steps like a frightened child for all his tall stature. It was strange face, mri-like, white even to the lips, and eyes of pale blue, shaded blue around the lids. Paint, Niun decided. It was paint. It livened the eyes, made their expression gentle and vulnerable.

"Go away," the elee said in a faint voice, much-accented.

Niun almost laughed. "Where is your Mother?" he asked, expecting a flare of defiance at least at this question. But the elee slid a glance toward the farther corridor for answer, and at that all the Kel murmured in disgust. "Walk with us," Niun said, and when the elee tensed as if to flee: *"We take no prisoners.* Walk with us."

The elee looked in one moment apt to break with terror, and in the next assumed a smile, made a graceful gesture of his long hands and offered them the way ahead.

Niun looked at his comrades, looked at Melein, who had veiled herself in this place of tsi'mri. "Ask his name," she said.

"Mother-of-mri, it is Illatai."

Weapons moved. Tsi'mri did not speak to her, save in peril of their lives; but she bade them stay, looked at Niun. "Tell this Illatai he must take us to the she'pan of elee."

Illatai glanced about him, at his folk who stood staring, and there was consternation in his face, the smile threatening to fade. The dusei stirred and moaned.

Tsi'mri, Niun thought, who even after so long, did not know mri. He considered, took the delicate sleeve of Illatai by its edge, and led him; the graceful man went with them, looked from one to the other with smiles for all they were veiled, nor did his eyes miss the beasts, nor the smile change. Niun let him go and let him walk as he would.

It was dream and nightmare, the halls of carven boulders and glass lit from glass structures of jewel colors, which light stained the floor of patterned stone and dyed the white manes and skins of elee and profaned Melein's robes too. There was no word from the Kel, none, for here were tsi'mri, and they were too proud; but elee talked behind their delicate hands and shrank from their presence, hiding themselves behind their monuments and their pillars of living stone and their jewel lamps. Here were columns rising to the ceiling, serpents wrought in gold, which crept up carven rocks and held the ceiling up, or crawled across it, writhing from this side to the other.

And beyond an archway of glass, and moisture-misted doors, a place where plants grew rife, and water flowed on stone walls and broke off glass panes. Plants bloomed, in warmth and mist. Vines hung thick, and fruit ripened, lush and full of moisture. "Gods," someone said in the ja'anom mu'ara. It was on them all, the dazzlement of such wealth; *this*, Niun thought, *this was Kutath once, before the seas fled*.

And more practical things: "Pumps," Duncan muttered very low. That must be so, that they had sunk deep as the basins to draw up such plenty.

More glass, panels and screens, prism colors: he remembered rainbows, which Kesrith had had and Kutath had forgotten. Doors yielded to the forceless hands of Illatai; his smile persisted, his moving was neither quick nor slow, but fluid as the water streams. Beyond the doors more elee clustered, and here gathered to bar the way, creatures delicate as lizards, whose robes seemed of greater weight than themselves, more alive than they, figured with—he realized it now—flowers, and beasts, and serpents.

Beautiful, he could not but think so. Beautiful as humans were not. He stopped, and the Kel stopped, before the white out-thrust hands, the frightened eyes which threatened nothing and pleaded defenselessness.

So also Illatai, who hovered between, as if to beg reason of either side.

"We shall go through," Melein said. "Say that to them."

"No," said Illatai. "Send. I shall carry messages."

Niun scowled at that, signed at Hlil, and toward one of the

delicate lights. Steel flashed, and crystal shards tumbled in ruin. The elee cried out in dismay, as out of one throat, and ward-impulse from the dusei began to build like storm.

"We go through," Niun said, and the elee stood still, clustered still before the doors. Blades were ready. Rhian and Elan were among the first to advance, and the elee simply shut their eyes.

"Do not," Niun said suddenly. "Move them."

It was not to anyone's taste, to lay hands on men and women who had chosen suicide. But lesser kel'ein performed that task, simply moving the elee aside; and as for Illatai, he turned his beautiful eyes on them all and gestured diffidently toward the inner hall.

The hall beyond blazed with gold, with colors, with the green of living things; and one elee there was in silver and gold, and one in gold and one in silver, amid others in colored robes: a gasp attended their entry, and elee tried ineffectually to prevent them, thrusting white hands before edged steel: they bled as red as mri and humans.

"No!" cried an aged voice, and the one in gold and silver held up her hands and forbade her defenders. The gold and the silver stayed close by her, the gold male, the silver young and female, who seated themselves in chairs as the eldest did, whose unity tugged unpleasantly at the senses: chairs, as if they were all of such rank. The bright-robed younger folk clustered behind them.

"Who speaks?" Niun asked.

"She is Mother," said Illatai softly, making a bow and gestures to either side. "Abotai. And mother-second, Hali. And Husband-first, T'hesfila. You speak to them, mri prince."

He looked back in profound disturbance, such that the dusei caught it. An order like their own; and not: a Mother who was not alone, who—he suspected—was not chaste. Melein folded her hands, unperturbed. "Among elee," Melein said as if she spoke in private council, "they have different manners. Abotai: you understand why I have come."

"To take service," the old elee said, and a frown came on her face. "You have thrown the world into chaos, and now you come to take service. Do so. Rid us of this trouble you have brought."

Melein glanced about her, cast a look at the elee, walked to one of the monuments and traced the delicate carving of a stone flower which bloomed out of living stone. "Tell the bearers-of-burdens, kel'anth of the ja'anom, that her existence is very fragile. And that An'ehon is in ruins; likely ruin belts the world, into cities beyond the basins. Tsi'mri have come from outside. And doubtless she knows this. This delicate place . . . stands; it did not link itself to An-ehon in the hour of attack, no. It was apart. Protected."

"Did the elee hear?" Niun asked coldly, though by the flickering of the membrane in the elee's eyes he knew that they were understood.

"Do you not know me?" Melein asked.

"I know you," the elee Abotai said, her old voice quavering with anger.

"And yet you let me in?"

"I had no choice," the elee acknowledged hoarsely. "I beg you, send your war away. It has no place here."

"Eighty thousands of years . . ." Melein murmured. "Eighty thousand years of voyaging . . . and to hear that we should go away. You are of persistent mind, Mother of elee."

"You will ruin us," the mother-second cried.

"Listen," said Abotai, and made a trembling gesture to her companions. "Show them. Show them."

A young elee moved, stirred several others into motion, a glittering of jewels, a nodding of white heads so swiftly moving that Niun clenched his hand on his gun and watched well where hands were. Light and colors flared, an entire jeweled wall parting upon a screen which came alive with images . . . black, and fire . . . dead mri, a tangled field of corpses, an edun in ruins; an edun fell in fire, and figures ran, swarming like corruption over the dead. . . .

—came closer, showing naked human faces.

—changed again, ships over ruins, and Kesrithi landscape.

And a human face dominated the screen, young and familiar to them. The Kel went rigid, and dus-sense lashed out. "No," Duncan said beside him, and Niun set a hand on his shoulder. "No. This is nothing humans have sent."

"Regul," Niun said, loudly enough for Melein, and the possibilities set a great dread into him. Melein's face had lost all humor.

"Open your machines to me," she said.

"No," the elee she'pan said. "Go fight from the dead cities."

"We have not come to go away at your bidding. If we fight, we will begin here."

The old she'pan's lips trembled. After a moment she rose up, and the mother-second and the Husband with her. She made a move of her hand; elee opened farther doors, and Niun gazed in amazement at a machine like and unlike that of An-ehon . . . like, for it had the same form; and unlike, for it was almost lost in ornament, in precious metal embellishments, in glass, in jewels.

"Come," said Melein to the few of the Sen who had come with them; they walked alone into that place, and the she'pan of the elee sought to follow.

"No," said Niun quickly, gestured, and kel'anthein moved at once to sweep their own contingents this way and that about the hall of the she'pan of the elee, setting their own bodies and their weapons, between the elee and the machine that was Ele'et.

"It will kill you," Abotai cried. "Our machine does not speak the hal'ari."

Melein turned, small and white against that metal complexity, walked back within the doorway. "Will it? Then you remind me of something even I had forgotten, Mother-of-elee: that elee know how to lie."

There was silence.

"Let her come," Melein said. "You may all come."

Niun hesitated, made a slight sign to the others, walked with Duncan and Hlil and Ras into that place; with Kalis and Mada and Rhian keeping close guard upon what elee strayed in and others holding the room behind.

Melein stepped within the white area of the floor, bathed at once in light that set her robes agleam; and Niun's heart clenched in him at the meaningless words that came.

"Na mri," she answered it, and again: "Le'a'haen! An-ehon! Zohain! Tho'e'i-shai!" Banks began to light, all but one. "A'on! Ti'a'ma-ka! Kha'o!" More flared into life, and there was an outcry of consternation from the elee present. Melein's voice continued, a roll call which set banks alight from one end to the other of the vast hall . . . the cities, Niun realized with a stirring of the hair at his nape: she was summoning the minds of the cities all about the world, names he had heard her name and names he had not—dead witnesses, the past springing to life about them, the guardians of the World.

And with every bank but two alight, with the thunder of machinery working, Melein spun in a swirl of white robes and pointed the finger at the she'pan Abotai with the blaze of triumph in her eyes.

"*Ai*, tell me now, Mother-of-elee, that I have no claim, tell me now that this place is yours, Mother of wars, Devourer of life! Now take the machine from me, elee!"

The elee stepped forward, stopped, at the edge of the light, her white face and white mane and metal robes agleam with it.

"The machines," Melein continued, her arm outstretched, "hold what I have given them, assume the pattern I built, as it was, as it *was*, elee she'pan. It holds the past of Kutath and the past of my own kindred, not, elee she'pan, not of Kutath; the Mysteries of those-who-went-out are within the net as well, my working; and it speaks the hal'ari, elee she'pan."

"Ele'et!" the elee cried.

"I am here," the machine responded, but it answered in the hal'ari, and the elee seemed shaken by that.

"Duncan," Melein said.

There was silence then, save for the machines. "Sov-kela," Niun murmured, touched Duncan's arm, received a distressed look, to which he nodded, indicating the circle to which he was summoned. "Leave the dus, sov-kela, for its sake."

Duncan entered the circle, and the dus stayed. "I am here," he said.

"This is the shadow-who-sits-at-our-door," the machine answered. "An-ehon remembers."

"Kel Duncan," Melein said. "Are you mine?"

"Yes, she'pan."

"I have need of a ship, kel'en. From here, it would be possible for you to contact humans. Do you think they will come to your request?"

"To take it?"

"That you will do for me too."

There was a moment's silence. There were five of them who felt that pain; and Niun swallowed heavily, trying to remain in contact. Duncan nodded assent; Melein reached to the board nearest and made some adjustment, looked back again.

"You have only to speak," she said. "An-ehon, give kel Duncan access for a transmission."

"He has access."

There was a moment when Duncan stood still, as if paralyzed; dus-sense purged itself, grew clear.

"SurTac Sten Duncan code Phoenix to any human ship, please respond."

He had spoken the human tongue. Niun understood; Melein would; there were no others, and the Kel and the elee shifted nervously. Duncan repeated his message, again and again.

"Flower *here*," a human voice returned. *"Duncan, we copy; what's your location?"*

And another voice, supplanting it, female: *"Duncan, this is Boaz. Where are you?"*

Duncan looked at Melein; she nodded slightly.

"Shuttle one, this is Flower." It was a different voice, older. *"Boz, don't jeopardize your position: keep silence. You may draw fire."*

"Tell them otherwise," Melein said.

"This is Duncan. The cities will not fire, if you do not provoke it. I can give you my location. Boaz, is a shuttle out?"

"We have two. Galey's down here; you know him, Sten. We'll come in if you'll let us. No firing. Where are you?"

"Terms," the voice from *Flower* cut in. *"What guarantee of safety? Duncan, are you speaking under threat?"*

"Your name is Emil Luiz, sir, and if I were under threat I would not give you a correct answer. —Boz, from the ruins nearest Flower, *southeast to some low hills; you'll see pillars, Boz, and a city within the rocks. Do you know that site?"*

"We can find it. We'll be there, Duncan. Be patient with us."

"Understood, Boz. You'll be safe to land. You only."

"Cease," said Melein.

"Transmission ceased," the machine echoed.

"Aliens," Abotai hissed. "You deal with aliens."

Duncan pulled his veil aside, and there was a void in the dus-sense; a cry went up from the elee, for it was the face of the image. He seemed not to regard it, but looked at Melein. "Is there else," he asked, "she'pan?"

"When they come," she answered.

"Aye," Duncan said, and the void persisted, a gap and a darkness where Duncan had been. A touch fell on Niun's shoulder; it was Hlil. He felt all of them, Ras, Rhian, Taz. Only Duncan was not there, for all that Duncan returned to him, and looked nakedly into his eyes, and stood among them.

"Veil yourself," Niun said, "sov-kela."

Duncan did so, and he and his beast went aside, into the other room, among the others who waited.

They rested . . . must, finally. Galey sucked in great breaths from the mask, bowed over, uninterested in the ra-

tions the others passed among them. A drink of water, that
he took, and bowed down with his head against his arms. His
knees ached and his temples pounded. He rubbed at eyes
which ran tears that never stopped.

More such to go: the city of the mri dead . . . that one
next, he reckoned.

"Sir," Kadarin said. And when he responded lethargically:
"Sir . . ."

He looked up, rose, as the others scrambled to their feet.
There was a ship coming. He stared at it, blank and terrified;
and there was no place to go, no concealment in the vast flat:
it was coming low.

One of their own. He blinked, no less disquieted, heard the
same realization on the lips of Magee and Kadarin.

It was coming for them, coming in fast.

"Treachery," Nagn hissed, her color gone white around the
nostrils.

Suth sat still, his hearts quite out of phase, stared at the
screens on which shuttles and *Santiago* were moving dots, all
his calculations amiss.

"Bai," Morkhug pleaded.

Suth faced his sled about. His attendant crouched in the
corner, attempting invisibility. Suth considered, regarding his
mates who looked to him for decision . . . suddenly keyed in
the control center, where a contact to *Saber*-com was
maintained continuously.

"Bai Koch," he requested of his own younglings, and
slowly calmed his breathing, suppressed the racing heartbeats
with reason. The human face suddenly filled his screen:
Koch, indeed: Suth knew him by the ruddiness and white,
clipped hair.

"Bai Suth?" the human bai asked.

"You are undertaking operations without consultation, bai,
contrary to agreement."

"No operations; maneuver. As you have an observer near
the world, as you have received transmission, as we have. We
are moving more reliable monitoring into position. We
confess surprise, bai Suth; we are not yet ready to address
policy."

"What action are you taking, bai?"

"Meditating on the matter, bai Suth."

"What is your installation onworld doing?"

A hesitation. "What is yours doing?"

"We are not in contact. They are pursuing previous instruction. Doubtless they will not act beyond those instructions."

"Ours likewise, bai Suth."

Suth sucked air. "Is your intention to accept this offered contact, reverend ally?"

There was a second hesitation. "Yes," Koch said.

Suth's hearts left synch again. "We . . . urge the bai to enter urgent consultations with us."

"Most assuredly. You are welcome aboard."

"We also . . . must contact our onworld mission."

Koch's face remained impassive. There was a slight flaring of his nostrils; what this meant in a human was disputable.

"We advise you," Koch said, "to stay clear of Kutath; we do not mean to have lives endangered. We would take very seriously any approach to Kutath, bai Suth."

"We wish to send a shuttle to your ship."

"I have said that you are welcome."

"I am entering arrangements. Favor, bai Koch, maintain a full flow of data to our offices."

"Agreed."

"Favor."

"Favor," Koch murmured in turn, and faded.

Suth sucked a deep breath, puffed it out with a flutter of his nostrils. "They wish me aboard."

"Bai?" Tiag mourned, visibly disturbed.

"Secure ship," Suth said. And when they delayed in confusion: "Leave onworld to onworld; secure the ship. *Saber* . . . is *here*."

"Enough," said Melek in horror; Magd killed the message which played over and over in the recorder. There was the thump of the pumps in the silence, the furtive scratching of some night-wandering crawler at the plastic dome.

They were alone, they two, senior. They had killed their assistants, a grim matter of economics. They hungered almost constantly in their terror; and Magd looked on Melek with continual fear. It was next, when it came to seniority.

"There is a way out," said Melek.

"I am listening." Magd's belly hurt. It really existed on short rations, pampering Melek, beginning to die slowly in the hope of living longer. Its skin flaked; its joints were whitening. More than anything it desired to please; its thoughts were nightmare, of hunger on the one hand, being refused survival by the elder Suth if it dared leave its post; of slaughter at Melek's hand, merciful and more immediate. It could not think. It wanted life, clung to hope, scrabbled after this one, that Melek itself offered.

"Orders," Melek said, "require we observe and find this youngling Duncan. That we stir up the mri and destroy this youngling if we find it. This is our way out. Listen . . . *listen,* youngest! Will this message have gone out and *Shirug* not know? Is not our time shortened here? They will send us orders; we finish here; we *finish.* Then we can come back; then Eldest will welcome us and make us favorites, feed us of his own cup. Both . . . both of us. If we do this for him. If we finish."

Magd had no inner confidence. Magd's hearts labored and its mouth was dry, its tongue sticking to the membranes, so that water and soi were the only coherent desires. Magd knew the trap: that yielding food to Melek, Magd was no longer strong enough to resist, no longer keen-witted.

"Yes," it said, desperate, paid anxious attention as Melek brought up charts on their screens.

"Here," Melek said, indicating a place near hills. "This is the place. We must be ready; we must work out all the details. You will lead in, youngest."

"Yes," it said again.

It would have agreed to any instruction.

XVII

It was an hour for sleeping. Perhaps some within the elee city did so, but none within the hall of the elee she'pan, nor anywhere about it. Niun sat still, at the feet of Melein, his dus and his companions by him, while certain kel'ein, mostly hao'nath and ja'ari, walked the corridors of the city, wandering by twos and by threes, to observe the things which passed among the elee. None offered them violence. None challenged them, or alarm would have been raised in the halls of Ele'et, and blood would have flowed: it did not; and the most part of the Kel sat quietly in attendance on the she'pan.

"You must call them back," said Abotai of the kel'ein who ranged the city corridors. "They must not—must not harm Ele'et."

"They do not," Melein said softly, and stilled any protest of Sen or Kel with an uplifted and gently lowered hand. "And we go where we will."

"Understand . . ." Abotai's lips trembled, and she held the hand of the Husband who sat beside her. "More than lives . . . these precious things, she'pan of the mri."

"What things?"

Abotai gestured about her, at the hall full of carved stones, flowers in jade, ornate work over every exposed finger's-length of surface, works in glass, statues in the likeness of elee and mri and lost races and beasts long forgotten, whether myth or truth. "Of all Kutath has made, of beauty, of eternal things . . . they are here. Look—look, mri she'pan." Abotai slipped from her ornate robes a pin, passed it to the youth Illatai, who sat in a chair near her. He leapt up to bring it, but Niun gestured abruptly and intercepted it. It was a translucent green stone, the likeness of a flower even to veins within the leaves, and a drop of moisture on a petal. He handled it most carefully, and passed it to Melein.

"It is very beautiful," Melein said, and passed it back at

once the same route it had come. "So are live ones. What is that to me?"

"It is an elee's life," said Abotai. "A sculptor spent his life to perfect that flower. Each thing you touch . . . even to the stonework under your feet . . . is the life of an elee, a perfection. Ele'et is a storehouse of all the millions of years of the meaning of Kutath, not alone of elee. *You* are here, wrought in stone, written in records, as we are."

"You are generous, then. A manner of pan'en, a holy thing. We shall tread lightly on it, this stonework. But we care nothing for it."

"It is all here," said Abotai. "All the goodness of the past. All perfection. Saved."

"For whom?" Melein whispered. "When the sun fades and the last lake of the last sea is drunk, and the sand is level . . . for *whom,* mother of elee?"

"For the Dark," said Abotai. "When the Dark comes . . . and all the world is gone . . . these things will stand. They will be here. After us."

"For whom?" Melein said yet again. "When the power fades, when there is not even a lizard left to crawl upon your beautiful stones—what is the good?"

"The stones will be here."

"The wind will erode them and the sand will take them."

"Buried, they will survive any wind that blows."

"Will it matter?"

"They will exist."

Niun drew in his breath, and there was a murmuring in the Kel.

"Is that the end," asked Melein, "of all the races and the civilizations, and the dreams of the world, to be able to leave a few stones buried beneath the sands, to tell the Dark that we were here? Leave us out of your pan'en, she'pan of elee. We want no part of it. Consumer of the world's substance, was it this, was it this for which you ate all the world and let the ships go . . . to leave a few stones to say that you were here?"

"And what gift do you leave?" Abotai pointed to the kel'en by a serpent pillar, at Duncan. "*That,* and the beasts? Aliens, to come here and see these things, and steal them, or destroy them?"

Duncan had looked up, and for a moment, a brief moment, he was back with them, a touch of pain in the dussense.

"He," said Melein in a still voice, "is more to Kutath than you, or your children, or the fine trinkets you have made to amuse the Dark. You gave me a flower in stone to touch, and it was the life of an elee. Duncan, kel'en, shadow-at-my-door . . . come here. Come here to me."

No, Niun pleaded with her in his mind, for Duncan had borne enough, had more yet to bear; but Duncan rose up and came, and sat down again at Melein's feet, his dus settling disconsolately against him. Melein set her hand on his shoulder, kept it there, while Duncan bowed his head. "He is not for your touching," Melein said. "But he is *our* gathering, elee she'pan, and far more precious than your stone flower."

"Abomination!"

"There are builders and there are movers, mother of elee; and in the great Dark—the builders have only their stones." She touched Duncan's shoulder, rested her hand there. "We went out, to find a way for all to follow. The great slow ships in which generations were born and died . . . took Kutath as far as our generations could reach; there was no hope, so few the ships, so many those left behind, on a world with no means left for ships—your doing, elee. But the ships of humans, that leap the Darks so blinding-swift—one such, only one; and perhaps eyes will live that will *see* these pretty stones of yours. And desire them. And scatter them, perhaps, that all the universe will wonder at the hands that made them."

"No," Abotai hissed.

"Then close your eyes, mother of elee. You are bound to see things you will not like at all. We do not serve to your service any more. And first, a ship, ai, kel'en-my-brother's-brother?"

Duncan looked up. The edge of his veil was damp and his eyes filmed. "Aye," he said.

She bent and kissed his brow. "Our Duncan," she murmured, and whispered: "If lives of humans come into our hands, take or give: I pass them to you. I do not ask more of you than the People need. And you will not do less."

"She'pan," he replied.

Time passed, that the elee murmured together in the edges of the hall, that elee brought food and drink, and offered to them; but they were not guests, and would not take. Elee ate and drank; those of the People that hungered drew what they needed of their own supplies, and if cups of water tempted them, pride forbade, and the law. They took nothing, not one.

And suddenly it came, the machine voice out of the other hall, advising them of movement in the skies of Kutath. Melein sprang up, all the People rising. "Stay," she bade them, and went with Sen only; and in the frightened whispers of the elee, the Kel settled back again.

"It has come," Niun said, hearing from the other room the advisement that it moved their way. He reached out, touched Duncan's sleeve. "Sov-kela?"

The void in the dus-sense filled, slowly, remarkably calm.

"We ought to go out there," Duncan said. "Not have them come in among elee; no knowing what could result of that. I should be out there, myself."

"So," Niun agreed.

"And you. If you would."

"I shall ask that," Niun said. Other dus-sense came to them, Taz, anxious and concerned; Rhian, who moved to join them and sank down on his heels, silent, solid.

Ras came. "Are you well?" she asked, touching at Duncan's arm; and Duncan murmured that he was. Strange, Niun thought, that there was affinity between these two, but there was; and Hlil drew near, who had no love of tsi'mri things . . . but he had lost his distaste regarding Duncan. Taz moved to them. *Always so,* Niun thought, *on Kesrith, that we and the beasts sat together; one never wondered there, whose was the need.* There was a numbness, a blessed lack of pain, the slow song of dusei—then disturbance, a sense of distance, of looking heavenward.

"The wild one," Duncan murmured. "It warns us. We have to go out now. We have to go."

"Not all," Niun said. "You and I. A few hands of others. I want some dusei left here, for safety." He rose up, hastened unbidden to the machine hall, stood there an instant until Melein turned her face to him.

"I set it in your hands," she said, "and Duncan's. They are coming in."

Elee watched them in their passage through the halls. The kel'ein ignored elee in their haste, hands empty of weapons; and Duncan spared them only an anxious glance, white, blue-eyed faces which stared at them forlornly and listlessly and perhaps . . . perhaps had self enough left to worry for their own brief lives and not for their treasure. He shuddered at them. They shrank away in equal terror whenever a kel'en brushed close to them.

And when it was clear they meant to go out, a frightened group of the jewel-robed citizens held up hands to stop them, hastening to show them a door that they might use, well-hidden in a trio of carved and living stones.

"They are jealous of their glass walls," said one-eyed Desai, when they were out in the dark and free. There was a muttering of laughter, for mri hated barriers, borders, and locked doors. The way that they had come in, letting the wind into the halls . . . that was a satisfaction to them, mri humor, equally grim.

Dawn had begun; it was a logical time for meetings, and the logical place was before them, the wide expanse of sand between the city and the carved pillars: room enough there for landings. Duncan walked, and Niun stayed beside him, with the others at his back, nothing questioning. The sand ahead writhed and rippled with life which fled the ward impulse of their two dusei. And when they had come most of the distance he stopped to wait.

Niun stood close, having moved between him and the wind. Desai did so from the other side, setting a hand upon his shoulder; and the ja'anom, for they were mostly ja'anom in the company, stood as close as they might, as if to shelter him, caring for him as for a child. He was always colder than they, and they seemed to realize his tendency to chill.

Sometimes, Niun had taught him early, a kel'en might find himself regretting friendships out-of-House, caught in a tangle of obligations and debts: best never to form them. When one did, there was one clear law, one service above other services, and that was the she'pan's will; if one was mri, one believed that.

There were two lights in the sky, brightening steadily out of the north.

"Shuttle's aboard, bay one," the secretary reported.

Koch took note of it, impatient, more interested in the flow of data from *Santiago*, which had moved closer to Kutath, within the critical limit. Regul visitors aboard were not to his taste; not now. They were here and they had to be welcomed. Averson would be coming up at any moment, to handle interpretation where needed. He had prepared information to satisfy regul curiosity and quiet their fears. Degas was scanning what further materials Averson planned to send the allies to be sure they were clean and clear of sensitive items. That was a hasty job, and critical. And it had to be ready; with regul on the ship, they were out of time.

He reached for the panel, coded in Degas's office.

And suddenly alarm lights flashed red.

"Sir," the bridge cut through. "Damage to landing bay one."

He stabbed the reply button, ignoring other lights which began to flash on his board, an urgent pulse from Degas's channel, the muffled babble of information from the operations contact. "The regul shuttle? Was it involved?"

"Yes, sir; we don't know details; we don't get com down there; the whole bay is breached. Casualties undetermined. Cause undetermined. Crash team is on its way, and med and security. The section sealed."

"Sir," Zahadi's voice overrode. "*Shirug* is moving our way."

Panic slammed into him. *Fire,* instinct advised him, xenophobic; politics was more cautious. "Get in touch with them," he said. "Advise them keep clear. Advise them we're doing what we can with the shuttle and they're to stay back."

A moment passed. He opened contact with Degas. "Take charge in-ship," he said, and broke off. His eyes were on scan, where each sweep jumped them nearer. There was a tiny blip out of *Shirug's* front, a shuttle, flea-sized between the warships.

They were not stopping.

"Bai," said a regul voice suddenly. "This is youngling Ragh, favor, bai. What is the situation? What has happened to the shuttle? What is the extent of damage?"

"Stand off, *Shirug.* Stand off at once. We don't know what has happened down there yet. We do not permit any closer approach. Stand off or expect strong action."

"Were there deaths, bai Koch? What of casualties?"

Koch darted a glance aside to scan, stabbed in a code for *Santiago.* RECALL. RECALL. CODE RED. "We are determining that now, youngling. Who is in command of *Shirug?* Was bai Suth on that shuttle?"

There was silence from the other end. The regul were at the limits of their shield; if they came closer, *Shirug* itself would penetrate that critical perimeter; it was fire or permit approach. The shuttle was already inside it.

Peace or war, on a word, an act.

"Sir." It was Degas, breaking through on red-channel. "Sir—"

"Back us off!" Koch ordered Zahadi. *"Up shields!"*

They hit maneuver without warning. Lights flashed everywhere on the boards.

"We don't have full shielding," Zahadi's voice returned. "The damage in bay one—"

There was a shudder in *Saber's* framework. Scan flicked to another image, pulsing warning. The shuttle within their perimeter was coming at the base line, at their kilometer-long midsection.

"Fire on the shuttle," Koch ordered. "Fire!" And then a second look at rapidly altering scan.

All the instruments jumped; a shock quivered through frame and hull like the blow of a fist.

"Hit," command relayed. "Damage—"

"Localize command!" Koch shouted into com, handing it to Zahadi entirely. He reached for the desk, for the restraint.

Scan went out.

Suddenly pressure hit, and red dissolved to white like the tearing of a film.

They were dead. He had time to know that.

The ships came in, one, and the other of them, in close sequence. The Kel regarded this with no outward show of emotion . . . this their first close sight of ships, and strangers who had struck at An-ehon, at them, and killed kin of theirs.

Two ships. They had expected one.

"Let me go out alone," Duncan asked, received in reply a pressure of Niun's hand on his shoulder.

"When they are in full sight," Niun said, "then whatever you will. In this, you say what should be, sov-kela."

The hatch of the first was opening. Men came down, with black scarves tied on their blue sleeves—strange combination to mri eyes; and masks which made them fearsome, like machines; last came a familiar woman, small and broad and wearing a gold scarf.

"Ai," muttered the kel'ein at one breath, for none sent out sen'ein to a prospective quarrel; it was a good sign.

"She is Boaz," Duncan said, "sen-second. I know her."

He touched his dus, to bid it stay, walked forward on his own. The second ship had opened its hatch, and a black man stood alone in the hatchway; he did not know him, only the two: Boaz, and the man by her, whose tangled reddish hair he recognized despite the masks.

"Boz," he said in meeting, "Galey."

"Duncan," Boaz said, and drew down her mask to speak, breathing the thin air. "Do we get the meeting we came for?"

"Come with me; bring all your company with you."

"We leave a guard," Galey said.

"No," Duncan said softly. "You do not. Lock no door to a mri. That is the way of things."

"Do it," Boaz said.

"Boz—"

"You can't have it by human rules," said Duncan. "Maybe you can speak to the she'pan; I will do as much as I can in that regard, and likely you can; but an argument will diminish your chances. Come. Don't delay here."

"Trust them?" Galey asked.

"You might," Duncan said, "if you could explain your meaning to them. A mri is himself; trust that. It's all you will get. *Shon'ai*, they say: cast and catch. You cannot play the Game with a closed fist. And you lock no doors to them; they never will with you. It's important to realize that. Come. Come with me."

"It's what we came for," Boaz said to Galey and the two men with him. "Haven't we taken worse chances, with less assurance?"

Galey nodded after a moment. "Do you want our guns?"

"No. Just come. Keep your hands off them. And if you know any names among them . . . be wary of using them."

"Niun is here?" Boaz asked. "And the she'pan?"

"Expect no recognition. Likely he would not remember at all. He is not grateful for human help; and some of it was not help, Boz. You know what was done to him. Do not presume any gratitude or any grudge. Come."

"Harris!" Galey shouted across to the other ship. "All of us out. Come on out and leave the hatch open."

There was some hesitation at that; they came down finally, and the hatch stayed open . . . three men in that group.

Duncan turned and led them across the sand to the black line of the Kel. There was neither welcome nor threat. Hands stayed visible and at sides.

"He is Niun s'Intel," Duncan said to Boaz at that meeting. "Kel'anth of the ja'anom tribe and of the she'pan Melein. The city is elee, but you have nothing to do with them. The kel'anth understands all that you say; don't expect him to admit to human speech: it's enough he comes out here to meet you."

"Offer him and the she'pan my respect and my thanks for meeting us," Boaz said. "We appreciate his courtesy."

Niun inclined his head, but in the same moment kel'ein moved out toward the ships. "Hey," Galey exclaimed in outrage, and two of his men moved hands to weapons.

"No!" Duncan said sharply; and before Galey could object further, for mri hands were equally poised, and quicker: "You have lost them, Galey. Let it be. You can fight challenge: that is what they offer. Or I don't doubt you could walk away into the desert, with your weapons and provisions. *Owning* things, except what one can wear . . . this is not their reckoning. If you have a point, it is much wiser to come in and talk about it."

Galey slid a look at Boaz. She nodded, and Galey signed his companions to let be.

"The machines," Duncan said in the hal'ari, "belong to their authorities. They feel offended, but they were sent to talk, and they agree to come and do that."

"Is that translation?" Niun asked dryly, who had understood every word. "They are very eloquent."

"I know these two," Duncan said, "Boaz and Galey, and they have known you. They feel some obligation to reason on that account."

Niun's eyes flickered, memory, perhaps, of a long nightmare. "And these others?"

"If Galey chose them, they are sensible. And if Boaz is here, it is her choosing. The mri have no better friend among humans."

"Ai," Niun said, and with a darting glance toward the human company: "Walk with us," he said in the human tongue. "We ask."

"Sir," Boaz murmured, glancing down in courtesy, and gestured the others to come.

There was an easier feeling as they walked along, amber eyes which acquired expression, which frankly admitted curiosity. They had not gone far before whispers began to be passed in the Kel, remarking on their varied looks and statures and their clothing and their manners, which, for all it was not courtesy, was a step toward it: mri would discuss a man long before approaching him.

Easier, Duncan thought, moved, *that they have become*

used to me; for one said: *Our Duncan knows them,* as if that settled some essential question.

They neared the city, and the open doors. Then Duncan recalled the elee, and that matter, opened his mouth to explain.

Suddenly there was an impulse from the dusei, a vague disturbance. He stopped; Niun did, likewise troubled . . . looked skyward at the same instant Duncan felt the same impulse. The whole Kel had paused, looked, whether by curiosity to them or that they also felt it, the darting apprehension.

"Duncan?" Boaz asked.

"Niun," Duncan said, a sinking feeling in his gut. "Something's moving in. It's not the she'pan's alarm. It's out there. The outwalker sees it."

"Tsi'mri trick," Niun exclaimed.

"What is it?" Boaz asked louder, and then stopped, for there were visible now two dots in the sky, eastward, for all eyes to see.

"Regul," Galey breathed, which needed no translation. "O God, *they're* downworld too. Duncan, the ships . . . the ships . . . caught on the ground—"

"Go!" Niun shouted suddenly, and pushed at Galey, toward the shuttles. Galey ran, nothing questioning; the black man spun about unhindered and ran too; and the others after, all but Boaz, for Duncan seized her arm. "Desai!" Niun shouted. "Run tell the kel'ein let them go at once—*run,* kel'en!"

He gripped Boaz's arm too hard; he realized it and pressed her hand instead, held it for comfort. He might have gone . . . *he* . . . but the hal'ari was between him and such ships, hands not in practice, mind divorced from such realities. He watched; it was nightmare, the slowness with which frightened humans could run in advance of oncoming ships. The two stranger ships were distinguishable now, coming fast. Desai sped to the kel'ein by the ships in advance of the humans; and the kel'ein let them through, Galey's to the nearest and the black man and his crew to the second, the kel'ein already running back as the hatches sealed one after another. The ships were obscured for a moment in their own dust . . . . . . lifted.

"Ai!" the Kel exclaimed, sensing the import of that race for the sky; the ships streaked up, aloft.

"They have made it," Duncan said past the tautness in his throat. He realized the grip of Boaz's hand on his cold fingers, saw the ships roll and evade, the oncoming craft veering aside.

One human ship headed for them in pursuit; the other kept climbing, up and up, and beyond sight.

"He's going for help," Boaz cried. "Duncan, they're not ours, I swear they're not; and he's after help. Tell them that."

"Truth?" Niun asked.

"Boaz believes it," Duncan answered. "And she could well know."

Niun spun about suddenly, gestured the kel'ein toward the doors of Ele'et. "Come. Quickly!"

They moved, Boaz panting into her mask; Duncan seized her arm and belt and dragged her along; kel Merin took her other arm, and they entered the city corridors, past wide-eyed elee faces, nigh running, which mri did not do.

Dus-sense enveloped them, Boaz's fright, Niun's pain, his own . . . it was one. They had too many enemies, and too little of time. The odds had come down on them.

Came suddenly a shriek of air and the hall beyond exploded in shards of rock and glass.

They were hit. Something had gotten through.

"Run!" Niun shouted. They plunged through wind-borne smoke and over glass and blood-soaked elee bodies, for Melein and the rest of the Kel sat trapped at the heart of it.

"She'pan!" Rhian exclaimed at the shock, but Melein stood firm within the circle of light, staring up at the screens, trying to stay with the flow of data which poured out from Ele'et, and the voice which reached out to them, as desperate as the voices about her.

"She'pan," it said through Ele'et's voice, sexless, magnified, human. "She'pan, are you there? Do you hear?"

"I hear," she replied.

". . . under fire. Requesting . . . the firing. . . ."

"Repeat," she said steadily, for all that the foundations of Ele'et quaked, and glass shattered. "This attack is not our doing, human sen'anth."

"Regul," the voice returned, audible for the moment. "Do you understand that? Regul warship. . . ."

"This is Harris," another cut in on the frequency. "I'll get him. Galey's gone for—"

There was abrupt silence. "Harris?" the human voice pursued.

A light vanished from the screen. Fire shook them.

"Strike at the aircraft," Melein said. "Ele'et, strike!"

It vanished. The screen was empty.

"Regul fire," the human voice continued, appealing to her. "Orbiting . . . if you have weapons . . . them. . . ." The voice went out in prolonged disruption.

She looked about her, at anxious faces, at ruin in the hall beyond, shattered pillars, broken glass and carvings. "Return fire!" she called to the machines. "All cities, return fire to any ship which fires at us."

It would destroy the cities; there was no hope; she knew it.

"Not in range," the remorseless voice of Ele'et replied. "Seeking target."

"It is your doing," Abotai wailed, from without the circle. "Pull us out! Pull us out of the network! Ele'et is worth a thousand of the other cities. Bate the power and hide us."

"It is irony," Melein said. "You are honored to become warriors in the world's last age; and you avoided it so zealously until now."

"Ele'et!" Abotai cried, and lunged forward into the light, at her. Melein sprang aside, startled, looked up at the flash of a firearm in an elee hand . . . moved, kel-quick.

Kel Mada sprang for it; his body took the shot; and an instant later the sweep of a path'andim sword cut the elee Illatai half asunder. Abotai screamed, and Melein spun on her heel at the sting of something from back to arm; struck, with a shout of anger, and Abotai sprawled in her jeweled robes, neck broken.

Elee screamed in anguish; some fled; some struck blows with glass shards. And Hlil and Ras and Dias were instant with a fence of blades. Dusei launched themselves. What elee were within reach of those paws died worse than the others.

A section of the board went out, a city dead.

And by that dead panel, the Husband and the she'pan-second died. Kalis of the ka'anomin killed them, and the several elee who had fled, armed, into that corner.

"Coming up on target," the city Ele'et droned. "Priorities: shields or fire?"

"Shields," Melein said at once. She had killed; white-robed, she had struck in anger; she was dazed by that enormity—at the touch of sen'ein, who seized up her arm and tried to stanch her wound she realized that blood was running freely off her fingers. And beyond the hedge of kel'ein were others . . . Niun was back; and Duncan; and with them a strange small woman. Melein stared at her, at success and failure at once, while the city rocked with fire which sent the sound of breaking glass everywhere at once. She flinched, as they all did, despite dignity, stood still again as a sen'en bound her arm.

"Your ship is under fire," Melein said to the human who wore sen-color. "I have spoken with your sen'anth. They accuse regul; two ships lifted from here; I permitted. But one was destroyed."

"We are holding the way open," Niun said, came to her, took her good hand. "Come. Please, let us get you out of this place, while there is time."

She hesitated, reason persuading her that he was right; and if there was Sight, he was wrong. She leaned upon it, that inward turning which she had constantly distrusted.

Intel's kind of madness, she thought; it had launched them in the beginning, a she'pan's vision.

"Come!" Niun pleaded with her. "If this can be fought, humans are fighting it. For once, we cannot."

"We can," she insisted, but reckoning the cost. She turned from him, and from the sen'ein, looked up at the machine. "Ele'et. Location of the enemy. Show me."

Screens leapt to life. She saw the world, and a point above it which flashed in alarm, another point, stationary, a third, indistinct.

"Fire on ships which fire at Kutath."

"They have passed this range," Ele'et said. "Coming up over Le'a'haen. La'a'haen priorities: shields or fire?"

"Fire," Melein said. The membrane hazed her eyes a moment, cleared again. She watched the steady advance of the enemy.

In time another set of lights began to flicker on the boards.

There was nothing for the moment, only the dark and the stars, and change-over. Galey struggled with suit-fastenings, locked on his helmet; it was an exhausting exercise in the tight space of the shuttle, trying the while to keep an eye to scan.

"Not getting anything," Shibo muttered, fussing with com with one hand and working at his helmet with the other.

There was, ominously, something on scan.

It was *Santiago,* by its size; and it gave no answer to hailing.

"Where's *Saber?*" Kadarin asked. "What's going on, that

Saber's not up here doing something? They wouldn't have let regul through to us."

"Didn't let them, I'm thinking." Galey freed both hands, kicked in full toward the silent object in scan. Computer signal raised nothing. "No more com," he said. "Hold it. Let's give no one anything we can help. All we have for protection is being too small to spot."

They had visual finally, stark shadow and stark metal-glare in the light of Na'i'in. It was *Santiago,* hard to recognize, for the black shadow was in the wrong places on its hull, and it was rolling very slowly, describing its own peculiar dance about the globe of Kutath.

"Dead," Shibo whispered through the suitcom. "O God, we're up here with nothing. *Santiago, Saber* . . . both gone."

"Not our regul allies," Kadarin said, a thin, cold sound. "They're here, I'm betting, somewhere around the curve. Pounding the surface into rubble. And *Flower* . . . *Flower's* all we've got can get us home."

"What do we do?" Shibo asked. "Sir?—We dive back down there?"

Galey took several quick breaths, trying to think, with nausea heaving at his stomach. "The regul have to be close in," he said. "If *Shirug's* firing on the surface, they have to be close in as they can get; and they don't like to do that." The silver and black hulk of *Santiago* filled all their view now; he put the shuttle under comp, to match with its roll. From the others there was not a word, only careful breathing hissing over the suitcoms. It was an ugly operation, matching the tumbling hulk; comp did most of it. He jerked control back again at the last, contacted the flat plane aft with a jolt and grappled, trying not to look out the ports or at the screens which tumbled and spun with them.

"We're going in?" Kadarin asked. "Its armscomp can't have lasted."

"Easy," Galey muttered, his mind too muddled for argument. He applied power carefully, biting blood from his lips as the shuttle strained to control the derelict, sliding and grating metal on metal. It began to have its effect, a gradual stability, easing over to come level in the concealment of shadowside.

"We got us a ship," Shibo muttered. "And what, sir?"

"Hang to it," Galey said. He heaved himself out of the cushion and slung hand over hand aft, toward the hatch. "I'm going in to see if the E-system's active. If I can move her, we'll see."

"What are *we* supposed to do?"

"Aim her; keep her straight at them."

Shibo's voice and Kadarin's exclaimed protest; he did not stop, did not argue orders; it was not a thing that bore thinking, what there was left for them to do.

Shirug was due over that horizon sooner or later, down-world from them.

He was acrophobic, always had been, mildly. He seized a handjet from the locker, vented himself out the lock, looking steadily at *Santiago's* surface and not the stars, nor Kutath. There was no need to use the lock for entry; the gaping hull afforded access. The big ships were never meant to land, fragile compared to the tough downworld probes and the shuttle-workhorses: she had blown badly. The blackness inside was absolute, and his light showed barren ruin . . . no bodies, no gee, no power, no atmosphere, dead metal. He used the handjet in total dark, walls and bulkheads and hazards careening insanely past in the momentary contact of his suit lamp . . . fended a jagged edge of metal with his boot, bounced a wall in his haste, hurled himself through a hatchway and against another hatch. He used manual, and it opened, without the blast of atmosphere he had braced for. There was void, gaping ruin here too: the bridge had blown. Comp was down; the cold had got it. One light still showed, a red eye in the dark, on a panel at the right.

"Got some life," he sent back into the static. "E-light's lit. Think I can get her moving. You ungrapple when I do. Get yourselves downworld."

There was faint acknowledgment. He eased over to the panel. His stomach kept trying to heave and he swallowed repeatedly, sweating in the suit and cold at the same time. He found the whole progress of it like a bad dream; kept thinking traitor thoughts of taking them all and diving downworld to live: they did not know, in fact, whether *Flower* herself survived, whether the whole exercise had any use at all for anyone, any use.

Only he was *Santiago's* sometime pilot; she was his ship, and there was no one else.

Think job by job, he urged himself, held the handgrip. With a punch at the glowing button, other lights flickered in, an emergency-powered trickle of life in the vital systems.

Waiting: that was hardest. He held still, staring at the panel and trying not to think at all.

"You need help?" a thin voice came, lifeline to reality. "Sir?"

"Stay put, you copy? You see if you can't line us up real carefully when they show; I don't know what I have for directionals: you're my guidance. And don't you miss. Or hang on too long. I'll do what I can for myself."

There was prolonged silence.

"Shibo, you copy?"

"I copy clear, sir. We'll do it."

And a moment later: "We got a ship in scan, sir. Think it's *Shirug*."

A small anomaly fixed to the flat surface of a dead ship, a hulk which had been gently rolling: he hoped the regul were paying more attention, for a few moments, to Kutath. He imagined the angles for himself, the curvature of the world, the likely course of the regul over the major sites. Hoped . . . hoped, that it was not for nothing.

That was the hardest thing: that he would never know.

He looked out, holding the handgrip, letting his body drift until he could see the stars beyond the rent . . . the vast deep. He suffered the old inside-out wrench, the down-up-sideways of the senses trying to remember which way was which. It was a trick of the mind, human stubbornness. He knew with a curiously certain sense which way Kutath lay; goblin whispers urged at him, stirring at his neck.

Down . . . as far as a man could fall.

There was a shifting of the stars which attended movement, a fine adjustment.

"Now," Kadarin's voice hissed. "God help us."

He pushed the main thrust in, and *Santiago* started to move in earnest, with the emergency systems full. It was meant for pulling a crippled ship out of proximity to some mass; it was good for one long run.

"Closing," Kadarin's voice said. "Straight as she bears, sir."

"Cast off!" he shouted into com, sick at heart. "Cast *off!*"

Fire flung the bridge into blinding white. He reckoned he had done what he could, scrambled hand over hand for the gaping hole forward, one desperate chance.

A black wall blotted out the stars before him. It was *Shirug*.

Fire hit again, flung him back, drifting, with cold spreading through his legs.

"Evade!" Suth screamed into the unit, felt the wrench as *Shirug* made an abrupt maneuver.

"Fire does not stop them," the youngling voice of command wailed, breaking in panic. "They do not react—"

There was impact. It grated, rang through the whole of the vast teardrop; the sled-console went chaotic.

"Eldest!" Nagn cried; and Tiag and Morkhug tried to break through on their channels, drowned in static.

"Leave orbit!" Suth ordered. "Witless, leave orbit!"

There was no response. There was a lightness, a feeling that the least movement would unbalance things, his own great bulk, the sled itself, for all it was locked down.

"Command!" he ordered. Across the room the youngling Ragh, ghastly in its pallor, attempted to reach him, holding to furnishings which were fixed in place.

"Command!"

Nothing responded.

"See to it," he bade Nagn. Fearfully she detached from safety, trundled across the carpet, disappeared from his vision. Ragh reached him, held to the sled, moaning.

Gravity was not what it had been. Suth sat very still, his hearts persistently out of phase; there was sudden silence, the air circulation cut off.

Eventually the lights dimmed. He punched buttons frantically and received only chaos.

"Youngling!" he cried, but Ragh had sunk down by him, huddled down in a ball, out of his reach. "Youngling!" he kept shouting and punched buttons until he knew that no one would answer.

Then he began in his terror to go to sleep, to slow his pulse deliberately, shutting down, for there was a strange sensation of descent, whether truth or madness he had no experience to know. He wished not to know.

For a considerable time they would descend, as the orbit decayed.

All but a last handful of lights went out on the boards. Niun watched, crouched, his arms about his knees, in this dimmed hall which they held at the cost of lives. Duncan was by him, the dusei, and the others of his comrades of the several tribes. The doors were guarded, that to this room and that of the one beyond, all that they did hold securely, for the elee found courage to fight when their treasures were threatened, and no few of them had distance-weapons.

Melein turned from the machines, in the dimming of the world's cities, of Ele'et itself; signaled wearily. Young kel'ein hastened to bring her a chair and she settled into it, bowed her head, her injured arm tucked against her, a silence in which none dared intrude.

The woman Boaz was there, sitting in the corner where elee dead had lain . . . and mri, until kel'ein had carried out all the dead which profaned the she'pan's presence. An elee robe sheltered the human, for she was beyond youth by some few years, and very tired, and the air was, for a human, cold. Niun had ordered that himself, the plundering of a dead elee, of which they had numerous.

Outside was dark, night fallen . . . dark in the hallways of broken glass and shattered monuments, where elee scurried about gathering possessions, furtive scavengers, armed with distance-weapons, in which they had no great skill, but then, the weapons needed little. Some of them had come into mri hands. *Honor does not forbid*, Niun had told his Kel plainly. *If tsi'mri fire them at you, fire back, and do it better.*

They learned aim very quickly; and practiced on injudicious intruders.

More such fire came from outside. The sen'e'en Boaz lowered her head into her hands, looked up when it was done. "Is there no talking with them out there? Could I try?"

"Tsi'mri," Niun muttered.

"Tsi'mri," Boaz echoed him. "Is there no talking—ever—with you?"

"Boz," Duncan said, "be still. Don't argue."

"I'm asking them something. I want an answer. I want to know why they don't want to reason . . . why a hundred twenty-three worlds are dead out there, and this one has to be added to the list. I want to know why. You face regul, and you take on the elee and us too. Why?"

Niun frowned, anger hot in him; he took a moment, to gather self-control.

"I answer you," Melein said, startling him. "You ask me, sen Boaz. Of the dead worlds?"

"Why?" Boaz asked, undaunted when she should have been. "Why? What could make a reasonable species do such a thing?"

Niun would have spoken, but Melein lifted her hand, preventing. "You were at Kesrith, sen'e'en?"

"Yes. I was there."

"What happened there . . . to the mri?"

"Regul . . . turned on you; we had nothing to do with—"

"Why did regul do this thing, when regul do not fight?"

"For fear."

"That we would go away?"

Boaz grew quiet, thought proceeding in her dark and human eyes. "That they couldn't control you any longer; that you . . . might go to us. That you were too dangerous—to leave loose at the end of the war, not obeying them."

"Ah," said Melein. "And when the People have served, sen Boaz, always we ask a place to stand, where only our feet and theirs walk; when the agreement is gone, we go—The dead worlds, sen Boaz, . . . were *ours*. You have seen Kesrith. In Kesrith—we defended while we could; at Nisren—we might have left regul service, and did not, to our great sadness—I suspect, because we had no means to rescue a thing . . . very precious to us. We used regul; we took a new homeworld. Nisren is a dead world; Kesrith is almost so. Who made them dead? We? You are the killers of worlds. Among the hundred twenty-three . . . are many Nisrens, many Kesriths. And you have come to make another."

There was profound silence. Of those who could have understood, there were three, but dus-sense translated something of it, that sat in the anguished eyes of Boaz, of Duncan.

"We have lost the shields," Melein said in the hal'ari. "We might survive another pass here; the living rock is over us here, and more stubborn than stones that hands have set. But I think of the camp, of Kath and Sen. We cannot send a messenger to them from here, through the elee; and any who tries to reach us will be murdered in their treachery. I weary of this place. The rocks outside can shelter us. And reaching them . . . cannot be too difficult, with the walls broken out. We will go there. We will learn whether our Kath and Sen survives. And you other tribes, go, if you will, but I ask otherwise."

"Let us," said kel Rhian, "send messengers each to our own tribes, to know how they fare. But the hao'nath stay."

"So do the ka'anomin," said old Kalis. Other kel'anthein nodded, Elan and Tian and Kedras.

"What for our dead?" asked the path'andim second. They mourned their kel'anth Mada, and no few of their number, for in their rage at the elee, they had been forward in the defense. "They will be butchered by elee hands."

"Can the ja'anom dictate to any?" Niun asked. "We go with weapons in our hands and as quickly as we can, to pro-

tect the she'pan. We do not quit serving when we are dead;
for me, if I fall, I am glad if the elee waste their strength on
me, and if my brothers save what I would save if I lived."

"Ai," muttered the path'andim. "We hear."

"Ai," the murmur ran the room. Niun stood up, and
Duncan, and all the others, sen Boaz last, and uncertainly.

"We are leaving the city," Duncan translated for her.

"Our ships will come," Boaz insisted, looking from him to
Melein. "We should wait *here*. They will come and help,
she'pan."

"Then we should be alive when they come," said Melein,
honoring her with a touch of her hand. "Come with us, sen
Boaz. Walk with our Sen."

She opened her mouth as if she would dispute; and closed
it, bowed her head. When they prepared to go out, she
wrapped her elee cloak about her and adjusted her mask, and
set herself where other sen'ein put themselves, inward of the
Kel, with Melein.

Swords came out, a whisper of steel. For his part, Niun
drew both gun and kel-sword; so did Duncan; and those who
possessed elee weapons held them ready. They walked quietly
into the next room, where path'andim and the patha of
Kedras held the door.

"They are massed out there," the patha second said softly,
"all in hiding. Behind the pillars, behind the rocks both small
and large. Some of the dead are not dead, to our reckoning,
but wounded who fear to move."

"Ai," Niun said, taking that danger into account. "Then we
make sure of them."

"We are at your back," said Rhian. "We follow ja'anom
lead."

"Aye," said Kalis. "I am senior and I say so." There was a
whispered agreement of other voices.

"Then follow," Niun said. He moved, first kel'anth, first to
go, with the others at his back. He laid down fire and fire
came back: someone by him fell, and his dus screamed rage
and scrambled forward into that dark hall with a pace he
could scarcely match on the polished floors. He fired where
he saw fire; by his side was another with a gun, and another
dus: Duncan, Duncan was by him, a kel'en well-accustomed
to this manner of fight.

The dusei hit glass, breached the walls into the moisture of
the gardens, admitting the Kel: elee fired from cover there
and then fled. More fire came from the door beyond, and of

a sudden one of the dusei roared with pain and lunged forward, gone berserk, a madness the others caught, and the youth Taz with them. Taz plunged ahead, riddled with elee fire, and took several elee in the sweep of his blade before more shots brought him down.

"Yai!" Duncan shouted at the dusei, bidding for sanity . . . Ras took a hurt: *they* felt it; and Taz's maddened dus plunged into elee like the storm wind. Niun went after it, holstered the failing gun and hewed with the sword whatever opposed him, foremost of a wedge which broke and reformed around the monuments, the carven stones, the statures, sweeping the hall of life.

There were exits; they did not take them . . . rushed, killing, as the dusei killed, after Taz's beast, for its kel'en was dead, and it was mad. Dus-sense filled the halls, the elee fled, screaming, abandoning weapons, casting off the weight of their jeweled robes, whatever hindered them; the Kel ran over broken glass and pools of blood and the jeweled fabric of elee garments.

"*Out!*" Niun cried, trying to break from the madness, that felt like desertion. The dus was dying; it wanted . . . *wanted*, followed the essence of Taz into the Dark, and drew the living Kel after.

He stopped, buffetted by bodies of his own kel'ein, seized at them, turned them for the open air, for the nearest breach in the walls, and out into the clean wind and across the sands. Dusei joined them. They ceased running outside, walked, with the dusei among them. Niun walked backward a moment, taking count . . . saw the white form of Melein; felt Duncan safe, and all the others dus-linked, all alike filled with horror for the beast which still pursued its crazed way apart from them, ranging the shattered halls of Ele'et, screaming its anguish and killing. Sen Boaz was with them, half-carried by two kel'ein, her elee robes stained with dark gouts of blood, but none of it, seemingly, her own. Melein's white was stained with more blood, as all of them reeked of it. They walked, a space apart from the city, up a slope to the carven rocks of the hills, where the hurt and the old might sink down and breathe in safety, ringed about by weapons.

The dusei crowded together; they who were linked with them did so, and Niun sank down among the others and held to his beast, its blood on him, for it was burned and glass-cut and shuddering in its misery.

Of a sudden there was a break, a cessation of hurt, like storm lifted.

"It is dead," Duncan said hoarsely, and Ras and Hlil and Rhian of the hao'nath held close to their dusei, shivering with them.

"*Mi'uk,*" Niun said. "Dus-madness. It almost took us all into the Dark. Gods . . . gods . . . gods."

His mind cleared, still numb, remote. He pushed himself to his feet, the few steps to Melein's side, to kneel and take her hand, frightened for her state of mind; but the calm came from her to him, a slight pressure of her fingers, a steadfast look. "What loss?" she asked him.

"Kel Taz; his dus—" He looked about him in the dark, questioning with his look . . . heard names others murmured, of those left behind.

Dias was lost, and Desai. He bit his lip, sorrowing for him in particular. A double hand of the ja'anom had perished; four hands plus two of the path'andim including the kel'anth Mada; one hand three of the patha; Kalis of the ka'anomin and two hands of her kelein; a hand three of the ja'ari; two hands one of the mari; four hands two of the hao'nath.

"My blessing on them," Melein said, looking suddenly very tired, and drawing her wounded arm more closely to her side. "Now we must see how the camp fared."

"Better than here," said a voice, very young and female. There was a stirring from the hindmost ranks near the rocks, and an unscarred, veilless, worked her way through in haste. She knelt down by Melein and bowed for her touch . . . looked up as Melein lifted her head with her fingers.

"You are—"

"Kel Tuas, Mother. Kel Seras sent us, when the fire stopped; it came near, but never hit the camp; I do not think it hit it since. I ran and hid in the rocks, to see what I could learn: my truebrother . . . went in. And I do not think by what I saw—"

"He did not reach us," Melein said.

"I thought that was so," Tuas said very faintly. "I have waited—some little time. May I carry word to Seras, Mother, that you are safe?"

Melein took her face in her hands and kissed her on the brow. "Are you able, kel'e'en?"

"Aye, Mother."

"Then run."

The kel'e'en sprang up and returned the kiss, turned in

blind haste; but Niun caught her arm, took an Honor from his own robes and pressed it into her cold hand. "Kel'anth," she murmured. She was ja'anom; he recalled her now, an innocent like Taz. The tribe was vital; it lost lives and gained them again in the young.

"Run," he said. "Life and honors, kel Tuas."

"Sir," she breathed, and parted their company, passed the ranks of those gathered about, serpent-quick. She was not the only messenger sped; others ran out, through the hills, shadows, young and swift of foot.

And those of them who remained, settled, reassured for what small news they had, that Ele'et had drawn the fire and the camps gone unscathed. They caught their breath, began to bind up wounds: Niun felt a growing ache in his lower arm, and found a bad slash, which Duncan bound for him. Ras had taken a wound in the shoulder, and Hlil attended it; Rhian had taken a minor hurt on his arm; there was hardly a kel'en in all the company entirely unscathed, and the dusei moaned and keened piteously with their own hurts, burns and lacerated paws. None of them would die, neither dus nor kel'en. Dusei licked at their own wounds assiduously, and at wounds of kel'ein where they might. Niun accepted it for his own, and it helped the pain.

Sen Boaz sat among them. "Are you hurt?" Duncan inquired of her, but she denied it, sat bowed, breathing great gasps from her mask, her elee robe wrapped about her and glittering with precious stones in the starlight.

And it was not the only such robe in sight.

"Look," said Rhian of the hao'nath, pointing toward the city, where elee stirred forth, pale faces and white manes and jeweled robes showing clearly in the dark among the huge rocks about which Ele'et had its shape.

"Let them come," kel Kedras said, "if they have gone entirely mad. I weary of elee."

"Aye," a number of voices agreed, and Niun himself sat with the blood pounding in his temples and an anger for the dead they had lost.

But the elee below wandered the near vicinity of their city as if dazed, and some of them were small: children. The anger of the Kel fell when they realized that, and the air grew calmer. Kel'ein talked then, grimly. but not of killing.

Niun bowed his head against his dus and felt all the aches in his body; and those of the dus; and those of the others. There were moments when dus-sense had no comfort to give, when the beasts needed, more than gave; and he comforted it such as he could, with a gentle touch and what calm of mind he could lend.

"They do not come," he said at last to Duncan. "Neither regul nor humans. Gods, I do not know, sov-kela; I think—" He did not dare to voice despair; the Kel was about them. He slid a glance instead to the human sen'e'en. "She says they will come; but she does not know. *Ai!*" he said sharply, looking up, and all the company looked heavenward. For a moment he both hoped and feared.

A star fell, in the west, over the basins.

That was all.

"They will come," Melein said.

"Aye," they all murmured, as if hoping could make it so.

Duncan settled down, and Ras, and Rhian and Hlil; he did, and laid his head against the shoulder of his dus, for warmth, and for comfort of it. The dusei made a knot, all touching, spreading warmth even beyond their circle.

Only the lightness, the shyness which had been Taz s'Sochil was gone from them. Somewhere up in the hills was the wild one, the only wild one.

There should be one, Niun thought, one which went apart.

"Ai," someone murmured, toward the dawning, and *Ai!* came the cry from the height where the sentries sat.

The whole Kel came awake, and Niun scrambled to his feet as the dusei surged up, among the others. Melein stood, and the sen'ein, and the human Boaz, last and with difficulty . . . eyes lifted toward the skies.

It began as a light, a brightening star overhead, that became a shape, and a thunder in the heavens.

"*Flower!*" Boaz cried; and if the Kel did not know the name, they saw the joy. "*Ai,*" they cried softly, and excitement coursed through the dusei.

The elee below had seen it. Some which had come out to spend the night at the edge of the ruin fled indoors again. Others ran for the rocks, their fine robes and white manes flitting as a pallor in the dawn.

Then *Flower* came down, ponderous, ungainly, settling near the city; it extended its strange stilt legs and crouched down to the sand like some great beast. The dusei backed around behind the shelter of the line of the Kel and moaned distress, snorting in dislike of the wind it raised.

The sound fell away; the wind ceased, and the whole ship

crouched lower and lower, opened its hatch and let down the ramp.

Waited.

"Let me go down to them," Boaz asked.

There was silence.

"If we say 'go' " Melein said finally, "you enter your ship and go away—and in what state are we, sen Boaz? Without ships, without the city machines, without anything but the sand. Humans would understand our thought . . . at least in this."

"You want to bargain?"

There was another silence, longer than the first. Niun bit at his lips until he tasted blood, heat risen to his face for the shame that mri should face such a question.

"No," Melein said. "Go down. Send us out a kel'en who will fight challenge for your ship."

"We don't do things that way," Boaz protested. "We can't."

"So." Melein folded her hands before her. "Go down, then. Do what you can."

The sen'e'en looked uncertain, began to walk away, with more than one backward glance at the beginning, and then none at all, hastening down the slope.

"They are tsi'mri," Duncan said out of turn. "You should not have given her up; she would have stayed. Call her back."

"Go to them yourself," Melein said in a faint voice, "if you see more clearly than I. But I think she is much like you, kel Duncan. Is she not?"

He stood still.

And after a little time the sen'e'en Boaz did, halfway down the slope to the ship. She looked back at them, then turned to the ship again, cried out strange words, what might be a name.

In time a man appeared in the hatch, came out, and down the ramp. Boaz walked toward him. Others came out, in the blue of the human kel'ein.

They stood in the open a time, and talked together, Boaz, a man who looked to be very old, and two like those who had been with the kel'en Galey.

Then they turned, with Boaz and the old one arm in arm, and began to walk up the hill, toward the People, bringing no weapons at all.

XVIII

Boaz came. Duncan was glad of that, on this last morning
. . . that it was Boaz who came out to them.

He ceased his work, which was the carrying of very light
stones, for the edun which should stand on the plain of the
elee pillars, in this place where the game was abundant and
elee machinery still provided water. He went out from the
rest, dusted his hands on the black fabric of his robes,
weaponless but for his small arms, as the mingled Kel generally went unburdened in this place of meeting. Ja'anom,
hao'nath, ja'ari, ka'anomin, mari, patha and path'andim; and
now homa'an, kesrit, biha'i; and tes'ua and i'osa, up out of
the depths of the great western basin, three days' hard climb
. . . all the tribes within reach lent a few hands of kel'ein to
this madness, this new edun on an old, old world; and to the
she'pan'anth Melein, the she'pan of the Promised.

Even elee, who could not leave their ruins, who languished
in the sun and found the winds too harsh for their eyes and
their delicate skins . . . labored in their own cause, retreating
by day to shelter, coming out to work by night, peopling the
plain with strange stones, statues, likenesses of themselves,
setting their precious monuments out in the wind and under
the eyes of mri and humans, as if to offer them to the elements, or to strangers, or simply to affirm that elee existed.
They did not come near the tents of mri or the edun; would
not; never would, likely; but they built, that being their way.

Six hands of days: the edun walls stood now high as a
kel'en's head. They began to build ramps of sand to ease the
work, for it would someday rise high as that of An-ehon, to
stand on a plain of statues, a fortress against the Dark.

"Boz," he greeted her as she came, and they walked together, khaki clothing and kel-black, casting disparate
shadows. His dus moved in, nudged at Boaz, and she spared
a caress for it, stopped, gazing at the work.

"Galey should have seen this," she said.

"I will tell you a thing," he said, "not for your records: that among things in the Pana of the mri, in the tables . . . there are three human names. His is one." He folded his hands behind him, walked farther with her, past the lines of children of the Kath, who carried their loads of sand for the ramps. "Yours is another."

She said nothing for a space. Beyond them, the tents of the camp were set, shelter until the edun should rise, and that was their direction.

"Sten. Come back with us."

"No."

"You could argue the mri's case . . . much better than I. Have you thought of that?"

"The she'pan forbids."

"Is that final for you?"

"Boz," he said, and stopped. He loosed his veil, which kel'ein still would not, before humans . . . met the passing shock in her eyes, for the scars on his face, which had had time to heal. And perhaps she understood; there was that look too. "Between friends," he said, "there is no veil. Truth, Boz: I'm grateful she refused."

"You'll be alone."

He smiled. "No. Only if I left." He started again toward the tents, put down a hand to touch the dus which crowded close to his left as they walked. "You'll do well for the People. I trust that."

"We're going to set markers up there; you'll not be bothered by visitors until we can get through."

"Human visitors, at least."

"Regul didn't get the tapes, only the chance to tag us, and that information died here so far as they're concerned, along with their chance. I don't think, I truly don't think human authorities are going to make free of mri data where regul are concerned. It was unique circumstance that brought them with us. It won't be repeated."

"We will hope not." He veiled himself again, half-veil, for they walked among the tents, among kath'ein and children. They were expected at the tent of the she'pan; sen'ein and kel'ein waited there, and walked in behind them, through the curtain.

Melein sat there, with a few of the sen'ein about her; and with Niun, and Hlil, and Seras, with two more of the dusei.

Hlil rose as they walked in, inclined his head.

"You do not have his service," Melein said to Boaz, "but he will be under your orders as regards his presence on your ship. He is my Hand reached out to humans. He is Hlil s'Sochil, kel-second; and the beast that is Hlil's: it goes with him too."

"We thank you," Boaz said, "for sending him. We will do all we can to make him welcome."

"Kel Hlil," Melein said, kissed him and received his kiss, dismissal; and from that distance: "Good-bye, sen Boaz."

It was dismissal. Formalities between mri and tsi'mri were always scant. Boaz gave him one look, a touch of the hand, walked away alone, and Hlil summoned his dus to him, paused to embrace Niun, and walked after.

Only beyond him he paused yet again, at the curtain, to look on a certain kel'e'en. "Life and honors," he bade Ras, lingered a scant moment, walked on, with wounding in the dus-sense. By Melein's side, Niun gathered himself to his feet. But Hlil had gone, with brief reverence to the Holy.

"Permission," Ras said, a thin, faint voice. "She'pan."

"You ask a question, kel Ras?"

"I ask to go."

"It is not," said Melein, "a walk to the rim and back. And do you serve the People, kel'e'en—or why do you go?"

"To see," she said; and after a long moment: "We are old friends, she'pan, Hlil and I. And I ask to go."

"Come here," Melein said; and when she had done so, took her hand. "You know all that Hlil knows. You can agree with my mind. You can do what I have bidden Hlil do."

"Aye," Ras said.

Melein drew her down, kissed her, was kissed in turn, let her go, with a nod toward the door. "Haste," she said.

Ras went, her dus after her, with a respect to the Holy and a quiet pace: she would surely have no difficulty overtaking a small, plump human.

Melein sank back in her chair, looked at Niun, looked out at Duncan, and suddenly at other kel'ein, with a quick frown. "Ask among all the Kels," she said. "Quickly: whether there is not one in all this camp, a kel'e'en who will go with them, that they can have a House. Kel Ras is right; they ought not to be alone among strangers."

It was the kel'e'en Tuas who went, who went striding out to the human ship in the last hour before their parting, and the camp turned out to wish her well; paused again in its labor when the ship *Flower* lifted, to watch it until it was out of sight.

"They will see Kesrith," Niun murmured, that night before they slept, in Kel-tent.

"Would you have gone?" Duncan asked. "Have you not had enough of voyaging?"

"A part of my heart went." Niun sank down on his arm, and Duncan did, and the dusei settled each at their backs. There was now besides them, only Rhian's, in the hao'nath camp, and the wild one, somewhere in the far north. "I have wondered," Niun said, "why the dusei chose . . . why ourselves, why Rhian, why Ras and Hlil, and Taz. I thought it might be for your sake, sov-kela; you have always had a strange way with them. But look you—look you: they chose those who would go out. Who would meet strangeness. Who would look longest and deepest into the Dark. That is how they always chose. I think that is so."

Duncan did not answer for a moment . . . gazed at the dus, at him. "No more. Only we hold it off here. Long enough."

"We wait," Niun said. "And we hold it off."

It was a larger city, after so many years: sprawling buildings and domes and covered avenues in the place of regul order. The scent of the wind was the same: acrid and abrasive; and the light . . . the red light of Arain. It must have rained that morning. Puddles stood at the curb before the Nom, and Boaz stopped a moment to stare about her, to reckon with change.

The three kel'ein with her did not make evident their curiosity. Doubtless they were curious, but they were under witness, and did not show it. It was much from them, that they all came, leaving the dusei on the ship . . . her asking.

Governor Stavros was dead, years ago; she had learned that even while *Flower* was inward bound. And there were changes more than the buildings.

"Come," she bade her companions, noting sourly the escort of military personnel which formed for them, with guns and formalities; she had her own, she reflected with grim humor. They walked through the doors of the Nom and into the once-remembered corridors, into a reception of officials, outstretched hands and nervous smiles for her, simply nervous looks for her tall companions.

"The governor's expecting you," one advised her, showing

her the way to offices she remembered very well without. She went, and the kel'ein walked after her.

Stavros dead; and more than Stavros. The uniforms were different, the official emblems were subtly changed. There was a moment's feeling of madness, to have come back to the wrong world, the wrong age. There was a new constitution, so they had said at station: civilian government, a dismantling of the powers that had been AlSec and a reorganization of the bureaus; a restoration of institutions abandoned in the war, as if there was any going back. Kesrith had become a major world, an administrative headquarters for wide regions.

For a moment she yearned for Luiz, for his comfort; and that was gone. He had died by a world of a yellow star, whose name humans did not know, and probably the kel'ein did not . . . died in jump, still lost in the vertigo of no-time, in a place where human flesh did not belong, between phases. Luiz had always leaned on the drugs. She had, until the last, that she and some few of the crew risked what the mri did, to take jump without them: she played at shon'ai with the kel'ein, as the sen played, with wands, and not with weapons.

Your hands are not apt to weapons, they told her.

She blinked, offered a handshake to the middle-aged man who was introduced to her. Governor Lee.

And uncertainly Lee offered his hand to the kel'ein. She opened her mouth to warn, sensed laughter behind the veils, a slight crinkling of Hlil's amber eyes as he touched the offered hand with his fingertips. So Tuas touched. Ras would not, but stood with hands behind her; that was courtesy enough.

"Mri representatives," Lee said. "And the report is—a mishap overtook the other ships; and the regul."

"A mishap, yes," she said. "I understand regul are scarce here."

Lee's eyes slid from hers. He offered her and the mri chairs, seated himself behind his desk. Boaz sat down in the chair, but the kel'ein sat down on the carpet, against the wall where they might see the governor, which was for them more comfort.

"It is open knowledge," Lee said, "that the regul have—detached themselves. We don't know why, or in what interest. They've gone from Kesrith, abandoned worlds nearby, left every human vicinity. They explore in their own directions, perhaps. You can't answer . . . from your own viewpoint . . . or from events where you come from—*why*, can you?"

"They don't like us," Boaz said.

"No. Clearly they don't. Many who stayed here . . . many who were closest in contact with us . . . suicided." He shifted uncomfortably. "The mri envoys . . . do they understand?"

"Every word."

"They agree to peace?"

Boaz shook her head slightly. "To contact. Across an expanse wider than you imagine, sir. And regul are mightily afraid of them. A virtue—as anxious as I've heard the colonies are, out here. But the mri are explorers . . . from here to the rim."

"And mercenaries," Lee said. "On *our* side? Is that the proposal?"

"We have been mercenaries," Hlil said, "if that is the use of the hire we offer."

"But there is cost," Lee said.

"Always," Ras answered.

"What cost? In what—do you expect payment?"

"A place to stand," Ras's quiet voice pursued. "For that, the Kel is at your bidding, so long as you maintain us a world where only your feet and ours touch. And supplies, of course. We are not farmers. And ships; we shall need them."

Lee gnawed at his lip. "So you offered the regul. What benefit did they have of the bargain?"

"Ask," Boaz said, her palms sweating. "You are on the wrong track, governor. Ask *why;* ask why, and you will get a different answer."

"Why?" Lee asked after a moment. "Why do you make such a bargain?"

"For the going," said Ras very softly. "The going itself is our hire. Use us wisely, human sen'en, for we are a sharp sword, to part the Dark for you. So we did for the regul, I have heard, giving them many worlds. And when we have gone far enough, and the tether strains . . . bid us good-bye, and be wiser than the regul. We are the Face that Looks Outward. We are makers of paths, walkers on the wind; and the going itself . . . is the hire for which we have always served."

Boaz pressed her lips together, thinking for one cold moment on the dead worlds, about which human councils would have to know, the course of mri homeworlds, destroyed beneath the mri in fear, fears which had to come to former wielders of the Sword: dread that mri might serve others, one's near neighbors. Fear. Fear had killed the worlds between.

To use the mri, one had to play the Game, to cast them from the hand and let them go.

The belief that it would be different . . . this, she cherished, as she believed in humankind.

She played the Game.

It was a quiet place, the morning on the heights of the carven rocks, looking down on the plain of statues and on the Edun of the People, the heights where there was only the wind for company, the wind and the hope of dusei, which sometimes ventured in for the good hunting, to the terror of the elee.

Merai Niun-Tais hunted here many a morning, and many a morning wasted moments, in this place of the best view of all, from which one could survey all the land from the northern flats to the hazy depths of the basins westward, out of which the great winds came.

He was a dreamer of dreams, was Merai. Patience, the she'pan counseled him; he had yet to win his scars . . . save one that his truefather had dealt him in the Game, to mind him of discipline, and the vice of rashness, to venture the blades with a Master.

But each night he listened to the songs in Kel; and the songs were true. He knew that they were, for Duncan was with them, and talked sometimes, when they could persuade kel Duncan to tell them the tales; the tales made all their hearts burn to hear them, and made them look at the stars with hope.

From the days that he had been in Kath until he took the black robes of Kel he had climbed this height to hunt, and to think of far worlds . . . and secretly, to tease the dusei which came—sometimes—maddeningly close. Forlorn hope: they did not come to kel'ein now; they were all wild, all the dusei born of the great pair of the ja'anom Kel, and the one belonging to old Rhian of the hao'nath—even it had gone wild, in Rhian's passing.

There was one which came most persistently. He had hoped for it this morning, secretly, shamefully, had concealed a tidbit of meat to take to it; but it failed him. He set about his hunting, moving carefully among the rocks, skin out the creatures which sheltered at the deep places, near the watering of Ele'et.

And in hunting, he looked up. There was a star, a star in daylight, that burned.

He stood staring while the brightness became a glare, and the glare a shape.

Then he began to run, racing toward the edun, his heart pounding against his ribs. He was late to bear the news, for all the Kel had come out to see. He slowed his step in the sight of his trueparents and of Duncan; and of the she'pan, for even the Mother had come down out of her tower; and the sen, theirs of the ja'anom and the visitors of other tribes.

The ship settled, obscured in sand, crouched low and waited still for a time, until the sand had settled. Then a hatch opened, and a ramp came down to them.

Kel'ein; they were kel'ein foremost of the strangers, black-robes with dusei at their sides, three of them, striding out across the sands in haste toward the Kel.

He knew their names; they had been sung all his life. And the Kel stood still only for a moment more, then walked faster and faster to meet them, with the kel'anth and Duncan far in the lead.